The Soul Bearers

SYLVIA MASSARA

License Notes

This novel is entirely a work of fiction. The names, characters, and incidents portrayed in it are the work of the author's imagination. Any resemblance to actual persons, living or dead, events, or localities is entirely coincidental.

Published by Tudor Enterprises
Australia
(61) 419 492 623

Revised edition 2016
First published by
Tudor Enterprises in 2010

ISBN-13: 978-0-9875475-1-4

Copyright © 2010, 2013, 2016 Sylvia Massara

Sylvia Massara asserts the moral right to
be identified as the author of this work

DEDICATION

To Didier for sharing his story;
To Rosepurple for believing in my idea;
And to Ron: May your soul be soaring in the Heavens;
Having been borne there by a beautiful Soul Bearer.

Titles by Sylvia Massara

Romantic comedy:

Like Casablanca
The Other Boyfriend

General fiction:

The Soul Bearers

Mia Ferrari mystery series:

Playing With The Bad Boys
The Gay Mardi Gras Murders
The South Pacific Murders

Sci-fi romance:

The Stranger

For more information on Massara's novels, both in eBook
& paperback editions, plus participating retailers;
or for latest novels or to contact the author, please visit:

www.sylviamassara.com

CHAPTER 1

Alex shivered as the wind blew through the city and echoed the coldness inside her. She huddled deeper into the blanket about her shoulders and looked out the window of her hotel room at the branches of the trees, waving back and forth in the park across the road. Her thoughts were in turmoil, and she studied the piece of paper that lay on the small writing table in front of her. The poem she'd written earlier in the evening reflected her dark mood on this particular moonless night, and the soft glow of the table lamp did little to cheer her.

> **In the darkness of night,**
> **He hovers.**
> **The cry of the innocent**
> **He does not hear.**
> **Death stalks near,**
> **Out of reach ...**
> **Yet it does not come.**

An image of another moonless night years ago flashed before her, and the cruel smile directed at her terrified her. Alex shut her eyes and felt panic engulf her as adrenaline coursed through her body and her limbs went weak. Her breathing became shallow and she stood abruptly, knocking over the chair she had been sitting on. A black fog threatened to engulf her in its cold infinity.

Through the chaotic thoughts flooding her mind, Alex clutched at the air in front of her until her fingers made contact with the edge of the writing table. She held on for balance and managed to whisper, despite her dry throat, "I ... am ... safe. I am safe." The black fog lifted momentarily, and she made her way to the bathroom on unsteady legs. A box of Valium sat on the vanity, and she popped two tablets into her mouth and swallowed them without water. She waited with eyes shut until she felt the adrenaline rush subside, and when she finally opened them, it was to find her face reflected in the mirror.

"My God!" she exclaimed as she took in the tear-streaked and blanched cheeks, her deep amber eyes reflecting fear.

"It's okay. It's okay. You're safe now," she said to her image. Then, she went back to the bedroom, where she straightened the chair she had knocked over earlier and draped the blanket over her shoulders once more. She looked down at the poem on the writing table. The words jumped out at her. *Death stalks near ...* But why hadn't it come for her?

She pushed away the thought and looked around the room where she had been living during the past week. It was about time she found something less expensive. The small hotel in the city had suited her purpose when she'd first arrived in Sydney, but she needed more time to decide whether to stay on in her hometown, and she couldn't go on paying hotel rates.

In fact, she wasn't even sure if she should have come here in the first place. She had been away for close to twenty years, and could have stayed away forever, but something deep inside her told her she had to face her fears. She couldn't keep running away from her stepfather indefinitely; and the only way to exorcise this stubborn ghost was to confront it. Easier said than done, she thought, knowing she owed it to herself to at least try to put the past behind her for good.

Her eyelids suddenly grew heavy with the effect of the tablets, and though she tried to keep her thoughts focused on her problem, she could not help but fall asleep on the unmade bed.

* * *

It was early morning when Alex awoke to find sunlight shining on her face. She felt rested and eager for the new day. The rustle of a newspaper being pushed under her door spurred her into action and she slipped out of bed and retrieved the paper; but first, a much needed shower and breakfast.

Once she was comfortably ensconced in the hotel's café, she spotted the advert in the "share accommodation" section: **SURRY HILLS—to share with gay couple**. She looked up from the ad, knowing instinctively this would be a safe haven for her, and she

2

hurried through breakfast so she could race to her room and make the call.

A soft male voice answered the phone, and Alex introduced herself and expressed her interest.

"Yes, it's still available," the voice on the other end of the line informed her. "If you want to come over this afternoon and have a look, you can meet both of us. I'm Steve Wicks and my partner's name is Matthew."

"Is two o'clock suitable?" Alex asked while she jotted down the address Steve gave her. "Great, I'll be there." She rang off with a feeling of optimism.

Privacy was very important to her, so Alex didn't want to share with females, who were bound to bring their boyfriends home; and definitely not with heterosexual males. But a gay couple was just right. She doubted they would pay much attention to her, and all she needed was a place where her privacy would be respected, where she could concentrate on pulling herself together, and at the same time get on with her work in peace.

Alex had been writing for newspapers and magazines as a freelancer for close to ten years now, and enjoyed a good reputation with her editors. Twenty years of travelling around Australia, never putting down roots, had served her well in her career. She'd left home at age fifteen and gone to the outback where she managed to find work at various sheep and cattle stations. Here, she spent several years doing the kind of gruelling work that took her mind off other, more dangerous, thoughts. She had tried her hand at everything— mending fences; herding in sheep and cattle; general maintenance around the station and homestead; cooking for the boys during shearing season; and she even had a go at shearing herself.

During this time in her life, she met some wonderful people. Fond memories of Harry, an old shearer with a tanned face full of lines and skin rough as cowhide, came to mind. Harry had been a good friend to the lonely and shy teenager she had been at the time. In fact, he had been like the father she'd never had, taking a protective interest, and teaching her the way around the station where she had first worked.

Those had been good days—days of hard work, but also of friendship and fun; days of shearers and cattle hands swapping tales of the outback. Tales Alex had absorbed and compiled in her diary while she travelled to places off the beaten track; tales that would one day turn into amusing and endearing stories. These were the tales that eventually found their way into discerning travel magazines and newspapers, and finally earned her a reputation and living as a travel writer. And this had been the beginning. Alex had then gone on to write about her travels through wine country, lush green rainforests, and endless miles of open ocean beaches as well as the many cities of the vast continent that was a part of her. But during all this time, travelling, writing, and living a gypsy kind of life, she had never returned to Sydney—until now.

Surprisingly, she was happy to be home. Sydney had changed dramatically in the last twenty years, especially so since the 2000 Olympics. The harbour city had turned into a hive of never-ending activity with an ever-changing skyline, and Alex looked forward to becoming a part of it all, immersing herself into this place that was in her blood.

* * *

Steve Wicks was a gentle-looking man in his mid-thirties; slight of build, bordering on the skinny side, and with thinning brown hair. Alex's first impression of him was of a person truly at peace with himself. Steve had a look of serenity about him that revealed itself in his soft brown eyes—eyes that shone with an indefinable quality Alex had never seen before except in paintings of Renaissance angels. She felt instantly at ease with him.

"Alex Dorian?" Steve greeted her in a friendly voice. "Please come in. We're just making tea. It's such a chilly day today."

He was right, Alex thought as she followed him into the house. Although it was only April, autumn had turned out to be very chilly this year, and despite the sun shining in full force, the cold wind from the previous night lingered on.

The house was a two-storey Victorian terrace in pale yellow with traditional Federation green trellises and balcony railings. It was charming, and Alex liked it immediately. Once inside, she caught a glimpse of tasteful, contemporary furniture complemented by antique pieces before she was led into a kitchen with a strong French provincial influence. But it was not the pleasant atmosphere that caught her attention when she entered the room; it was the young

4

man who stood at the breakfast counter pouring hot water into a Mexican earthenware teapot.

It took all of Alex's willpower to stop herself from staring at the vision in front of her—for when her eyes had first rested on him, she'd thought she was looking at an angelic being disguised in human form.

"Hello," the vision spoke to her. "I'm Matthew Davis. Would you like a cup of tea?"

Alex nodded, dumbfounded by the beautiful young man. She was captivated by his tall, tanned figure with the perfect athletic build. Piercing blue eyes gazed back at her from an extremely attractive face, which was almost boyish and yet strong, framed by golden light brown hair casually swept back from his face. An aquiline nose and sensual mouth with perfectly white teeth completed the picture.

"Alex, please have a seat." Steve broke the spell as he gestured toward the rustic kitchen table. Matthew finished with the tea things, and he and Steve joined her.

The sun seemed to shine from Matthew's eyes, and Alex felt tongue-tied for the first time since she had been the shy teenager who had left home. She quickly reminded herself that the guy was gay; and in any case, she was immune to the attentions of men. At this thought, a shadow from the past threatened to rear its ugly head, but this time she was able to control the beginning of one of her panic attacks and instead accepted the mug of tea from Matthew.

"Thank you." She figured his age to be somewhere in his mid to late twenties.

"You mentioned on the phone that you're a writer." Steve addressed her in his soft voice.

Alex forced her focus back on him. "Yes, I freelance. I write travel articles."

"So you must move around quite a lot." This from Matthew.

"For the last twenty years or so, yes." Alex responded with trepidation, hoping they weren't going to ask her too many questions.

"You don't sound very excited," Matthew observed. This earned him a reprimanding look from Steve.

"Perhaps Alex is tired of travelling and wants to put down roots."

Steve was very perceptive, Alex thought, or perhaps she was easy to read. "You're both right," she replied. "No, I'm not that excited about travelling anymore; and yes, I'm looking to settle down now."

"Sorry," Matthew apologised. "I didn't mean to pry."

"It's okay," she assured him. "You have a right to be curious about me." But she secretly wished he wouldn't become too curious.

"Well, as for us," Steve explained, "I work in the hospitality industry as a functions and events supervisor, and Matthew's an actor."

Alex noticed the special pride in his voice when he referred to his partner and saw Matthew blush under his tan as he gently corrected Steve, "A hopeful actor at this point."

Alex had a sip of tea and managed to avoid his eyes. Instead, she turned to Steve when he continued speaking. "Tell me, Alex, how do you feel about living with a gay couple?"

She coloured at his direct question, knowing she would have to offer a convincing response. "I hadn't actually thought about it that way." She felt guilty because she couldn't exactly tell him the real reason she wanted to share with a gay couple. She liked Steve and didn't want to start their housemate relationship with a lie, but she could not help it. This was not the time for her to start talking about her past.

"As a writer, I need privacy," she suddenly felt inspired to say, "and I figure sharing with other females won't give me the solitude I need. You know, a lot of the time girls will bring home boyfriends and such, plus they like to chat a lot, too." She looked from one to the other to see how this was received and hoped Steve and Matthew did not find this too lame an explanation.

Steve gazed back at her with an understanding look that suggested he knew she was hiding something. This unsettled her. Matthew, on the other hand, looked suspicious, and she felt even more uncomfortable under his scrutiny.

"Let me show you around." Steve came to the rescue, and Alex was silently grateful to him.

"Thanks for the tea," she said to Matthew and stood to follow Steve.

Matthew nodded in response, and she had the feeling he disliked her. This made her feel inexplicably sad.

Steve motioned her out of the kitchen and made his way down a hallway with polished floorboards, which led to a staircase. Opposite the stairwell was a set of French doors leading to a tastefully furnished loungeroom containing a mixture of antique pieces and a couple of modern cream-coloured leather sofas.

"Upstairs we have two bedrooms and a bathroom. Unfortunately, we don't have an ensuite in our room, so we all have to share."

They reached the top of the stairs where the hallway's timber floor was covered in what looked like a fine antique Persian rug. The walls were painted in a burnished gold tone and dotted here and there with French impressionist paintings, giving an effect of elegance with a touch of Olde World charm.

The main bedroom's walls were painted in the same colour as the hallway. The furniture in the room was once again a mixture of old pieces and contemporary ones: a Queen Anne writing desk; a modern built-in wardrobe with sliding timber doors; an antique dresser that looked Georgian; an early 20th century queen-size bed with an elaborate brass bedhead, crowned with a canopy of white mosquito netting. Here again, the walls were decorated with French impressionist paintings.

Alex liked the style of the room even though it was rather eclectic, and she warmed to Steve for showing her around his inner sanctum. She already felt a strong connection between them.

"Who's your favourite painter?" she asked while taking in the different pictures.

"Monet." With a smile, he added, "Of course, I wish these were real instead of reproductions, but beggars can't be choosers."

Alex laughed. "I know what you mean," she uttered, thinking of all the years she'd spent living out of a suitcase with not a great deal of money to show for it.

Steve closed the door to the room and led the way to another doorway. "This is the spare room."

Alex took in the modern theme of the room. The colour of the walls was the same as the upper part of the house, but here the built-in had sliding mirror doors, and the double bed was framed in Oregon pine with a matching writing desk nearby. A window with timber venetian blinds looked down onto a surprisingly large back garden, lovingly landscaped, which gave way to a small sandstone terrace with a rustic outdoor dining set of wrought iron.

"What a gorgeous garden! Do you look after it yourself?" Alex admired the neat flowerbeds bordering a large pink frangipani tree.

"Yes, I'm the gardener in the family. Matthew doesn't go anywhere near the plants. It's a shame."

"I know what you mean," Alex replied. "Gardening can be very therapeutic."

"I was just thinking the same thing."

Alex turned back to look around the room and liked the feel of it. Adorning the walls were modern prints that were very colourful and full of life—all except the one hanging above the bed. This one, was an enlarged black and white print from a photograph of two perfect male bodies facing each other—two attractive faces in profile and two bare torsos, almost touching down to naked hips—exuding a raw sexuality Alex couldn't explain. Sudden fear gripped at her throat, and she gazed at the print as if mesmerised.

"Alex?" Steve called out gently but received no response. "Alex," he called out a little louder this time, finally getting her attention.

"Oh! I'm sorry … I sort of wandered off there, didn't I?" She sounded a little breathless.

"If the print bothers you, we can take it down."

"Um … No, no, it's okay, really … I was thinking of something else." She knew she made a poor liar, but was thankful he did not comment further.

"Well, that's it then. The tour's complete. If you have any furniture you want to bring along, we can store all of this away."

"No, it's okay. I don't have furniture." She had recovered her composure by now.

Steve walked her back downstairs and to the front door. "We have a couple of other people who'll be dropping by to see the room. If you leave me your contact number, I'll call you once we make a decision."

"Of course. By the way, I think I should tell you that I'm looking at accommodation for the short term—maybe three months or so. I'm not yet sure whether I'll be settling down in Sydney. It's difficult to decide where to put down roots." She felt she had to be truthful about this much at least. She really wanted the room. She liked Steve and even the disturbing Matthew. She liked the house and the suburb. But she wasn't so sure about that unsettling print in the bedroom.

"We're flexible with the time frame." Steve's voice intruded into her thoughts. "This is the first time we've ever considered having a housemate so it'll be a testing time for us, too. It's probably best to have a short term arrangement."

"Okay. Then, I guess that's all. When will I hear from you?" She tried not to sound too eager.

"We'll make a decision by tomorrow."

Alex took out one of her business cards and gave it to him. "Right now I'm staying at the Phoenix Hotel. If I don't get the room, I'll have to look for something else fairly quickly. Hotel rates are not very kind to the pocket, so I would really appreciate a reply either way."

"Don't worry, you'll have one. I'll call you tomorrow morning," Steve reassured her.

"Thank you. It's been great meeting you and Matthew. Until tomorrow then." She stepped out onto the small front garden and admired the beautiful roses bordering the street fence. "I see you also keep this in tip-top shape."

"It keeps me fit," Steve replied. "Nice to meet you, Alex. We'll talk soon."

"Goodbye." Alex stood on the sidewalk and waited until he closed the front door. Suddenly, she felt alone.

CHAPTER 2

It was evening by the time Steve and Matthew finished showing the room to other interested parties, and they were both tired when they finally settled down to a pizza in front of the TV.

Matthew enjoyed having Steve at home on a Saturday evening. It was rare for him to get Saturdays off from his hotel job since most functions took place during the weekend, but Steve had requested this particular weekend off well in advance so they could show the room together.

"You lost weight again," Matthew remarked casually, pretending to watch the animal documentary playing on the television.

Steve nodded, helped himself to another slice of pizza, and leaned back against the comfort of the leather sofa. Matthew sat cross-legged on the floor by the coffee table.

"You haven't even told me how you're feeling lately," Matthew persisted.

"I'm fine," was the reply. Steve knew his partner worried about him, but he was too weary to get into their usual "you have to watch your health" debate.

"I meant since you left the hospital," Matthew went on.

Steve sighed tiredly. "I'm fine, Matthew; don't worry."

Matthew turned his attention once more to the program, but Steve noted the look of frustration on his face.

"This pizza's delicious," he said, hoping to distract Matthew from his brooding mood.

Matthew's response was heated. "How can you be so cool about all this?"

Looking at him with love in his eyes, Steve remarked, "I'm at peace with myself."

Matthew's eyes filled with tears, and it wrung Steve's heart. He would give anything to be able to avoid hurting his loved one, but the fact was he didn't have anything left to give—his life was already given. Instead, he motioned for Matthew to join him on the sofa and held him as a mother might hold a frightened child. He could at least give him all his love and hope it would be enough to sustain him in future.

"What did you think of Alex?" He changed the subject, once again trying to shift Matthew's attention.

"The writer?" Matthew was diverted for a moment. "Too intense, I thought."

"I liked her."

"Why's that?"

"She values her privacy and therefore will respect ours." Then, Steve added thoughtfully, "Plus I think she's really hurting inside."

"How can you tell?" Matthew sounded surprised.

"I just know. She's intense, as you say, but she's also trying to appear confident at the same time. She's hiding some big hurt. In fact, she's a lot like you, you know."

"No way!" Matthew protested. He hated it when Steve saw too deep into his soul, and he seemed to have the gift for doing so.

"Whatever you say," Steve indulged him. "In any case, I think we should rent the room to her."

"If you want to, it's fine by me. I only hope she can cope with all of this."

Matthew's tone reflected the petulant child he could sometimes be, and Steve humoured him. "Cope with what?"

"You know, the illness—everything. I just wish we didn't have to do this."

"We need the extra income now that I can't work long hours anymore."

"I can go to work, too, you know!" Matthew burst out.

"I'm not going to let you give up your dream for me. You're young and have a good chance to make it big."

"Steve, I can still work at some job. We don't need to take in a stranger, truly."

"No. We agreed you'd concentrate on your acting. I don't want to see you throw everything away for nothing."

"For nothing?" Matthew exclaimed, a hurt look in his eyes. "How can you say it's for nothing? I love you, and I'll do whatever it takes to—"

11

"I know, I know, and I love you back," Steve interrupted gently. His voice was so soothing it had a calming effect on his companion.

Matthew leaned into him, and Steve caressed his hair. And Matthew felt his anger dissolve. "I'm sorry. The last thing I want to do is upset you, but you know we can still work this out without taking in a stranger."

"Let's just give it a go for my sake. Alex told me she wanted to have a flexible arrangement, and this is a good thing. It'll give us the opportunity to see how we like sharing, and if things don't work out either way, we can call it quits," Steve pointed out, and added, "Besides, I think Alex would benefit from our help."

Matthew sighed, frustrated. "You're the only person I know who thinks about helping others when others can't help you."

Steve smiled wisely. "All the more reason to do it."

Matthew regarded him questioningly, not understanding his meaning. But Steve remained silent, and Matthew saw the infinite kindness in the soft brown eyes he loved so much.

* * *

Alex was in her hotel room writing an article on the city of Perth for an in-flight magazine while the wind outside echoed with the strength of the previous night's. She felt cold and poured herself another cup of coffee from the jug she'd ordered earlier from room service.

It was close to ten, and she knew better than to drink strong coffee so late at night, but she was not in the mood for sleep. Images of Matthew Davis kept intruding into her mind, and the more she thought about him, the more disturbed she felt—so much so, that she gave up her repeated attempts at writing and went to stand in front of the full-length mirror in the bathroom.

A woman in her mid-thirties looked back at her with long black hair and amber eyes, a legacy of her Irish ancestry. Alex didn't know if she was attractive although men had found her so in the past. She knew she wasn't beautiful, but there seemed to be something about her exotic colouring that appealed to the opposite sex. As for the rest of her body, she avoided looking at it, especially when naked. After all, this was the body that had attracted *him,* and she was angry at it.

The skinny child's body she had possessed years ago had

matured into a full female form, and though she acknowledged her present body had nothing to do with what happened in the past, she made sure no one saw or touched it. Since leaving home, she had gone out of her way to avoid anyone who showed the remotest interest in her and had taken to dressing in baggy clothes to hide her form as much as possible. Only after she took these measures had she begun to feel a little safer.

Now, the memory of Matthew's mesmerising blue eyes popped into her head. What was the matter with her? She turned from the mirror and went to sit on her unmade bed, wrapping her arms around herself. She'd seen good looking males in the past, but none had affected her like Matthew did.

She admitted he was the most attractive male she had ever seen, but this should not make any difference. In fact, she should feel as fearful of him as she had of all the others. Then, in a rare moment of insight, the answer came to her—Matthew was gay, and therefore safe to look at, safe to appreciate. He wasn't interested in her.

This was obviously the reason why she had found him so disturbingly sensual and why he aroused such strange feelings in her—because it was safe for her to fantasise about him as he was off-limits to her. The realisation brought colour to her face.

Here she was, thinking about sex—that horrible, terrifying, three-letter word she had avoided thinking about for so long, and anxiety reared its ugly head. She suddenly jumped up off the bed and ran back to the bathroom where she splashed cold water on her face and reached for her magic Valiums just in time to stem off another panic attack. Then, she slowly made her way back to lie on the bed, curling up in a fetal position.

Visions of Matthew haunted her until the drug-induced oblivion took over.

* * *

She ran. Her legs felt heavy and moved in slow motion. The fear permeated through her body and threatened to paralyse her limbs, but she knew she must keep running. Up the stairs she ran, toward her room. She would lock the door and climb out the window to the safety of the busy street below. But she must hurry. *Hurry!* She urged her legs as she heard the footsteps following close behind her.

After what seemed an eternity, she reached the landing outside her room and went to open the door. Too late! Another body came up from behind and shoved her into the room with brute force. She was sent sprawling to the floor, and fear choked her throat. She could not scream nor could she move. She turned and looked up at the figure standing over her and begged softly through her tears for him to stop. But he was deaf to her pleading.

He locked the door behind him and approached her crouched form while he unbuckled his belt. Then, miraculously, she was able to move again and tried to get up. This resulted in a stinging slap across her face that split open her lip. She tasted the warm blood as it trickled into her mouth, and she became enveloped in a paralysing panic.

She knew nothing could stop him now as she lay on the cold uncarpeted floor, tears running down her cheeks. She closed her eyes and begged death to come and claim her this very moment. But death did not hear her plea. Instead, the familiar wounding pain shot through her female parts as the organ entered her and started its horrific rhythm: hard, hurting and plundering. Just when she thought she would split in half, she felt the warm liquid run down her inner thighs. The deed was over, and he left her immediately, closing the door gently behind him. He was satisfied—until the next time.

Alex sat up in bed, drenched in sweat. It was daylight outside, and the nightmare was just that, a nightmare—an evil entity that came for her once in a while even after all these years.

Tears of anger and rage rolled down her cheeks as she pictured the monster who took her innocence away when she had been seven years old. She realised these were the tears she had kept inside her for so long, only to be brought to the surface because she had allowed herself to find a man attractive.

Thank God he was gay, so she didn't have to confront her past right now. She knew she wasn't yet ready to face the ghost. She could stall a little longer. Her past was dead, and would remain so for now. The present was all she needed to worry about; and in the present, there were no evil men out to get her, only the disturbing image of Matthew. But she had everything under control, didn't she? Of course she did. Living alongside of him would be fine because his attentions were only for Steve.

Her mobile rang and jolted her out of her thoughts. She

answered immediately. "Hello?"

"Good morning, Alex." It was Steve.

"Hi, Steve, how are you?" She felt normal again.

"Very well, thanks. Matthew and I have made our decision, and if you're still interested, we'd like to offer you the room."

Her heart lifted at the news. "That's great! Thank you. I'm so glad! I can help you with the gardening, too. I've got a bit of a green thumb, you know." She knew she was babbling in her happiness but didn't care.

"I'll take you up on that." Steve laughed at the other end. "So when do you want to move in?"

"Any time, really. I only have one suitcase and my laptop." She hoped to move today if possible.

Steve seemed to read her mind. "If you can manage it, today would be best. We're both at home and we'll help you settle in. I go back to work in the morning."

"Yes, today's just fine." Alex was relieved that she wouldn't have to spend another night alone.

"Come around three this afternoon. We'll get a set of keys cut for you, too."

"I'll be there. Thank you, Steve. I look forward to living in a real home." The statement was out before she could do anything about it.

"I'm glad we can be a home to you, my dear," Steve said gently. "Well, I guess we'll see you this afternoon."

"Yes, thank you once again. I'll see you later." Alex pressed the off button on her mobile with a big smile on her face.

CHAPTER 3

Steve set to work on his roses and felt a sense of happiness in the moment. He had long ago learned to appreciate the present and detach from the past without worrying about an uncertain future. Matthew had told him he had become very spiritual since the onset of his illness, and he agreed this was the case.

Since he'd discovered his spiritual self, he had found peace and acceptance of whatever was to come. He paused for a few seconds to take in the warmth of the sunshine in the bright blue sky and listen to the twittering of the birds in the trees nearby. He breathed in the fragrance of the plants and flowers around him. This communion with nature gave him a sense of being part of the whole. He closed his eyes to capture the moment a little longer, but was brought out of his reverie when Matthew stepped out onto the courtyard.

He was dressed in faded blue jeans and a crisp white cotton shirt that made his tan stand out as an attractive contrast to the whiteness of the garment and his piercing blue eyes.

Steve paused to take in the picture he made, standing there so unselfconscious. He was convinced Matthew did not realise just how very good looking he really was. His naïveté was part of his overall appeal. Matthew possessed a "little boy lost" look that people, both male and female, found irresistible.

"I'm off," Matthew announced. "Wish you would come."

Steve smiled faintly. "I don't think your mother wants to see me somehow."

Matthew frowned. "If she expects me to visit more often, she'll have to accept my way of life."

"Give her time, Matthew."

"You mean nine years isn't long enough?" Matthew remarked sarcastically.

"Not for some people," Steve replied in his soft voice. He

understood exactly how Matthew's parents felt about their son being gay, and he knew some people would never accept it. His own parents certainly hadn't.

"What are you going to do while I'm gone?" Matthew always worried about leaving Steve alone when he went out.

"I'll potter around the garden for a couple of hours. Then, I'm meeting Gazza for lunch. Don't forget Alex arrives at three."

Matthew shot him a sullen look. "How could I forget? First my mother, and now a stranger intruding into our lives."

"Alex isn't an intruder. She's just a housemate. I'm sure she'll keep pretty much to herself." Steve did not understand why Matthew had taken such a dislike to her, but perhaps it was not Alex so much as the fact that they would have a new person living with them.

"Okay, okay. I'm sorry. I'm sure she'll keep to herself. She's just a little weird though," he commented.

This aroused Steve's curiosity. "How do you mean?"

"Didn't you notice the way she was dressed the other day? Baggy jeans and a pullover three times the size of her. No sense of style."

Steve was amused at the description. Matthew was obsessed with fashion. He was so fastidious that when they planned to go out, he often changed outfits three or four times before he was satisfied. "Maybe she doesn't have your sense of style," he pointed out, grinning.

"I'll say."

"Well, don't worry about it. Just because she has no dress sense doesn't mean she's weird," Steve chided gently.

"God, Steve, sometimes you really get on my nerves. You're so ..." Matthew was at a loss for the right word.

"So *what?*" Steve prompted him.

"So ... accepting of things," Matthew accused him.

"You mean tolerant, don't you? Well, you should know more than anyone else that my motto is 'live and let live'; otherwise, how do you think I put up with your throwing dirty socks and underwear all over the bedroom floor when you change?"

Matthew made a face. "I'll see you this afternoon, and don't overdo it with the gardening. You know how it tires you out," he admonished.

"Nag, nag. If I didn't know any better, I'd say I was living with my mother," Steve teased, rolling his eyes. "And heaven forbid that!"

Matthew departed, and Steve's mind wandered in contemplation. He thought of his own parents, now deceased, and how they had never accepted his way of life. He'd had no siblings, and as the only child of a church minister and his devoted wife, the shock had been too much.

He had only just turned eighteen when he announced to his parents he was gay. This was the last time he ever saw them. His father ordered him out of the house, calling him the devil's spawn. His mother cried with disappointment at the fact that her only son would never give her grandchildren.

Steve had not attempted to justify his way of life to them. He had always believed in "live and let live" so he simply packed his clothes and few belongings and moved in with his first and only lover at the time, an older man by the name of Patrick. He left his contact number with his parents, but they never called.

Ten years later, a lawyer contacted him to let him know his parents passed away. They had gone within a few days of each other. His father had suffered a fatal stroke, and his mother died a week later from a heart attack. The only thing Steve was left in their will was the Bible his father had used for Sunday services. The family home, monies, and personal effects had been left to the church.

Steve did not attend the funeral nor did he feel grief at his parents' passing. He merely felt sadness for them and pity at the fact that they had shut him out of their lives. Then, shortly after his parents' death, his partner, Patrick, succumbed to a long-standing illness, and Steve inherited the house in Surry Hills along with a small mortgage. He decided to keep the house where he had lived for so long, and where Matthew later joined him when they met about a year after Patrick's death.

During the first couple of years they were together, Steve and Matthew took out a further loan to renovate the house and restore it to its present glory. It was around this time that Steve discovered he had not only inherited Patrick's house, but also the disease that killed his first love. He tested HIV positive shortly after he and Matthew commenced renovations.

Steve was not surprised. In a way, he had been expecting it, and he thanked God that from the time he became involved with Matthew, they had practised safe sex. Steve knew Patrick had been unaware of his condition when they had first become lovers, and he simply felt destiny had stepped in and taken a hand.

Matthew took the news well at the time, and although Steve encouraged him to leave for his own safety, Matthew had stuck by him. Their love possessed a strong bond no disease could ever break. So they stayed together and gone on practising safe sex. This was five years ago, and their mutual love had grown steadily stronger since.

Steve was grateful Matthew was with him as he himself had been there for Patrick. His biggest consolation was that Matthew had remained healthy and would live on long after he left this world. This was the main reason for his peaceful state of mind.

* * *

Matthew was not in a good mood while he drove his old and rather beat-up Toyota Corolla to the luncheon appointment with his mother. Steve had mentioned buying a new car this year, but with his illness getting worse and their dwindling income, it had not been possible.

What he could not understand was Steve's determination that he should persist with his acting and forget about working on a more regular basis. He knew heaps of actors who held part-time jobs to make ends meet, but Steve argued he should attend acting classes to keep up his craft and concentrate on attending auditions as much as possible.

Matthew made a mental note to drop in on his agent sometime the following day and see whether there was anything going. Besides, Brent had not yet contacted him over the audition he had attended the previous week.

To date, Matthew had been fairly lucky in obtaining work. He was usually selected for modelling jobs, but the work was not steady, and this was not where his dreams lay. He wanted to act on TV or film, but so far his only work consisted of commercials and several one-off roles in soapies. The audition he attended the previous week was for a small part in an American movie being shot on location in Sydney, and he really wanted it. This could be the break he had been looking for. The previous year he'd missed out on a substantial role in a big American blockbuster, which could have meant an opportunity for him to get into mainstream film, and he had been down in the dumps for weeks afterwards.

Steve constantly urged him to go to Los Angeles for a few months to try his luck, but Matthew was not prepared to leave him behind. So the dream was put on hold. In any case, with the increasing number of American films being shot in Australia in recent years, Matthew figured he had a good chance at making a name for himself locally.

As he daydreamed about his future, he steered the car automatically toward his parents' home in Darling Point. He veered left into winding Yarranabee Road and stopped outside a large Spanish style villa by the waterfront surrounded by a myriad of exotic plants and trees, and enclosed within high black wrought iron gates.

Matthew's mood was no better now than when he'd left home, especially as he was about to face his mother. Two young females walking past on the sidewalk ogled him with admiring eyes, but he took no notice of them. He was used to getting such looks, and it irritated him that people seemed to regard him as some sort of beautiful object. Even as a small child, he remembered being "put on show" by his mother. He had done modelling even back then, and he learned most humans who came into contact with him wanted to get close simply because of the way he looked. As a result, he had come to hate his image and had grown up impervious to the effect his looks had on others.

Even though he acknowledged he was attractive, Matthew could not understand what all the fuss was about. Over time, he had learned to identify those around him who were only responding to his looks, and he had stayed away from their superficiality. Then, he had met Steve—his dear, gentle, loving Steve, who did not judge and who saw deeply into his soul.

Steve had taken him under his wing, away from the shallow kind of world in which he had grown up. The world of the rich—his parents' world—was a world of high power and social events where only the crème-de-la-crème were seen. It was a world Matthew shunned, one where, due to his mother, he was still remembered as "straight." In his mother's world, there was no place for homosexuals.

As he made his way to the gate and rang the security doorbell, the young girls on the sidewalk were still turning around, trying to snatch a good look at him. Matthew ignored them.

"Davis residence," said a heavily accented voice on the intercom.

"My lovely Conchita, it is I, your favourite man!" Matthew teased the Davis' Filipino housekeeper.

"Oh, Mr Matthew!" was the delighted reply as she buzzed him in.

She was waiting on the doorstep to the main entrance when he appeared through the dense foliage of the front garden. Conchita was a diminutive woman in her late fifties with chocolate-brown skin and a wide smile, which was warm and welcoming.

"Mr Matthew, it's been so long. How are you?"

Matthew reached out and kissed her on the cheek. "Conchita, my life's not the same without you." He beamed a happy look at her, feeling his dark mood lift.

"You are such a flirt," she chided, but blushed with pleasure. Conchita had fallen in love with her "Mr Matthew" on the day she'd first met him as a four-year-old. "Mrs Davis is in the loungeroom waiting for you."

"Thanks, Conchita." Matthew entered the house.

"And Mr Matthew," she called out after him, "next time don't stay away so long."

His heart warmed toward her. "I'll come visit just for you, my dear Conchita." Matthew left her smiling at the front door and made his way along a hallway filled with contemporary paintings and sculptures. He then paused outside heavy wooden double doors, knocked and walked into a large modern loungeroom decorated in blacks and whites with expansive windows overlooking a wide balcony and the glory of the harbour.

"Hello, Mother," he said to the slim and elegant figure of Dora Davis.

"Darling, you made it!" Dora smiled at her beautiful son from behind the bar where she was pouring a scotch on the rocks. "Anything for you?"

"A Pellegrino, thanks." Matthew threw himself down on an immaculate white leather sofa and watched his mother get the drinks ready.

She looked very good for her age. At fifty-one, Dora still retained the classical good looks she had passed on to her son. She was tall and willowy slim like a catwalk model. Her hair was platinum blonde, and she had the same piercing blue eyes as Matthew. She was dressed in white silk slacks and a shimmering pale blue shirt that accentuated her beauty.

She joined Matthew with their drinks and took a seat on the sofa opposite his. "Darling, you've been a long time coming," she admonished gently and had a sip of her scotch.

"You could've come to visit me for once." Matthew hated going through this routine. It was the same conversation he had with her every time he came to visit.

"You know how it is," she remarked. "I've been busy with my charity work, plus your father—"

"How *is* Father?" Matthew cut through the pretence of his mother's lame excuses.

"He's fine. We're both fine, dear." Dora's tone sounded a pitch higher than usual, and Matthew knew she was lying. "You're looking well. How's your acting work?"

Matthew indulged her by not asking anything further about his father. "Nothing major's come up."

"Well, they don't know what they're missing. You're so good looking—can't they see that?" she exclaimed with indignation in her voice.

Matthew sighed. "Looks aren't everything, Mother. So why did you call me over, anyway?"

Dora was momentarily taken aback by the sudden question. "Can't I ask my son to visit me?" The high-pitched tone again.

"Only when you want something," was the rejoinder.

"Really, Matthew, sometimes you sound just like your father," she berated. "But now that you mention it, there is something I have been meaning to ask you."

Matthew waited patiently. If anyone should have been an actor in this family, it was his mother.

"The Taylors are hosting a big fashion event, and they asked after you. I thought you'd ask their daughter to partner you."

Matthew sighed with irritation. "Mother, when are you going to face reality? I'm not interested in Marjory or anyone else. I'm in a relationship already."

"With a man!" she declared, exasperated.

"Do we have to go through this again?" Matthew wished he had never come. He knew this would happen.

"Darling, how can you waste yourself like this when you could have any woman in the world?" Dora entreated. "Besides, your …

um … partner … well, he's dying. Doesn't it worry you?"

Matthew's face flushed with anger. "I'll always regret the day I told you about Steve's illness. I thought my own mother would understand." He rose from the sofa, slamming his glass on the coffee table and started to make for the door. "I'll see you around, Mother. Say hello to Father if he's interested in knowing I'm still alive."

"Wait, darling, wait!" Dora ran to him. "Do you need money?"

A look of distaste crossed his face. He could not believe his own mother would be this cold and calculating, trying to buy him. "Save my father's money. I'm sure he can well spend it on his latest girlfriend." He knew this would hurt her, but she deserved it.

"You leave him out of this." Dora was suddenly on the verge of tears.

Matthew's conscience pricked at him. "I'm sorry, okay? I didn't mean it. It's just that … Well, it doesn't matter. I have to go. I'll call you sometime." He opened the door.

Dora clutched at his sleeve. "Matthew, there'll be interesting people at the fashion do. I hear some big American film director will be there."

Matthew shook his head in exasperation. "Save it, please. Even the Queen of England couldn't get me to go unless, of course, Steve's invited as well."

"You take delight in hurting me." Dora released his sleeve.

Matthew retorted sarcastically, "And of course you don't!" With this said he left her standing at the door and slammed out of the house.

* * *

Alex arrived on the dot of three with her suitcase and laptop. The front door was opened by Matthew.

"So you're here," he said by way of greeting, his mood still affected by the earlier encounter with his mother.

Alex did not know how to reply to this. Thankfully, before she could say anything, Steve appeared.

"Alex, welcome! Please come in. Matthew will take your suitcase upstairs." He ushered her inside the house with Matthew following and carrying in her suitcase. Alex looked after him in confusion when he started up the stairs.

"Don't worry about him," Steve remarked, sensing her feelings. "He had a bad day, and I'm sure he didn't mean to be rude."

Alex produced a weak smile in response. Matthew's reception had hurt. She had been looking forward to moving in, and the last thing she wanted was to get off on the wrong foot.

"Come on through to the kitchen. Dump your computer anywhere, and we'll make a cup of tea."

Dear Steve, Alex thought, *the peacemaker*. "That'll be nice, thank you."

The kitchen was bathed in the bright light that came in through the windows and the French doors leading to the back garden. Alex looked outside.

"I see you've been working in the garden again. You pruned that tree over there." She pointed to a plum tree standing near the back fence.

Steve smiled, but before he could reply, Matthew entered the kitchen.

"Steve works too hard, and he'll wear himself out. Perhaps, we can give him a hand sometime."

Alex assumed this was his way of telling her he was sorry for his surly welcome, and she felt better immediately. "Definitely," she replied brightly. "I was telling Steve when he showed me around the house that I have a bit of a green thumb."

Matthew smiled, and suddenly the world was a much better place. "You're on then," he said.

"Matthew hasn't got a single green finger on either hand, let alone a thumb, Alex. But he does make great tea," Steve stated bluntly but in good humour.

Matthew got the hint. "All right, all right. I'll make the tea. You two sit down and chatter away."

This, they did. They sat at the kitchen table, and Alex recounted some of her travel adventures at Steve's request. It was obvious both men found her tales of old Harry really interesting because by the time she finished talking about her old shearing friend, the sun was setting and the kitchen was enveloped in the advancing dusk of early evening.

Noticing the time, Alex exclaimed, "My God! I talked my head off and wasted your whole afternoon. I'm so sorry."

"Don't be silly. We had fun. Your stories are really great," Steve said sincerely.

"Yes," Matthew agreed. "I love to hear about the outback. Can you believe it? I've lived in Sydney all my life and the only time I ever travelled was overseas. It's funny how we take for granted the beauty we have at home," he observed.

"Well, I'm glad you enjoyed listening to me. I generally don't talk my head off, but you two have been a wonderful audience." Alex smiled, feeling happy.

"And your wonderful audience will cook dinner for you in your honour," Steve announced and before she could protest, added, "but don't worry; we'll let you do the dishes so you feel needed."

Alex laughed. "It's a deal."

"Why don't you go up and get settled now? I left some towels and linen in your room. We'll eat in about an hour."

Matthew commented as soon as Alex was out of earshot, "You look beat. I'll cook."

"I must admit I overdid it in the garden this morning," Steve returned gratefully.

"Go lie down. I'll call you when dinner's ready."

"Okay." Steve threw him a warm smile and left.

Matthew looked after him as he disappeared down the hallway. His biggest fear was that Steve would succumb again like last time and would have to go to hospital. Matthew didn't think he could cope if anything happened to him.

CHAPTER 4

Russell Davis enjoyed the warmth of the sun on deck of his fifty-foot yacht, which bobbed gently on Rushcutters Bay. In his mid-fifties, Russell was tall and attractive in a rugged sort of way with green eyes and dark blonde hair, but he possessed none of the classical beauty of his son Matthew.

He looked after himself and kept trim by working out every day and jogging at least three times a week. His body was deeply tanned, and he had been lucky his skin still retained the suppleness of someone a lot younger.

On this particular afternoon, Russell was preoccupied as he lay sunbathing next to the twenty-three-year-old beauty by his side. His wife had told him Matthew would be coming around to lunch and Russell, not wanting to see him, had gone out sailing.

He was now thought about the waste that was his son—so much potential but such stupidity. His disappointment in Matthew still hurt him deeply.

"Honey, when are we going to take the holiday you promised?" Joanna intruded into his thoughts as she leaned forward on one elbow so she could see his face, her long honey-blonde hair brushed his chest.

Russell looked at her bare pink-tipped breasts, which were sporting a soft tan, and felt himself grow hard, but he resisted the urge to drag her downstairs to the cabin to fuck her. "Not now, Joanna, I'm too busy." His tone was harsh while he tried to do battle with his body.

Joanna glanced at the erection showing through his swimmers, and she leaned closer to him so her breasts lightly touched his chest. Her fingers travelled playfully and slowly toward his navel. "You promised, honey. You said we'd go to the Caribbean this year." Her voice was that of a pleading little girl.

Russell felt his organ begin to ache. If he didn't do something about it soon, he'd burst. "So I did, my sweet." He rose and brought her up with him. "Come with me." His thoughts about his son quickly left him.

They made their way to the cabin below, which was decked out with a double bed amidst modern décor in pastel blues and greys. Joanna lay back on the bed, her arms raised above her head in order to display the glory of her perfect breasts. Russell drew in his breath at her beauty and with one single movement ripped off her brief bikini panties and then divested himself of his swimmers. His penis was rock hard, and he plunged into her body like a desperate animal. Joanna's hips rose up to meet his deep thrusts, and in less than a minute he exploded inside her.

God, that felt good, he thought while he lay on the bed feeling spent. It was then he realised he had not given Joanna enough time to orgasm. "I'm sorry, sweet. I just couldn't help myself," he apologised.

Joanna was not perturbed. She moved so that her face was close to his spent member and her buttocks almost touched his face. "Lick me," she ordered, and then took his penis into her mouth and began to suck on it, swirling her tongue around it.

Russell groaned with pleasure as he tasted her, and his tongue plundered into her very essence. This time, they both came, and later, as they lay back on the bed, their thoughts could not have been more diverse—Russell was totally and absolutely intoxicated by his young girlfriend, and already planning a romantic holiday, while Joanna wondered how much longer she would have to put up being fucked by an old man before she could get some serious money out of him.

* * *

After a delicious dinner of chicken curry prepared by Matthew, the three housemates settled down to watch a movie, and Alex thanked her lucky stars she had been guided to this household. Somehow, this reminded her of the good old days with Harry when she was able to enjoy male company without feeling threatened.

Later in the evening, she did the dishes after Steve excused himself to go to bed. She thought he had looked a little pale throughout dinner, but she'd refrained from asking what was wrong. She had just moved in and reminded herself she must respect her housemates' privacy as much as she expected the same from them.

Soon after Steve went to bed, Matthew followed suit, telling her he wished to have an early night. Being left on her own was nothing new to her, and Alex enjoyed the quiet of the house while she cleaned up in the kitchen. She'd had a pretty exciting day and enjoyed good company. She could ask for nothing else.

The house settled down around her, and by the time she finished the dishes, it was past ten o'clock and she realised how tired she was. She checked all windows and doors to ensure they were securely locked and switched off the downstairs lights except the one in the hallway. Steve had told her earlier that they left it on every night in case someone had to rush down the stairs. Alex had wondered at the time why anyone would need to come down the stairs in such a hurry, but she had not questioned him about it. People had their little eccentricities, and that was that.

Delighting in the knowledge that for now this was home, she made her way to her room to grab a towel with the intention of taking a quick shower before bed. As she turned to leave the room, she noticed the reflection on the wardrobe mirror of the offending photo print of the two male bodies. Steve had offered to have it taken down, but she had insisted it didn't bother her and the print should stay where it was. Now, she wasn't so sure.

What was it about the picture that unsettled her mind? She tore her eyes away from the offending bodies and made for the bathroom down the hall. She wasn't in the mood just now to delve into unwelcome thoughts.

* * *

A door slamming down the hallway woke Alex with a start. She glanced at the clock on her bedside table and saw it was still early, just past four in the morning. She sat up in bed, and for a moment, memories of other doors slamming came into her mind. She cringed under the covers and waited, holding her breath.

Nothing happened. Her door remained shut, and no one came for her. Then, she heard a noise she recognised immediately—that of someone retching. She knew the sound well because this was exactly how she had sounded after a visit from *him*.

With a sinking heart, she realised it was Steve throwing up in the bathroom. Alex tiptoed out of bed and opened her bedroom door just enough to be able to hear what was going on.

'It's back, Steve!" Matthew's voice was raised in concern. "I told you to take it easy in the garden."

Steve replied in between retching. "It's nothing. Go back to bed!" More violent retching followed.

'I'm calling Dr Benning." Matthew's voice.

'No! Go back to bed." Steve managed to say just before he was overtaken by yet another bout of retching.

Alex closed her door and got back into bed with the sudden realisation that Steve was dying. It was obvious: the fragile countenance, the tiredness, Matthew's concern, and the fact this had happened before. Most of all, it was Steve's eyes that had communicated to her he was not long for this world. They had been full of love, full of peace—he was a person who had faced his illness and accepted it.

Without a second thought, Alex did what she had not done since childhood. She got down on her knees by the bed and said a prayer on Steve's behalf. Then, she lay back down and tried to shut out the sounds coming from the bathroom. Eventually, she slept.

* * *

Later that morning, Alex entered the kitchen to find a subdued Matthew and a sickly-looking Steve picking at his breakfast.

"Good morning!" She tried to sound bright and cheery, but somehow the effect was not achieved.

Steve smiled at her wanly, and Matthew, wanting to keep busy, jumped from his chair and went to the kitchen counter. "Want some coffee?"

She nodded. "Thanks."

"More toast?" Matthew asked Steve while he poured Alex a mug of coffee.

"No, thanks." Steve pushed his almost untouched plate of scrambled eggs away from him. "I have to get ready for work."

"You're not going in?" Matthew exclaimed, astounded.

Alex took the mug of coffee from him and sat quietly, listening to the interchange between the two men.

"I have to, Matthew. I have a big function on this evening."

"So let them run it without you. You hardly slept last night!"

"I can't do that. Besides, I feel better now," he stated not too convincingly.

Matthew sighed in exasperation, knowing once Steve made up his mind to do something, there was no stopping him. "What if—"

Steve did not let him finish. "Nothing is going to happen. I'm okay. Believe me." He suddenly realised Alex was still in the room, so he turned to her. "Just had a bad night. Maybe it was Matthew's curry," he uttered jokingly, but no one laughed. "Well, I better go and get ready. I'll see you both later." He was out of the kitchen and up the stairs before Matthew could say anything else.

The silence after his departure grew long, and Alex sipped her coffee, not knowing what else to do. Matthew remained at the table and pretended to sip his, all the while listening to Steve move around upstairs while he prepared for work. Finally, they both heard footsteps coming down the stairs and the front door open and close. Steve was gone.

Alex gazed at Matthew's face; he was frowning. "You know, if the wind changes, you'll stay like that," she teased and was rewarded with a smile.

"Your mother tell you this when you were a kid?"

Alex's own smile suddenly faded, and a shadow crossed her face. "I don't remember." How could she tell him she had never been a kid?

Matthew watched the interplay of emotions on her face and for the first time wondered what it was that brought on the haunted look he had observed several times. The previous night, when the three of them had sat in the kitchen with her recounting her travel tales, he had caught the same look from time to time.

Perhaps Steve was right when he'd said she was hiding a big hurt, and Matthew wondered what it was. Steve had told him he and Alex were alike in many ways, and Matthew now thought he knew what Steve had meant. Was he himself hiding a big hurt? An image of his parents popped into his head, but he dismissed it instantly.

"I'll do the dishes," Alex said, breaking into his pensive mood.

Matthew regarded her, as if for the first time, and realised here was another human being suffering inside—just like him.

Alex noticed his eyes on her and became self-conscious. She felt safe in her usual garb of jeans and oversized pullover, but Matthew's eyes were penetrating, and even though he was gay, he was still a man looking at a woman.

"Is ..." Her mouth felt dry. "Is something wrong?"

"I'm sorry. I was staring, wasn't I?" he apologised. His beautiful smile dispelled any fears she might have had. "I guess I was lost in my own thoughts and didn't realise it. I'm running down the road to see my agent and check on a few things with him, but when I get back, do you want to do some grocery shopping with me?" he asked, aware of the beginning of a warm feeling of friendship toward her.

Alex felt the prick of tears behind her eyes. It was ridiculous to feel this way about a gay man, but her need for his approval was so strong, and for the life of her, she could not understand it. "I'd like that."

"Good. We'll go as soon as I get back because I have a class this afternoon."

Matthew had earlier told her he attended acting classes three afternoons per week. "Suits me fine. I have to do some writing later on," Alex replied.

"See you in half an hour then." He threw what looked like a smile her way and disappeared out the door, leaving a dazed Alex behind.

* * *

Brent's office was not far, and Matthew strolled down the street in the cool morning bathed in sunshine. Men and women could not help glancing his way, but he ignored the appreciative looks. His thoughts were filled with concern for Steve's condition.

Last time he had one of his attacks, he ended up in hospital, and Dr Benning warned him to take it easy. Now, he was working long hours again in that blasted hotel. Matthew knew he had to get more of a regular income if he was to be of any help. It was time Brent got off his arse and found him more work. If he couldn't come up with the goods, Matthew decided he would simply look for another agent.

He reached a white terrace with maroon trelliswork where several chrome plaques displayed the names of different businesses. One of them read: BJ Management. Matthew entered the building and went straight up the stairs to Brent's rooms on the first floor.

The agent's office consisted of a small anteroom, where a

receptionist manned the phone and greeted clients, and two back offices where Brent and another agent worked. Larisa, the receptionist, put on her best smile when he entered.

"Hi, Matthew," she said in a coquettish manner.

"Is Brent in?" Matthew asked, disregarding the coy look she gave him; she was just another one of those who reacted to his looks.

"Take a seat. I'll tell him you're here." Not put off by Matthew's cold manner, Larisa disappeared behind the wooden partition leading to Brent's office. She was back in a moment. "You can go through."

Matthew barely acknowledged her with a nod of his head before making his way to Brent's office.

Brent Perry was a plump, balding little man in his mid-thirties with thick-framed glasses and a snub nose. Every time Matthew saw him, he couldn't help but think that if Brent ever decided to go into acting, he'd be typecast as a child molester.

"Matt, this is a surprise. I was gonna ring you today about the audition. The bastards finally got back to me," Brent announced in a breathy, excitable voice that was the norm whether he had good or bad news to impart to a client.

"And?" Matthew was used to his agent's excitability.

"Sorry, Matt, we missed out. Too good looking, they said. Too angelic! Can you believe it? Since when do they turn down attractive actors? Anyway, it turns out they wanted some macho-looking fucker for the role, a more rugged type. But I wouldn't be too disappointed about this one. The movie's low budget shit. It's B-grade rubbish. Won't go anywhere."

"It still would've gotten me some exposure," Matthew pointed out.

"The wrong kind," Brent stated firmly. "You don't want to be associated with these movies where you're always fucking some chick or you have to show your cock on screen."

Brent knew Matthew was worth more than a porn movie. If only he would make the decision to go to LA like he suggested to him repeatedly. He knew people over there who might have an interest in his client, but Matthew refused to go—something to do with his partner being ill. Brent had nothing against gay men, but these faggots pissed him off sometimes—too emotional for their own good.

"Brent, I need more regular work," Matthew said, breaking into the agent's thoughts.

"Okay, okay. If you don't object to doing more TV commercials and some modelling, I can keep you busy. But Matt, when are you going to think about the big move? You know you're limiting your chances in Australia."

"We've been through this before, and I'm not in a position to leave the country just now. It'll have to wait."

"Well, don't wait too long. You're twenty-eight, mate. Your career should be established by now and rising," Brent warned.

Matthew regarded him thoughtfully, torn between his dream and his love for Steve. He knew if his career was to have any sort of chance, he would have to move to LA, but the thought of leaving Steve was unbearable. He simply couldn't do it. Therefore, if it meant missing out on the "big one", then so be it. He would carry on being a low paid actor in Sydney.

"Do the best you can, all right? I have to go now." He turned toward the door.

"Okay. Just give me a couple of days and I'll make some phone calls." Brent would get Matthew more work and hoped eventually to get him off to LA. Matthew had a real chance if he played his cards right, and Brent was going to try to make sure he did.

* * *

When Matthew returned home, Alex was ready to go shopping and they set off toward the supermarket, which was a five minute walk from the house. While they strolled in companionable silence, Matthew felt his mood lighten, especially after the meeting with Brent. He was sure his agent could get him more work, and this would ease the financial burden. Plus coupled with the rent money Alex paid, he would ensure Steve worked fewer hours at the hotel.

Meanwhile, Alex was happy to walk quietly beside Matthew and observe the envious looks she received from passing females. If only they knew, she thought with a smile.

"What's that for?" Matthew caught her smiling.

"I'm being silly, that's all." She felt suddenly shy.

"So tell me anyway."

"Okay," she said, suddenly feeling self-conscious. "It's just that ... Well, I don't know if you've noticed, but ..." As she was trying to explain, another female walked past and eyed Matthew appreciatively before giving Alex a disdainful look.

Matthew laughed. "Oh, I get it. You mean the looks, don't you? I don't notice them anymore."

"Yes, but ... Well, they're also looking at me as if to say, *what's that baggage doing with him?*" Alex laughed, and Matthew liked her the better for it.

"You're not baggage. Don't ever say that about yourself," he chided her passionately.

Alex was surprised by his reaction.

Matthew saw the questioning look on her face and explained. "I grew up around the 'beautiful people', who put good looks above everything else. My whole life was based on superficiality until I met Steve and learned that true beauty is inside the person."

Alex felt touched. "Steve *is* a beautiful person, isn't he? He's kind, gentle, and funny; and even though he's dying ..." Too late! She realised with horror what she had just said. "I'm sorry, I'm so sorry! I didn't mean to say ... I ...um..." She was at a loss for words and felt terrible when she noticed the brightness in Matthew's eyes from the tears he held in check.

He stopped walking and stood still for a moment until he was able to control his emotions. Alex wanted to give him comfort, throw her arms around him and tell him she understood what pain felt like, but she dared not touch him. She stood quietly, waiting for him to say something.

"How did you know?" Matthew finally asked.

"I guessed. There's a look of peace in his eyes—a look that seems otherworldly, somehow. Then, there are the physical signs ... I'm so very sorry," she uttered softly.

"No need to apologise, Alex. I guess we should've told you from the beginning. Not everybody wants to share a house with someone who's dying of AIDS," he spoke harshly.

Alex realised the bitterness was not aimed at her, but at life. "Steve's a great soul; and no matter what happens in the future, I'm happy to have met him," she stated without hesitation.

Matthew felt as if a small weight had been lifted off his shoulders. Here was someone who did not judge and was supportive—totally unlike his parents. He resumed walking, and Alex followed.

"Like I said, beauty lies inside the person," Matthew commented, and this time he meant Alex. "Still, you may want to rethink the wardrobe," he teased her with a smile.

Alex did not take offence because she knew he meant well, and she understood his fastidiousness for dress. Steve had made fun of him, telling her it usually took him two hours to get ready to go out; and this was on a good day! "I thought oversized pullovers were in," she teased back.

"Not so, darling, not so!" Matthew replied in a posh voice. "Perhaps, I can persuade you to look at the latest collection from Paris? We have the trendiest designer fashions, and grunge is in this year."

They laughed aloud and passersby looked at them, wondering at the young Adonis with the woman in the baggy clothes.

CHAPTER 5

The mild days of autumn gave way to winter, and the season set in with surprisingly warm temperatures. The sun shone brightly in deep blue skies and Steve's garden flourished with Alex's help. The three housemates had settled into a seemingly harmonious existence, and Alex no longer thought of this as a flexible arrangement. She was truly happy in her new home.

There was still the matter of Steve's illness, but since the attack he'd experienced when Alex first moved in, his health had settled somewhat, and though he still looked frail at times, he seemed to be feeling better.

During their regular gardening sessions, Steve and Alex developed a close friendship, which made it natural for them to confide in each other—and this is how Alex learned about his personal history.

Steve told her about his contracting AIDS and how his deep love for Matthew was the only thing that really kept him going. Alex wondered how he felt about the risk involved in the sexual relations he still shared with Matthew, but she could not ask something so personal. However, this, too, came out in the course of their conversations.

It was during one of their early gardening sessions when Steve brought up the subject of his illness.

"I guess by now you know I have AIDS," he'd said in a matter-of-fact tone.

"I kind of guessed the first night I was here when you were ill."

"So Matthew and I did wake you after all. You know, he argued you didn't hear a thing." He smiled at the thought of Matthew trying to protect him from any more concerns than he already had.

"I'm a light sleeper." A temporary shadow crossed Alex's features. "I mean, sometimes living in the outback, you have to be a light sleeper in case dingoes decide to pay a visit."

Steve picked up a certain hesitation in her quick explanation but did not pursue it. He believed she would disclose what she chose in her own good time. "Anyway, Matthew finally told me you'd guessed. Apparently, you told him the day you went shopping for groceries, after I left for work."

Alex remained silent, waiting for what he had to say next.

"I felt then it was okay to let things be. I didn't see the need to go over all the woes of my tale of hardship, but I want you to know your support's meant a lot to me. You took over the cleaning of the house, which is great as we both know Matthew can be a bit of a pig." They grinned at each other; then Steve continued. "You also helped me with the garden, and since I shortened my hours at work, I've been feeling more rested and spoiled by the two of you. You guys won't even let me cook or do the dishes. So I want to thank you for this, and also for not being judgemental and running off in terror."

"Why would I do that? You've become a friend."

"You'd be amazed at the number of people who disappeared from my life once they found out about me." He felt sad, thinking of so-called friends who had cut off contact with him.

"Well, I say good riddance to bad rubbish. Isn't it during times of adversity when a person finds out who their true friends really are?" Alex's eyes clouded for a moment, far away in thought.

"And who are *your* friends, Alex?"

Steve surprised her with his direct question, but she didn't feel threatened by it. "Just old Harry. I still write to him, you know. He's like the father I never had ... And of course, you and Matthew are friends, too. You guys accepted me the way I am. Matthew keeps asking me why I wear baggy clothes all the time though." She grinned. "But you haven't said anything to me."

"I figure if you want me to know, you'll tell me when you're ready. Matthew's young and a bit brash at times, but he does have a heart of gold; he just doesn't know it."

Alex had no doubt Matthew had a heart of gold, at least where Steve was concerned. He had stuck by him through thick and thin.

"The one thing I'm truly grateful for," Steve went on, "is that ever since he and I got together, I always insisted on safe sex. Even so, I still worry a condom might break. Thank God this never happened."

"Matthew loves you very much," Alex remarked to hide her embarrassment at his intimate remark.

"I know, and this is why I'm so lucky. There are people out there who go through their whole life feeling unloved, and then they die." Then, almost as if talking to himself, he added, "At least I'll die knowing both Patrick and Matthew loved me. I've been twice blessed." With what seemed a feeling of contentment, he turned to work on the rosebushes in front of him.

Alex was left with her own thoughts. Who had loved her? Maybe old Harry, and perhaps now Steve and Matthew were beginning to care for her. Other than this, there was nobody.

Her real father had died when she was two years old, and her mother could not possibly have loved her; otherwise, she would have guessed what had happened with *him*. A cloud blocked the sunlight and Alex shivered. Even after twenty years, the ghosts of the past had the power to haunt her.

Thankfully, since she had moved in with Steve and Matthew, the ghosts had visited her thoughts and dreams less often; she had not had a single panic attack since the night at the hotel. For the first time in her life, she began to feel safe and content. Steve's health seemed better, and she was happy she had contributed to it by taking on most of the housekeeping duties. Her work was going well, too, and she was currently working on a three-part piece on camel trekking through Central Australia for a well-known travel magazine.

As for Matthew, her friendship with him was growing nicely, and he seemed a lot happier now he was working on a regular basis doing TV commercials, modelling and small parts in a few of the soapies. His free time was spent with Steve; and he hadn't visited his mother since the time when Alex had first moved in.

Alex knew this because Mrs Davis commented on it whenever she telephoned; and since Matthew never took her calls, it was usually Alex who had to deal with her. For a time, Mrs Davis took an interest in her, asking who she was and what she was doing there, but her curiosity soon wore off when Alex informed her she was not Matthew's girlfriend, only a housemate. Alex assumed at the time Matthew's mother either did not know her son was gay or she was simply living in denial. She had no way of knowing for sure because Matthew had not discussed his parents with her.

* * *

The past reached out to touch Alex once again on the first truly cold and rainy night that winter.

Alex retired to her room early, leaving Matthew and Steve watching a film downstairs. Not long after, she heard the telephone ring and Matthew calling out to her, "Alex, you still awake?"

She opened the door of her room and peeked out. "What is it?"

"A call for you. Take it in our room if you like."

There was a telephone in the main bedroom and she went to it, wondering who could be calling at this time. All the editors had both her mobile and landline number, but they certainly had no need to call this late.

"Alex Dorian speaking."

"Alex, at last!"

The voice at the other end of the line sent chills down Alex's spine. Her legs turned to jelly and she sat on the edge of the bed for support. "Hello, Mother," she responded, her voice devoid of feeling.

"You haven't written in ages. John and I were worried about you. Then, I saw one of your articles in a magazine so I called the editor, who told me you were in Sydney," her mother explained, hardly pausing for breath.

"Who gave you this number?" Alex asked coldly.

"My dear, there's no need to get upset. I am your mother after all. I deserve to know you're okay. Why, you never keep in touch—"

"How did you get this number?" Alex interrupted.

"Well, it's like I told you, I got the number from this editor I rang. I had a time convincing him it was an emergency, of course, but as you listed this as your alternative business number, in the end he saw no harm in letting me have it. I tried your mobile first, but it was switched off."

Alex did not speak.

"Are you there, dear?"

Her mother could be very pushy when she wanted, Alex fumed; yet she played the helpless, delicate flower in need of protection when she was around men.

"Alex, answer me!"

"What do you want?" Alex remarked abruptly.

"Really! Is this how you're going to greet me? You don't write for close to six months. Last time I tracked you down, you were over in Perth. Now you're in Sydney, and not even a call to find out if I'm still alive."

The indignation pouring out of her mother's mouth was too much for Alex. She was very good at playing the wounded parent, Alex thought resentfully, but she wasn't going to let it get to her. "So how are you, Mother?" Alex did nothing to keep the dryness out of her tone.

"I see you don't care much about family. Heaven only knows how long you've been in Sydney, and to think you didn't even bother to make contact. You could've at least dropped in to see us."

"I don't want to *drop in* to see you; you know that."

"No, I don't know why you never visit us."

Alex sighed. Her mother was either a real innocent or she was just playing dumb. "Well, you try and figure it out." She paused as an idea popped into her mind and then added, "And if you truly want to see me, you can meet with me alone."

Although she had kept in touch from time to time, Alex had not actually seen her mother since she had left home at age fifteen. At the beginning, she tried to get her mother to meet with her; she'd even offered to pay for the plane ticket to get her to fly out. Her mother, however, was always ready with excuses such as being too busy with a charity event for church or insisting she simply couldn't cope travelling without John.

Alex would rather die than see *him* again, so she stopped asking her mother to meet up, and the years had slipped by.

"Of course I want to see you, dear," her mother declared, interrupting Alex's thoughts. "John and I can drive up to town and—"

"No, Mother. I said alone."

"Alex, what's your problem? Why don't you want to see John?"

Did she not get it? "John's not family," Alex blurted out. It was the first thing that came into her head.

"Honestly! I don't know how you can say that. He raised you as his own, for God's sake. How can you be so ungrateful?" her mother berated. "What sort of a daughter did I raise? Why, I bet you don't even go to church these days."

Alex rolled her eyes in exasperation. Her mother came from a

40

family of devout Catholics, and Alex remembered being dragged to church every Sunday with her and John. They made the perfect picture of a religious and dutiful family, taking part in all the church activities.

Small wonder Father Timothy hadn't believed the shy, eight-year-old Alex when she once tried to explain what her stepfather was doing to her. In all fairness to the priest, she hadn't exactly come right out with it. She had felt too awkward and frightened to do this, but she had hoped that by hinting her stepfather liked to play games with her, Father Timothy would've asked her to be more specific. Instead, the priest said something about Alex having to come to terms with the fact that John was now her dad and she had to honour him as she would a real father.

"Alex, what's the matter with you? Are you still there?" Her mother's voice brought her out of her reverie.

"Yes, yes, I'm here. Look, if you want to see me, I'm happy to meet with you alone. The choice is yours."

"Okay. I can't say I understand your reluctance to see John; but yes, I'd like to see you."

"All right then. How about this coming Sunday? We'll have coffee at the Hyatt—say three in the afternoon?"

"That's fine. I'll meet you in the lobby. I only hope I can recognise you." The wounded parent tone again.

"Please, Mother," Alex stated drily. "We both know my photo always appears alongside my articles. You know very well what I look like. And please, don't call this number again. If you need to talk with me leave a message on my mobile."

Her mother realised self-pity was not going to work with her daughter as the girl was devoid of all feeling. "All right then, I'll see you on Sunday."

Alex hung up without saying goodbye and released a sigh of relief. She noticed the tension that had built up in her body while talking to her mother, and her muscles felt like they would give way on her, so she remained sitting on the bed, giving herself time to recover.

She did not know how long she sat there, trying to shake off what seemed to be the beginnings of a panic attack, so when Matthew suddenly appeared beside her, she was startled.

"Are you okay? Not bad news, I hope." He saw the familiar

haunted look on her face and became aware she was shivering. "You're cold." He sat down next to her and placed a hand on her shoulder.

Alex almost jumped off the bed. "I'm ... I'll be okay." His hand seemed to burn through her with a searing heat she could not bear. "It's just ... well ... it was ...."

She was not very coherent, and Matthew became concerned. Perhaps something awful had happened. He placed his other hand on her other shoulder and felt her trembling like a creature caught in a trap. "Alex, what's the matter?"

Alex could not think as a myriad of emotions exploded within her. She had not been touched by male hands for twenty years, and Matthew's touch was doing all sorts of inexplicable things to her. She felt frightened, and his nearness was threatening to her. At the same time, her body was consumed with a feeling of exhilaration like she had suddenly been set free, her spirit soaring through the heavens.

Then, reality took over and she knew she had to get away from his touch. She pulled back gently and forced herself to sound composed. "It was a call from my mother. I guess she has this effect on me." As she said this, she was not to know just how much she and Matthew had in common.

"Well, I can certainly relate to that. Don't let it get to you, but if it ever does remember I'm here."

Alex was surprised at his response. She looked into his eyes and saw a hurt in them that mirrored her own. She had no idea what type of relationship he had with his mother but knew that whatever it was, it had the power to wound him deeply.

"Thank you. I really appreciate it. I better be off to bed now." It was time to get away from his strong physical presence.

"Sleep well," he said as she left the room. Remaining behind, he looked after her thoughtfully.

Once out of his sight, Alex raced to the bathroom and locked the door behind her. A hot shower was the only way to release the tension in her muscles. She caught a glimpse of her face in the mirror and saw the haunted look in her eyes. Would she ever be free of the past?

* * *

42

Cecilia Dorian-Hunt put down the phone and turned to find her husband standing behind her, a cup of coffee in hand. She saw a gentle-looking man with fair hair and green eyes who had aged before his time. John looked more like a man in his late sixties than someone who had just turned fifty-four, and for the first time, she wondered what it was that had aged him so.

They had been married for twenty-six years, and though there were no children, Cecilia felt theirs had been a good marriage. John was Catholic like herself and just as devout. Their life together had been one of contentment and companionship where sex played a small part.

Cecilia learned from the beginning that John was not overly enthusiastic about sex, but she had fallen in love with his gentleness and kindness to her and her child at a time when it was difficult for a widow to survive without a man. So she had accepted the good with the not so good. Sex had never really been the main feature in her own life although she had enjoyed it during her younger years when she was married to Alex's father, Jason.

Jason had been passionate about life, love, and sex. He had been a wonderful husband to her, and they had been truly happy. Alex's birth was a real blessing and a source of extreme delight for Jason. He loved the sight of his baby girl the minute he laid eyes on her, and for the two years he was alive after her birth, he'd poured his love on her as if he knew he would not be around for long.

Jason was a miner and had lived in the mining community of Wollongong all his life. He had also died in that community in a work-related accident. Cecilia, being a miner's daughter, had remained in the town after his passing, and in the house they had purchased when they'd first married.

Thankfully, Jason's insurance payout had covered the mortgage on their home, but Cecilia had to provide for her and her daughter as best she could by working as a sales assistant in a ladies fashion store. Alex's grandparents on both sides were deceased, and the young widow had had to struggle on her own for close to five years until John Hunt came into her life.

John was what people referred to as a drifter. He seemed to have no past. He had simply drifted into town one day, and shortly thereafter met Cecilia in the supermarket where he worked as a packer.

From the time they met, John was pleasant to the young widow and her six-year-old girl. He always looked out for them and helped them take their groceries out to the car. As time went by, John and Cecilia began to date, and a year later they married.

With John's wage, he being a supervisor at the supermarket by then, Cecilia's burdens eased enormously and she felt happiness come back into her life. She knew very little about her new husband's past, but she loved him all the same, and this was all that mattered to her.

John had been orphaned at a young age and had moved around the country working odd jobs since he left school. He was born in South Australia in a small wine-producing community and had lived there with an aunt after his parents' death in a car accident.

Cecilia was not concerned with the past, however, and only knew John was a good, hardworking man who provided for her family. This was all she needed to know. So it never bothered her that he wasn't overly enthused about sex. On the occasions when they were intimate, he was always gentle and loving, and though she was barely ever left satisfied, she resigned herself to the fact that it was pleasant enough.

Cecilia's thoughts now turned to her daughter. Alex had at first accepted John readily into the family, excited at the prospect of having a daddy, but after about six months she began to change toward him. Cecilia could have sworn her little girl positively hated her stepfather.

She followed his every move with wary eyes and hardly ever spoke to him. Alex had always been shy, though, and Cecilia had put it down to the child's personality. Children could be strange at times, and though Cecilia tried on numerous occasions to get her daughter to be more receptive toward John, she never got a response from Alex.

John bought Alex all sorts of gifts to try to win her heart. He lavished her with all the attention and love a parent could give a child, but Alex remained stone cold. Cecilia became upset with her over this and ignored her pleas that she did not want to "play games" with John anymore.

What an ungrateful child she had been, Cecilia thought, feeling vexed even now. Here was John, buying her all sorts of toys and games, and Alex always refused to play with him. In fact, she was so rude at times that Cecilia took to slapping her across the face whenever she caught her being disrespectful. John had always chided her not to be so tough on the child, but Cecilia could not help it; she wanted Alex to accept her stepfather.

As Alex grew up, she became very wild, often staying out of the house for long periods of time—supposedly bushwalking or climbing at a reserve nearby. She must have taken some falls, too, which explained her unkempt appearance and her often-bruised skin. Cecilia felt her child had turned into a real heathen, and in the end it had been a relief when Alex ran away from home. Finally, Cecilia could have a more peaceful life with her husband.

John took Alex's absence badly and for a long time kept asking after her, wondering what she said in her letters to her mother. Poor John, he had so wanted to be a father to Alex, but she had never let him.

Now, as she faced him, Cecilia said to her husband, "That was Alex. She's in Sydney."

John was surprised and looked alert. "How is she? What does she say?"

"Nothing much, as usual. She's agreed to see me, though."

"Oh. When? Want me to drive you?" He seemed uneasy, and Cecilia put it down to his memory of Alex's rejection.

"No, it's okay. I'll catch the train, love."

Wollongong was approximately a ninety minute ride by train from Sydney, and it would make no sense getting John to drive her all the way only to have to wait in the car while she met up with Alex.

"I don't suppose she wants to see me?" John asked casually.

"I'm sorry, love. You know how she is." Cecilia hated to hurt his feelings, but there was nothing else she could do.

John nodded absentmindedly, continuing to watch his wife while she made herself a coffee. Cecilia was still attractive enough at fifty-three: petite with short dark hair, and large amber eyes, just like Alex's. Lately, however, she had put on some weight and become quite plump. John wondered what Alex looked like these days. Was she still as slim as she had been when she was younger? He felt himself grow hard at the thought of her young body fighting him off. Banging his coffee cup down on the kitchen table, he walked off to the bathroom and heard Cecilia calling after him. "Are you okay, John?"

"Yes," he called back before locking the door behind him.

He pulled down his trousers and shorts and looked at his hard cock, erect as ever. For a moment, he thought of his wife and felt repulsed by her. He only desired a young, firm body under his, but in the absence of one he would have to make do relieving himself with his hand.

When he came, he thought about the young thing he was fucking from the supermarket. She was a girl of fifteen who reminded him of Alex. She allowed John to use her body while he paid to maintain her little drug habit. It was expensive but worth it.

It had been a very long time since Alex's departure and during the years that followed, he had played the model husband to Cecilia. His life had been quite comfortable, but since Cecilia did not satisfy him sexually, it had been difficult for him.

Then, Wendy had come to work at the supermarket and it wasn't long before he discovered her drug habit. He gave her a choice: do as he said and keep her job and drug habit, or get out.

Wendy was no novice to sex, so it was an easy choice for her to make.

CHAPTER 6

Alex awoke to a sunny day and felt her spirits lift after a bad night spent tossing and turning. She'd had a dream where her stepfather burst into her room, and just as she was about to scream out in fear, two hands at her shoulders steadied her and she found herself face to face with Matthew. The look in his eyes told her he was there to protect her, and then she fell into the safety his arms.

Now, Alex jumped out of bed, not wanting to relive the dream. The thought of Matthew touching her felt too disconcerting and she wasn't able to deal with it right now. After a refreshing shower, she made her way downstairs where she found Steve and Matthew at breakfast. "Morning," she greeted them.

"Good morning," they each replied. "How are you today?" Matthew asked.

She coloured, once again remembering the feel of his hands on her shoulders. "I'm fine, thanks." Then, she turned to Steve. "My ... um ... I heard from my mother last night."

"I hope everything's well."

"Yes, of course. It's just ..." She didn't know how to explain the rest.

Steve handed her a cup of coffee and bade her sit next to him. "Alex, whatever it is, you don't have to say anything unless you feel you want to," he said kindly, patting her hand.

His touch was reassuring and, combined with the sun shining in through the kitchen window and the genuine concern on her housemates' faces, Alex relaxed.

"I'm going to see her for the first time in twenty years, you see," she finally stated. "I guess I'm nervous and scared of the memories." She took a sip of her coffee; she could not tell them any more at this stage.

"Do you want to see her?" Steve probed gently.

"I suppose so." She sounded unsure.

"Well, maybe one of us can give you a lift and hang around," Matthew suggested. He knew exactly how uncomfortable it felt to meet with an estranged parent.

The knight in shining armour, Alex thought. "Thanks, but I think this is something I need to do alone."

"Well, remember what I said last night," he reminded her. "I'm here, and so is Steve."

"Thank you for that. I really appreciate it." She felt so confused she buried her face in the coffee mug, and sensing her discomfort, Steve changed the subject altogether.

"I'm only working half day today, so what do you say to a little gardening later on this afternoon?" He knew she enjoyed their gardening sessions.

"You're on." Alex was silently grateful to him. She did not want to think about Sunday, only two days away now, or her mother.

* * *

Russell Davis leaned over the balcony rail and gazed at the harbour lights in the cool of the evening while he enjoyed a cigarette. Dora joined him, a glass of scotch in hand. "Want a drink?"

"No, thanks."

They both looked into the night sky for a moment, wrapped in their private thoughts. Dora was first to break the silence. "Matthew hasn't returned any of my calls."

Russell remained silent and took a drag from his cigarette.

Dora continued, "I think I really upset him last time he was here. He wasn't in a good mood to start with. Not enough acting work, I think he said."

"Let his fairy boyfriend pay the bills, for God's sake!" Russell snapped harshly. "Don't you give him any money, you hear?"

Dora was shocked at the savage tone in his voice. "How can you say that? He's your son."

Russell exploded. "I don't have a son! Not since he decided to take up with those poofs!"

"Russell—"

"Enough, Dora! We go through this every time I'm here."

"Which is not often!" she exclaimed in retaliation to his attack.

"You can't stop me from helping Matthew. He needs money now that Steve's ill."

"I said *enough*. I don't want to hear about Matthew or his faggot boyfriend!"

This infuriated her. "No, of course you don't. All you care about is your young slut!"

Russell flicked the cigarette over the balcony rail and threw his wife a look of contempt. "Get a life." He made to turn into the loungeroom, but Dora grabbed him by the sleeve of his shirt.

"I've been a faithful wife to you, damn it! I think I deserve some respect." She was holding onto her self-control and hoped he would not see her cry.

"You're a drunk. I don't respect drunks."

"And I don't respect cheats!"

Russell removed her hand from his sleeve as if her touch repulsed him. "That makes us even then, doesn't it?" He strode into the loungeroom and across to the double wooden doors leading to the corridor. "As I said before, get a life," he called out and slammed his way out of the room.

Dora's internal dam broke and tears spilled out. She finished her drink in one gulp and made her way toward the bar for a refill.

* * *

That same evening, Steve and Matthew were getting ready to watch a DVD. Matthew walked into the lounge with three mugs of hot chocolate.

"Is Alex coming down?" Steve asked.

Matthew set the mugs on the coffee table. "I'll go get her." He moved across to the bottom of the stairs and called out Alex's name. There was no response, so he climbed the stairs and made his way to her room.

The door was standing ajar. "Alex?" he called softly. Again, no response. He listened for a moment and realised she was in the bathroom with the shower running. He was about to knock on the bathroom door but instead found himself entering her room. He felt guilty intruding in on her privacy, but curiosity got the better of him. Since Alex had talked about her uneasiness at seeing her mother, he had been wondering why this was the case.

He cast a quick look around the room, but saw nothing out of the ordinary until he spotted the picture hanging above her bed. It was covered by a piece of cloth. He moved closer and lifted a corner of the cloth to peek underneath. It was the photo print of the two naked male figures. He wondered why she'd covered.

Turning from the print, a piece of paper lying on the desk caught his attention. He picked it up and read:

When man savagely takes,
The victim's soul is not marred,
The spirit rises above the squalor,
Rescued by death.

"Is something wrong?" Alex remarked from the doorway, startling him so that he dropped the paper to the floor.

He turned to her, looking guilty. "I came to look for you. We're ready."

She looked at the piece of paper as he picked it up and placed it back on the desk. "I didn't know you wrote poetry. I'm sorry. I didn't mean to pry."

She nodded, accepting his apology. "I'll be right down."

"Yes, well, there's hot chocolate waiting," he said and quickly exited the room, squeezing past her at the door.

It was only after he left that it occurred to Alex he might have noticed the covered print.

* * *

Matthew thought Steve looked rather tired and felt like berating him for having spent all afternoon in the garden, but Steve loved his plants. Gardening was a source of joy to him, so Matthew said nothing. At least, Alex helped out now, and this meant Steve did not have to work so hard. It was just after nine, and Steve had dozed off while Matthew read in bed.

"What are you reading?" Steve's voice asked out of the semidarkness.

"I thought you were asleep. Do you want me to switch off the light?"

"No, it's okay. I like a little light in the room. I only wondered what you were reading."

"Some audition pieces," Matthew replied, and then, "Steve?"

"Yes?"

"Are you feeling okay? I thought you looked a bit tired earlier."

"Too much gardening, I think; but Alex was a great help. You know, she's so emotionally fragile." Steve managed to steer the topic away from his state of health.

For once Matthew was distracted. "How do you mean?" he uttered with curiosity.

"She puts on a brave front, but deep down there's a terrible hurt. I can see it in her eyes. Maybe it's something to do with her mother."

"Earlier, when I went to get her, she was in the shower. I looked inside her room and noticed a poem on the desk; it was hers. It was so ... dark, I guess. She wrote about being rescued by death or something."

Steve turned to look at him, sitting up slightly against the pillows. "I'll ignore the fact that you spied on her," he admonished, while trying to hide his amusement. "Hmm—*rescued by death*," he repeated as if he understood what it meant. "I know she's hurting inside. I only wish I could help, but I can't unless she confides in me."

"And another thing," added Matthew, "you know the print above her bed? She covered it with a cloth."

"She covered it ... You mean the print with the two naked males?" Steve asked quickly, an idea flashing into his mind.

"Yes."

"I could be way off here, but I think I know what's haunting her," he said, almost to himself.

"Well?" Matthew prompted.

"Don't you see? The way she dresses; the fact that the naked male figures disturb her; the poetry—*being rescued by death*."

"No, I don't see. What does it mean?"

"She's been hurt by someone—a man. She dresses in a way that'll repulse any male interest in her. When she first came to look at the room, remember she mentioned she specifically wanted to share with a gay couple? I think it was because she felt safe with us."

"My God! Do you mean to say she was molested or something?" Matthew was suddenly shocked at the idea that this was what may have happened to their housemate.

"I don't know, but this meeting with her mother after twenty years? I mean, why leave it so long to see her, unless the person who hurt Alex was someone close to the mother? It could be someone like a male friend. She did say this Harry fellow, the shearer, was the only father she ever knew. So I'm assuming her father's out of the picture, somehow. Perhaps, Alex lost him when she was young and her mother remarried or had a boyfriend."

"Or it could still be the biological father for all we know. Poor Alex." Matthew frowned. "And to think I teased her about her fashion sense. God, what an insensitive idiot I am! But how was I to know?"

"Don't feel bad. You were only teasing, and I'm sure she understands."

"I hope so because I'd hate for her to think I was being a bastard."

"I'm sure she doesn't. In fact, she seems to like you."

"She likes you, too."

"Yes, I know, but I was referring to your looks. She reacts to you," Steve commented.

Matthew suddenly felt uncomfortable. "What? Calling Dr Freud! How would you know she reacts to my looks?"

"Don't take it badly. She's not after you in *that* way."

"Well, what do you mean then?"

"I'm only saying she may think it's safe for her to feel attracted to you because you're gay. So it's okay for her to look. My God! I wonder what this monster did to her."

Matthew wondered the same thing, and to his surprise he found himself feeling protective toward Alex. She was, after all, a good person. She didn't judge them for being gay nor did she judge Steve for having AIDS. And she'd taken the household under her wing to ease the pressure off them. She had become a good friend. "Well, whoever this son of a bitch is, I'd like to—"

"Calm down." Steve was amused by Matthew's chivalry, his heart of gold coming to the rescue once again. This was the reason why Steve loved him so much. "We don't know if this is really what happened. I'm only speculating, but the signs are certainly there. In any case, for the moment, we can only be her friends and hope that over time she'll reach out to us. Until then, we carry on being there for her."

"You're right," Matthew agreed.

Steve yawned. "I'm going to sleep now. I'm tired. Good night." He snuggled back down and turned away from the light.

"Good night," Matthew replied, deep in thought. He now understood the reason why Alex had trembled after taking the call from her mother, and he also wondered whether his own touch had frightened her.

* * *

Steve still looked tired and rather pale the following morning, giving Matthew cause for concern. He sat out in the courtyard, enjoying the morning sun and watching his garden, while Matthew prepared breakfast and peeked at him through the kitchen window.

"Hi." Alex entered the kitchen. "Need any help?"

"Just the coffee. We're having breakfast outdoors if you want to join us."

"That'll be nice." She made herself busy but noticed Matthew seemed worried and kept glancing at Steve every few seconds. "Bad night?" she asked.

"Not really. Although he was rather tired. But this morning he looks terrible." His frown confirmed his concern, and Alex felt for him.

"Why don't you let me finish up in here while you go and keep him company?" she suggested.

"Thanks, I appreciate it." He beamed at her and went out to join Steve.

Alex finished the scrambled eggs he had started to prepare and served portions for all of them with toast and grilled ham. This reminded her of the old days in the outback when she cooked for the shearers, although in those days, she had cooked for at least thirty hungry men.

She manoeuvred two of the plates and the coffee mugs out to where the boys were sitting. Steve did look pale. "Good morning," she said to him. "Eat while it's hot." She put down the plates and mugs and went back inside to get her own.

"Thank you," Steve uttered when she rejoined them.

"No problem. I'm used to cooking for more than three people."

"Well, then, maybe we could open up a café," Matthew teased.

"Now, there's a living for us. Hey, I could even play the maitre'd!'"

Alex noticed Steve did not respond with his usual humour. Instead, he sat quietly and did not touch his food. "Oh, I don't know that my culinary skills would stretch to such an enterprise. I think the café would soon go broke, even with a maitre'd who's an aspiring actor." She grinned at Matthew.

"You underestimate yourself, Alex," he replied, stealing a glance at Steve.

There was still no response from him, so Matthew turned his attention to the food and ate in silence.

Alex could tell he was bursting to say something, but he seemed hesitant so she decided to come to the rescue. "Steve, you're not doing justice to my cooking. In that case, I guess the café idea is definitely out of the question."

Steve did not reply. He was watching over his garden as if he were the only person present. Alex noticed he was following the moves of a beautiful, bright blue and black butterfly, which was flying about from flower to flower, seemingly enjoying the morning sun.

Alex saw Matthew throw her a look of concern, and she turned to Steve. "Steve—" She started to say.

"When I was a kid," Steve spoke suddenly, but the look in his eyes remained distant, as if he saw something the other two could not see. "When I was a kid," he said again, "my mother told me it was a sin to catch or kill a butterfly."

Alex and Matthew listened in silence as Steve continued, "She told me when a person died and their soul was waiting to move onto another plane of existence, the soul lived in the butterfly temporarily until it was freed to move on to its divine source. So if one caught or killed a butterfly, they would be interfering with the soul's passage."

The two housemates watched the butterfly as it landed on one of Steve's roses and rested there for a few seconds. A chill of foreboding ran through Matthew's body. Alex was mesmerised by the story, although she sensed Matthew's reaction.

Steve talked on while his breakfast slowly grew cold. "Ever since then, I became fascinated by these 'Soul Bearers'—that's what I used to call them; and I'd sit there and watch them flying around our garden for hours. I loved the blue and black ones the best; they were so majestic somehow. It was then I promised myself when it was my time to die that my soul would travel on one of those beautiful creatures toward eternal happiness." Steve watched the butterfly as it came away from the rose it had landed on earlier and now hovered above the other flowers.

Alex felt a tear run down her face. She felt moved by the touching story and sad for Steve. Matthew was silent. His look of desperation told her he was already thinking ahead to the day when Steve would be gone, and instinctively she knew that day was not too far away.

"Steve," she spoke gently, "your breakfast's getting cold." She felt she had to break the tense moment for Matthew's sake.

Steve finally noticed her and gave her a serene smile. "I'm not so hungry, after all, Alex. I'll just have my coffee, thanks." He picked up the mug and took a sip as his eyes rested once more on the butterfly.

Alex started to clear the table. "Matthew, why don't you help me?"

Matthew seemed grateful for something to do. He instantly jumped up and followed her into the kitchen with his own plate and coffee mug, leaving Steve to his silent contemplation.

CHAPTER 7

Alex did the dishes while Matthew dried and put them away. He worked in silence, and once again Alex sensed his mood. She seemed so in tune with his emotions these days that she felt she could literally reach out and touch them.

How was it that she had become so close to his thoughts? It was like a part of her existed inside of him. She had always believed two people could be soul mates in friendship, and she wondered whether Matthew believed in the same thing.

From a young age, she had developed beliefs about karma and reincarnation. She once read that people tended to reincarnate in groups: so if in one lifetime a person was one's husband, in another they might be a brother or a friend; and in yet another, they could be an uncle or a teacher, and so on. Somehow, all this was meant to be decided before people reincarnated. The people involved apparently agreed upon the roles they would play once on earth and what lessons they would learn from each other.

For a chilling moment, Alex paused, wet plate in hand, and thought of her stepfather. Could she have possibly agreed for him to reincarnate so he would torture her the way he had? She'd also read negative karma had to be worked off. So basically, a person who committed negative or evil deeds would have to pay off somewhere down the line, but not necessarily in their present life; it could happen in another one. This explained why so many innocent people suffered in their present life without necessarily having done something wrong or evil. It simply meant it was time for them to work off some of the negative karma accumulated from past lives.

If this was the case, then Alex had worked off a lot of it by suffering at her stepfather's hands. This belief helped her understand why she had to go through her ordeal, and the thought was somewhat comforting. If she had already paid off in this life, she would never have to go through that particular experience again.

Her mind then wandered over to Matthew and what role he had played in relation to her in a previous life. They might have been lovers and agreed to come back as friends in this lifetime. The thought of Matthew as her lover brought colour to her cheeks and she felt her face grow hot.

"Something wrong?" Matthew had been observing her quietly, noticing the changing expressions playing across her face.

Alex managed a smile as she dismissed her private thoughts. "No. Just thinking about things, I guess." She then changed the subject. "I suppose you're worried about Steve."

"I can't help thinking the worst." He expressed exactly what she had been thinking earlier in the garden, and a feeling of déjà vu went through her.

"I know that nothing I say will make you feel any better, but I want you to know, whatever happens, I'll be here if you need anything." Then, she added hastily, "If you want me to be, that is."

Matthew was secretly relieved to hear this. When she had first moved in, Alex said she might only stick around for three months, but now it seemed like she was finally putting down roots. He acknowledged that in some way both Steve's and his own friendship toward her had been responsible for this. He believed she drew comfort from knowing she was safe with them, and he was sure she now considered them to be the family she never had. "Does this mean you're not moving on?"

To Alex's surprise, Matthew came out with her secret hope—the hope she would be able to stay on, even after Steve was gone. She did not, however, know how to reply to his question. If she said she was staying on, he would think she was being presumptuous; but if she said she did not yet know, he might think she did not value their friendship or that she couldn't make up her mind.

"Well ... I ... well ..." She felt uneasy about how to respond so she looked to him for a cue and found him smiling at her, certain in those few seconds that he had read her thoughts.

"Of course I want you to stay. You're part of the family now, you know," he declared with such sincerity that she was left in no doubt he needed her and she, in turn, needed him.

"Thank you," she uttered shyly and went on doing the dishes, making every effort not to get too emotional.

Matthew resumed his drying up duties and let her be. He knew he had touched her deeply.

Alex composed her emotions and thought about the way things had turned out. Steve was a dear man, and so much more sure of himself. He seemed at peace with the knowledge he was dying, and his only concern was whether Matthew would be strong enough to get on with his life once he passed on. From a spiritual point of view, Alex figured Steve did not need any support; he was highly spiritual already and seemed to know his purpose on earth. He was here to share his love with Matthew, and now with her; and to teach them that if a person was at peace with themselves and the world, then they had nothing to fear. Alex felt moved and humbled by this realisation. She and Matthew were the needy ones, drawing strength from Steve—and he was their rock.

Steve was so wise about things, and so very loving and understanding that she was not surprised his eyes shone with the light of pure and unconditional love. Instead, Matthew was the one who needed all the love in order to get over the pain of his parents' rejection, and now the loss he may soon have to face. Matthew had been lucky when he had found this kind of supportive love in his soul mate, Steve.

Then what, Alex wondered, did Matthew need from her? If he had Steve's love, what was it he needed from the friend she had become? She could not see this as clearly as she saw the Steve-Matthew relationship. Furthermore, what did she need from Matthew? At this point, Alex forced her mind to go blank. To pursue this line of thought any further would only confuse her and bring up all sorts of emotions about the past.

Matthew noticed the changing expressions on her face once again and knew this was the time to interrupt. "By the way," he remarked, "I'm organising a surprise birthday party for Steve. He turns thirty-six in two weeks' time. I hope you're going to be here."

"Of course! I wouldn't miss it for the world. Do you need help with anything?" Alex offered excitedly, relieved to be rescued from her reverie.

"You know I do. Can you imagine me cooking for sixty people?" They laughed. Matthew's cooking skills were limited to scrambled eggs and chicken curry.

"What were you thinking of doing?"

"Well, if the weather holds out until then, I thought we'd have a backyard barbecue. So all we need are salads and stuff. I can handle the rest."

"Sounds great. I'll make the salads, finger food, and desserts," Alex volunteered, already caught up in the party spirit. "What about entertainment?"

"We'll leave that up to Gary and his partner." Matthew smiled at her enthusiasm before explaining, "Gary is Steve's best friend— typical queen, by the way. He and his partner, Barry, will know what to do. They're both in the entertainment business."

"I look forward to meeting them."

"When you do, call them Gazza and Bazza; everybody calls them that."

"Gazza and Bazza? It sounds like a circus act."

"Almost," Matthew laughed good-naturedly. "They do a drag queen show at Stonewall on weekends and they have a really great act—though half the time they're not acting; it's the real thing, you know? They're great boys."

Alex had heard about Stonewall. It was a trendy bar/nightclub in the heart of Sydney's "gay city" at Oxford Street, and though she had never been there, she knew it was a popular venue with all sorts of people, gay and straight.

"So when's the big day?"

"Two Saturdays from now—July second."

"Good. That'll give us plenty of time to get things ready and ..." Alex paused when she saw him smirking. "What?"

"Look at you, already planning and scheming. Typical female."

"Get out of it." She dismissed him jokingly to shake off her elation at being included in his plans.

"Oh, and another thing," Matthew added, "I'm shooting a TV commercial tomorrow at Dee Why beach. I thought if you had nothing to do, you may want to come along and watch. This way, we can plan Steve's party in detail. I don't want him around the house while we're talking about it."

"I'd love to come." She tried not to sound too excited at the proposed outing. "It might even inspire me to write something new."

"You mean you'll write about me?" he teased her.

"You wish," she came back at him with a quirky smile. "I meant the beach. You know, one of the many surfing beaches of Sydney."

He feigned disappointment. "Oh, and I thought you were going to give me some press."

"I wouldn't dream of inflating your ego any further."

It felt good to be able to tease and laugh with him, and Alex rested in the knowledge that they truly were soul mates in friendship.

In the afternoon, while Alex was in her room typing away on her laptop, she thought about the commercial shoot the following day. God, what was the matter with her? She was carrying on like a schoolgirl with a major crush. She admitted she enjoyed Matthew's company; it was infectious and she was happy whenever she was with him, but he was gay. To think of him in any other way was pure madness.

She sighed and shut down the computer. She could not write another word while she was in this frame of mind. Outside, the sky was a beautiful azure blue and looking out her bedroom window, she saw Steve pruning the rosebushes.

After the morning's strange breakfast, Steve had gone to his room for a rest, and had remained there right through lunchtime. Alex still felt the beauty and sadness of his story about the butterflies, and she hoped against hope he could beat this disease and get better. She had read about people who'd been able to do it.

Steve noticed her watching him and waved. Alex opened the window and called down to him. "How are you feeling? Do you want me to fix you some lunch?"

"Thanks for asking. I had something to eat already, but how about a cup of tea and your company?" He sounded like his normal self again.

"I'll be right down." Alex hurried to the kitchen where she put the kettle to boil and joined him. "I'll give you a hand with those as soon as the tea's ready."

"No need. I'm almost done. I thought you might enjoy a cuppa in the sun. You've been shut up in your room for hours." He finished the pruning and took off his gardening gloves.

"I have a deadline to meet so I had to shut myself away. Did you rest well?"

"Yes. I caught up on my sleep and I feel better now."

The kettle whistled from the kitchen and Alex went inside to make the tea while he put away his gardening tools. They then sat at the outdoor table, soaking up the afternoon sun.

"Thanks. This is just what I need," Steve declared as he sipped his tea.

"Well, it's good to see you're feeling good."

"I am; for the time being, anyway." A little of the morning's mood came creeping back in his voice.

"Steve—" Alex started to say but was interrupted by him.

"Promise me one thing."

"Anything." She held her breath in anticipation at what he was going to say, though her sixth sense told her exactly what it was he would ask of her.

"Promise me you'll stay on with Matthew after I'm gone."

"I knew you were going to ask me this," she answered. "And of course I'll stay. You don't need to worry. But you're not going anywhere!"

"Maybe not so soon, but you know I'm going, Alex." There was conviction in his voice. "I'm not afraid of death, you know. I'm at peace with everything." He paused and gazed at her more closely. "The only missing piece was you."

Alex was struck by what he said. "What do you mean?"

"Matthew's very vulnerable. You know he takes his family's rejection quite badly, though he rarely speaks of it. I feel he draws his strength from me, but once I'm gone he's going to need you."

Somehow, what he said made perfect sense, and Alex began to see a purpose in her life. "I promise that for as long as Matthew needs me, I'll stay with him," she reassured him.

Steve looked relieved. "I know it's selfish of me to ask you to put your plans on hold, but—"

"I have no plans, Steve," she cut in. "I've been drifting around for years, running away from my worst fears."

"And now?"

"And now I think it's time I face them, though I don't exactly know how. This may sound strange to you, but with you and Matthew, I feel safe. I found the anchor I needed all this time, and I feel a little bit braver about facing the past. So maybe there's hope for me yet." Alex was surprised at her admission.

Steve took hold of her hand. "Nothing you say sounds strange to me, my dear. From the time we met, I knew you were on a par with our thoughts and feelings although you may not have known it then."

Alex regarded him in amazement. She had the feeling he had known all along about her. Not so much the details of her life, but the hurt, the fears, and the sadness. Tears gathered in her eyes and she did nothing to stop them from falling.

Steve pulled her to her feet and hugged her, and she returned the hug because it was the most natural thing for her to do. Besides, she needed to be touched by another human being.

"I think I know what you went through," Steve stated with reassurance, "and believe me when I tell you this monster will have his day of judgement."

Alex pulled back a little and gazed at his kind face through her tears; then, something gave way inside her and she confessed, "It was my stepfather. He ... He hurt me so much. He hurt me so very much." For the first time in her life, Alex burst into tears in front of another person, and it felt good—all the other times, she had cried alone.

Steve held her and let her cry, and Alex cried for her lost childhood and for the pain she had carried with her all this time. After a while, she felt some of the darkness lift from her and the tears subsided. "I'm sorry, I soaked your shirt," she uttered in a croaky voice.

"No worries, I've got plenty. Come on, let's go back inside. It's getting cold out here."

They picked up the tea things and went into the kitchen. "We're here for you, too, Alex. You're part of our family now," he told her.

It was twice in one day that Alex had heard these words, and she felt safe.

CHAPTER 8

That evening, Alex ate a sandwich in her room and caught up with the work she had put off in the afternoon. The boys had gone to dinner at Gazza and Bazza's house, and she suspected Matthew would find the opportunity to pull them aside and have a quiet word about Steve's birthday party.

It was past ten o'clock when she hopped into bed, exhausted from the afternoon's emotional outpouring. Overall, it had been a strange day for the three of them—first with the butterfly episode and later with her outburst in the garden.

Her eyes closed, heavy with sleep, and for the first time in a long time, she did not mind the darkness in the room around her. She felt relaxed and safe in her home and in the knowledge that she had at last found a real family.

She must have slept quite deeply because she was startled by the heavy rap on her door, and Matthew calling out, "Alex, are you awake?"

She glanced drowsily at her clock and realised she hadn't heard the alarm. It was now five-thirty in the morning and if she didn't hurry, they would be late. They were supposed to be at the location for the shoot by half past six.

Alex jumped out of bed. "Give me fifteen minutes." She rummaged through her wardrobe for clean underwear and clothes, and in ten minutes she was showered and fully dressed.

It was going to be a cold day at the beach so she wore black corduroy jeans with a big, bone-coloured alpaca wool pullover and a black leather jacket. She tied her hair back from her face and wrapped a black wool scarf around her neck for good measure. Finally, she threw a lip balm stick into her bag and raced down to the kitchen where she found Matthew dressed in a dark blue winter tracksuit with a heavy black leather jacket over the top. He held out a cup of coffee to her.

"Relax." He seemed amused by her whirlwind entrance. "We've got enough time for coffee and a piece of toast." The toast popped out of the toaster as he said this and he spread peanut butter and strawberry jam on it. "Hope you like this."

"Yeah, it's okay." She took the toast from him. "How's Steve?"

"Seemed much better last night, though I think he suspects something's going on. He caught me talking to Gazza and Bazza in the bathroom, and we all looked guilty as hell." He laughed at the memory. "Anyway, even if he does suspect, he's going along with it because on the way home he didn't raise a peep."

"That's good."

"He told me you guys did some gardening yesterday afternoon. Perhaps the exercise made him feel better," he remarked.

"Is that all he told you?" Alex asked warily.

"Yeah, why?" He popped the last bit of toast into his mouth and finished his coffee.

Alex breathed a sigh of relief. "Nothing. I thought he might have said something about the butterfly episode."

"No, he didn't say anything. Steve can be very private that way. I know he'll tell me about it if he wants to, so there's no point asking. Are you ready?" He placed his cup in the sink and snatched his car keys from the kitchen table.

Alex finished her coffee in one gulp and placed her cup next to his. She was grateful Steve had kept the scene in the garden between them. For reasons unknown to her, she did not yet want Matthew to know about her past.

The day would come when she would tell him, but at this point it was one step at a time and she sent silent thanks to Steve for keeping her secret. "Let's go," she said and followed Matthew out to the car.

They made Dee Why in under half an hour, and Matthew was called to go in to make-up immediately upon arrival. "Just hang around. Have something to eat if you like. They're setting up the coffee station now."

A young guy in a catering van was setting up for morning coffee and people began to gather round for their first cup. Even though the sky was now a brilliant blue, the cold wind kept everyone in small huddles here and there to keep out the cold. All of those present were wrapped up warmly.

Alex felt a little out of place. "You're sure it's okay for me to hang around?"

"Yeah, I told the director you're my girlfriend and doing a write up for one of your magazine articles—you know, behind the scenes at a commercial shoot."

"God, Matthew, you could get into trouble!" She was surprised he had lied to get her onto the set.

"Don't be silly. I'm the star of this shoot, and I'm allowed to bend the rules a little."

Alex flushed at the thought of being considered his girlfriend by other people, but did not have the time to ponder on this for long because one of the production assistants came to fetch him.

"Matt, make-up's waiting." The young girl seemed to know him, probably from other shoots, and Alex saw her eyes light up while she regarded him. It seemed every female was attracted to Matthew.

"Okay, coming," he replied. Turning to Alex, he said, "I'll talk to you later."

Alex found a sunny spot near the coffee station and sat down to watch the action around her. Matthew had told her earlier the commercial was for a brand of surfboards, popular worldwide, and it would be screened in most English-speaking countries.

People were running around setting up lights and sound equipment on the sand close to the shore; others discussed the shooting script with the director; and both the make-up and wardrobe vans buzzed with activity. It seemed the only person who had nothing much to do besides herself was the catering guy, who had just finished setting up the coffee station and was now sitting a few feet away from her smoking a cigarette.

Half an hour later, Matthew rejoined her. He wore a wetsuit under his jacket and his face was covered in the customary theatrical make-up, which made him look more tanned than usual. His eyes sparkled bright blue in the morning sun.

"Wow," was all Alex could say. She was mesmerised by the brilliant blue of those eyes and the whiteness of his teeth when he smiled. He was beautiful.

"Wow, what?" he uttered, totally unaware of the effect he was having on her.

"I mean, how come you're wearing a wetsuit?" she improvised, hoping he wouldn't pick up on how she felt.

"Most surfers wear a wetsuit. Mind you, the top half will be hanging off me, like it's a hot day. I'll be coming out of the water carrying my surfboard and two girls come running down the beach toward me and stop to admire it. Basically, they're supposed to be attracted to me because of the surfboard I use."

Alex laughed.

"What?" He threw her an enquiring glance.

"Well, let's just say it's not the surfboard that's of interest to them," she said in a moment of boldness.

He looked confused and then laughed. "You're a tease, you know that?" He ruffled her hair, and she would have fallen off her seat if not for his quick move to steady her.

Just then, two tall and attractive girls approached them. Alex realised they were the models who would be playing the girls on the beach. One was a platinum blonde with straight hair, falling to her waist; the other had long and wavy auburn hair.

"We're all gonna freeze, Matt," the blonde declared when the girls reached the spot where he was standing.

"I know. You'd think the weather could've been a little kinder to poor talent like us," he responded in the easy manner of someone who was familiar with them.

Perhaps, he had worked with them before, Alex thought. This was soon confirmed when Matthew turned to her. "Alex, this is Cindy, and that over there is Carol." He introduced the blonde first, then her companion. "This is my girlfriend, Alex," he said to the girls.

Alex was sure her face turned red as a tomato, but there was absolutely nothing she could do. "Hello," she uttered in a soft voice.

The girls gave her lukewarm smiles and turned their attention back to Matthew. "Are you coming to Carol's housewarming? You got the invite, right?" Cindy's smile was anything but lukewarm right now.

"That's right, Matt. I left the invite with Larisa at your agent's office." Carol spoke like a little girl asking for candy, Alex noticed. "Say you're coming to my party," Carol added in a whiny tone.

"Sorry girls, I didn't get any invite," Matthew answered, and Alex detected a tight tone to his voice.

The girls did not seem to pick up on this. "C'mon, Matt, you know you don't need an invite anyway." This was Cindy again. She stepped closer to him and her hips swayed gently as if trying to beckon his body to hers.

Alex felt uncomfortable with the interchange while Matthew looked irritated. "I'm busy," he stated a little sharply.

"We haven't even told you the date yet," Cindy persisted.

"Never mind, I have long-standing plans." This time his voice was quiet, but deadly serious.

Alex now understood why he disliked people reacting to him. The girls were insincere and superficial. They were flirty and pushy, enough to irritate anyone without an inflated ego, gay or not.

"Well, try and make it, Matt. All the people from the agency are going to be there," Carol told him.

"It's on Saturday, second of July," Cindy added. "Say you'll be there, Matt. It wouldn't be the same without you."

Matthew ignored the girls' pleas, looked in Alex's direction for a moment, then turned back to them. "No can do, but thanks all the same," he replied, flatly.

The girls finally got the message, made some excuse about having to go to wardrobe, and walked off.

"They're rather insistent," Alex commented.

Matthew threw her a strange look.

"What is it?" she asked, thinking she'd said something wrong.

"Not just insistent, they were rude to you," he pointed out, looking upset. Alex gave him a puzzled look, so he explained further, "Although they believed you were my girlfriend, Alex, they only asked *me* to go to the party, totally ignoring the fact that you were sitting right here. It was an insult to you."

Alex was stunned. It had never occurred to her the girls had been insulting toward her. However, she had never been in a normal girlfriend-boyfriend situation where things like this might happen. She'd never had a boyfriend, not even a pretend one. "Oh."

"You're a real innocent, aren't you?" Matthew still sounded upset. "If I were you, I'd be really pissed at their behaviour."

"I ..."

"Look, forget it," he said more gently. "It doesn't matter. They're just bimbos who don't know any better. I have to go now. I'll see you later."

He walked off in the direction of the beach, leaving her alone with her thoughts. How could she expect him to understand her lack of anger at the girls' behaviour? She really was an innocent.

* * *

Alex did not get to see Matthew for the rest of the morning. The director had him repeating the scene where he came out of the water over and over so they could shoot from different angles. From what Alex could see of him in the distance, he looked extremely cold. She moved closer to where the shooting was taking place, huddling against the strong wind, and noticed it was much colder close to the shore. A make-up assistant kept going up to Matthew in between takes to retouch his face and spray his hair with water to give him the "wet look". His naked torso was perfect in every way though at present covered in goose bumps from the chill wind. Alex noticed Cindy and Carol huddling close to him in their skimpy bikinis and stamping their feet in an attempt to keep warm.

"Okay, people, we'll do one last take of this one," the director called out, "but first we'll have a coffee break. You guys need to thaw out." He was mainly referring to Matthew and the girls.

One of the production assistants threw Matthew's jacket to him and gave Cindy and Carol a blanket each with which to wrap themselves. Meanwhile, crewmembers started walking briskly toward the coffee station.

Matthew looked tired, and Alex was about to join him when the director pulled him aside. She decided to go and get him a cup of coffee instead and started to make her way up the beach with the rest of the crew. Cindy and Carol were walking a few feet ahead of her, and Alex could not help but overhear their conversation as it carried in the wind.

"What a body! He really makes me wanna fuck him," Cindy was saying.

"Well, it seems he's not interested in either one of us, darling. If it weren't for that poor excuse of a girlfriend, I'd say he was gay," Carol remarked spitefully.

"She looks like such a hag, doesn't she? I bet she's older than him, too. And that baggy top of hers—no taste whatsoever." Cindy was on a roll now. "I reckon she's a doormat to boot. I mean, she only said one word during the whole conversation, and did you see

68

how she flushed when he introduced her?"

"Well, you know what they say, 'still waters run deep'," Carol commented.

"What's that supposed to mean?"

"God, you're dumb! I mean, her looks aren't much, but she must have something that attracts him to her."

"Like what?"

"Like a great cunt!" The girls laughed maliciously.

Alex felt bile rise to the back of her throat as a mental picture of her stepfather loomed up to meet her. A shrill scream of fear went off inside her mind, and suddenly she was running blindly. She ran and ran, not looking where she was going. She only knew she had to get away from this place.

She left the beach behind and reached a bus stop, her breath coming out in short rasps as if she could not get enough air into her lungs. She was hot and cold at the same time and shivered with the rising panic.

"Are you all right, dearie?"

Alex turned toward the voice to find an elderly lady with kind eyes regarding her. "You look very pale. Can I help in any way?" the elderly lady added in a gentle voice. Her concern touched Alex and had a calming effect on her rising panic.

"I'm ... I'll be okay, thank you," Alex responded, still trying to pull herself together.

The lady patted the bench in the bus shelter to get Alex to sit next to her. "I'm waiting for the bus. It's due in a few minutes. Are you from around here?"

"No. I live in Surry Hills." Alex felt the shivering begin to subside.

"Well then, you're a long way from home, aren't you? I'm going into the city to see my daughter. She works in a law firm, and today she invited me for afternoon tea." The lady chatted happily as if she had known Alex all her life.

The trivial chitchat dissolved the demons inside Alex's head. "That's really nice of her," she said to the old lady. "Is this a special occasion?"

"It's my birthday next week, you see, but Mary's going away with her husband and the kids on a short holiday, so we're celebrating early. The kids will be there this afternoon. I just love to see them.

Graham is five, and Deirdre is only three, but a naughty girl all the same."

Alex smiled at her companion while she spoke about her daughter and grandchildren. When the bus arrived, they both boarded it together and shared a seat all the way into town, and the old lady did not stop to draw breath once.

This was exactly what Alex needed to give her nerves a chance to calm down. By the time they reached the city, she was back in control and silently grateful to her companion for keeping her company. They both got off at the same stop and Alex helped the old lady alight from the bus.

"Thank you, dear. You look much better now. I knew my chatter would help. Nerves can be very nasty," she said knowingly, taking Alex by surprise.

"But how ...?"

"Dearie, I've suffered with panic attacks for over forty years and I learned a few tricks to stave them off. Chatter always works." She smiled.

Alex kissed her on the cheek. "Thank you, I'm really grateful. And happy birthday for next week."

"Bye bye, dear, and keep your chin up." The lady gave her one last smile and walked off.

Guardian Angels came in many guises, thought Alex as she watched her saviour go. She then hailed a taxi to take her home.

CHAPTER 9

Upon her return to the house, Alex found a note from Steve stating he was off to work and that he would be back late. Although he had now reduced his working hours to two days per week, Matthew kept at him to quit altogether. Much to Matthew's annoyance, however, Steve wanted to keep working. Alex knew it was not so much the money, but his need to maintain contact with the outside world that kept Steve from quitting altogether. Matthew, on the other hand, was just being protective.

It was early afternoon when she finally fixed a sandwich for lunch. Aside from the coffee she had consumed at the shoot, she'd eaten nothing since breakfast. She ate quickly, not realising how famished she was until now. The whole day had so far been a long and disastrous one, she thought, and it was not over yet. She berated herself for leaving the beach without telling Matthew, but he should not have lied about her status to everyone on the shoot. Had he left things alone, Cindy and Carol would not have made those comments about her.

Matthew had been upset at the models' rudeness toward her, but Alex could not find it in her heart to be angry with them. They were irrelevant to the situation. It was Matthew she was upset with for playing a role involving her without her consent. At first, she'd thought it harmless, but since she had been the one at the receiving end of his actions, she knew better now. To a certain extent, she blamed herself. After all, she had gone along with it even though she now felt inadequate and stupid for reacting in such a childish way. She should never have taken off the way she did, but it was too late to dwell on it now. The best thing was to put the whole episode behind her.

She went to her room to do some work, but like the previous day she found her thoughts wandering and could not concentrate.

Frustrated, she shut down the computer and decided the best tonic for her condition was to do something physical. Therefore, when Matthew returned home, he found her furiously dusting around the loungeroom.

There was a big gust of wind when he opened the front door, sending several message slips, which had been resting on the telephone table, flying through the air. His eyes on Alex, Matthew did not notice them.

"What happened to you?" He was obviously annoyed. "I turn around and there you are, racing up the beach as if the demons from hell were after you."

Alex was polishing one of the bookshelves so hard she thought she might actually rub a hole in it. "I had to leave," she replied in a controlled tone. She felt like crying, but this would not do.

Matthew watched her wiping away at the bookshelf with her back to him, concentrating on the task as if her life depended on it. She had not even turned to look at him.

"Will you stop that? I'm talking to you!" His voice came out sounding harsh and angry.

Alex ignored the warning bell inside her head and kept polishing. "Well, I don't want to talk," she snapped. Anger was always the best antidote for tears.

This did not exactly have a calming effect on Matthew, and he felt his temper get the better of him. He strode across the room, snatched the polishing rag from her fingers, and physically turned her to face him by pinning down her arms against the sides of her body. He felt the sudden urge to shake her. "Look at me when I'm talking to you, damn it!"

Alex was not going to back down. She looked right up into his flashing blue eyes and allowed her anger to have its way. "How dare you play games?" she shouted. "Those models said horrible things about me because they thought I was your girlfriend. You placed me in that position!"

"Just as I thought," he responded in a calmer tone and released her, his temper burst quickly dissolving.

Alex felt stung. "Well, I don't care what you thought. You had no right to do what you did, and furthermore—"

"Alex, I only lied to get you on the shoot. I didn't know it was going to cause problems," he explained.

"Of course you didn't! How would you know anything at all when you get admiration wherever you go? I bet no one thinks you look like a hag." She was dangerously close to tears, the biting remarks of the models coming back to sting her.

Matthew almost smiled. "Is that what they said? You can't possibly believe any of their crap. They're just bimbos." He could see how upset she was, and his heart went out to her.

"They said a lot more you wouldn't know anything about, so you can just leave me alone." She snatched back the polishing rag from his hand. "Please go." She knew she was carrying on like a child throwing a tantrum, but she did not care.

"You're afraid," Matthew came back at her with a challenging look.

Alex was amazed at his nerve. "Afraid? Afraid of what?"

"You're afraid you're not good looking enough to attract a man."

His reply grounded her, the childish manner dropping away immediately. "What are you saying?"

"Don't you get it? They were jealous of you because they thought you were my girlfriend! Of course they were going to make catty remarks about you. So unless you're afraid you're not good enough to attract a guy, why take what they said personally?"

Once again anger was her only refuge. "And what makes you think I'm afraid, Mr Psychologist?"

Matthew ignored her sarcasm. "For starters, look at the way you dress all the time."

"What's that got to do with anything? So I like baggy clothes, okay?"

"Sure you do, because you feel it's safe to hide inside them. Why don't you wear a dress and make-up for a change? You just might surprise yourself."

Alex threw the polishing rag at him, hitting him in the face. "And since when did you become Versace?" She left the room abruptly, leaving behind a surprised-looking Matthew.

* * *

Alex ordered a pizza in the evening and ate in her room while she worked. Steve was still at work and she did not want to face

Matthew on her own. She had not spoken to him since their argument that afternoon, and it was obvious he was also steering clear of her.

When she had gone downstairs to pay the pizza delivery guy, she'd noticed Matthew reading in the loungeroom. He had seen her, too, but had made no attempt to communicate. Once the pizza guy left, after giving Alex some change, she heard Matthew pottering around the kitchen and she put away any thoughts of reconciliation.

It was after ten when she finished her work and decided to have a bath before bed. She knew Matthew had gone to sleep because she'd heard him coming up the stairs to his room earlier. In the bath, she relaxed almost immediately. She closed her eyes and immersed her mind in the peaceful quiet of the house around her. It was not long, however, before the events of the day returned to intrude on her newly found calm. The comments made by the models were now forgotten, but not what Matthew had said to her during their argument.

"*You're afraid you're not good looking enough to attract a man,*" had been his words. Alex felt her muscles stiffen automatically. Was she really afraid of this? No. This wasn't true, she concluded. Matthew didn't understand how she felt. She knew she wasn't a beauty, but she wasn't unattractive, either. The real problem was that she was afraid of attracting *unwanted* male attention. She sadly admitted that thanks to her stepfather, she would never be able to love a man in a physical way—the thought of sex absolutely terrified her. So what was the point in looking attractive?

She sighed and forgave Matthew for his comments. He had meant well, and had even been upset at the catty models' behaviour toward her. She relaxed once more, realising she couldn't stay upset at him. He was her friend and had acted in her best interests.

After the bath, she slept soundly with her mind at peace until she was woken by the sound of someone vomiting in the bathroom. Steve. It was not yet dawn, and she heard Matthew talking rapidly. Although she could not hear what was being said, she detected the concern in his voice as Steve kept retching.

* * *

When she made her way to the kitchen later that morning, Alex knew she would find a very pale-looking Steve. She was not wrong. His pallor was terrible, the skin on his face devoid of all colour. Matthew was sitting at the table opposite him, looking serious, and there was total silence in the room.

Alex felt it inappropriate to greet them cheerily, so she sat next to Steve and regarded him with concern. "Hey, can I get you anything?"

He smiled wanly. "Did I wake you earlier? Sorry about the noise."

"Don't be silly! No one can help feeling ill. Why don't you let me make you a soft-boiled egg and some toast? You need to get your strength back."

"I'm not hungry." Steve sounded tired.

"I think he should be in bed," Matthew interjected, knowing Steve usually listened to Alex when it came to health matters. He always told Matthew not to fuss, but when advice came from Alex, he tended to follow it without too much prompting.

As if reading his thoughts, Alex took up the cue. "Matthew's right. What time did you get in last night? I didn't even hear you."

"This morning, around two," was the reply.

"Well, no wonder you're not well. God, if I kept those kind of hours I'd fall apart at the seams," she said for his benefit, not wanting him to feel like he was a weakling because he was ill. "Why don't you go and lie down? I'll make you some hot soup for lunch."

Steve smiled. "You're real pushy, aren't you?" he uttered affectionately. "Okay, I'll go and get some sleep, Miss Bossy."

Matthew threw Alex a look of gratitude. "C'mon." He turned to Steve. "I'll take you up."

"No need to fuss, Matthew. I'll be okay. Why don't you go and do the groceries instead? That way, Alex can make me some of her delicious tomato soup."

Alex was amused. "Just like I used to cook for the shearing boys?"

"You got it, lady." He winked at her and left the kitchen.

"Thank you," said Matthew once Steve had gone.

"No problem. Someone's got to fatten him up."

"Alex, about yesterday ..."

"Don't worry about it. I shouldn't have reacted the way I did. Thank you for caring."

Matthew appreciated her candour. "Well, I'm glad you don't hate me."

"Of course I don't hate you," she declared, and then added with an impish smile, "but if you want me to wear a dress, you'll have to buy me one. My wardrobe's limited to baggy tops and pants."

He saw the laughter in her eyes, teasing him, and went along with it. "You're on then. I'll get you something if you promise to wear it next Saturday at Steve's party."

"Sure, sure," she dismissed his comment, not taking him seriously. "Now, why don't you go and buy me some groceries?"

* * *

Steve felt much more rested after his morning nap and the lunch Alex had prepared for him, so in the evening the three housemates decided to get a pizza and sit in front of the television to watch a DVD. While her companions watched the film, Alex found her mind jumping to the following day's meeting.

On Sunday afternoon she would be seeing her mother for the first time in twenty years, and she wondered why she had been so impulsive in suggesting the meeting in the first place. Surely there was nothing to talk about after such a long time. Besides, she found she had no feelings for the woman she called Mother. Did Cecilia even suspect what John had done to her daughter? Did she ever wonder why Alex avoided her stepfather and why she had never wanted to see him again after she left home? It was difficult to believe her mother had no inkling at all about her husband's behavior. Obviously, she did not because John was one of the main topics that came up in most of the conversations she had with Alex.

There was a little routine her mother went through whenever Alex talked with her on the phone—first, she reproached her for not calling often enough; then, she moved on to recount the latest news and activities relating to the church, making sure each time to include an exclusive account of her stepfather's active participation in whatever was happening.

This was one of the main reasons why Alex had not kept in touch with her on a regular basis. The last thing she wanted to hear was *"John did this and then he ..."* It hurt Alex that her mother rarely ever asked her about how she was feeling or whether she was happy.

She simply did not seem to care about the life Alex led. The one thing she did care about, however, was why Alex did not want to come and visit. She was forever saying, *"John misses you, dear. Why are you so ungrateful to him? He raised you like his own daughter."*

Like a daughter! If she only knew the half of it. A long repressed anger surfaced inside Alex, and it occurred to her that perhaps it was time her mother found out the truth about the monster with whom she shared her life. If she never really suspected anything, it was time to tell her she had been living under a delusion.

Alex was not one to seek revenge or to set out to ruin anybody's life, but surely the truth had to come out sometime. Even if there was no love between her and her mother, the truth needed to be told. The whole reason there was no love in the first place was because of her stepfather's influence over his wife.

Alex had been so caught up in her thoughts, she failed to notice the film ended and Matthew and Steve were gazing at her questioningly.

"Oh. Did you say something?" She came out of her reverie and saw the boys sitting on the sofa next to hers, waiting.

"Obviously you missed the twist at the end, right?" This was Matthew.

"The twist?" Alex knew she sounded idiotic.

"The movie. The surprise ending with a twist?" he persisted.

"Perhaps Alex has other things on her mind," Steve interceded, always the more insightful of the two.

"God, I can't believe you missed it! The guy was dead, all the time he was dead; only, he didn't know it!" Matthew could not believe Alex hadn't seen *The Sixth Sense* in all these years, and now that they'd rented it for her benefit she'd missed the twist at the end, not to mention half the movie.

"Oh," was all Alex said.

"Matthew, leave it alone. Alex can always watch it another time." Steve knew that not everyone shared Matthew's passion for films.

"Sorry, I'm afraid I was deep in thought," Alex apologised.

"It's okay. Just ignore him. You know what he's like." Steve rolled his eyes and made her laugh.

"What did I do now?" Matthew asked.

"Never mind." Steve sighed.

"Oh, I get it." The penny dropped. "It's about tomorrow, isn't it?"

Alex nodded. She knew Matthew and Steve were aware she was dreading the meeting with her mother, so there was no point in pretending everything was okay.

"Hey, let me drive you over. I'll sit in the car and wait for you till you're done," Matthew offered immediately.

Alex looked at Steve for his opinion. Perhaps, it was a good idea for someone to go with her.

"I think he's right," Steve affirmed. "At least if you feel uncomfortable, you can leave straight away and won't have to wait for a taxi."

He was right. If things did not go well during the visit, it would be awkward for her to walk out of the hotel and wait for a taxi with her mother possibly going in the same direction. And what if her stepfather had driven in with her mother and he was out there somewhere, waiting for his wife? Alex felt terrified at the thought of running into him.

"Okay. If you don't mind, I'd really appreciate it," she told Matthew.

"Good, I never liked the idea of your going on your own."

Alex was touched by his concern, and that night before she fell asleep it occurred to her that this must be what it was like to have a caring family around her.

CHAPTER 10

Sunday dawned cold and clear, and Alex was up by six. She was so nervous about the forthcoming meeting that she had slept very little and in the end spent most of the night tossing and turning. By dawn she gave up trying to sleep altogether and decided to take a hot shower, cook breakfast for herself, and leave something hot for when the boys got up.

She was surprised, therefore, to find Steve already up and reading the paper when she walked into the kitchen. "God, you gave me a fright. I thought you'd still be fast asleep," she said when she saw him, noticing he looked a little pale.

"Morning," he greeted her. "Water's hot. I just made some tea."

Alex fixed herself a cup. "So you didn't sleep much?"

"No. I had leg cramps during the night and didn't want to disturb Matthew, so I got up and came down here."

"How long have you been up?" She joined him at the table.

"Since three."

"Isn't there something you can take for the cramps?"

"Not really, unless I want to take more drugs than the ones I'm already taking." There was a weary tone in his voice that put her on the alert.

"Is there something I can do?"

"You're doing enough already, my dear," he assured her. "You took over the household, for which I'm grateful. You know if we left it to Matthew, we'd all be wading in dust and little green things growing out of the fridge." He grinned at this last comment.

Alex laughed. "Well, how about something to eat then? I bet you didn't have any breakfast."

"I suppose you'll force me if I say no."

"You have to eat, Steve. You've been losing weight lately."

"You sound just like Matthew."

"Well, I promised him I would fatten you up, and fatten you up I will!" She went to the fridge and took out various ingredients. "I'll make us a traditional brekkie."

"Okay, boss. It looks like I have no alternative."

"Exactly. But you do get to choose between tea and coffee," she teased him.

"Wonderful," he replied in the same mood.

Alex started preparing breakfast while Steve chatted to her about various things, and then he asked suddenly, "So what progress are you making for my surprise birthday party?"

"You sneak!" Alex yelped. "Matthew's going to be upset when he finds out that you know."

"Then there's no need to tell him. He's not the only actor in the family, you know. I'll just pretend I'm surprised."

"Well, I'm not going to tell you anything, so you'll just have to wait and see."

"Fine. I'm a patient fellow. I suppose there's a whole crowd coming?" he fished.

"Uh-uh! My lips are sealed. Better change the subject."

The aroma of frying bacon and eggs wafted through the kitchen, and Steve realised he was indeed quite hungry. "That smells great. I think I'll go with coffee this time," he declared and joined Alex at the kitchen counter. "I'll make it," he offered. "You want some, too?"

"Make it three," came the reply from the doorway as Matthew walked in.

Alex wondered how long he had been standing there and whether he'd heard anything about the party. If he had, he gave no indication of it.

"How're the cramps?" he asked Steve.

"Did I wake you?"

"No, you didn't."

"So how did you know?"

"You're always up early when you get them," he replied as he plopped down on one of the chairs and started flipping through Steve's newspaper.

"Well, I feel better, and Alex is cooking up a storm."

"Good, I'm hungry as a bear, so get a move on." Matthew smiled and looked over to where Alex was already adding extra eggs and bacon into the frying pan.

"Yes, massah." She grinned.

He made a face at her, and it was in this jubilant mood that the three of them sat down to Sunday breakfast, all worries temporarily forgotten in the warmth of the kitchen enveloped in winter sunshine.

* * *

Steve went to lie down after breakfast and Matthew was roped into doing the dishes while Alex disappeared into her room to decide what to wear for the meeting with her mother. She rummaged through her wardrobe for something suitable and in the end came up with a pair of black pants and a red turtleneck pullover. Wardrobe decided, and it had just gone ten. Alex sighed and frowned at the thought of what she would do with herself until it was time to leave. She went back downstairs and found Matthew wiping down the kitchen counter.

"We'll leave around quarter past two. Is that okay?" he remarked.

"Sure."

"In the meantime, I have some shopping to do," he announced.

"Want me to come along?" She jumped at this, but was soon disappointed when he refused.

"I'm not shopping for groceries," he said mysteriously.

"Oh?" She did not know what to make of this, but guessed he was going shopping for Steve's birthday present and wanted to be alone. "Well, I'll do some gardening then. I'm making vegetable soup for lunch. Are you going to be back by then?"

"Sure will," he replied and was out of the kitchen.

Matthew certainly had a secretive air about him when he went out, Alex thought. She had heard him go upstairs for a few minutes and then was out the front door. She shrugged her shoulders and made her way out to the garden. This was the best therapy for nerves, in any case, and she was soon lost in a world of pruning and digging out weeds.

Steve came back down just as Alex finished cooking the soup; not long after, Matthew reappeared. Alex noticed he was not carrying any packages when he walked in, and she figured he had snuck upstairs to hide his booty before making an appearance. As the boys wolfed down the soup, her appetite waned and she only managed a few spoonfuls. If Steve and Matthew saw this, they did not comment.

"Thanks, Alex, that was wonderful," Steve said when they finished eating. "I'll do the dishes"

"I'll help," Matthew offered.

Alex went to get ready. She was keen to get the meeting over and done with, and the best way to do so was by putting her best face forward. So for the first time in a long time, she decided to wear make-up. Make-up was always a good camouflage; it made one feel more confident.

She dressed carefully, adding a fine gold chain around her neck and small hoop earrings in her ears. Then, she brushed her hair back from her face into a loose plait. For make-up, she applied a fine foundation and outlined her eyes with brown eyeliner followed by black mascara to accentuate her long eyelashes. A little blush powder and dark red lipstick added the finishing touch. When she inspected herself in the mirror, she was satisfied.

This was Alex, the writer. The Alex her mother would have seen in the photographs attached to her many articles. The worldly, confident Alex who showed she had nothing to fear. This was the only Alex her mother knew, and she would play the part. It seemed there were now three actors in the family, she mused.

"Wow!" Matthew exclaimed when she entered the kitchen where the boys were having coffee.

Alex felt colour rush to her face. Any admiration from a male made her feel extremely self-conscious. Steve threw Matthew a warning look; he sensed how Alex felt, given the circumstances of her childhood.

"You look very confident, Alex," Steve commented, trying to put her at ease.

"What do you mean, confident? She's totally transformed!" Matthew blundered in, much to Steve's annoyance.

Alex regarded them with a look of anxiety in her eyes. "Too much make-up, right? I'll take some off." She made to turn to go back upstairs.

"No. No!" Steve reassured her. "You look just right. Don't mind Matthew and his big mouth. You know how he carries on," he added, throwing Matthew another warning look.

"Oh, I'm sorry, Alex." Matthew finally got the hint. "I only meant to say that you look very good—and ready for this meeting," he remarked, trying to sound casual.

Alex fidgeted with her clothes. "Are you sure? I don't look ... you know, overdressed or anything?" She had added an elegant cashmere jacket to her outfit at the last minute and now wondered whether she'd overdone it.

"Of course not," Steve replied before Matthew could offer further comment. "You look like the worldly writer you are—so go get 'em!"

This was what she needed to hear, and she turned to him with gratitude. "Thank you. I was hoping you'd see that."

"Shall we go?" Matthew asked.

"Yes, we better. We won't be long, Steve. I'll be back in time to cook chicken curry for tonight." In fact, she couldn't wait to get back home and cook whatever the boys desired.

"You've cooked enough for today, my dear," he smiled at her. "Matthew can make the curry."

"Hey, hold on a minute—" Matthew started to protest.

"Yes, he will," Steve insisted, his gaze still on Alex, "and you can relax, knowing your meeting is behind you."

On impulse, Alex went to him and kissed his cheek. "You always understand. See you later."

"Good luck," he said affectionately.

* * *

In the car Alex sat rigidly, looking ahead.

"Relax; my driving isn't that bad," Matthew teased and was rewarded with a smile.

"I'm really nervous, you know, but I'm glad you're here," she said shyly.

"Hey, if you feel this badly, I can come in with you."

"Much as I'd love you to, I need to see my mother alone." Alex realised that her voice lacked conviction but knew she had to go through this on her own. "Maybe you can wait for me in the lobby," she suggested hopefully.

"No problem." Matthew treated her to one of his smiles.

Alex felt more reassured, though a little confused at the feelings his smile invoked in her. "Thank you." For the rest of the trip she remained silent.

Matthew wondered why Alex had such a problem meeting with her mother, but now was not the time to ask. In fact, thinking of mothers, he had not seen his own in months. Was she ever going to accept his lifestyle or would she live in denial forever? He sighed and stole a peek at his companion. Whatever Alex's problems with her mother, he didn't blame her for being nervous about seeing her. Why was it that parents always wounded their children even when they didn't mean to?

They were fortunate to find a parking spot across the road from the Hyatt Hotel at The Rocks. A spot this close was a miracle or, as Alex chose to think of it, a good omen.

They walked over to the building, deep in their own thoughts and oblivious to the beautiful day that was a backdrop to the Harbour Bridge looming to the left of the luxurious hotel. The hotel lobby welcomed them with a mixture of marble and various objets d'art surrounded by floral arrangements that complemented the luxury décor.

Alex was blind to everything as she looked around nervously, hoping against hope her mother wouldn't show up. "I don't even know if I'll recognise her," she told Matthew.

"Where did you arrange to meet?"

"Around the lobby; but perhaps she's near the café. Why don't you wait here, and I'll go find her?"

"Okay. I'll be sitting by the window along there." He pointed to several glass windows overlooking the harbour. "If I'm not there, I'll be outside having a cappuccino at the café." The café had an outdoor service area set up on timber decking overlooking a popular tourist walk, which extended past the restaurants and cafés that were part of the historic Rocks area.

"I shouldn't be longer than an hour," Alex said, glancing at her watch and noticing it was already five minutes after three. "Wish me luck."

Matthew reached out and kissed her cheek. "You'll be fine, and like Steve said—go get 'em!"

Alex smiled through her nerves, feeling her face flush, and walked off in the direction of the café, hoping he had not noticed. Why did Matthew have such an effect on her? She didn't feel this way when Steve touched or held her—like on the day she had poured her heart out to him in the garden. Annoyed, she pushed away the thought. Now was not the time to analyse her physical attraction to Matthew. She had more important things on her mind.

Nearing the café, she glanced toward its entrance and saw a petite figure that looked familiar. Her heart skipped a beat as she realised it was her mother.

Cecilia looked older and plumper, Alex noticed, but time had been generous to her and she was still attractive. Her mother recognised her and was looking back in her direction with a smile on her face.

"Alex, dear, you look wonderful! I never thought you'd grow up to be such a beauty." Cecilia greeted her daughter with a peck on the cheek. She wanted to take Alex in her arms, but sensed from the slight withdrawal in her daughter's body language that she had done the right thing in not greeting her in a more effusive manner.

"Hello, Mother." Alex managed to sound pleasant while she ignored her mother's rather insincere greeting—a beauty indeed!

"You look more like your father than ever, except for the eyes. They're the image of my own dear mother; God rest her soul."

Alex was surprised at the mention of her real father. In all the years she lived in her mother's home, she never remembered her mother talking about him.

"Shall we go in?" Alex led the way into the café and informed the hostess of their reservation. They were shown to a table by the window overlooking the harbour, and Alex was glad of the sun streaming in to warm the chill that had sprung up inside her body.

A waiter came up immediately to take their order. "May I tell you today's specials?" he addressed Alex.

"Just a cappuccino for me, thanks." She turned to her mother. "How about you? Do you want to order anything to eat?"

"No, no, I must watch the figure." Cecilia said, and then addressed the waiter. "I'll have Earl Grey with some lemon slices on the side."

"Perhaps I can interest you in our scones with extra-light clotted cream," the waiter suggested, eager to be of service.

"Well, that sounds very nice." Cecilia did not take much convincing. "Yes, thank you. What about you, Alex?" She was all charm.

"Just the cappuccino, thanks," Alex spoke directly to the waiter. He took their order and left them alone.

"So what does one say after these many years?" Her mother came to the point, her tone not so charming anymore.

"It all depends on what it is you want to talk about. If you're going to lecture me about the reason why I didn't visit in all this time, then it's best to say as little as possible." Alex could not keep the hardness out of her voice.

"Really, Alex, you sound as uncaring as always. You know I wanted to see you."

The wounded parent speaks again, thought Alex. "You had plenty of opportunities to do so. I even offered to fly you over at my cost several times."

"But I never understood why you didn't want to visit at home, dear. John's missed you terribly," Cecilia persisted in the same tone.

Alex felt like running away. Just the mention of her stepfather's name conjured up enough fear to make her want to scurry for cover. "Mother, don't you want to know how I've been all this time?" She forced herself to remain calm and ignore her mother's last remark.

"Well, of course, I do, dear. A mother always wonders why her daughter takes it into her head to run off at such an early age."

There was just enough wounded sarcasm in the remark to get on Alex's nerves, but she maintained her calm demeanour.

"I meant to say don't you care what I've been *doing* all this time?" The need for approval was evident in Alex's voice, and she hated it. Why couldn't she sound more confident?

"Okay, so what have you been doing all this time?" There was not a trace of approval or interest in Cecilia's tone, and Alex's heart shrank with disappointment.

Meanwhile, Cecilia did not know where this was going. All she knew was that her daughter had always been an ungrateful child, and it appeared she had grown into an equally ungrateful adult. The girl was never going to be thankful for the things dear John had done for her.

Trying to cope with her own feelings at her mother's uncaring attitude, Alex was unaware of the thoughts going on inside her parent's head, so she simply replied to the question even though she knew her mother did not really care.

"I travelled a lot, as you know; and my writing is doing well," she said for the purpose of having some conversation between them.

Just then, the waiter arrived with their order, and this gave Alex a chance to recover a little of her confidence while pushing away feelings of inadequacy.

"Mmm! I simply love scones, don't you? Would you like to try one?" Cecilia offered as she bit into a fluffy scone loaded with strawberry jam and cream.

"No, thank you." Alex stirred sugar in her cappuccino; the thought of food at this moment almost made her gag.

"Well, that's very nice, dear," Cecilia remarked in her charming voice again.

"What's nice?" Alex was momentarily confused.

"That your writing's going well," her mother replied with a sugary smile. "What about young men?"

The question took Alex by surprise. "Well ... I ..."

"Too busy with your career, I suppose." Cecilia did not wait for a response. "Young people are all the same these days, always career before romance. Then, who was that nice young man who answered the phone the night I called?"

The penny dropped, and Alex realised her mother missed nothing—except the fact that her dear husband had molested her daughter from early childhood. "That was my housemate," she replied, her voice flat.

"So you live with a male housemate?" Cecilia became curious now.

"Two, actually." Alex thought she might as well shock her mother out of her little Catholic socks. "They're a gay couple."

This had the intended effect, and she had the satisfaction of seeing her mother spill some of her tea onto the tablecloth.

For a moment Cecilia was speechless, but she soon found her voice. "Well, really!"

"Is something the matter?" Alex uttered, innocently.

"Now, Alex, don't play games. Didn't I teach you anything?" Cecilia sounded genuinely upset.

"What do you mean?" Alex felt genuinely confused. She did not remember her mother teaching her anything at all—ever.

"Well, one simply doesn't mix with these people. It's not natural! Two men living like that. The church doesn't allow this sort of thing." Her voice was full of indignation.

"So?" Alex said carelessly.

"So! How can you say that? You're living with sinners, God help me!"

And so are you, dear mother, so are you, Alex said to herself and chuckled at the irony of it—and her manner seemed to upset Cecilia even more.

"What could possibly be so funny?" A deep frown appeared on her mother's face.

"Funny? Nothing, Mother. It's hypocritical, that's all."

"Hypocritical? What are you talking about?"

Cecilia was either totally blind to her husband's behavior or she was a superb actress. This enraged Alex. "Why don't you ask John?" The words escaped her lips before she could stop them, and she was not so sure she had wanted to stop them in the first place. It was inconceivable that her mother had no idea about her husband.

"What's John got to do with any of this?" Cecilia uttered. Then, an idea occurred to her and she sounded suspicious, "Have you been doing something you shouldn't?"

Alex could not believe her ears. Burning anger rose up through her body and she was shaking with it. "Are you suggesting I pursued your husband in any way?" she whispered harshly, in total disbelief.

Cecilia gave up any pretence at being social as her long-term suspicion reared its ugly head inside her mind. "What other reason could there be for your insolent behaviour toward John? You wanted him for yourself, you little slut!"

Her vicious tone stung Alex like a hard slap across the face.

Cecilia, seeing the changing emotions in her daughter's eyes, assumed her suspicion had been right all along and added savagely, "And when he wouldn't pay you any mind, you ran away from home to fornicate with whomever would have you!"

Alex was stunned. This was her mother's final betrayal—not only total denial at what had truly happened, but also the swift condemnation of her own daughter. A wave of nausea engulfed her and with what felt like super human effort, she stood up and managed to say, "I don't think we have anything further to talk about. Not now. Not ever."

Alex left an indignant Cecilia behind and made her way out of the café as quickly as her legs would carry her. She had to put distance between her and the ugliness that was her mother. A feeling of deep fear threatened to overtake her with a panic so dark it seemed to be coming straight from hell. The only logical thought that managed to surface in her frightened mind was that she had to find Matthew. She ran blindly toward the hotel exit, her mind a jumble of images from the past: her stepfather pursuing her, his hands clutching at her body, her clothes being torn off, strong hands prying her legs open ...

Alex slammed into a solid body and two strong hands reached out to steady her. A scream rose to her throat, but she subdued it in time when she recognised Matthew's concerned eyes looking into hers. "What's wrong?"

"God, Matthew, please get me out of here," she cried and collapsed into his arms as she willed her mind to go blank.

She felt herself being propelled out of the hotel, and within moments she was seated inside the car and in the safety of Matthew's arms. Her panic attack subsided, only to be replaced by a torrent of tears. Matthew held her against him while her body shook with violent sobs. After a while, she stopped crying and realised she was clutching at his shirt. She pulled away slightly and noticed she'd torn it open and a couple of buttons were missing.

"Oh, my God, I'm sorry! I tore your shirt. I'm so sorry. Please, forgive me ..." Alex was still in a highly emotional state and the thought of what she had done to his shirt disturbed her out of all proportion.

"Hey, it's nothing. Don't worry about the shirt. It's you I'm worried about," Matthew cried with concern. "You have to tell me what happened in there, Alex. I think it's time!"

Alex stayed within the circle of his arms. She could not look at him for the shame of what she was about to say. "I thought Steve might have told you by now."

"What's that, honey?" His tone was so gentle and caring that Alex knew she could confide in him.

"My stepfather ... he ... he ..." Her voice failed momentarily. She tried again. "I was sexually molested for some years, you see. This is why I ran away. My mother ... Well, she thinks I was the one who ... She called me a slut, Matthew!" Her eyes grew wide with distress. "How can I be a slut when I'm terrified of sex?" At this, a fresh flood of tears poured out of her eyes and she sobbed once more into his chest.

"Oh, baby, don't cry!" Matthew soothed her. "No one can ever hurt you again. I promise. Besides, the woman's blind. She doesn't know what she's talking about."

While she sobbed desperately, Matthew's heart hardened with hate toward the unknown man who had violated his friend's young body and the mother who ignored her daughter's silent pleas for understanding. The woman was obviously in denial about her husband's role in all this—another parent in total denial, just like his own.

His heart went out to Alex. They *were* two of a kind: both betrayed by their parents; both denied the love they craved and the approval they needed to have; both hurt emotionally by the rejection of their truth.

When they returned to the house, Alex went straight to her room and stayed there for the rest of the afternoon. She was emotionally spent and grateful when sleep claimed her. It was early evening when she awoke to a soft knocking sound at her door.

"Alex, it's me," Steve called out. "May I come in?"

Alex sat up, hoping she didn't look a total mess. She had not even washed her face since the torrent of tears earlier that afternoon, but she guessed most of her make-up had been washed off by the weeping, and the rest would be clinging to Matthew's ruined shirt.

"Come in," she called and switched on the bedside lamp.

Steve entered the room holding a mug. "Here's some chamomile tea. I want you to drink it before dinner. Matthew's in the kitchen cooking the curry."

"But—" she began.

"No buts. This time, I'm the one who gets to boss you around. It's payback for all you do for me," he admonished gently and handed her the mug. "Go on, drink up."

"Thanks." She gave in and patted the bed. "Sit awhile."

Steve did so. "Matthew told me what happened. It must've been horrible for you," he remarked, sympathy in his voice.

"Yeah, well; that's life, I guess." Alex felt empty thinking about her lost youth. "You know, I always thought one day I would to get the chance to tell my mother what truly happened. I even had a speech prepared in my mind and I thought when I told her, she was finally going to understand and she would ... love me." She paused, fighting back the tears.

Steve waited quietly while she had a sip of the tea and took a few moments to check her emotions. "Anyway," she continued in a more composed manner, "the last thing I expected to hear was that she thought I was coming on to *him*. I was so shocked when she said it that I knew if I didn't get out of there, I was going to make an even bigger fool of myself." She paused again as she relived the scene in her mind. "The worst part of it is I never got the chance to tell her the truth."

Steve watched as Alex tried to keep a tight rein over her emotions, and his heart ached for her. "You know," he said gently, "some people are too terrified to acknowledge the truth, even when it's staring them in the face. I think if you'd told your mother, she wouldn't have believed you."

"Well, I don't suppose we'll ever know now." Alex sounded defeated.

Steve patted her gently on the shoulder. "For what it's worth, Matthew and I are here for you, and while our love can't replace that of a mother's, we're still your family."

Alex was touched. "Steve, you always know when I need to hear things to comfort me. I'm really grateful. And since I don't know what it's like to have a mother's love, yours is the only love I need."

"I'm sure deep down your mother loves you, Alex," he reassured her.

"Maybe; maybe not. All I know is she became a different person when my stepfather entered our lives." Her voice held regret. "But we're all authors of our own destiny, and what we ultimately become is our own responsibility. I don't blame my mother's behaviour on my stepfather; she simply chose to be who she is."

"You're right. But bear in mind that although we all choose to become who we are, sometimes we don't choose wisely," Steve pointed out.

"What do you mean?"

"Just that we need to leave a little room in our hearts to forgive ourselves and those who've hurt us."

Alex gazed into his eyes and saw in them a deep compassion that touched her. She wondered what made a man facing a death sentence become so open to love. "I hope one day I can learn to forgive both of them," she said quietly.

"You will, my dear, and when you do, you'll feel like a big weight has been lifted off your shoulders." Steve's kind smile soothed her troubled emotions.

91

Alex was able to imagine being able to forgive her mother one day, but when she thought of her stepfather, all she saw was a dark, evil force enveloping her. She shook her head at this as if to banish the image from her mind. "Thank you for the tea and talk," she uttered. "I'll be down to dinner in a few minutes."

"Good for you." Steve walked over to the door and then turned momentarily. "You'll be all right, Alex," he assured her in his gentle way and left the room.

Alex looked at the closed door and could only wonder from what source Steve drew his inner strength.

CHAPTER 11

Over the next few days, Alex settled back down after her maelstrom of emotions and worked in the garden, often with Steve. Matthew had another TV commercial to film and was away for three days.

The commercial was to do with outdoor fashions, and he would be appearing in camping and hiking scenes in the Blue Mountains. Since the location was a couple of hours' drive west of Sydney, the production crew and talent were staying locally. Alex was grateful for his absence. She still felt sensitive about her reaction to the meeting with her mother and was not yet ready to face him. It had been easier to discuss her feelings with Steve. He had a gift for making people feel at ease in his company whereas every time she was around Matthew, she felt self-conscious.

Matthew had left early Monday morning and was to return late Wednesday. He telephoned on Tuesday evening, however, when Steve was at work.

"Steve's doing a function tonight," Alex informed him.

"I know. I rang to talk to you," he said.

"Oh?" She was surprised.

"Don't worry. I didn't call to abuse you for ruining my precious shirt," he teased. He sensed that a little humour would put her at ease about any feelings regarding her mother.

"Okay, I know fashion is everything to you, but could you possibly be any more superficial?" Alex responded, feeling more relaxed talking over the phone with him rather than face to face.

"Just disappointed," Matthew replied. "It was a good shirt, but I forgive you, my darling girl."

"Are you by any chance flirting with me?"

"A poor boy like me can only try," was his cheeky response.

"A poor *gay* boy, you mean." Alex laughed.

"Ah! I knew I forgot something, but we can't all be perfect."

This brought another laugh from Alex. "So why are you calling?" She was curious.

"To discuss final arrangements for the party; plus I also need you to contact Gazza for me." He went on to explain what needed to be done during his absence while Alex wrote out a list.

"How's the shoot going?" she asked after they finished discussing the party arrangements.

"I'm freezing, that's how. We had a sprinkle of snow today."

"Wow! No wonder it's so cold down here."

"Yeah, well, let's hope the weather improves by Saturday," Matthew remarked.

"True or we'll freeze in the backyard." Alex immediately thought of Steve's frail countenance.

"I hope it won't come to this; otherwise, you won't be able to wear your dress."

What was this? "Dress?" she asked, puzzled.

"Yes."

"What dress?"

"The one under your bed." With this, he hung up laughing.

Alex ran up the stairs to her room and looked under the bed, all the while thinking Matthew had played a practical joke on her; but there was a parcel wrapped in gold paper waiting for her. She pulled it out and ripped open the envelope attached to it. Inside was a white card with Matthew's handwriting scrawled across it. It read: *You promised to wear it to the party. So guess what!*

Alex was astounded. She recalled their argument after the commercial shoot at the beach and how Matthew had said he would buy her a dress if she promised to wear it to Steve's party. Now, it seemed he had actually gone out and bought her one! Then, she recalled his mysterious shopping trip on the day of the meeting with her mother.

Sweet, crazy, adorable Matthew! She felt tears of joy spring to her eyes. Never in all the years she'd been on her own had she received a gift from anybody. She'd had the odd editor send her a bunch of flowers when one of her articles received positive feedback, but that was all. She thought about all the Christmases spent alone when the shearing boys went home to their families. The feeling of desolation had never left her, and not once over the years had she experienced the love behind a gift given with sincerity.

She now looked at the parcel on the bed. What was she waiting for? With the eager fingers of a child opening her first present, she ripped at the paper and pulled out the garment wrapped inside.

The dress was made from terracotta-coloured wool. It had long sleeves and a calf-length free-flowing skirt. An Aztec design in turquoise and black was woven into the bodice of the garment, which was framed with small dark bone buttons down the front. The dress was beautiful and earthy, exactly what she would have selected for herself.

Alex threw off her clothes and tried on the garment in front of the mirror. It fitted perfectly and she noticed the colour of the fabric accentuated the reddish brown tones of her long hair. She looked very feminine and for once, she felt good about being a female.

The telephone rang and she raced to take the call from the boys' room. She knew it would be him. "Oh, Matthew! It's beautiful. I love it! Thank you so much."

"I thought you'd like it." He seemed pleased with her response.

"What can I say, except it was a crazy thing to do?" Alex laughed happily, wanting to throw her arms around him.

"Don't say anything. Just enjoy it. Enjoy being a pretty woman. I want that for you. I know the past hurt you very much, but don't let it destroy you," he spoke with sincerity.

She felt a lump in her throat and knew she was going to cry, grateful that at least he could not see her tears this time. "Thank you, my dear friend. Thank you for caring," she uttered in a croaky voice.

"I'm glad you like it." Matthew sensed her emotions and quickly shifted the mood. "Remember, you promised to wear it on Saturday night. I'm expecting a whole bunch of guys to come courting at your feet."

Alex exploded with laughter. "Yeah, right, at a gay party!"

"Steve's hotel friends are coming, too, you know; and they're all straight, and some are even single. So watch out!"

Alex sobered up. "Oh. I didn't know."

"Well, don't go worrying about it. I'm sure with Steve and I, you'll have plenty of chaperoning."

"You're making fun of me."

"Of course I am, silly. Gotta go now, early start in the morning."

"Okay. Have a good night, and thank you once again."

They rang off and Alex returned to her room to change, carefully putting the dress away. She thought about what Matthew had said—straight males; some of them single—and for one unrealistic moment, she wondered whether she would meet anyone interesting.

* * *

The day of the party dawned sunny and clear, and the temperature was mild for a winter's day. This pleased Alex and Matthew while they sat sipping cappuccinos at a local outdoor café.

"So what did you tell Steve?" Alex remarked, enjoying the aroma of the fragrant coffee.

"Nothing," was the reply. "I snuck out while he was still sleeping and left him a note saying we went shopping."

"And what happens when we get back?"

"By that time, Gazza and Bazza will have dropped by to drag him off to brunch. They won't bring him back until it's time for the party." He smiled in anticipation.

"Isn't Steve going to think it a bit strange that he hasn't seen you all day on his birthday?"

"To tell you the truth, I think he knows something's up," he confided, a smirk on his face. "C'mon, Alex, cough up! What did he say to you?"

"What do you mean?" Alex played the innocent.

"I know he's been talking to you. What did he say?"

Alex could not resist the glint in his merry eyes. "All right, all right! He took me by surprise a few days ago and asked how things were progressing for his birthday party."

Matthew laughed. "I knew it! Did you tell him anything?"

"Of course not!"

"Well, there you go. Then, he won't think anything's strange today. He knows we have the party on tonight, and he'll be ready for it."

"So what do we do now?"

"We wait. He'll be out of the house by ten. Then, we go back and start preparations. Some of the boys from the hotel are coming over this afternoon to help us set up. Do you think we have enough meat for the barbecue?"

Alex nodded. "I think we bought enough to feed an army. You're going to have to cope with the barbecue without my help, though. I'll be too busy preparing the salads and desserts."

Matthew didn't seem troubled by this; his thoughts were somewhere else. "And then, you'll be wearing the dress."

"Yes. Then, I'll be wearing the dress." Alex blushed.

"You're not going all shy on me, are you?" He grinned, showing his irresistible smile, but this time Alex was not giving in to self-consciousness.

"Not if you promise to dance with me at least once," she returned boldly.

"It's a promise."

A group of young men arrived at the café and sat at a table nearby. Alex noticed one of them ogling Matthew, hoping to catch his eye. Matthew did not notice.

"So what did you get Steve for his birthday?" She turned her attention back to Matthew.

"A gold watch. I had it inscribed with a special message."

"Sounds beautiful. I got him a book on French impressionists."

"He'll like that, especially now that he's got so much more time to read."

They both went silent for a moment, each wrapped in their own thoughts. It was obvious to Alex they were thinking about the same thing: Steve's illness. Alex watched the young man who had been ogling Matthew give his partner an affectionate kiss. Matthew saw it as well, and a frown crossed his face.

"Steve's very lucky to have you," Alex commented, wanting to give comfort for what seemed to be troubling thoughts.

Matthew did not reply. He simply drank his coffee.

* * *

By six that evening, the house was transformed into a beacon of light, with coloured fairy lights decorating the front garden and welcoming the soon-to-arrive guests. The backyard was equally lit up, with lights bordering the fence around the back garden while others were threaded through trees and rosebushes.

Bunches of balloons formed multi-coloured bouquets and were tied randomly to trees along the fence line. More balloons decorated a raised platform in one corner of the backyard, which would serve as a stage for the entertainment. The rest of the yard was set up with trestle tables for guests to sit and eat and with a long buffet table full of salads, finger food, and desserts. A smaller table stood close to the buffet and served as a bar. Matthew had rented a large portable gas barbecue, which now stood near the bar, piled high with platters of raw meat and sausages waiting to be cooked.

Everyone had worked tirelessly through the afternoon and now they were having a quick drink before going to dress. Matthew served the drinks, while Alex felt uncomfortable, sitting at a table surrounded by Steve's hotel friends.

There were four men in total: Michael, a thirty-something married man with a kind face; Bruce, tall and lanky, also married; and Mark and Dennis, single and within the same age group. Dennis was short with a thatch of red hair and a face covered in freckles while Mark was as tall as Matthew, with a lean and muscular build. His straight dark hair was swept back from his face and he had lively hazel eyes.

Alex became very aware of Mark's presence and reacted to his handsome masculine features with mixed feelings—discomfort, and something she could only describe as attraction.

"How long have you been living with these two troublemakers, Alex?" Michael asked. Up until now, the boys had been talking shop while she had sat quietly, wrapped in her thoughts. Now, the attention had turned to her, and Alex blushed.

"Oh." She felt nervous, and her eyes shot to Matthew. He smiled encouragingly. "Just a few months," she said.

"Do you work in the hotel industry?" This came from Bruce.

"No, I'm a travel writer," she informed them quietly.

This aroused interest among the four males and she was peppered with questions from all sides. Matthew took one look at her blanching face and decided to intervene.

"Okay, guys, Alex will grant interviews later during the party," he remarked lightly and got a laugh from the boys. He turned to Alex, "Perhaps, you want to go up and dress now."

Alex did not need further encouragement and was out of her chair in a split second. "I guess I'll see you all later." She turned to make her way inside the house, but not before she caught the look of interest in Mark's eyes.

She dressed with care, leaving her hair loose except for the two mother-of-pearl combs that swept back the sides from her face. The only jewellery she wore consisted of small hoop earrings and a fine gold bracelet that had belonged to her grandmother. When she was ready, she examined herself in the mirror and could not help thinking she looked attractive, especially with freshly applied make-up.

She was aware that about half the guests had arrived by now but was reluctant to go down. Better to wait a little longer so she could join the full throng without being too conspicuous.

As she peeked out the window to the yard below, she counted approximately twenty people gathered around and greeting Steve. Gifts were piled up on a small table, and Matthew was busy getting the barbecue started while two men, who looked older than the rest of the group, set up microphones and lights on stage. Alex guessed they were Steve's close friends, Gazza and Bazza. Dennis, the self-appointed barman for the evening, served drinks while guests moved about and mingled with one another.

There were a few females present, Alex observed with relief, two of which stood close to Michael and Bruce, and Alex assumed they were the men's wives. Her eyes roamed over the rest of the crowd and finally came to rest on Mark, who helped Gazza and Bazza with the equipment on stage. She noticed his dark handsome looks and agile body while he moved here and there, and she pulled away from the window abruptly and sat on the bed while her face burned hot. Just then, there was a knock on the door and Matthew's face peeked in.

"Just popped up to see where you were. You look great!" There was sincere praise in his voice.

Alex tried to hide her flaming cheeks by looking around the room as if she had forgotten something.

"What are you waiting for?" he exclaimed, sensing her hesitation. "Come down. You'll be just fine; trust me."

"I'll be down in five," she replied.

* * *

Steve's party was in full swing by the time Alex put in an appearance. There were now around fifty people in total; some gathered in small groups to talk while others danced to popular music.

Matthew was circulating around the crowd when he spotted her. "About time," he said when he reached her. "We're going to eat soon."

Alex noticed Bruce and Dennis manning the barbecue. "And I see you delegated the cooking duties."

"Well, you know how it is; I have to host for Steve. He's too busy having fun. Now, come with me; you have to meet Gazza and Bazza." He took hold of her hand and led her to a group of people standing close to the stage. "Hey, everyone," he announced, "this is Alex, our housemate. Alex, you know Michael already, and this is his wife, Elaine."

Elaine was an attractive petite blonde. Standing next to her was Mark, with his disturbing looks, and next to him, the two middle-aged men Alex had seen earlier from her bedroom window.

"Mark you know," Matthew stated, "and these are Gazza and Bazza, the stars of Stonewall."

On closer inspection, Alex thought the two men looked to be in their early fifties. Both were of stocky build with good-humoured looks on their craggy faces. They seemed more like kindly uncles or older brothers than a gay couple; and they were so similar in looks, they could have passed for twins.

"Not stars, darling, drag queens!" corrected Gazza in a surprisingly deep voice. "Nice to meet you, sweets." This, to Alex as he threw his arms around her and planted a kiss on either side of her face.

Alex smiled a little uneasily, not used to such close contact with a stranger.

"And hello, Alex." This was Bazza, whose only distinguishing feature from that of his partner was his hair, which was a darker shade of red. Gazza's was carrot orange.

Bazza hugged and kissed Alex, and Gazza, meanwhile, turned to Mark. "My dear Mark, aren't you going to get the lady a drink?"

Mark nodded. "Of course. What will you have, Alex?"

Alex coloured under his gaze. "Nothing yet, thank you. If you'll all excuse me, I have to find the birthday boy." She moved away from the group to go in search of Steve before someone noticed her blushing. She found him talking to a group of people and excused herself as she drew him aside. "Just wanted to wish you a happy birthday," she declared, giving him a hug.

Steve hugged her back. "Thank you, my dear. I know how hard you worked to put all of this together, and I appreciate it."

"Matthew worked hard, too," she replied.

"Yes, I'm sure he was really busy *supervising*," he returned, tongue-in-cheek. They laughed, but this was the extent of their conversation because Gazza and Bazza appeared at his elbow and each grabbed one of his arms.

"Excuse us, Alex, darling. We're going to borrow the boy for a moment," Bazza said and with this, they spirited Steve away.

Alex watched them go with a smile. The boys truly were a dear pair. She turned in the direction of the bar with the intention of getting herself a drink when she came up against a tall figure with a pair of hazel eyes.

"How about that drink now?" Mark smiled at her.

Alex felt the self-consciousness return but managed to give the impression she was cool and collected; even her tongue worked when she replied, "Thanks, that'll be nice."

They made their way to the bar and Mark poured her a glass of red wine, as she'd requested, and grabbed a beer for himself. "Steve tells me you pretty much took over the running of the household. It's very nice of you, considering his situation."

Mark surprised her with this knowledge, and Alex felt herself prickle. "And what else does Steve tell you?" She tried not to sound too defensive; after all, he was a good friend of Steve's.

"Only that you're great at handling the housekeeping duties and you're a mean gardener," he replied with a glint in his eye.

This made her smile. "Well, I suppose I do have a green thumb." She responded to his charm. "How long have you known Steve?" she asked before he had a chance to tell her something else he had learned from Steve. It seemed Steve trusted his friend enough to tell him all about her, and she suddenly felt somewhat annoyed with her housemate.

"We've worked together for over four years. He's a really great guy." Mark was sincere in his appraisal of his workmate and friend.

"Yes. He's a very special person," Alex agreed.

"True, and because Steve's such a special person, I trust everything he said about you."

His eyes were flirting with hers, and Alex became guarded. She didn't like where this was going. "And what exactly did he tell you?" This time, she could not hide the defensiveness in her tone.

Mark seemed to become aware of it and explained quickly, "Please don't get me wrong. It's not like he told me any deep, dark secrets. He simply said you're a very warm and attractive person, and that I should meet you."

Alex could not believe her ears. Since when had Steve started to play cupid? "He said all of this?" She was suspicious. Perhaps, Mark was making it up to flirt with her.

"Yes. And why shouldn't he? I can see for myself it's true, and I'm glad we had the chance to meet."

"Why?" On the defensive again.

"Why?" he exclaimed, a little confused at her attitude. "Why does a man want to meet a warm and attractive woman? So he can see if they can be good friends. It's nice to have good friends, isn't it?"

"I see." Where did she go from here? And why had Steve talked to this man about her, anyway? Right now, she could have easily pushed him into one of his prized rosebushes!

"So what do you say?" Mark asked her, cutting into her thoughts.

"What do I say to what?" Alex was aware the tone of her voice did not sound very friendly. She looked around the crowd and saw that Steve had seen them and was making his way over through the throng of guests.

"Look, I'm sorry if I said something to upset you." Mark seemed truly puzzled at her behaviour. He could have sworn Alex had found him as attractive as he had found her. "Like I said, Steve thought I should meet you."

"Well, Steve thought wrong! Excuse me." Alex did not understand what came over her. All she knew was that she had to get away before Steve reached them. She walked off on the pretext that she had to go to the bathroom and murmured this intention to no one in particular just before Steve reached them.

"What happened?" Steve asked when he saw the look on Alex's face as she disappeared through the crowd.

"I guess she's not interested," Mark informed him. "Pity."

"Maybe I did this all wrong." Steve sighed, looking concerned. "Please don't take this personally. She's mad at me, not you."

"No worries, mate. She's a female." Mark shrugged, rather bemused by Alex's behaviour.

Reassured by his friend's comment, Steve was happy he did not have to make further explanations. He could hardly tell Mark the truth about Alex's past. He had noticed earlier that Alex seemed to find Mark attractive, and he'd hoped she would allow herself to get to know him better. He wished in time she would be able to overcome the fear she had of being involved with a man. Judging by tonight's performance, however, he was not so sure that day would come any time soon. Poor Alex, he thought; was she destined to go through life without someone to love because of what she had suffered in the past?

Suddenly, his happiness at the evening began to wane.

* * *

Alex ran to her room and locked the door behind her. She didn't want anyone to know where she was so she left the lights off. In the darkness around her, the reflection from the fairy lights below made colour patterns on the walls of her room, giving the effect of a soft rainbow. She was not in the mood, however, to admire this just now; she had to sort out her disturbing feelings.

She was no longer upset with Steve for playing cupid, but was angry at the way she had reacted. She'd made a complete fool of herself in front of Mark, and in the heat of the moment, she had blamed Steve for starting all of this.

Alex walked to the window and peeked out, careful not to be seen. There they were, almost under her window, Steve and Mark, discussing something she was sure involved her. But with the noise of the merrymakers filtering into her room, she could not be sure of this. She could only assume she was the topic under discussion.

This was unbearable. Her life had been a lot simpler before she'd agreed to wear a dress. She should have never listened to Matthew or even Steve. This was what happened when someone made the effort to look attractive—all of a sudden, they became a beacon for men like Mark.

Just the thought of where this might have taken her brought up fears from the past, but before she could give way to dark thoughts, she sprang into action. She practically ripped the offending garment from her body and jumped into one of her comfortable tracksuits. Then, she grabbed a handful of tissues and wiped the make-up from her face as best she could without bothering to go to the bathroom for cleansing cream. She took off her jewellery, kicked off her shoes, and finally, pulled back her hair into a rough ponytail.

It was only after she had done all this that she relaxed a little. Downstairs, the music had stopped, and she heard Matthew's voice come through the loud speakers. She went back to the window to peek down and saw him on stage, making a happy birthday speech to Steve.

"We're here to celebrate Steve's thirty-sixth birthday," Matthew stated, amidst cheers from the crowd and congratulations being thrown Steve's way. "I just want to say, happy birthday, Steve. May you have many more!"

The guests broke into applause. "And for the surprise of the evening ..." He paused until the noise subsided. "For the surprise of the evening—and no, it's not the cops coming to tell us we're being too noisy." This brought a bout of laughter from the crowd. "The surprise is that our superstars from Stonewall are here to entertain you. So put your hands together for Gazza and Bazza, the Queens of Stonewall!"

Again, the crowd broke into applause and cheering as Gazza and Bazza stepped on stage wearing the most colourful and glitzy gowns Alex had ever seen. They were dressed Carmen Miranda style, with long and impossibly tight skirts ending in a gush of ruffles and with midriff tie-up blouses covered in multi-coloured sequins. On their heads, they each wore a brightly coloured turban decorated with plastic fruits and enhanced by huge silver hoop earrings. The boys' make-up was heavy, and even from where she was watching, Alex could see the fake eyelashes loaded with black mascara.

One of the boys came up to the microphone; Alex could not tell which one. "Thank you, Matthew darling!" he declared as he turned and gave Matthew a kiss on the lips.

Matthew almost fell off the stage, and everyone laughed.

"Ooohhh, what a luscious young buck!" cried the Carmen Miranda imitation.

"Darling!" The other imitation joined his partner. "You're forgetting this is Steve's birthday, so don't go kissing the wrong guy."

"Oh shush, you bitch! You're just jealous," the first imitation purred.

It was obvious the guests enjoyed the spectacle as they clapped and cheered the queens.

"Now, Stevie, sweet cheeks," continued the first imitation, "you've turned thirty-six, darling; and now you're a vintage queen, just like me."

"What are you saying?" the other imitation cut in. "Stevie might be vintage, but you're positively ancient, my dear!"

More laughter from the crowd. "All right, you pushy cat-thing, you! No need to embarrass me in front of this lovely crowd. Let's not forget you're in the age of decay, too," was the comeback.

"Well, I may be a cat-thing in decay, sweetie, but you're one declining old pussy!"

The guests roared with laughter as bright spotlights shone on the boys and a lively South American tune blared out from the speakers. This was the cue for them to get on with their act, and they broke into a ridiculous salsa-type dance, which had the whole crowd going.

Suddenly, Mark and Matthew appeared on either side of Steve, who had been standing near the stage, and lifted him up, depositing him next to the two queens who pounced on him and made him part of the act.

People began moving in time to the rhythmic music while on stage, the boys danced with Steve and encouraged the crowd to join in. Alex pulled away from the window. The fun downstairs was infectious, but she was no longer in the party mood. She lay on her bed, feeling tired after the day's activities and soon, she slept.

* * *

There was knocking at the door, and Alex sat up in fear. Her stepfather didn't knock; he always slipped into her room without warning. Maybe, it was her mother coming in to tell her off for being a slut.

She watched as the door slowly opened and a dark figure peeked in wearing a dark hood that hid his face, except for the hollow of his eyes, which were looking directly at her. Here was death at last.

Then, the figure dissolved into that of her stepfather and Alex felt a scream at her throat, but nothing came out.

"Alex! Alex, open up!" her stepfather called out from the other side of the door.

Alex wanted to scream for death to return. Why did it go away?

"Alex!" The insistent knocking slowly found its way into her dream, and her eyes flew open. Alex found herself sitting up in bed, the room in darkness, and she was safe. Thank God!

There was the knock again and Matthew's voice, "Alex, open the door!"

She looked at the clock—3:11a.m.—and slowly got out of bed, groggy with sleep. She unlocked the door and came face to face with Matthew, who strode into the room without asking for permission. "So what happened to you?" His voice was harsh with anger.

Alex's temper flared up despite the grogginess. "How dare you come barging in here at this time? It's none of your business what happened," she spat back at him. She felt inexplicably annoyed at his attitude and at the fact that he might be able to see her face in the dark. She probably looked a real mess with her half-smeared make-up.

Matthew was as annoyed with her. "You're a real chicken, you know that? The minute a man flirts with you, you run off like he was the devil."

"And what do you care? It's none of your business! I'm fed up with your telling me what to do and what to wear; and with Steve, who's playing cupid now as well. Why can't you just leave me alone?" Alex felt close to tears.

Matthew ignored her plea. "When are you going to face the fact that you're an attractive woman and you need a man?" He was angry for her, not at her.

"And when are you going to start facing your own family's rejection instead of trying to fix up my problems?" she shouted back, enraged. Then, she froze at the look in his eyes. Even in the dark she could see his reaction to her comment.

Matthew was speechless, and the wounded look he gave her said it all. He simply stood there, face to face with her, his anger burning inside him.

Alex realised she had gone too far. Unfortunately, it was too late to take it back. She stood facing him, fully expecting Matthew to hit her across the face, but he simply gazed into her eyes, lost in his own thoughts.

It dawned on Alex just how much she had hurt him with her words. She immediately wanted to apologise, but before she could say anything, he strode from the room, slamming the door after him. Alex grew weak at the knees and sat down on the bed, tears rolling down her face. The look in Matthew's eyes would haunt her for a long time to come.

CHAPTER 12

During the days that followed Steve's party, Alex and Matthew maintained a surface civility toward each other for the sake of domestic harmony. They greeted one another good morning; they consulted on household bills and tasks to be done; they greeted each other good night. Their daily communication did not go beyond this point.

Steve became aware something was wrong between the two housemates but thought it prudent not to interfere, hoping the two would resolve their differences. The one thing bothering him was that Alex's behaviour might have something to do with his own initiative to try and throw Mark in her path. Yet, Alex seemed quite normal around him; it was only when Matthew was anywhere near her that she went quiet.

When a couple of weeks passed, and he saw nothing change between the two, he decided something had to be done. His opportunity came on a rainy Monday morning when the three of them happened to be having breakfast at the same time. They all had engagements to attend to that day: Steve was going in to work for a lunchtime function; Matthew had an audition; and Alex was meeting with one of her editors.

"You must've been working really hard these past few days," Steve addressed Alex. "We've hardly seen you downstairs."

Alex threw a quick glance toward a silent Matthew before she replied, "I had a number of articles to write for this particular editor, and I had to meet a tight deadline." She felt somewhat uncomfortable offering this explanation even though it happened to be true. She had been busy, but knew she could have made time to spend with Steve and Matthew. It must have seemed strange to them that during the past couple of weeks, she had only come down for dinner twice; the rest of the time, she had survived on junk food.

"Well, perhaps you'll have more free time now. I take it you finished your work?" Steve persisted.

"For the time being," she answered and focused on her breakfast in order to avoid his all-seeing eyes.

Steve sighed, feeling he was not getting anywhere. He then turned to Matthew. "And what's this audition of yours about?"

"Just a small part in one of the soapies," Matthew replied, totally ignoring Alex's existence. He had not even looked her way once.

Steve gave up with a sigh and remarked, "It's a shame we're having heavy rain when we all have to go about our business." Stilted conversation was something he disliked immensely, and he wished the other two would snap out of their moods and come out with whatever was bothering them.

Breakfast was finished in silence, and while Alex offered to do the dishes, Matthew escaped upstairs to get ready. Steve waited until he was out of the way before he addressed her once more. "Alex, what's troubling you?"

"Nothing," she lied as she got busy clearing the table.

"Hey, this is me, remember? I know it's none of my business, but it pains me to see you at loggerheads with Matthew."

"Who's at loggerheads?" she remarked, a touch too lightheartedly.

"Okay, you don't have to tell me about your problems with him." Steve decided to let the remark pass. "But you do have to tell me whether I did something to offend you."

He sounded quite concerned, and Alex felt guilty all of a sudden. "Oh, Steve, you didn't do anything, really. This is just a silly thing between Matthew and me. Let's just say we had a difference of opinion."

"But what about Mark?" Steve asked, surprising her.

"What's Mark got to do with it?" Alex thought she could stall for time, but Steve came right to the point.

"C'mon, don't play games. I know you were upset because you thought I was trying to set you up."

"And weren't you?" She threw back at him, a tad resentfully.

He smiled at her directness. "Okay, I admit it. I was hoping you'd want to meet a nice guy."

"Steve, please don't take this the wrong way, but I really don't need help to meet guys. I'm simply not interested," she explained. "I know you meant well, but I'd rather forget about it."

Steve looked disappointed. "All right, if you say so. I could've sworn you found Mark attractive, and I was hoping the two of you would get together."

Alex smiled. "I know you meant well, and Mark is an attractive guy, I agree. It's only that I'm not ready for this."

"How can you know when you don't give it a chance?"

Steve could be like a stubborn little terrier sometimes, yapping at one's ankles until he was picked up and petted. The thought amused her. "Let's just say I know," she stated, picturing a little terrier with Steve's face barking up at her. She laughed.

"What's so funny?" He was bewildered by her reaction.

"You don't want to know, believe me," she replied, a merry look in her eyes.

He gave up. At least, she wasn't angry with him. "Fair enough. I'll leave you to your secrets, my dear. But promise me one thing, think about what I've said and don't cut yourself off from finding happiness."

Alex sobered up at his comment. Surely happiness was something meant for other people—normal people.

"I'm off now," Matthew suddenly called from the doorway, interrupting the mood in the kitchen. He was looking straight at Steve, and Alex sighed with regret. The cruel words she had said to him on the night of the party came back to haunt her.

"Good luck with the audition," Steve uttered, and Matthew was gone. Steve then turned to Alex. "Don't worry about him. Whatever happened between the two of you will heal in time."

Alex looked at him gratefully. Steve was an eternal optimist.

* * *

The meeting with her editor was over before noon, and Alex was dismayed at the torrent of rain pouring down when she exited the office building. In the rush to get ready that morning, she had forgotten her umbrella. Now, standing under a small portico, she toyed with the idea of calling for a taxi even though she didn't like her chances of getting one. She was about to dial the taxi service on her mobile when a voice made her heart skip a beat.

"Alex, is that you?"

Alex looked up to meet the eyes of the man Steve had thrown her way. "Mark! What a surprise." Suddenly, she felt mortified at the abrupt way in which she had parted from him.

"How are you?" Mark sounded pleased to see her, and Alex felt an inexplicable excitement. She noticed his dark hair was damp from the rain, making it look darker; a contrast to his attractive hazel eyes.

"Fine. I've been fine, unlike the weather, as you can see." The lighthearted remark worked at hiding her nervousness, and it brought a laugh from him. Immediately, she felt more at ease.

"What are you doing in the city on a day like this?"

"Just had a meeting with my editor and now I'm looking for a taxi. I forgot my brollie at home."

"Well, I came well prepared," he declared, gesturing to the large burgundy and gold golfing umbrella in his hand. "Compliments of the hotel."

"Aren't those supposed to be client giveaways?" she teased him.

He gave her a conspiratorial look. "Just borrowed it and forgot to return it, I guess. You won't tell, will you?"

"No." She laughed. "Besides, you're advertising their name all over town."

"Precisely," he agreed. "Mind you, they've changed corporate colours recently and," he confessed, "they truly did give these away to the staff."

"Ah, and I thought I'd come across a real smuggler." Alex found she enjoyed the playful banter.

"Sorry to disappoint you; but why not live up to my name and allow me to *smuggle* you off to lunch?"

This had a sobering effect on her, and she felt her uneasiness return.

Mark seemed to sense her change of mood. "C'mon," he invited with a cheeky smile, "I promise I won't bite. Besides, you'll never find a taxi in this rain. Admit it, you're stuck with me."

He was persuasive, and Alex relaxed again. Why not? Steve had told her to give it a chance. Well, this was the perfect opportunity—and in no way contrived. "Okay, that'll be nice," she said to her surprise and saw his face light up.

"Wonderful! There's a nice café around the corner, and if you stick close by me, the umbrella will cover us both." He opened the umbrella and led her gently by taking hold of her elbow.

They walked in silence until they reached a cosy Italian café on one of the side streets, away from the noisy city traffic. Though the café was crowded with the usual lunchtime crowd, they managed to find a table tucked away in a corner. Alex was glad when a waiter appeared immediately with menus as this gave her a chance to collect herself without having to make conversation. She stole a peek at Mark while he glanced through his menu and noticed how attractive he looked in his faded jeans and dark green pullover. She hoped she looked presentable in her black pants and red wool jacket. She didn't have many attractive clothes, but this outfit was okay, and she was thankful she had decided to wear make-up for the meeting.

"Do you know what you want yet?" Mark's voice intruded into her thoughts.

"Yes," she answered. "I'll go for the vegetarian focaccia and a coffee."

Mark nodded and signalled for the waiter, and Alex regarded him while he ordered their meals. He seemed confident and in control, whereas she felt like a confused little girl, wondering what to say next.

"Well," said Mark when the waiter went away with their order, "lucky thing I decided to come into town today; otherwise, I wouldn't have run into you."

"You're not working then?"

"I have a few days off, so I'm running some errands." His eyes held hers, and she felt a niggling in her conscience and knew before they could continue to have any sort of discussion, she must get a little something out of the way.

"Mark," she uttered, her voice somewhat hoarse due to nerves, "about the night of the party—I didn't mean to be rude or abrupt."

"Hey, don't worry." He put her at ease with his charming smile. "I think Steve was playing cupid and though he meant well, I can see how this may have made you feel uncomfortable."

He was right of course, and Alex was grateful to him for his insight. "Well, I'm glad that's out of the way."

"Good, so we can start all over again and introduce ourselves. Hello, my name's Mark Templeton, and you are?" he prompted her, and she played along.

"I'm Alex Dorian." She grinned at this charade.

He shook her hand. "Lovely to make your acquaintance." They

laughed at their play-acting and received a curious look from the waiter who brought their coffees. They laughed again after he left.

"He must think we're really strange," Alex commented.

"I'm sure he's seen a real mix of nuts in his trade," Mark responded, amused.

For some reason, this had them laughing again. It was Mark's easygoing and humorous manner that made Alex relax and allowed her to enjoy the company of an attractive male without feeling threatened.

She had fun listening to stories about people at his work, and she even shared some of her own travel tales. Therefore, she was amazed when she caught sight of a clock on the café wall and noticed it was past three in the afternoon. They had been in there for close to three hours, chatting and laughing as though they had known each other for years.

"Oh!" she exclaimed.

"What is it?" Mark wondered what had happened to break her easy mood.

"It's past three. We've been here for ages."

He smiled, unconcerned. "Is that all? Well, you know what they say, time flies when you're having fun."

"Yes, you're right. It's been fun, but I really have to go now; and I'm sure you have things to do as well."

Mark was going to tell her he did not and that as far as he was concerned, he had the rest of the evening and night free. But something told him she would not respond well to being rushed, and he certainly did not want to spoil their budding friendship. Not only did he find her attractive, he had really enjoyed his time with her and wanted to make sure he saw her again. So he signalled to the waiter for the bill and frowned when he saw her taking out her wallet.

"Lunch is on me."

"But—" she started to protest.

"No buts. It's the least I can do for a lady who has graced me with her company—and pleasurable company at that." His eyes held an impish look as he regarded her.

Alex smiled at his play-acting, for surely he could not be flirting with her. "Why, thank you, sir. Had I known earlier, I would've ordered the whole menu," she joked, feeling a sense of boldness; but her humour backfired when he took her at her word.

"And so you shall, my lady," returned Mark with a wide grin. "You can order the full menu when you allow me to take you out to dinner, say, this Friday evening?"

Alex was dumbfounded. She had walked right into that one. How naïve she was in the ways of men. "Well, I ..." She looked for a polite way to refuse.

"Please, Alex, no strings attached," Mark assured her before she could change her mind. "I really would like to get to know you better if you'll let me."

Alex did not know how to get out of the situation and was not sure she really wanted to, so she accepted.

"Great!" Mark's enthusiasm showed his pleasure. "I'll give you a call during the week."

"Okay, but I really have to go now. Thank you for lunch, it was lovely." She got up to go.

"Wait for me and I'll walk out with you. The waiter will be back with the bill in a moment."

"No need. The rain's stopped and I really have to go. Thank you once again."

Mark knew when he was beaten. "You're very welcome, and I really enjoyed your company. I'll talk to you soon."

Alex left the café and was lucky to find a taxi almost immediately upon reaching the street corner. She sat comfortably in the back seat of the cab and as they sped through the city traffic, she relived the events of the afternoon.

She had enjoyed Mark's company very much, and there was no doubt in her mind about the attraction she felt for him. She was excited he wanted to see her again and certain his attraction for her was strong, too. But what would happen then? One dinner would lead to another and to yet another, and then what? How could she manage a growing friendship? How would she react when their relationship became physical; for she had no doubt that it would. The fire behind those hazel eyes told her Mark Templeton was a passionate man and he was interested in much more than a platonic friendship.

For the rest of the ride home, Alex fought against rising images of a naked Mark with his hands caressing her body. She gasped in shock at the violent feelings this brought out in her and felt her stomach contract in fear. Suddenly, Mark's face changed and became that of her stepfather's. The hands that had been caressing her so lovingly were now prying open her legs in preparation for another assault on her innocence. Alex gagged and was brought back to reality when the taxi screeched to a halt on one of the streets close to her home.

"Are you okay, Miss?" The taxi driver regarded her with concern in his eyes, and Alex realised she must look a mess. Her face was covered in sweat, though the day was cold, and she imagined it was devoid of all colour.

"I'm sorry, I ... I think I'm coming down with the flu," she lied.

"You do look rather pale. Do you want me to drive you to a doctor?" the driver offered.

"No, it's fine, really. I'm feeling better now, and I'm close to home. I just need to lie down."

The taxi driver nodded. "We're almost there, only two minutes away. Nasty thing, the flu. Only got over it myself last month and felt weak as a kitten."

They were on their way again, and Alex leaned her head back on the headrest. She would be home soon and then she could hide away in the safety of her room to think up an excuse for not going to dinner with Mark Templeton.

As it turned out, she did not have to think of an excuse. Fate had other plans.

CHAPTER 13

Alex arrived home, went straight to her room, and fell into a deep sleep. She was exhausted by her emotions and did not want to think about Mark or their upcoming date on Friday evening. She slept deeply and dreamlessly and awoke to a dark room. It was just after eleven, and the house was quiet. Matthew and Steve had gone to bed.

She headed to the bathroom for a shower and afterwards made her way to the kitchen. She was famished, having missed out on dinner, and was beating eggs to make an omelette, when Matthew rushed in, startling her so much that she almost dropped the bowl.

"Alex, can you make some tea? Steve's throwing up again." He did not wait for a reply before rushing back out.

Alex put the bowl aside, hunger forgotten, and heated water for chamomile tea. While she waited for the water to boil, she heard sounds of retching intermingled with the sounds of the wind and rain coming from outside. A chill spread through her body, and she was suddenly afraid for Steve. How much more of this could his body take?

When the tea was ready, she rushed upstairs to find him in his room, lying in bed and looking very pale. Matthew watched over him, wiping at his brow with a wet cloth.

"Come in," Matthew called out, knowing she had paused in the doorway.

"How is he?" She brought over the tea.

"It's under control, but he's dehydrated and needs to drink. The tea should help settle his stomach."

"You fuss too much," Steve uttered in a weak voice.

"Nonsense. You know you always get ill when you work long hours. I can't understand why you don't give up that damn job!" Matthew gave vent to his frustration.

116

"I'll help Steve drink his tea if you like," Alex addressed Matthew. The last thing they needed now was an argument about Steve's working hours.

Matthew looked like he was going to argue further but seemed to think the better of it and relinquished his place by Steve's side so she could sit down. Alex helped Steve sit up against the pillows and held the cup to his mouth while he sipped the tea.

"Matthew, we need to rehydrate him properly. Get a litre of water mixed with four heaping teaspoons of sugar and a half teaspoon of salt."

"Okay."

Matthew left the room, and Alex turned to see Steve with a smile on his face. "What?"

"You—Miss Order All. I don't know how you do it, but Matthew always jumps to do your bidding."

"I hardly think so." Alex was amused at the thought. "However, where your health's concerned, I'm inclined to agree. Now, drink up and be quiet."

"Yes, Miss Order All." He made an effort to have a few more sips and then brushed away the cup. "I need a break."

"Come on, Steve. You have to drink plenty of fluids. Vomiting dehydrates a person severely," Alex protested, "and the last thing you want to do is ruin your kidneys."

"Is your rehydration formula an outback remedy?" Steve remarked to draw her attention from fussing over him.

"Yes. Dehydration in the desert can prove fatal, so people better know how to replace their fluids fast."

"Why the sugar and the salt; why not just water?"

"The glucose in the sugar helps with the absorption of fluid and salts in the body."

"Well, you learn something new every day," Steve commented, sounding tired.

"How many times did you vomit?"

"Can't remember anymore... Just want to sleep."

"You have to finish the tea before you sleep. And I'll wake you in a while so you can drink some of the solution," Alex told him as she brought the cup to his lips again and practically forced the drink into his mouth.

Matthew returned holding a jug full of liquid and a glass. "How's

117

the patient?"

"He'll be okay as long as he replaces his fluids. He can start on the solution in a little while."

"My God! Two fussy, order-all people. What's a guy to do?" Steve teased weakly.

"A guy's to drink and be quiet," Alex gently admonished him.

"Okay, I can take a hint. Pour some more down my throat, woman." He resigned himself to her care.

Matthew and Alex exchanged a smile at his comment, and at that moment they felt their feelings of enmity for each other dissolve into thin air. Neither one had the need to say anything. It was like a silent message passed between them.

Steve finished the tea and leaned back on the pillows. He fell asleep almost instantly, and the other two went back down to the kitchen.

"You must be starving," Matthew remarked.

"How did you know?"

He gestured toward the eggs in the bowl, still sitting on the bench. "I think you were preparing something just as I came in."

Alex laughed. "That's right. I forgot all about it. I was making an omelette since I didn't have any dinner."

"I know. We didn't see you there," he stated.

"I fell asleep. I was tired after all the work I've been doing lately." Alex suddenly wanted to confide in him about Mark but could not bring herself to do it.

"We had pizza, and there's heaps left in the fridge. Why don't you reheat it and save yourself the trouble of cooking?"

The idea sounded attractive so Alex stored the eggs in the fridge for later use. "Good thinking. Want to join me?"

"Why not? I didn't eat much earlier on so there's plenty left over." He drew out a box from the fridge, which held a whole pizza inside.

"How many pizzas did you end up getting?"

"Two large ones. Steve thought you might want some later. Besides, he hardly ate any."

"I'll make the coffee if you heat up," Alex offered.

"Deal."

A few minutes later, they sat down to hot coffee and reheated pizza, and ate companionably. Alex was happy to be friends again, and even her tumultuous feelings about Mark failed to spoil the moment.

"How did the audition go?" she asked, taking a bite of pizza.

"Well, I think. I won't know for a few days yet, but I've worked with this particular director before and things look positive."

"That's great. I hope you get it."

"I think I will. The part's spread over three episodes so the money's quite good."

"What's the part?"

"A doctor. Well, an intern, to be exact, and he gets framed for sexually harassing one of the nursing staff."

Alex smiled. "And how will you like playing that?"

"If she's a blonde babe, I won't mind at all," he teased, and they burst out laughing. It felt good to be close again. "How did your meeting go?"

"I think the editor was happy with my efforts, so now I can take a little holiday."

"How come?"

"The article, or series of articles, I should say, will pay well. I've got enough money saved up now to live at leisure for the rest of the year if I wish. So I thought a break of a few weeks might be good."

"What about saving some of it?"

"What for?" She asked in earnest.

"Well, you have to have some money put aside for emergencies. Look at what happened to Steve and me. We didn't plan on his falling ill, and now we have the mortgage to pay."

"Yes, but I don't have a mortgage or a home of my own. So I can live on what I make as I go along."

"Don't you ever want to buy a house and settle down somewhere?"

"Maybe, but I never plan long-term. I figure life is unreliable enough as it is. How many times do you make plans and think everything's going to work out, only to have it all blow up in your face?" Alex sniffed cynically. "So now I live for the moment, and spend for the moment, too."

"I suppose if you look at it that way, then you're right," Matthew replied, but in his heart he was sad for her. To be so alone must be frightening.

Alex read his thoughts. "Don't you go feeling sorry for me. I enjoy my single status, and besides, I have you and Steve." She became pensive. "Mind you, one shouldn't be lulled into a comfort zone, either, since everything's in a constant state of change."

They sat quietly, each reflecting on the concept of impermanence. Matthew was the first to break the silence. "That kind of view is really depressing."

"Life can be really depressing," she remarked.

"Yes, but you're not giving it a chance. You arbitrarily made up your mind that life is depressing."

"I don't know about *arbitrarily*. My view of life is based on past experience."

"Okay, I can see that," Matthew agreed, "but aside from what happened with your stepfather, you must've had some good times." He persisted, wanting her to see life was also about positive things.

"I did have some good experiences, I guess; but everything I do is overshadowed by the past." She sounded sad. "So I've learned not to set high expectations for myself about anything anymore. This way, I won't be disappointed if good things don't happen."

"I'm sorry you feel that way. I wish I could help."

Alex regarded him thoughtfully, taking in his beautiful looks: the perfect body, the handsome face and those large, innocent-looking blue eyes. He seemed so untouched by life, and yet, he was living with the rejection of his family and the imminent death of his partner. Her heart felt like breaking at the thought of what was ahead for him, and she wanted to reach out, take him in her arms, and protect him from the evils of the world. She felt a hundred years old next to him, but before she gave in to depression, she snapped out of her dark thoughts.

"Why don't you check on Steve while I tidy up?"

"Will you look in on him later, too?" Matthew sounded like a little boy lost.

"Sure. I'll be up in ten minutes. Meanwhile," she reminded him, "make sure he drinks a minimum of two glasses."

He threw her a boyish smile and left the kitchen. Alex felt good about being needed. This was her family now.

* * *

When she went to check on the boys, Alex found Matthew fast

asleep next to Steve. Steve's gentle breathing also suggested he was sleeping, and she turned to leave the room.

"Alex," Steve called out softly. "Got a minute?"

"Of course." She approached his side of the bed and crouched down close to him. "I thought you were asleep. How are you feeling?"

"Still queasy, but I managed to drink some of the solution."

"Well, you need to rest now. I'll leave and look in on you later."

"Please stay for a few moments." He reached out for her hand.

"Can I get you anything?" Alex asked, taking his hand in hers.

"No, I just want to talk."

"All right." She waited.

After a pause, Steve said, "Mark rang me at work this afternoon. He told me you had lunch with him."

Alex knew it would come out sooner or later, and she did not mind Steve knowing. "I happened to run into him, and he invited me."

"I'm glad," he remarked. "He really likes you, and he told me you're going out to dinner this Friday. So I just wanted to say I'm happy things worked out in the end."

Alex sighed, wondering whether this was the time to tell him she had no intention of going out to dinner with Mark, but she did not have the heart to do it. "It's early days yet. Mark's only a friend, anyway." With this, she dismissed the topic. "Now," she added in a bossy tone, "you're talking far too much when you should be resting." She made to get up from her crouching position, but Steve held onto her hand a little tighter.

"One other thing; I'm glad that whatever happened between you and Matthew is over."

Alex glanced at the sleeping figure of Matthew and then back at Steve. "How do you know?"

"He told me when he came back upstairs. I couldn't stand seeing the two of you being indifferent. He needs you, especially now that I'm—"

"Now that you're getting better," she interjected, "because Matthew and I plan to pamper you all the time."

Steve smiled and let go of her hand. "Go get some sleep. I promise I'll drink up like a good boy."

She kissed his cheek and stood up. "I'm not sleepy. I'll be

reading in my room. So call out if you need anything."

* * *

In her room, Alex settled back on the bed with a book on the history of medieval England. History was one of her passions, and she loved the thought one could get lost in it, especially among the turmoil and intrigue of the dark ages. Besides, she always found history a good antidote to help her forget about her own life, even if it was just for a short while.

She read for about an hour and eventually felt her eyelids grow heavy with sleep. The wind and rain still raged on outside, and the warmth of the blanket she had wrapped around her weaved a safe cocoon. She relaxed, content in her little world, and soon she fell asleep.

A loud crashing noise startled her awake and she opened her eyes to find Matthew pulling her out of bed.

"Alex, wake up! Steve's really ill. The ambulance is on its way. We're going to hospital with him." His eyes were wide with fear.

Alex noticed he was only dressed in a pair of tracksuit pants. The crashing noise had been the door of her room, which Matthew had thrown open with such force it had swung back, banging against the wall. "What happened?"

"No time now. Quick, get ready," he uttered and rushed out.

Alex was already dressed in the dark green tracksuit she had been wearing when she fell asleep so she put on a pair of sneakers and grabbed a heavy jacket. She was in the boys' room in less than two minutes.

Steve was throwing up again, this time into a bucket by the side of his bed. Matthew held his head to support him in between bouts of retching.

"Let me do that while you dress." Alex nudged him out of the way and took over. She looked into the bucket and was shocked to see red droplets. There was very little vomit left in Steve, it was mainly bile flecked with blood. Her heart skipped in fear. "When you're ready, help me get him into a dressing gown. It'll be freezing outside," she told Matthew.

While Matthew searched in the wardrobe for a dressing gown, Alex helped Steve back on the pillows and wiped his pale face with a

122

wet cloth. "Steve, can you hear me?"

Steve nodded weakly but kept his eyes closed.

"We're here with you," Alex continued as calmly as she could. "The ambulance is on its way, and we have to get you ready. We're going to put a dressing gown on you."

Matthew came back with a winter gown, and between the two of them, they dressed Steve with it. Alex grabbed a pair of thick socks from the dresser for him and then pulled out a blanket from the wardrobe.

"We'll wrap him in this. We can't afford for him to catch cold."

Matthew had Steve out of bed and held his limp body against his own. "He's really weak, Alex. God, please help him," he cried in a desperate voice.

They heard the sound of the approaching ambulance. "That'll be them," Alex declared. "I'll let them in. He's going to be okay, Matthew, you'll see. Stay calm. You need to for his sake, you hear?"

Matthew looked into her eyes and seemed to draw strength from them. He nodded. "I'm okay."

"Good." She threw him an encouraging smile and ran downstairs.

* * *

Alex brought coffee in two paper cups and joined Matthew in the waiting room at St Vincent's Hospital. She sat next to him and put one of the cups in his hand. "It's not exactly espresso, but it's hot," she spoke softly.

It was close to four in the morning and the waiting room was deserted, for which Alex was immensely grateful. Matthew looked a mess as he sat back in his chair. He had dressed hastily in black track pants, a white t-shirt, and a lightweight red windbreaker, but he didn't seem to feel the cold. The rain had not stopped and the wind howled ferociously outside. Alex shivered even though she was warmly wrapped up, and the heating inside the room did little to stop the chill spreading through her body.

Matthew sat in his chair without having moved for some time.

"Have some coffee. It'll do you good." She reached out and touched his hand. It felt frozen.

"I can't drink anything right now," his voice was croaky with emotion.

"Just a few sips. It'll help. Besides, you don't want Steve to see you looking like this, do you?"

The statement worked immediately and his eyes lit up with hope. "You're right. He can't see me looking exhausted." He took a sip of the coffee and held the cup with both hands to keep them warm.

"I'm going to find you a blanket. You look frozen."

He did not argue, and Alex left the room briefly. When she returned, she was holding a hospital blanket, which she threw over his shoulders. She was pleased to notice that during her absence, he had finished the coffee.

"Better now?" she asked, once again taking a seat next to him.

He nodded, and they remained with their own thoughts until the door swung open and a doctor strode in. Matthew jumped from his seat, the blanket dropping to the floor. "Dr Benning, how is he?"

The doctor was a kind-looking man in his fifties, who was short and plump and reminded Alex of a jolly clown rather than a man of medicine.

"Please, have a seat, Matthew. You look worn out," Dr Benning said gently, retrieving the blanket from the floor to throw it back around Matthew's shoulders.

He sat down next to Matthew and acknowledged Alex with a nod. "Steve is suffering from an infection of the bowels, which is affecting his digestive system. This is why he's been vomiting. There are also some complications with his kidneys and as you know, he's severely dehydrated."

"We tried to rehydrate him, doctor," Alex explained.

"Yes, but it wouldn't have done any good because of the complications I'm talking about. He needs to be rehydrated intravenously plus we need to treat the infection at the same time. He's going to be here for a few days."

"Is he going to be all right?" Matthew's voice sounded shaky.

The doctor smiled reassuringly. "You know we're doing the best we can. I wish I could tell you with more certainty what the outcome will be, but I can only say we'll do everything in our power to get him back on his feet."

Matthew looked so lost and fearful that the doctor put a comforting hand on his shoulder. "If you want to help him, you'll go home and get some rest. He's not going to be happy if you get ill."

Then, he addressed Alex. "Young lady, are you looking after Matthew?"

"Yes." Alex didn't have to think twice about her answer.

"Good," said the doctor. "Then, get him home and put him to bed. There's nothing he can do by staying here now. Steve won't be having any visitors tonight. I'll make sure to contact you as soon as we know how the condition is progressing."

"Thank you, doctor." Alex stood and pulled Matthew after her as the doctor bade them good night and went on his way.

"Come on, we'll call a taxi."

Matthew pulled back. "I want to see Steve first. What if I never see him again?" He was having trouble controlling his emotions, and Alex saw the tears gather in his eyes.

"Of course you'll see him again! He simply needs to rest." She was firm with him. "Let's go. You heard the doctor. If anything happens, he'll call us."

Finally, he allowed himself to be led away while Alex prayed silently for Steve's recovery.

CHAPTER 14

"Sometimes I wonder why we even exist," Matthew reflected from his reclining position on the sofa, mug of coffee in one hand.

Alex, who was sitting opposite him on the floor, sipped her coffee and waited for him to continue.

"I mean," he went on, "life's such a struggle, full of disappointments and suffering, and then we die. Where's the reward in that?"

"Who's to say there has to be a reward?" Alex could not help sounding cynical. She thought how ironic it was that hours earlier Matthew had been talking to her about focusing on the positive things in life.

Matthew studied her for a moment. "You're right. Maybe there's nothing out there; no meaning, nothing."

They sat in silence while dawn signalled a new day, though the light coming in through the loungeroom window was still dim. The wind and rain still raged on, with the outside temperature close to freezing. It was as though the beautiful weather had disappeared along with Steve's health.

Alex began to feel sleepy in the warmth of the room and fought against her closing eyelids. They had been sitting with the heater on since their return from the hospital, but neither of them wanted to sleep even though they were exhausted after the night's events.

"I think we owe it to Steve not to get too negative," she remarked. "He'd think we're heathens or something."

This brought a smile to Matthew's face. "He's not religious, you know."

"Yes, but he does believe in the hereafter. Remember his story about the butterflies—what did he call them—the Soul Bearers?"

"That's right. He said something about the soul waiting to be transported to another plane of existence." Matthew sounded skeptical.

"I don't suppose you believe in that." Alex sniffed as though the idea was nonsensical.

"Do you?" he challenged her back.

"I don't know what to believe." She was truly puzzled, not sure what to believe. "I guess I'd like to think there's something better than this, but who knows. Life's the biggest mystery of all."

"You mean death," he amended.

"Life, death, what does it matter?" She frowned. "You know, I've known people who were dead even when they were alive. They're the monsters that don't care about those they hurt." Her eyes clouded with troubled thoughts.

Matthew knew she was referring to her stepfather; and what she said made sense. The world was full of people who thought only of themselves and no one else. They thought of *their* needs, *their* feelings, and *their* image. His own father was a prime example of this; so was his mother with her misdirected love for her son. Yes, she loved him; at least, he thought as much, but it was a conditional type of love. Dora could only truly love him if he left Steve.

Alex noticed the changing emotions playing across Matthew's face and wondered what he was thinking. "Steve will be fine," she reassured him. "You'll see."

"I hope you're right."

"Why don't you get some sleep? You look tired." The strain on his face was plain to see.

"So do you."

"At least I got some sleep yesterday afternoon, but you've had an exhausting day and night," she argued.

"I don't want to sleep just yet. You go on. I'll call you if I hear something from the hospital."

"No. I'll keep you company," she declared, stubbornly.

Again, they lapsed into silence, and Alex regarded Matthew thoughtfully. He looked exhausted, and yet he still looked beautiful. He had an air of untouched innocence that made her want to reach out and touch him. She felt the blood rush to her face, and in confusion she blurted out the first thing that came into her mind. "How did you become gay?"

Matthew laughed for a moment. "You don't *become gay*; you just are," he answered, amused by her question.

"You know what I mean," she persisted.

He smiled and explained, "Well, it may surprise you to know that I was once engaged." He saw he had her undivided attention. "My parents picked her out for me. She was nice enough, I guess. Most importantly, she had the right background.

"I was all of nineteen at the time, and Erica's father owned one of the most prominent real estate development firms in Australia; so you can imagine how happy this made my father. Our marriage would've been a merger between two companies, and my feelings for Erica, or rather the lack thereof, didn't come into it." He paused and took a sip of coffee. It was cold, but he didn't notice; his mind was on the story he was relating.

"Anyway, I had been going out with Erica on and off. We went to the same university, and that's how I met her. Then, in less than a year, I was engaged to her—I don't even know how it happened. We had a good sex life—she was certainly no beginner—but I always thought there was something missing for me." He noticed how Alex averted her gaze away from his. "What's wrong, does this make you uncomfortable?"

"No, no, it's just ... I suppose I'm not used to people talking about sex so openly, that's all." Alex cringed whenever someone spoke of sex as if it were something to be enjoyed even though she knew this was true for most people. "Please, go on," she prompted him, eager to hear the rest of his story.

"One night, we went out with Erica's brother. We were celebrating something or other, and I found myself feeling so attracted to him that I was shocked. The urge was quite strong and I couldn't deny it. I guess at the back of my mind, I always knew I preferred men. Anyway, at the end of the evening, we dropped Erica off at her apartment. I made the excuse I was too tired to stay with her; and Julian, her brother, offered to give me a ride home.

"On our way, we decided to have a drink at a new nightclub. You know, it was a bit like a boys' night out. He didn't drink as much as I did because he was driving, but I was loaded by the time we left. When we arrived at my place, Julian had to help me out of the car and into the house.

"I'll never forget this part," he paused, a smile on his face. "We were in the garden at my parents' home—and this garden is like a tropical jungle—really dark and exotic-looking." He paused again and closed his eyes as if conjuring up the image in his mind.

Alex spoke again. "And?"

Matthew opened his eyes and smiled mischievously. "And as we were walking through the garden with Julian holding me up, I stopped, swung around to face him, and kissed him full on the mouth." He let out a laugh, one that sounded rather bitter. "My hand reached out to cup his crotch, too. My God, the guy was stunned."

"What did he do?" Alex was stunned, too.

"He punched me in the face so hard that I flew through the air and crashed into a palm tree. I thought he broke my nose. Then, he called me a 'fucking faggot' and left. I couldn't even get up off the ground; I was that drunk. I slept right where I was until my father found me the following morning." He laughed again, and this time Alex could have sworn he wanted to cry at the memory.

"By this time, it was midmorning. Julian telephoned the house and spoke with my father, telling him what I did. When the old man found me, he pulled me into the house like I was nothing but a sack of potatoes and gave me the beating of my life." There was definitely a teary look in his eyes now, and Alex went to him and sat on the edge of the sofa.

Matthew seemed to take comfort from her proximity and went on. "I slept most of that day, and when I woke up I felt like shit. I had the worst headache from the hangover and from the blows I got from Julian and my father. My stomach felt like it was pasted to my back and my muscles were so stiff from the beating, I could barely move." His voice was suddenly devoid of emotion as if the whole episode had occurred to someone else.

"Anyway, my father came to see me with my mother in tow, and it was obvious she'd been crying. He asked me if I meant what I did or whether it was just the alcohol. Up until then, I'd been too frightened and confused about what had happened with Julian to really think about it. But when my father came into my room demanding to know if I really meant what I did, and looking like he was going to give me another beating, my head just cleared, and I knew.

"I knew I was gay, and I wasn't going to be my parents' pawn and marry Erica. I couldn't love her as a man loves a woman, and I could never live under my father's thumb, either. So I told him I meant it, and there was nothing he could do about it." Matthew frowned but continued with his story. "Well, apparently there *was* something he could do about it. Right there and then, he pulled me from the bed and physically kicked me out into the street. I was still wearing the clothes from the night before. I remember my mother screaming for him to stop, but he was a man demented. When he shoved me out the front door, he told me not to bother coming back home—ever. And that was that."

Alex was horrified. Matthew's treatment by his father was just as brutal as what she had endured at the hands of her stepfather, and though sexual abuse was not involved in Matthew's case, the emotional pain was no less traumatic. Suddenly, she was aware of a tear rolling down her face. Matthew saw it, too, and reached out to wipe it away with his finger before pulling her into his arms. He felt a deep need for human contact; the kind that would help him erase the painful memories of the past.

Alex was surprised at his action but made no move to resist. "What did you do then?" She nestled closer into his chest, finding comfort in his warmth and not feeling the least bit threatened by her action.

"I had a few bucks in my pocket so I caught a taxi and went to a friend's place, a guy from university. He was gay and living with his partner, so he offered to put me up until I was back on my feet again. It's ironic how help can come from strangers rather than family, isn't it?" Matthew asked, but didn't wait for an answer. "Daryl gave me some clothes and let me stay in a spare room. His partner worked in a hotel and got me a casual job so I could earn some money while I put myself through uni.

"I stayed with them for over a year, and then I met Steve. He was a friend of Daryl's partner, and it turned out he was looking for a housemate. Daryl and his partner thought I might like to move now that I had more money. Their spare room was small and it was time for me to go in any case. So that's how I met Steve, and shortly after this we became lovers."

"Did you ever see your father again?" Alex hoped Matthew had not noticed the blush on her face when he talked of Steve and himself becoming lovers.

"Only if he happened to be in the house when I went to visit my mother. It took a couple of years for him to allow me to visit, and only because my mother begged him. Of course, he always made sure he was out when I came around."

"What about your mother—did she ever help you with money?"

"No. She may live in luxury, but my father holds the purse strings. I did get my clothes back, though. She mailed them to me a few weeks after I was kicked out. She couldn't accept my lifestyle, either; but she did try to help. I believe she still loves me in her own way." This last statement held a note of doubt in it.

"I'm sure she loves you." Alex saw the sadness in his eyes.

"Well, I'm not so sure anymore. But this is the way things are. She's always at me to go to the States and make a name for myself. She promises to help if I decide to do so." His voice held a hint of cynicism.

"So what's wrong with that?"

"On the condition I leave Steve," he added bitterly.

"Oh."

"Exactly."

Mention of Steve brought Matthew back to the present, and he felt a strong sense of sadness take over him. "We haven't made love for months, you know," he confessed suddenly.

Alex was amazed at his disclosure, but she realised talking so intimately had moved their friendship onto a new level. There was no denying that aside from Steve, she was the next closest person to him.

"I've been too afraid to hurt him," Matthew went on. "He's so frail all the time; and I just don't think it's right. But if he dies now ..."

"He's not going to die," Alex declared, sounding encouraging. "He'll get better and come home."

"Yes, you're right," he replied, trying to convince himself.

They were silent again, and the warmth in the room, combined with their own body heat, lulled them into sleep as they were— cradled together like two lost children in a savage storm.

* * *

The telephone rang, startling them awake. They looked at each other, still dazed with sleep, and then Matthew raced to take the call.

"Yes, this is he." Alex heard him say and knew it was news from the hospital.

She could not hear the rest of the conversation so she waited for him to return. In the meantime, she had a few moments to reflect on the fact that she had slept with her housemate, and although it was not in the intimate sense, the physical aspect of having slept in each other's arms had left her feeling tingly all over.

Alex indulged in this feeling because she knew Matthew did not look upon her as a sex object. Had the same thing happened with Mark ... Mark! She had forgotten all about her date with him. Friday was three days away and she had not yet come up with an excuse to turn him down. She had a feeling he'd be telephoning sometime today and had no idea what she was going to say.

A sudden laugh coming from the hallway told her things must be okay with Steve. Thank God, she sighed with relief. And this was when she knew what she was going to do about her date. Steve had to stay in hospital for a few days and she had to look after Matthew. A poor excuse, as Matthew could look after himself, but from an emotional support point of view, plausible enough.

Just as she settled on this idea, Matthew walked back in. "Steve's fine. He has to stay in hospital for a few days because they want to keep an eye on the infection, but he's fine!" He was smiling, and his eyes lit up like the sun.

Alex drew in her breath at his beauty. "That's wonderful news," she exclaimed. "And now I can finally say: *I told you so!* When can we see him?"

"No visitors until this evening, and then only one at a time."

"Understandable, I suppose." She felt disappointed. "Well, I guess you'll have to tell me how he's doing and send him my regards."

"It's okay. You can see him tomorrow during the day. I have an audition and would appreciate it if you could relieve me at the hospital."

"But of course—any time you want." She brightened up. "You need to take breaks, too, you know. The last thing we need is for you to come down with stress exhaustion."

"It's all settled then." Matthew was too excited to worry about his own health right now. "I'll go see him tonight and tomorrow morning, and you can relieve me in the afternoon."

"Good. Now, let's have something to eat."

Alex led the way to the kitchen, suddenly realising how hungry she was. But before they could start preparing their food, the telephone rang again and Matthew went to take the call. After a few seconds, he returned to the kitchen. "It's for you."

Alex knew who it would be even before she took the receiver in her hand. "Alex speaking," she spoke in a neutral tone lest he think she was happy to hear from him.

"Hi, it's Mark. How are you?" The voice at the other end of the line sounded chirpy. "Told you I'd call. Time to order the whole menu as you suggested," he said in jest.

Alex felt guilty about what she was going to do next, but she could not help it. In the long run, Mark would be better off without her. "Mark, I ..." her voice faltered, and she started again. "Mark, Steve's in hospital," she blurted out and saw Matthew's head appear from the kitchen doorway, regarding her with curiosity.

"My God, what happened?" His humour gone, Mark's tone was serious. "Matthew didn't say anything when he answered the phone just now."

"Steve took ill last night, but he'll be okay. He's staying in hospital for a few days recovering," she reassured him. "Anyway, I can't go to dinner Friday night." She swallowed hard. "The house is a mess plus I have to look after Matthew." It sounded so lame when she said it, and her eyes darted to Matthew and his inquiring look.

"Oh." Mark sounded disappointed. "Well, if you have to look after things ..."

Alex imagined him thinking what a poor liar she made, but there was no help for it. "I'm sorry, but I have to go now. We didn't get any sleep through the night and I'm really tired." *You liar!*

"Perhaps, some other time." Mark managed to keep the disappointment out of his voice. "Please send Steve my best wishes. Tell him the guys and I will drop by when the hospital says it's okay to do so. I'll see you around." He rang off.

Alex replaced the receiver and turned to Matthew with a look of guilt on her face.

"You're a shit, Alex," Matthew remarked in a voice that told her he saw right through her little charade. "You don't have to look after me. What a load of—"

"All right, I know! I used a little white lie to cancel the date."

He looked unconvinced.

"Well, it's true!" she insisted as she followed him into the

133

kitchen. "Steve *is* ill."

"Yes, that part's true, but you don't have to look after me and clean around the house. You scrubbed the whole place top to bottom two days ago, and I certainly don't need looking after. Besides, I'll be with Steve most of the time."

Alex went to the refrigerator and took out various ingredients for their lunch. "Yes, but Mark doesn't know this."

Matthew was amused. "I know it's none of my business, and I don't want you jumping down my throat; but if you didn't want to go out with him in the first place, why did you accept?"

"It just happened that way."

While they made lunch, she told him how she had bumped into Mark after her meeting at the editor's and the lunch that followed. "Anyway," she remarked when she finished telling the story, "it was a joke I made because he offered to pay for lunch. I said if I had known he'd be paying, I would've ordered the whole menu. I was trying to be funny, but he took it seriously and asked me out to dinner."

"You could've said no," Matthew pointed out.

"I suppose so, but I didn't have the heart to do it. It would've sounded ungracious."

He laughed. "God, Alex, you do beat all. Were you going to go out with him just because it would've been ungracious to turn him down?"

Alex looked at the sandwich she had made like it held some deep, dark secret.

"Well?" he prompted.

"I ... I don't know." She knew she sounded pathetic. The truth was she had wanted to go out with Mark, and now she'd chickened out. She wasn't going to admit this to Matthew, however.

"Do you like him?" Matthew probed cautiously.

"I suppose so, I ... Look, I'd rather we drop the subject."

Matthew, remembering their last fight, readily agreed. "Okay, but if you change your mind and want to talk about it, I'm here."

"Thank you," she said and buried her face in her sandwich.

CHAPTER 15

Steve was in good spirits, if a little pale, when he greeted Alex the following afternoon. Matthew had left as soon as she arrived to relieve him, and Steve confided in her jokingly, "Thank God! I was beginning to think he was never going to leave. He's been like a nursemaid since he arrived last night."

Alex smiled. "He means well, and he's been really worried about you."

"Don't I know it! He fusses about everything. Heaven help me if I don't take my medication." His eyes widened in mock horror.

Alex laughed. "And how have you been?"

"Better," was his too swift reply. They grinned at each other.

"Seriously though, how do you feel?" Alex knew Steve hated to complain.

"I feel like I've been through fifty-two weekends of army reserve training without the weekdays in between." He was still joking, and before he could go on, a nurse walked in.

"How's my favourite patient today?" she asked. The nurse was a plump, cheerful woman in her early forties with a good-natured smile.

"Still waiting for that dance you promised me, Sister," Steve replied.

The nurse laughed and turned to Alex. "He's such an outrageous flirt, this one. He has all the female nurses buzzing around him like bees to honey."

"And the male ones, too," Steve added, his expression deadpan.

This sent the nurse roaring with laughter. "Oh, you are a real case, love. Wait until I tell the boys," she remarked while she changed the bag of hydrating solution on Steve's IV drip. "With him around, we don't need to watch any more sitcoms," she told Alex and tossed Steve a smile on her way out.

"I see there's a wicked side to you," Alex observed.

"Well, you know how it is. It's either humour or despair. I opt for humour."

Suddenly, Alex was serious. "Do you really mean that? *Are* you in despair?"

"No, no," he reassured her. "What I meant was you can make the choice to see the glass half full or half empty."

Alex still looked doubtful.

"I'm all right, Alex. I promise you. I'm not in pain and I'm responding to medication. So now let's talk about you, my dear."

Alex reached into her bag and pulled out a couple of glossy magazines. "I brought you some reading material."

"Thank you," Steve said, taking them. "I suppose I'll find one of your travel articles in this?" He held up one of the magazines, which was on travel.

"Well, I can't be totally modest, can I? So yes, one of my latest articles is in there."

"I look forward to reading it then. But now it's time for the truth," he sounded mysterious.

"What do you mean?" she asked but knew what was coming.

"I received a call today, and guess who my caller was?"

Alex did not respond. She simply gazed at him with feigned interest and waited for him to go on.

"Our friend Mark," Steve announced enthusiastically.

"How nice of him," her tone was sarcastic.

"Come on, Alex, you know what I'm getting at."

It seemed Steve was not going to let her dismiss the matter quite so lightly, causing Alex to be inexplicably annoyed with Mark. "He had no right ringing you while you're in hospital to tell you I wouldn't go out with him! How insensitive is that?"

Steve was amused. "He didn't ring only for that. He obviously wanted to see how I was, and then we got talking about work and other things. Finally, he told me about your excuse for cancelling dinner."

"Well, he may have gone about it the long way, but in the end he told you the story just the same. This wasn't the right time or place to do it," she protested.

"Go easy on the guy. He's one of my good friends, and he can tell me anything he likes."

"So he said I made up an excuse, did he?" She sounded interested, despite her annoyance.

"It didn't take him long to figure it out."

She shrugged her shoulders. "I don't care anyway. I don't want to go out with him, and that's that."

"What are you afraid of?"

Just like Steve to go to the heart of the matter immediately, thought Alex. "I'd rather drop it if you don't mind."

"But I do mind," he insisted.

If this were Matthew, she would have found a way to have an argument of some sort to steer him off course, but with Steve it was different, so she remained silent.

"You do like him, don't you?" Steve persisted gently.

Alex sighed with resignation. It was obvious he wasn't going to give up—just like a little terrier with a bone. "Yes, okay. I do like him," she admitted, "but he frightens me."

"Why?"

"Well, he's a man for starters. I don't feel comfortable around men, you know this." She felt exasperated.

"You seem to feel just fine around Matthew and me," he pointed out.

"It's different with you guys. You're my housemates. Besides, you're ..." She paused and didn't know how to go on.

"We're gay. Yes, I know that," he finished for her. "But I also know you find Matthew attractive—in a sexual way, I mean."

Alex went beet red and wished she could crawl under the hospital bed. Steve laughed at the look of mortification on her face.

"Don't worry. I'm not going to scratch your eyes out, but it doesn't change the way you feel about him."

"How did you know?" she asked in a little voice.

"How did I know you find him attractive? Well, who wouldn't? He's a beautiful person, both inside and out." He paused and gazed into her eyes. "With you, though, it's different. I think you find him attractive because you feel safe with him. Besides, I'm not blind. I've seen the way you react to him."

"Oh God! Does he know this?" She cringed at the thought.

"I think he has a good idea."

Alex buried her face in her hands, wondering why she could not disappear into thin air. "Steve, why didn't you tell me this before?"

"Why should I? It's not a problem with me. Besides, I think it may do you good to practise on Matthew."

"Practise? What do you mean, practise?" She could not believe what she heard.

"You know, being with an attractive man." Steve sounded perfectly logical about the whole matter, and Alex looked on in disbelief. He smiled at her in a good-natured way, and she calmed down.

"Okay, but as you've said, he's gay so it doesn't count. And I do admit it—I *am* afraid of men, and the reason is because of the sex part. There! I've said it. Are you happy now?" She threw him a sullen look.

"Don't get upset. It's normal that you would be afraid of sex after what happened in the past. I just don't want you to crawl into a shell and be a nun for the rest of your life."

His kind manner did nothing to allay her fears. "Why not?" she challenged him.

"Because you have a lot of love to give and you shouldn't waste it. Love's a very special gift to have, and it should be shared with the right person."

Alex sat quietly, taking in what he said. True love, the soul mate kind, would be a wonderful thing. She had daily proof of this by watching Matthew and Steve.

"Well?" Steve intruded into her thoughts.

"Perhaps you're right, but I don't know how to face this fear. I mean, Mark hasn't even touched me and despite this, I'm always nervous around him. I just know if he does I'll flee in terror. How silly will I look then? Don't you see? He's better off without me."

Steve noticed the agonised look in her eyes and realised she was getting quite worked up about her dilemma, so he decided to let matters drop. "Okay, relax. You don't have to do anything you don't want to. Just remember one thing though, no matter what happens, I'm here for you."

"Matthew told me the same thing, and I thank you both. When I think about it, I don't know how I survived so long without you guys."

"The human spirit can adapt to many things even during the most trying of times," Steve uttered consolingly. "In any case, I'm sure when the time is right you'll do whatever feels natural, but for now don't give up altogether."

Alex looked thoughtful.

* * *

The next couple of days were quiet around the house. Matthew was at the hospital from morning to evening, and Alex hardly saw him. She kept busy, tidying up Steve's garden, cleaning the house, and doing the shopping. Steve would be coming home in two days' time and she planned to cook a welcome home dinner. She browsed through some of his cookbooks and settled on eggplant lasagna with Italian salad for mains and tiramisu for dessert. After making a list of ingredients, she decided to go shopping.

On the way to the market, she thought about the conversation she'd had with Steve about his insight into her attraction for Matthew and the reason behind it; plus her fear of intimacy with a heterosexual male. Steve had told her when the time came, she would do what was natural to her—and now she wondered what he'd meant. In her opinion, the natural thing was to recoil from any intimacy with the opposite sex.

Perhaps, what Steve had meant was that there would come a time when she would be able to face her fear. Unfortunately, she didn't see how this would ever come about and her hope turned to despair. Even when she saw couples in the street, walking hand in hand or touching in some way, she always shivered at the dark thoughts that rose to her mind, and she quickly looked away. Ironically, she had finally discovered the delight of being touched by a male, thanks to Matthew. However, he'd treated her more like a sister than anything else, and this had enabled her to develop a certain trust in him; hence the reason she was able to enjoy his touch. Matthew had no expectations of her whatsoever; but a heterosexual male would definitely expect something in return. And this was something she could not give.

"Well, well. It seems we're fated to meet yet again." A male voice brought her out of her reverie and Alex found herself face to face with Mark, who was carrying two shopping bags laden with groceries.

"So it seems." She tried to keep the annoyance out of her voice. It wasn't his fault they had bumped into each other, she thought. She was simply annoyed at fate for playing its little tricks.

"I saw Steve yesterday," Mark announced. "He's looking well and can't wait to get home."

"Yes. He's being released on Monday."

"And how have you been—busy?"

Was there a hint of sarcasm in his voice? "Quite busy actually," Alex lied. "It's amazing how much there's to do when one looks around; plus I want the house to be perfect for when Steve comes home."

"Sure. I guess the boys are lucky to have you. I know if it was left up to Matthew, there'd be fungus growing out of the carpet by now." This was said in jest, and Alex laughed, feeling more relaxed.

"You're right. I think he's allergic to any form of housework."

Mark's face went suddenly serious as he regarded her and he plunged into what had been uppermost in his mind. "Look, about the dinner date—"

"Please, Mark," she interrupted him. "The fact I cancelled has nothing to do with you. It's just that—"

"Prove it then," he cut her short.

"Prove what?"

"Prove that it's nothing to do with me. Come out to dinner this week sometime."

Alex sighed. She could not stop getting into trouble whenever Mark was around, and the thing was she really did want to go out with him.

"So what do you say?" Those wonderful eyes were waiting with anticipation for her answer.

Would one dinner really cause any harm? Alex tried to justify her desire to accept his invitation. Surely, he'd have no expectations after only one dinner; and this would be the perfect opportunity for her to start facing the fear that had paralysed her whole life to date. One dinner, she negotiated with herself. Then, she would not see him again. After all, Mark was a good looking guy and he would have no trouble finding other women. Her rejection would not hurt his feelings.

She became aware he was still waiting for an answer. "Okay," she said finally, "one dinner."

He looked at her quizzically, wondering what she meant by "one dinner". Surely, if they hit it off, there would be others. Just take it one step at a time, he thought. "Great. How about this Wednesday?

I'm off work. Say I pick you up at seven?"

"Fine," Alex committed herself.

"I'm looking forward to it." He threw her an irresistible smile.

Alex felt uneasy once more. "I have to go and do some shopping now."

"See you Wednesday." He smiled and went on his way.

* * *

They went to a Japanese restaurant in town where they were seated in a small private room with sliding screen doors and the floor covered in tatami mats. Alex sat on a floor cushion with her legs folded under a black lacquered dining table and with the folds of the dress Matthew had given her spread around her.

"I hope this is comfortable for you," Mark said. Alex reassured him it was. "I know I should've asked if you enjoyed Japanese food, but I took a chance." He sounded a little unsure.

Alex was not a big fan of Japanese cuisine, but she did enjoy certain dishes. "As long as it's not raw and it doesn't move, I'll try anything," she replied, reassuring him.

A waitress dressed in a brightly coloured kimono entered the room, placed a small bottle of sake wine next to each of them, and poured some of the liquid into small china cups. "You wish to order?" she asked Mark in a softly accented voice.

"Give us five minutes, please."

The waitress bowed her head and left them quietly, sliding the screen door shut behind her.

"They move so gracefully, don't they? The women, I mean," Alex observed.

"It's part of their culture. They're not as demonstrative as Westerners, and it shows in the way they carry themselves." Mark picked up his cup. "Here's to your delightful company."

Alex smiled a little uneasily at the compliment and took a sip of her wine. She loved the warm feel of the liquid as it slid down her throat.

The rest of the evening passed well with lively conversation and Mark's entertaining company. He made her laugh with stories about his work and life, and once again time flew for Alex just as it had the time when she had lunch with him. Before she knew it, she was finishing off her meal with green tea, and she felt light-headed and relaxed, which she put down to the sake wine.

"I have to apologise," Mark uttered. "I spent the whole evening boring you with stories about me and didn't give you a chance to say very much."

Alex was secretly relieved. "It's not a problem, really. I enjoyed hearing about the hotel business and what goes on behind all the glamour."

"Yes, but I don't know much about you," he countered.

"What's to know? You already heard some of my travel tales, and I have twenty years of the same stories behind me. There's nothing more to say."

Mark's look was enigmatic. "You haven't told me about Alex, the person; just Alex, the writer."

Alex coloured under his searching gaze. "Well, like I said, there's not much to tell. I've been travelling from an early age."

"But what about your family; do you have brothers and sisters? Where do you come from?" he persisted.

Mark had told her all about growing up in the beach suburbs of northern Sydney. His father was a lawyer; his mother made pottery and was a well-known, local artist. He had two brothers, both married and living in different parts of Australia. Mark was the baby of the family and had never been married, though he had been in a long-term relationship, which had come to an end the year before.

Alex listened to all this information, never once divulging anything about herself. She'd looked interested and encouraged him to talk about his life so she could keep him from asking about hers. Now, he was asking questions she would rather avoid, but she realised it would be rude to do so. Therefore, she told him as much as she could without compromising her privacy.

"I was an only child and my father died when I was very young. Born and raised in Wollongong, by age fifteen I got itchy feet and decided I wanted to see more of the world. So I took off and went to the outback. This is how I became a writer; I had plenty of stories to tell."

Mark did not look very satisfied. Luckily, he had the good sense not to push it further. Instead, he changed the subject altogether. "Did you enjoy your meal?"

"I did, thank you very much. The tempura was wonderful, and at least it didn't move." She grinned.

"More tea?"

"No, thanks. I think I drank enough liquid for one night, especially the sake. Any more, and I'll drown." She had meant to be funny, but he did not laugh.

He looked into her eyes for a moment as if he wanted to say something of importance but decided against it at the last minute. "In that case, I think we're ready to go."

"Yes," she replied, feeling somewhat let down.

It was close to midnight by the time Mark's car pulled up outside her place. The house was in darkness except for the porch light. Mark shut off the engine and turned to Alex. "Well, madam, you are safely delivered home."

He tried to sound lighthearted, but somehow it did not come out that way. To Alex, it sounded like he was disappointed, and she wondered whether he regretted having come out with her. She supposed it didn't matter so much as this was the one and only dinner she had promised herself.

"Thank you for dinner," she said. "I really enjoyed it." She went to open the car door, but his hand reached out and took hold of her arm.

"Wait, Alex, don't go in yet." His voice was soft, almost a whisper.

She turned to look at him and found his eyes pleading with hers. Her heart started to beat faster and her mouth went dry. His hand was still on her arm and he was only inches away from her, making her more aware of his male scent.

"It's late—" she started to say, but was cut short when his mouth swooped down on hers and she was suddenly in his arms.

His kiss was deep and hungry, and a shiver of excitement spread through Alex as his hands started to explore her body. His tongue invaded her mouth to entangle with hers in a delightful play that brought a rush of heat to her face.

Alex willed her body to relax and enjoy the erotic kiss; somewhere in the depths of her mind she reminded herself it was the sake wine that was giving her courage. The kiss grew deeper, more intimate, more forceful, and she met this force with her own. Her body responded to his touch, like a well-tuned violin at the hands of its master. Somehow, the fear she had kept locked inside her all these years did not rise up to spoil the moment. This gave her more confidence, and all she could think about was Mark and his hard body pressing against hers, his hands roaming and sending ripples of spine-tingling desire through her.

One of his hands travelled up inside her skirt and pulled down her pantyhose, finding its way to her panties. Alex moaned and pressed closer to him. Mark's mouth was on her neck, leaving a hot trail of kisses leading all the way to one of her breasts. He slid aside part of her bra and a pink tipped nipple was exposed, only to be devoured by his mouth. Alex moaned again and felt like she was going to explode from so many wonderful sensations.

It was only when his fingers broke past the barrier of her panties and found their way to her most intimate place that her mind suddenly cleared. The cloud of absolute bliss, which had been enveloping her, disappeared; and Alex was dropped back down to the ground with a loud thump. Her body stiffened, but Mark failed to perceive the change.

A stifling darkness descended upon her and in an instant she was transported back to her childhood bedroom—pinned down to the floor by her stepfather's knees while his hands pried open her legs. She screamed, "Nooooooo!"

The scream must have been real because when she opened her eyes, she saw a surprised Mark, his own eyes still glazed with passion.

"Did I hurt you?" he asked softly.

The reality of the moment came rushing back and galvanised her into action. She pushed him away, and her hand gripped the handle of the car door. "I can't do this. I'm sorry." She opened the door and got out.

Alex ran toward the house, her key miraculously in hand, and she did not look back when she heard Mark calling after her. She tried to insert the key into the lock with shaking fingers but dropped it on the floor instead. A sob laced with fear caught at her throat.

"Alex, wait!" Mark called after her.

She ignored him and retrieved the key to try again. At that moment, the front door opened and she came face to face with a sleepy-looking Matthew.

"What the—" he started to say, and then he noticed the state of her clothes and her tear-streaked face.

Alex threw herself into his arms and started to sob like a child.

Matthew automatically held her in a protective embrace while he observed Mark starting up the engine and talking to himself. Probably swearing, Matthew thought. Mark then leaned across to shut the passenger door, which Alex had left open, and with what looked like another oath on his lips, he drove off into the night.

CHAPTER 16

Alex was gardening while Steve sat in the courtyard enjoying the morning sun. He still looked pale, she noticed, and very frail. Since his return from hospital a few days earlier, he had slept most of the time and done little else. Matthew spent most of his time with him when he was not going to classes or filming the soapie episodes he had landed. During his absence, Alex spent time with Steve, either reading to him or just chatting while looking after his garden.

"You know you're a life saver," Steve said to her. "If I had to rely on Matthew to look after my roses, they'd be fit to be pressed in a book by now."

Alex smiled in amusement and replied, "He's busy these days. Besides, the work's good for him."

"I know, but even so, he doesn't have the magic green thumb." They grinned at each other in acknowledgment of this statement. "In any case," Steve went on, "I agree with you. It's good for him to be away from me at times."

"Why do you say that?" Alex spoke over some branches she had pruned from a rosebush.

"I think he's too dependent on me." Steve paused for a moment before continuing, "This worries me."

"You mean because one day he'll be alone?" Alex read his mind.

"I fear for him. How is he going to cope?"

"One day we're all going to be alone, Steve. Even couples who've been together for a lifetime are separated when one of them dies."

"I know this. It's just that Matthew's so young in many ways. He went from his family home to the friend who looked after him, and then to me. So even though he's been through some rough times, he's also been sheltered."

"We all have to grow up some day," Alex uttered wistfully, and added, "some of us sooner than others."

"I know." Steve smiled with understanding. "Don't mind me; I must sound like a mother hen."

"You've every right to be concerned, but I think Matthew has a hidden strength that will come to the surface when he needs it."

"I hope you're right, my dear." He sighed tiredly. "I think I'll go up for a nap now."

"Want me to wake you for lunch? I'm making quiche Lorraine."

"Then, how could I resist?" He smiled at her fondly.

Alex watched him go into the house, his steps slow and shuffling. It was like he had aged twenty years during his stay in hospital, but not once had he complained about how he felt. She wondered whether he knew death might not be too far away. The thought gave her the shivers; she shook her head and returned to the pruning.

* * *

After lunch, Steve went to lie down again, and Alex decided to read in her room. The afternoon had turned cold and windy, robbing the sun of its power to spread warmth. Matthew would be home late and he had told her not to expect him for dinner.

Alex was grateful he had been so busy lately. Since the fateful night of her disastrous date with Mark, he hadn't had a chance to ask her what had happened. When she flew into his arms, she had been too busy crying for him to get anything intelligible out of her, so he had no choice but to comfort her at the time. Then, the next morning, he had gone to his shoot early, and for the last few days he had been either filming or at classes, the rest of the time he had spent with Steve.

This suited her well because she felt stupid about the way she'd reacted to Mark's advances. She admitted none of it would've happened in the first place if she had stopped it earlier. However, a part of her had wanted to see how far she could go without chickening out. Her body had enjoyed Mark's touch, a fact she acknowledged with self-contempt.

In any case, she was certainly not going to allow a repetition of the episode with him in future. She'd tried and failed, and no matter what Steve said about confronting one's fears, she was not going to place herself in that kind of situation again. She had encouraged Mark by responding to him and then, like a slap in the face, she'd turned cold and run off in a panic. What must he think of her? She knew she had angered him because Matthew later told her about him driving off in a huff.

Despite this, Mark did telephone the following day, but Alex let the answering machine pick up the call while she stood by, listening to his deep and attractive voice, as he left her a message. "Alex, it's Mark. We need to talk. Call me at home tonight. Bye for now." Alex had not returned his call.

Two days later, he called again, and Matthew, who was on his way to acting class, answered the call. When he went to inform Alex, who was out in the garden at the time, she simply told him to take a message. He had looked as though he wanted to say something, but instead went back inside the house and did as he was bid while Alex hoped Mark got the hint that she didn't want to have further contact.

* * *

Alex was doing the dishes when Matthew arrived from his shoot that evening. It was after nine. "Hi, I'm back."

"Long day for you. Did you eat?"

"You sound like a concerned mother," he remarked cheerfully. "We had plenty of food, thanks. But if you're making coffee ...." He let the suggestion hang in the air.

"It looks like I am now." She made a face at him.

"How's Steve?" He peeled off his leather jacket and threw it on the nearest chair.

"He slept a lot today but kept me company in the garden for a while this morning. We watched a movie after an early dinner, and he went to bed about half an hour ago." Alex noticed Matthew was wearing a summery denim shirt. "Isn't that a bit light for this time of year? It's quite cold outside."

He grinned. "Alex, what's the matter with you? You really *are* acting like a concerned mother."

"I'm sorry." She didn't know what had come over her so she put it down to her concern for Steve's health.

"Hey!" Matthew took in her pensive expression. "I didn't mean to upset you. I'm just teasing."

"I know. I guess it was an automatic response because I'm so used to bossing Steve around," she tried to make light of it.

"You mean you boss *both* of us around," he teased again, and then was serious. "But what about yourself? You look tense. Maybe, *you* should take it easy."

She turned to the counter when the water boiled and prepared the coffee. This way, she could avoid his eyes. "I'm fine. Don't forget I'm taking a break from writing, so how could I feel anything but relaxed?"

"There are other things that could be stressing you," he pointed out.

She joined him at the table with the coffee but said nothing.

"Thanks," he uttered, taking his cup. "This smells good; not like the slop we get out of catering at the shoot."

She managed a fleeting smile. "That's the price you pay for being a star."

"Yeah, right."

"So how was the shoot, anyway?" Anything to steer him away from a subject she knew he was trying to broach.

"Last day today, so the director made us go through the scene heaps of times to make sure he had enough footage to work with. I think I must've repeated my two lines a hundred times." He took a sip of coffee and sat back in his chair, gazing toward her thoughtfully.

Alex stared into her cup as if the meaning of life was written at the bottom of it. Matthew had seen this look before, but this time he was not going to be put off.

"So what's this thing with Mark?"

There it was! She could not escape from it now. "Nothing."

"Nothing!" Matthew spluttered. "Alex, you don't come out of some guy's car looking like the very devil attacked you and call it nothing."

"You're exaggerating." She wished he would drop the subject.

"Right," he stated sarcastically. "So throwing yourself at me was just a *glad to see you, Matthew,* greeting."

Alex's eyes flashed in anger. "God, Matthew! If I knew you were going to carry on like this, I would've walked straight past you with my nose up in the air."

"That's not the point!" He was exasperated. "What I'm saying is you were really upset about something, and I was concerned to see you like that. Then, there was Mark, swearing like a sailor."

"I have no control over his behaviour."

He sighed resignedly. "You're really trying to avoid the issue, aren't you?"

"Yes." She was blunt.

"So you're not going to tell me what happened?" He felt irritated with her all of a sudden.

"Why do you need to know everything about me anyway? It's none of your business!" she attacked in a sudden spurt of temper.

Matthew was stunned for a second but managed to find his voice. "I'm sorry you feel this way. And next time you get into trouble, don't bother running to me because I won't be there."

He pushed away his cup and stood up, the chair making a loud scraping noise against the floor. He was at the door in two strides, then stopped and turned back to look at her. "You know what I think?" he commented but did not give her a chance to answer. "You're like an ostrich that hides its head in the sand. You won't face up to your problems, but you draw other people into them. Then, when they want to help you, you suddenly decide it's none of their business."

He was hurt by her attitude, but Alex did not realise this. As he made to walk out, she was upon him in a flash, clutching at his shirtsleeve. "How dare you sit in judgement of me? Who are you to tell me what I am and what I'm not? Look at your own faults before you go around pointing out the faults of others."

It was now Matthew's turn to lose his temper. "Oh, so we're back to that, are we? And I suppose you're going to start bombarding me with your little lecture about confronting the pain from my parents' rejection."

"You brought it up!" she exclaimed, a shade too triumphantly.

"Sure, because I know that's exactly what's going to come out of your mouth."

They glared at each other, neither willing to back down. The momentary silence in the kitchen was broken only by the ticking of the clock on the wall. Then, an unexpected thing happened—they both laughed at the same time. They laughed, and could not stop laughing. Soon, the tension in the air dissolved. Matthew spoke first. "Look at us; this is just like being in one of the soapies I'm filming."

Alex made her way back to the kitchen counter. "I think we need another coffee, don't you?"

He nodded in acknowledgment, and she took out two clean cups from the cupboard. "It seems between us we could write a soapie all of our own," Matthew observed.

"That may be an idea," she replied, no longer feeling threatened by the earlier scene. She poured the coffee and joined him at the table once more. "It's like another take, isn't it?"

"What is?"

"This. The coffee scene. A bit of chitchat followed by a temper eruption. Now, this is 'take two', except they rewrote our lines."

Matthew saw the humour in her comment. "And this time, there won't be any eruptions, right?" he remarked, feigning concern.

She smiled in response, knowing she could not stay mad at him for long.

"So you want to tell me about it?" he asked suddenly.

"You don't give up, do you?" she uttered, but this time she was not upset.

"It's a rewrite, remember?"

She sighed with resignation. "There's not much to tell, really. He kissed me and things got ..." She coloured and looked into her cup.

"Things got hot," Matthew finished for her.

"Yes." She was grateful for his help. "And the old fear came back, and I ..."

Matthew saw she was really perturbed, so he said gently, "I understand. You don't have to explain the rest. But why was he so upset?"

"I don't know. I suppose he thought me a tease." Alex felt distressed by the thought.

"Well, I can't answer for his way of thinking, but surely he wouldn't feel like that on a first date," Matthew reasoned.

"I have no idea, and it doesn't matter. The point is I should've stopped it before it went any further, and I didn't. So when I went cold on him, he obviously got a rude shock."

"Don't beat yourself up over it. It wasn't your fault. It wasn't anyone's fault. We're all human and we can't turn our emotions on and off at will."

Alex remained silent.

"Did you return his call yet?"

She shook her head.

"Maybe he wants to apologise."

"Maybe, but I don't want to see him again. It all got out of hand and I don't want to talk to him. I wouldn't know what to say. The thing is, I'm not good at the dating game. I've never had any experience."

She sounded sad when she said this, and Matthew reached out and took her hand in his. "Don't worry about it. There are no hard and fast rules; we all learn as we go."

They exchanged a warm smile and left it at that. It was time to change the subject.

"What about you? When are you going to see your mother again?" It was now her turn to ask the questions.

Matthew threw her a sheepish look. "I suppose I can't call you an ostrich unless I face my own problems, right?"

"Right."

He gazed at her for a long moment, and Alex could see his thoughts were far away. She waited silently until he spoke.

"Well, you've given me something serious to think about," he said finally.

CHAPTER 17

The discussion with Alex the previous evening prompted Matthew to telephone his mother. Dora's delight was such that she immediately begged her son to join her for lunch. She sounded so happy at having heard from him that Matthew could not refuse.

The weather was sunny and warm, unlike the day before, and Dora led Matthew out on the terrace upon arrival.

"It's so beautiful today I asked Conchita to set up lunch out here. I hope that's okay." Dora was at her most charming.

"Sure," Matthew responded, noticing for the first time the fine lines of stress in her otherwise flawless face. He felt some guilt at this and silently acknowledged his mother meant well even though she was still in denial about his relationship.

Conchita appeared with their drinks; a light beer for Matthew, a scotch and soda for Dora.

"Thank you, Conchita. Please give us a few minutes to talk before you bring out the salads," Dora said to the housekeeper.

Conchita nodded and sent a happy smile to Matthew on her way out. She was obviously glad her Mr Matthew had returned for a visit.

"Cheers." Matthew raised his glass to Dora, and she responded likewise.

"I'm so happy you called, darling. It's been so long." She regarded her son with proprietary pride in her eyes. She still couldn't get over how good looking he was.

"Yes, it has been a long time." Matthew saw his mother's eyes full of love for him and he began to hope that perhaps all she really needed was time to get used to his way of life. She had certainly greeted him effusively enough when he'd arrived, and she had not mentioned his last visit, which had ended so abruptly.

"Too long," Dora remarked and took a sip of her drink. "So tell me about your work. How's everything going?"

Matthew told her about the soapie episodes he had just finished filming, and she looked as excited as a little child. Even her face looked beautiful again, the stress lines disappearing momentarily.

"That's so wonderful, darling." She beamed with happiness, and Matthew thought she was going to clap her hands. "What's your next project?"

He smiled at her eagerness. "I'm not Harrison Ford yet, you know."

"But you could be—if only your agent would push a little harder."

"Brent's okay," Matthew defended his agent. "He's been at me to make the move to LA."

Dora's eyes were suddenly guarded, her voice careful when she asked, "And what do you think about it?"

"Well, I'm not really in a position at present, you know. Steve's been ill again."

"Oh, poor Steve! How is he?" Her concern seemed genuine, and Matthew gazed searchingly at her to see if she was for real. Did she truly care about Steve? Was she finally coming around? Before he could reply, however, Conchita appeared and asked if she could serve lunch. Dora readily agreed. The housekeeper brought out chicken and avocado salad and crispy French bread.

"Your favourite, Mr Matthew," she said when she placed a plate in front of him. "I made it myself."

"Then, I'm sure it'll taste like ambrosia." Matthew grinned.

Conchita's little brown face crinkled with pleasure. "Thank you, Mr Matthew."

Dora waited until the housekeeper was gone before she spoke again. "Honestly, Matthew, do you have to wrap her around your little finger all the time? She's constantly asking after you and won't give me a moment's peace."

"Conchita's a darling. Fancy her remembering I used to love chicken and avocado salad. Poor thing. I didn't have the heart to tell her these days I mainly eat curries and pizza."

"Still, you do keep in very good shape." She appraised his body.

"I work out at the gym after class and go for runs when I can. I barely drink and I don't smoke. So yes, I try to keep in shape."

Dora frowned for a moment. "I guess you're saying I drink and smoke too much."

154

"No, Mother, I'm not." He took a bite of chicken. "Mm, this is good."

"You don't care, then, that I drink and smoke?" She sounded hurt.

"It's your choice what you do with your body, and you don't need me to tell you how to look after yourself. But if it's any consolation, you look superb," he told her and meant it. With her trim figure dressed in a buttercup yellow pantsuit and her youthful good looks, Dora certainly had the power to turn heads. How much longer would this last, though, if she kept abusing herself? Matthew wondered silently.

"Well, thank you." She felt the sincerity of her son's compliment and fleetingly wished her husband would pay her more attention once in awhile, but she dismissed this immediately. She didn't want thoughts of Russell spoiling her lunch. "You were telling me about Steve." She went back to their earlier topic.

While they ate, Matthew told her all about Steve's latest illness and shared his fears with her. This felt strange to him because up until now, he had only been able to talk about Steve's condition with Alex. Alex had become his close friend and seemed to be the only person who understood him aside from Steve. Dare he hope now that his mother was truly accepting his situation?

Dora listened attentively as her son spoke, responding with all the right words in the right places. She realised by acknowledging Steve, she would be able to gain her son's trust, which might bring Matthew closer to her. Why hadn't she thought of this before?

They finished their lunch with freshly brewed coffee and an assortment of fruit and cheese. By this time, Matthew was relaxed in Dora's company. A surge of love for her welled up inside him and he convinced himself he had misjudged her in the past, and now they had turned over a new leaf. They could be mother and son again. His father's rejection could not hurt him anymore, not when he had Dora on his side.

"I feel very bad for Steve," Dora stated. "I can imagine how difficult it's been for you, my dear—both emotionally and financially."

"It was at first," Matthew admitted, "but things improved once Alex moved in. Her rental payments help with the mortgage, and she's been wonderful. She's taken over the house and even looks after Steve when I'm not there."

The fondness in his voice as he spoke about Alex piqued Dora's curiosity. "So what does Alex do for a living?"

"She's a travel writer. She freelances."

"That's an interesting career for a girl. I suppose she's going to move on soon?" Dora remarked casually.

"I don't think so. She promised she would stay for as long as I need her."

Matthew's admission took Dora by surprise. "Really?" Her brain went into overdrive. "But why would she do that? After all, it's not like she's involved with you." There was a faint note of hope in her voice. If there was a chance of Matthew becoming interested in a woman, she would even accept Medusa as his girlfriend. But her son's next words crushed all her hopes.

"No, no. It's nothing like that. Alex is just a good friend. She's been through a lot of emotional pain. Besides, she's not interested in men."

"You mean she's a lesbian?" Dora tried to keep the disgust out of her voice and must have succeeded because her son simply smiled.

"No, Mother. She just had a lot of man trouble, that's all. Anyway, as I was saying, now that Alex is with us, things are more bearable."

"And what will you do about LA?" Dora asked testily.

"Nothing. Not at this point, anyway."

"But why, darling?" Dora saw her dream slipping further and further away.

"I won't leave Steve."

Steve! Always, Steve! Dora felt like screaming at her son not to waste his time on a dying homosexual, but she knew if she wanted to get through to him, she must tread carefully. "You know I love you, Matthew, no matter what life you choose to live."

Matthew was about to tell her he loved her, too; but something told him to wait for her to continue.

"I want to help you with your career, darling. Nothing would give me more pleasure than to see your dreams come true." Dora paused, as if gathering her thoughts. "Perhaps, you should think about LA," she said, quickly adding, "not permanently, of course, but only for a while." She waited for a reaction and went on when there was none. "I have some money set aside for you, my dear, and you could give it a try."

Matthew remained silent. He felt himself going cold all over but maintained an outward calm. He did not want to be so quick to misjudge again.

Encouraged by his silence, Dora spoke again. "Your father and I are getting a divorce." She quietly noted his lack of surprise at this. "I suppose you saw it coming, but that's not what I'm trying to say."

Matthew grew impatient. "What is it, Mother?"

"Russell will let me keep the house and he's giving me a good settlement. So I've been thinking it's a chance to take time out for myself and go travelling. I thought I might rent a house in LA for a while. I have friends there." She stopped and noticed there was some liquid left in her fifth glass of scotch and soda. She swallowed it down in one gulp.

Meanwhile, Matthew kept a tight control over his spiralling emotions. He waited for Dora to finish what she had to say, but he knew what was coming and was already berating himself for the fool he had been.

Dora, totally unaware of her son's conflicting thoughts, kept on. "So you see, with a house in LA, you could come and stay with me for a while. You could try and realise some of those ambitions." She stopped and looked at him expectantly.

"And what about Steve?" Matthew's voice was very quiet, almost a whisper.

"Well, you said this friend of yours, what's her name ... Alex? She took over the household, right? So she could look after Steve while you're in LA."

Matthew closed his eyes lest his mother see the deep hurt in them. She had been manipulating him all along, and he, like a gullible idiot, thought she had accepted Steve. He wanted to explode right here and now, but he was not going to give her the satisfaction of another big argument where she got to play the victim.

He opened his eyes and regarded her, and all of a sudden she didn't look so beautiful anymore. She was a drunk and a desperate middle-aged woman who had replaced the mother he'd once known. "Thanks for lunch, Mother. It's been very enlightening." His voice was icy as he stood up.

"Wait, Matthew!" Dora followed him when he made his way into the house and across the loungeroom. "I know what you're thinking, and it's not like that. I do feel for Steve, really I do. But you need to work on your career, darling."

Matthew paused at the door leading to the hallway. "How do you know what I need?" He could not help the look of disgust he gave her. "I think from now on you should stick to what's really important."

"What's that?" Dora asked, a feeling of hope still within her.

"What *you* need. Isn't this what you've been doing all along anyway?" Matthew opened the door and walked out. This time, he knew it was forever.

Dora did not follow after him. She knew she had lost him, and the thought terrified her—first Russell and now her son. She was truly alone.

His thoughts in turmoil, Matthew walked out of the house and was surprised when he bumped into someone who was about to walk in. He looked straight into the face of Russell Davis. The two men regarded each other for a few seconds, and then Russell broke the silence.

"What are you doing here?" he said curtly.

Matthew felt nothing for the man he had once called Father. As far as he was concerned, he had no parents. "I have no idea," he answered in a cold voice, stepping around Russell to make his way to the street.

A pair of puzzled eyes followed him.

* * *

Russell had not seen his son in years. He had always made sure he was out of the house on the occasions he came to visit. So now he wondered if today had been a surprise visit since Dora had not mentioned anything earlier. But then he remembered; it had been this morning he announced that he was moving in with Joanna. He was sure this had made his wife forget everything else.

He walked into the loungeroom and saw Dora through the window, sitting out on the terrace, a drink in one hand, a cigarette in the other. He sighed with resignation; she was probably drunk again. Before he could walk back out, however, Dora turned and saw him. He had no alternative but to join her.

"I just saw your son leaving the house," he said by way of

greeting.

Dora was staring out at the harbour with unseeing eyes, and he wondered how many drinks she had been through.

"He's your son, too," she replied, her voice surprisingly firm.

"Biologically, yes, I'm afraid. Other than that, he's forgotten," Russell uttered rather harshly. The pain of Matthew's homosexuality still had the power to hurt him, and he would never forgive his son—even if it meant never seeing him again.

Dora sniffed contemptuously. "How convenient for you, Russell; first you forget you have a son, and now you forget you have a wife."

"Let's not start this again." He regarded her with distaste in his eyes. "Remember, you were the one who wanted the divorce. I was happy to stay in the marriage."

Dora laughed bitterly. "That's a new one!" She gulped down the rest of her drink and poured another scotch from the bottle, which was resting on the table near her. "Stay in the marriage," she repeated sarcastically. "What marriage? Since you took up with that trollop, you haven't been here long enough to take a piss in your own toilet."

Russell held his temper in check. He was not in the mood for a fight. "You made the decision, and now you're getting the divorce and a fair settlement to go with it. So don't throw a guilt trip my way. It isn't going to work."

"And what about your son?" Dora clung to the last thing that connected the two of them.

"My son, as you put it, made his choice long ago, and I want nothing to do with him. As far as I'm concerned, he doesn't exist."

"You're a real bastard!" She was close to tears. "How can you treat Matthew in this way?"

"I am what I am, Dora. So don't try to make me become the accepting father. At least, Matthew knew from the beginning that I didn't approve of his lifestyle. I wasn't the one dangling my riches in his face to try and entice him to come back and play the straight son."

"Are you saying I don't love him?" Dora was angry and wished her head did not spin so much from the effects of the alcohol she had consumed.

"All I'm saying is, I never pretended with him and he knows this. I didn't try to manipulate him in any way."

"You've said enough. Go back to your little tart and let me be. I may not be the best mother in the world, but I gave my love to Matthew, which is more than you ever gave him."

Despite her drunkenness and anger, she still managed to look like the beautiful woman who had once attracted him, thought Russell. He paused for a moment to admire her regal profile before going back inside the house. He had loved her to distraction once upon a time; she had been his golden princess until she turned into a bitter ageing woman whose love became conditional.

"I came by to pick up the last of my clothes. I'll be out of here in a few minutes," he said with a touch of pity in his voice.

Dora did not reply. She stared out at the harbour, drink in hand, looking into nothingness.

* * *

Alex noticed Matthew was quiet at dinner. Steve had told her he'd gone to visit his mother, and judging from the way he looked now, she concluded the visit had not been a successful one. She supposed everybody's life was touched by one disappointment or other. Some people had big problems to contend with, and some had little ones; but overall, everyone felt their own problems keenly, no matter whether they were big or small.

"There's plenty of curry left," she remarked, looking at Matthew.

"Thanks, I've had enough." He pushed his plate away from him and stood up. "If you don't mind, I have a few phone calls to make."

Alex watched him leave the kitchen and turned to Steve, who was still looking very pale. His plate was almost full. "I don't suppose you want any more either," she stated.

"I can't even finish this," he replied, looking a little distracted.

"I'll make us some tea."

She cleared the table and put the kettle on while Steve sat in his chair, regarding her quietly. "Mark called me today," he announced out of the blue.

"How is he?" She busied herself with the tea things.

"Don't worry. I'm not going to lecture you. He only wanted to know what he did to frighten you so much."

Alex turned to him, astounded. "You mean he told you what happened?"

He smiled. "Not in so many words, but I think I got the idea."

"Well!" she sniffed.

"Don't get huffy, Alex. He's only concerned because you won't return his calls, and he thinks it was his fault."

"Then, you can tell him not to worry. It wasn't anyone's fault. I'm just not ready, and I don't want to go out with him or anyone else for that matter." She brought the tea to the table and sat back down. "It's difficult when I can't tell him the truth about me, but he's just going to have to accept the situation as it is. I should have never gone out with him in the first place."

Steve took a sip of his tea and decided to drop the subject of Mark altogether. He knew deep in his heart Alex would work things out when she was ready. She was a strong person, and he was grateful she had come to his household at a time when she was needed. He remembered his father saying that God worked in mysterious ways, but Steve had never really believed it—at least not until Alex came into his and Matthew's life.

CHAPTER 18

It was past midnight, and Matthew could not sleep. He sat up in bed and switched on the bedside lamp, planning to read until he felt sleepy.

"What's wrong?" Steve's voice spoke out of the semidarkness.

"I'm sorry. I didn't mean to wake you. Are you all right?"

Steve sat up and gazed at Matthew's face. "She upset you again, didn't she?" He was referring to Dora.

Matthew felt tears gathering in his eyes. "I was so angry with her, you know. She wanted me to leave Alex to look after you while I joined her in LA." He paused, fighting back the tears, his voice bitter. "She really had me going for a while though. She was all caring and asking about you, and I really began to think she loved me and was accepting my way of life. But all the time she was looking for a way to get me away from you."

A tear rolled down his face and Steve wiped it off with his finger. "She may have gone about things the wrong way, Matthew, but I'm sure in her own heart she does love you."

Matthew's voice held the inevitable acceptance he had hitherto chosen to ignore. "No, Steve, you're wrong. She loves the idea of a 'straight' Matthew—someone she won't have to be ashamed of."

"I don't think she'd be trying so hard if she didn't feel anything for you," Steve pointed out.

"Do you want to know what I think?" Matthew was still smarting from the emotional pain at the thought of Dora. "She's simply a desperate and lonely woman. She drinks like a fish and is afraid of losing her looks. She already lost my father, and now she's afraid to lose me. That's the only reason she wants me around."

"She certainly sounds like a very frightened woman. It's like she's lost her soul," Steve remarked. He felt genuine pity for the woman he had never met.

"That's her problem!" Matthew uttered, almost savagely. "She chose things to be this way. She could've accepted our way of life and then would have gained a son and a friend."

"Sometimes people are afraid of change," Steve explained. "Look at my parents' reaction when they found out I was gay. They never came to terms with it."

"Exactly! So why should my mother be any different? At least, your parents disowned you outright, but my mother kept pretending she cared all this time just so she could get me to come back to her."

"People have different ways of coping, I guess. My parents couldn't cope at all."

"My mother only pretended she could cope for her own sake. She won't love me unless it's on her own terms." Matthew sighed with sadness.

Steve saw the tears in his eyes threatening to fall again and his heart swelled with protective love toward his sensitive partner.

"I came face to face with my father as well," Matthew continued. "For the first time since he threw me out, the old man spoke to me." His tone was bitter once more.

Steve was surprised. "What did he say?"

"He gave me a look of pure disgust and said, '*What are you doing here?*'" Matthew mimicked his father's voice. "I told him I didn't know and left. Great dialogue to have after so many years, huh?"

The hurt in his eyes was too much for Steve, but he didn't want to touch Matthew in order to comfort him just yet. He felt Matthew needed to get this whole episode out of his system. Steve resisted the urge to reach out to him, gently asking instead, "What would you have said to him had he asked how you were?"

Matthew was pensive for a moment. "I don't really know. I suppose I would've said I was all right."

"Is that the only thing you'd want him to know?" Steve probed.

A moment of silence from Matthew. "No," he stated finally.

"So what would you have told him?"

"I would've told him he's a gutless wonder. That he pushed me away from his life because I'm gay, but at least I had the balls to admit it. Meanwhile, he didn't have the guts to admit it to himself or anybody else." Matthew shook his head with exasperation. "It's ironic, but he's so well suited to my mother. He only loves on his own terms, just as she does." He felt the tears begin to spill unchecked down his face but made no attempt to dry them.

Steve gave him time to come to terms with his turmoil. When Matthew pulled himself together, he continued speaking. "After watching my mother being so manipulative today, I knew I could finally let go and disown both my parents." He sniffed back a few tears. "Up until now, I've been living with the secret hope that at least my mother would accept my lifestyle. What I finally realised was that I don't need her approval or his—not as long as I can accept myself as I am."

Listening to what Matthew said, it suddenly occurred to Steve that Alex had been right all along. Matthew was stronger than Steve had given him credit for.

Steve allowed a few minutes to elapse in silence before he spoke, changing the subject altogether. "I want you to sell the house after I'm gone."

Matthew looked at him in shocked surprise.

Steve went on, "Sell the house, and go to LA. That's where you should be. You need to fulfill your destiny. So promise me you'll do it."

Matthew was speechless. He gazed at Steve, his eyes full of love.

"You're a beautiful person," Steve went on, "and I thank God every single day that you're healthy. If you'd caught this—"

"Maybe it would've been better if I had," Matthew interrupted bitterly. He'd lost his parents and now he was losing Steve. What else was there to live for?

"Don't even say that!" Steve admonished him. "The only reason I can cope with this condition, and be at peace with myself, is because I know you're okay."

"I'm sorry. It's just that I don't know what I'll do without you," Matthew confessed. "I can't lose you!"

Perhaps, Alex had not been altogether correct, Steve decided. Matthew still needed to find his strength. "You'll never lose me," he said in a gentle voice. "I'll always be with you in spirit. Remember the butterflies when I'm gone. Then, you'll know I'm with you." It was the only consolation he could offer.

They looked at each other and Matthew's eyes filled with tears once again. Steve reached out and wiped them away as they fell. Matthew caught his hand and kissed it.

"It's been so long since we made love." His voice was soft. "I'm always afraid to touch you in case I hurt you in some way; and I don't want to hurt you."

Steve gazed deep into his eyes and saw the love written in them. It was the purest kind of love he had ever seen. He brought his face close to Matthew and kissed him tenderly.

Matthew responded in kind, a feeling of bliss permeating his body, and all the emotional pain about his parents was instantly wiped away. He had wanted this for so long, and he now gave himself up to the wonder of Steve's love. It was where he was meant to be.

* * *

Alex was choking. She couldn't breathe. An immobilising panic gripped her entire body and she lay helpless as an oppressive darkness descended upon her. Finally, a scream escaped from her throat and she gave way to it. Then, she was sitting up in bed, her face wet with tears. She breathed a sigh of relief, thankful her nightmare was over. Her mouth felt very dry and she needed a drink of water.

She went downstairs, saw the kitchen light from the hallway and wondered whether one of the boys had forgotten to switch it off. When she entered the room, she saw Matthew sitting at the table. He was wearing nothing except pyjama bottoms and she immediately dragged her eyes away from his muscular torso and made every effort to appear normal.

"Is something the matter?" She went straight to the sink and helped herself to a glass of water.

"No. I just couldn't sleep. What about you?" Matthew sounded tired.

"Bad dream."

"I suppose we've all been through a lot lately, haven't we? I'm not surprised you're having bad dreams."

"These things happen." She didn't want to ponder on her dream. "How's Steve?"

"He's not getting any better." The concern in his tone was evident.

"But he's had this sort of episode before, right?"

"Yes, and he always recovered fully in the past. But now he's so fragile." As he said this, he wondered whether he and Steve should've made love.

Though unaware of his thoughts, Alex noticed the worry in Matthew's face and the smudges under his eyes. "You haven't been sleeping all that well lately, either."

"I guess not. With all the work I've had since Steve's been in hospital, plus other problems I won't bore you with, I've been too busy to sleep. Now, I just can't seem to."

"Can I help in any way?" Alex guessed the "other problems" to which Matthew was referring had something to do with his mother.

"Thanks, but I'll be fine." His words did not succeed in belying how he felt.

"At least you don't have classes anymore," she pointed out.

Matthew's acting classes had ended a few days before, and he had decided to defer for a while so he could spend more time with Steve.

"What about you; weren't you taking time off from writing or something?" Matthew steered the conversation away from himself.

"Yes, till September. Then, I'm going to do a series of pieces on the trendy cafes of Sydney. I already have an editor who's interested."

"Sounds great."

They were silent for a moment, and Alex sensed he wanted to be alone. "Well, I'll go back up and see if I can get some sleep. Maybe, you should try, too."

"I'll go up later. Good night."

She hovered for another second and then left him alone.

* * *

Alex tossed and turned in bed, but sleep did not come. Too many thoughts crowded her mind: the impact of her nightmare, the effect Matthew's physical looks provoked in her, and her unresolved feelings about the episode with Mark. She recognised the hidden passion within her that craved release, but her fear always stood in the way.

What was it Steve had said? Something about doing what came naturally when the time was right. But how? She had run away from Mark. She had always run from life, and no matter where she went in future, she knew she would keep on running. She found no comfort in this realisation. She had once heard that some books were better left unopened. Mark was like one of those books and as far as she was concerned, he would remain unopened and unread.

When the first streaks of dawn filtered into the room, she got out of bed and had a shower. The water streaming down her body felt like it was washing away the ghosts from the night.

Downstairs, Matthew was still where she had left him, three empty coffee mugs in front of him. His head was resting on his arms while he slept at the kitchen table. Alex's first impulse was to keep him warm as the chill in the room had not yet dispersed with the first rays of the sun. She went to the linen cupboard and returned with a throw. The minute she placed it over his naked shoulders, his eyes opened and he gave her a sleepy smile.

"I guess I never made it upstairs."

"It's not even six yet. Why don't you stretch out on the sofa and sleep some more? I'll wake you when breakfast is ready."

He agreed without argument, and she saw him settled on the sofa where not so long ago she had lain with him, cradled in his arms. His eyes closed as soon as his head was down.

* * *

By nine o'clock the sun was pouring into the kitchen, enveloping the whole room in its warmth. Alex went out to the courtyard and was surprised by the unmistakable scent of early spring in the air. She took a deep breath and turned her face toward the sun with her eyes closed and a smile on her lips. Suddenly, she felt a presence behind her and immediately knew it was Matthew.

"It's going to be a magic day today," he said, stretching his arms. He had not yet changed, and his upper body looked golden in the morning light. "Why don't we have breakfast out here?"

"Good idea. Go shower, and breakfast will be waiting by the time you get back," she replied without turning around.

Two strong arms grabbed her from behind and she felt her body being slammed against a hard chest. She stiffened instinctively, but Matthew did not notice. "Are you saying I smell?" he remarked jokingly.

"No, that's not it. Let go, Matthew!" How could she tell him his touch sent a thrill of excitement coursing through her body?

"Oh, come on. You were the one who told me to keep warm."

"Then go back inside!" She tried to break his hold, but he was too strong for her.

"But this is more fun," he insisted, "and besides, you should count yourself lucky. You're being held by someone who some day may be a future star." He tickled her ribs, and she squirmed.

"Stop it! What's come over you?" She tried to sound firm but was laughing instead.

They were both laughing, and enjoying the physical play, and for once, Alex realised she was having fun.

Matthew had been aware for some time of the effect he had on Alex, and knowing about her background, it touched him deeply. From the beginning of their friendship, she had turned to him for physical comfort, and it had seemed the most natural thing for her to do.

Once he realised she was starved for the need of physical contact with another human being, he had been happy to provide it. He remembered how trusting she had been all those times she sought refuge in his arms, and he'd come to care for her. She had become a good friend to him and Steve and an anchor to his emotions when he worried about his partner. In truth, aside from Steve, he never thought he would find a real friend. Now, he was glad Alex was a part of their family.

Another squeal from Alex brought him out of his reverie. "Matthew, let go! We'll never have breakfast if you keep this up."

"That's right. And I hear we're eating out of doors." Steve was standing near them, and by the looks of it, he'd been watching silently for a while.

Matthew stopped tickling Alex but did not let her go. Alex could feel her face burning red.

"How are you?" Matthew asked his partner.

"More rested," he replied and then glanced toward Alex. "I think you can let our friend go now. She seems uncomfortable and in need of oxygen. Her face is positively red."

Matthew turned Alex around within the circle of his arms and examined her closely. "You're right. I must've been choking the life out of her without realising it."

Alex was still squirming to get away, her mortification unbearable. "Steve, please don't think anything strange is happening here. It's just that ..." she started to explain and stopped when she saw the strained look on his face. He was doing everything in his power not to burst out laughing.

"Oh, you two! You really had me going!" She slipped away from Matthew's hold and mock-slapped him around the head. "Troublemaker!" She huffed, spinning on her heel.

She walked off toward the kitchen, followed by her housemates' laughter, and smiled secretly. They were not the only ones who had enjoyed the fun.

* * *

Breakfast was destined to become brunch as it was almost eleven by the time Alex started to cook. Matthew was upstairs showering and Steve kept her company in the kitchen.

"Honestly, he's like a big kid!" Alex protested. "I was so shocked when you came out."

Steve was amused. "Don't worry, my dear. I know what he's like. He's always been a kid at heart, and this is why these last few years have been so hard on him. We used to clown around, too, before my illness got worse. Now, he can clown around with you."

"Well, I don't know about that, but you sure put on a good act like you disapproved."

"I was only pulling your leg. You need to laugh more."

Alex reached over and planted a kiss on his cheek.

When Matthew came back down, they ate and chatted companionably.

"If no one has any plans today, why don't we go to the beach?" Matthew suggested.

"It's not that warm, you know—at least not for a swim," Alex observed.

"I meant for a walk. What do you say, Steve, are you up for it?"

Steve did not reply. Matthew and Alex glanced at his face and saw a faraway look in his eyes. They had seen this look before—one morning, not long ago.

Suddenly, Steve spoke, "Right on cue."

The other two followed his gaze, and resting on one of his roses was Steve's favourite butterfly—its wings were bright blue and black.

CHAPTER 19

As things turned out, no one went to the beach that day. Shortly after their meal, fatigue settled quickly over Steve and after taking one look at his pale face, Matthew sent him up to their room to rest. Alex did the dishes and then decided on some gardening.

She was hard at work preparing a patch of soil in readiness for planting when Matthew appeared holding two mugs of coffee.

"Break time," he called out to her.

Alex joined him and they sat at the outdoor table sipping their hot drinks.

"What are you going to plant?" he asked.

"Jasmine." She added with a dreamy look, "There's nothing more fragrant than the aroma of jasmine on a sultry summer evening."

"Spoken like a truly talented writer with a good command of prose."

She laughed at his statement. "How would you know? I bet you didn't even read any of my articles."

"You're right. I'm terrible, aren't I?" he confessed, looking sheepish.

"Not really. There's no reason why you should," she pointed out.

"Only that Steve said they're excellent."

Alex laughed, remembering. "That's right. I practically forced the poor man to read my work while he was stuck in hospital."

At mention of the word hospital, Matthew's eyes clouded over with worry. "You had a sense of déjà vu at breakfast, didn't you?"

"You're referring to Steve's faraway look?"

He nodded. "It freaked me out. It's like he can see something beyond our scope of vision."

Alex had felt this, too, but did not admit to it. The last thing she wanted was to add to Matthew's worries. "Perhaps you're reading too much into it."

Matthew was thoughtful for a moment. "Maybe." He did not look convinced and finished his coffee in silence. When he spoke again, the fear in his voice was unmistakable. "I have a really bad feeling about this, Alex."

Alex gazed into his clear blue eyes and saw such despair in them she was reminded of her own haunted look after one of her nightmares. She reached across the table and took hold of his hand. It was the only comfort she could give him. Matthew held on to her fingers tightly as if they were a lifeline.

"I think the time's come and I'm not ready." He sounded surprised at his own admission. "It's like it's not really happening, but it is."

Alex could relate to his sense of the surreal. It was a mixture of denial and shock at something that was too awful to acknowledge, and yet it was happening. She felt helpless by not being able to make things better for him.

"I really don't think anyone is ever ready for something like this," she uttered softly. "It's the type of human experience we're always unprepared for."

There was understanding in Matthew's eyes. He breathed a sigh of relief, realising how crucial it was to have someone like Alex in his life at a time like this. "You're the only one I can talk to. I can't burden Steve with my fears; he already has so much to cope with."

"I know," Alex sighed, suddenly feeling weary. "Whatever happens, I want you to remember I'm here for you."

Matthew nodded; the look of worry still in his eyes.

* * *

It was when Matthew went to wake Steve for lunch that his worst fears were confirmed. Upon entering the bedroom, he found him throwing up on the floor, his vomit flecked with blood.

"I couldn't get to the bathroom in time," Steve managed to say before he collapsed, unconscious.

Matthew yelled for Alex and was on the phone calling for an ambulance when she appeared at the door. Between them, they lifted Steve back onto the bed and while Matthew cleaned his face with a wet towel, Alex packed a few essentials in an overnight bag. Neither of them spoke.

Steve looked deathly pale and Alex saw the tight control Matthew kept over his emotions while he readied his partner for the ordeal to come.

It wasn't long before the ambulance arrived and Alex went downstairs to open the door. Within moments, Steve was carried downstairs on a stretcher by two paramedics and placed into the back of the ambulance where his vital signs were monitored. Matthew went to climb in to be with Steve, but one of the paramedics stopped him.

"It's better if you go directly to the hospital and wait until you see his doctor," he said, putting his hand on Matthew's shoulder. "He's going straight to intensive care. Try not to worry; we'll look after him." He shut the back door and the ambulance drove off, leaving a dazed Matthew standing in the street.

Alex led him back into the house and bade him sit on the sofa. His face was devoid of expression and his eyes wore a glazed look.

"I'm going to make you a cup of tea and then we'll drive to the hospital together, okay?"

Matthew nodded, still dumbfounded.

"They won't have any news for a while, so we have time to get ready," she further reassured him, noticing he had started to shiver. She wrapped a throw around his shoulders. "I'll be right back."

She made the tea and was back by his side within minutes. "Here." She handed him the cup and watched him take it in silence. "Drink it as hot as you can." She sat next to him and put her arm around his shoulders. At least, he had stopped shivering.

Matthew sipped his tea slowly. The action of doing something so mundane invoked a small semblance of normalcy. "Sorry," he uttered. "I think I lost it for a while, but I'm okay now."

"Good." She kissed his cheek. "I'm here, remember?"

"Yes. I'm glad you're here." He still sounded a little detached from what was happening, but Alex thought under the circumstances, this was for the best.

* * *

They drove to the hospital in Matthew's car with Alex at the wheel. Upon arrival, they were told Dr Benning was attending to Steve and there were no further news. A receptionist at information directed them to the waiting room in the intensive care unit.

The room was small, almost claustrophobic, but luckily it was empty except for them. Alex sat next to Matthew on one of the hard plastic chairs and they waited in silence. In the meantime, she looked around her and wondered why it was that hospital walls and floors were mostly grey in colour. It was bad enough having to be in a hospital in the first place, let alone being surrounded by such a dull, lifeless colour. Perhaps, there was a psychological intent—grey representing hopelessness, she mused cynically.

She had never liked hospitals and didn't think too many people would disagree with her on this. There was something about the smell of antiseptic combined with the dull surroundings that made one feel like they were on their way to death. She shivered but managed to dispel her morbid thoughts as she stole a quick peek at her companion.

Matthew sat forward with his head in his hands, and Alex realised she could not possibly know how it was to have a loved one in danger of dying. She had never loved anyone that much, she acknowledged with a sense of sadness. The only love she remembered from the past was a vague memory; the one she had shared with her mother before her stepfather had arrived on the scene. Now, the only love she felt was the love of a close friend for her housemates.

A feeling of anger suddenly shot through her. She was angry at Steve's illness. She was angry because of the pain he must have endured all this time, and above all because of the waste of a young life. And what about Matthew? What was it like to know your partner was dying? She tried to imagine this but only felt emptiness inside. She silently cursed her stepfather, not only for killing her innocence, but also for robbing her of the chance to love as deeply as Matthew and Steve loved each other. She sighed for her lost youth and decided it was best to direct her thoughts to the present situation. The only way she could help Matthew was by being there for him.

It seemed like they had been waiting forever in the little room, but it was only just under an hour before Dr Benning walked in. The look on his face was not promising and Alex grabbed hold of Matthew's hand as they both stood up.

"Please, sit down," Dr Benning told them gently. He pulled up a chair and sat facing them. Alex felt a lump of tension in her throat.

"How is he?" asked Matthew, panic rising in his stomach. He wanted to know, but at the same time he was afraid of knowing.

Dr Benning took a few moments to reply. It was as though he was formulating the answer in his head so he could put it to them as simply and compassionately as possible. "I can't say it's good, Matthew," he said finally, his eyes regarding him kindly. "It looks like the complications he had with his last infection didn't clear up."

"What does that mean?" Matthew exclaimed reluctantly.

"It means the infection is not responding to the usual antibiotics we've been using. You see, Steve's immune system is greatly weakened and his body isn't coping."

Alex saw tears gather in Matthew's eyes, so she spoke for him. "What else can be done?"

Dr Benning took in their worried faces and thought how he hated having to do this. "I'm sorry, but you need to prepare yourselves. The condition's quite serious. Steve has developed septicaemia."

"What?" Matthew was too stressed to take in what the doctor had said, but he instinctively knew this was the end.

"Blood poisoning," Alex explained, thinking he did not know what the condition was.

Matthew's voice was devoid of all hope when he spoke. "How long does he have?" His manner was dead calm.

Alex was amazed at the sudden transformation—from pure fear and anxiety to full control, and finally, acceptance.

"Maybe a few days," replied the doctor. "We moved him to palliative care and still have him on the antibiotics, but he's not responding as we had hoped. I'm so sorry."

"You did all you could. Is he awake?" Matthew sounded detached, even cold.

"Yes, but he can't have visitors just now. We're stabilising him as much as we can, and he needs to get some rest. You'll be able to see him this evening."

"Okay." Matthew responded with a nod.

Through his cold demeanour Alex sensed his emotional exhaustion, but she wasn't sure what she could do to help him.

Dr Benning turned to address her. "Why don't you come back at around six this evening? You'll both be able to visit with him."

"Thank you," she spoke quietly as if to speak any louder would upset the balance of things around them.

"Matthew, is there anything I can get for you—maybe something to help you sleep awhile?" The doctor took in the smudges under Matthew's eyes and the look of pure fatigue on his face.

"No, I'll be fine. We'll be back later."

Dr Benning nodded sympathetically and left them alone. Alex realised Matthew was still holding onto her hand.

* * *

It was early afternoon when the telephone rang, and Alex rushed to answer it. Matthew was asleep on the sofa.

"Hello," she picked it up on the second ring, and her stomach did a somersault when she heard the voice at the other end.

"Alex, hi, it's Mark." As if she hadn't guessed. "I was expecting a call from Steve last night, but I haven't heard from him. I called several times today and the machine picked up, so I thought maybe you'd all been out."

Alex was relieved he made no mention of the fact that she had not returned any of his calls. "Steve's in hospital. That's where we were."

"My God! Is he okay?"

"I'm sorry to say he's not." She kept her voice soft in case Matthew woke up. "He's very ill, and—" She paused for a moment, trying to regain control of her emotions before she gave way to tears.

There was understanding in Mark's voice when he replied, "I think I know what you're trying to say. I'll contact the hospital for more information."

"Yes, please do. Matthew's sleeping so I don't want to wake him. He needs his rest."

"I understand. Is Steve allowed to have visitors?"

"I don't know. The doctor said it would be okay for us to visit this evening, but you'll have to ask the hospital about other visitors."

"I'll do that. Please tell Matthew how sorry I am. When you get to see Steve, tell him I want to visit him if allowed. My thoughts are with him." Mark sounded upset, and Alex suddenly felt bad about the way she had treated him in the past.

"I'll do that," she said softly. "I have to go now."

"Wait! How are you holding up?"

"I'm all right. Thanks for asking." So he was not angry with her after all, Alex thought.

"Alex, I know this isn't the time, but we need to talk soon. Please promise me you'll agree to talk with me."

"Okay." She did not sound too convincing.

"You mean it?"

She sighed with resignation. "Yes, I mean it."

* * *

When they arrived at the hospital in the evening, Alex and Matthew were informed Steve had been moved into a private room. Alex was thankful for this; at least, they would have privacy. The palliative care ward was quiet as they moved through the corridor in search of Steve's room.

Alex felt a chill run through her body. She could sense death all around her. She grabbed hold of Matthew's hand, not only for her own reassurance, but also to lend him support for what was to come. Matthew looked more rested, but his face reflected a deep sorrow that was hurtful to see. His eyes, usually so bright and full of life, looked dull and without expression.

They reached Room 205, where Steve was housed, and paused outside the heavy wooden door. "I'll come in to say hello and then leave you two alone," Alex told Matthew. "What time do you want me to pick you up?"

"I'll call you." He squeezed her hand in gratitude for understanding. "If you don't hear from me by ten, go to bed. I'll catch a taxi."

Alex gazed into his eyes for a moment, wishing she could wipe away the distress and sadness she saw there. "Ready?" He nodded, and they walked into the room.

The sight that met their eyes shocked them, and instead of letting go of each other's hand, their grip grew tighter.

Steve lay in bed with his eyes closed, his face gaunt. He was so pale he seemed almost ghostly. A number of tubes and wires were connected to his slight body, and this made him look like he had shrunk in size. Alex was quick to note the drip and a tube that ran from the bed cover and connected to a plastic bag unobtrusively placed under the bed in a special plastic holder. Steve had been catheterised. A peg with a long wire attached to his left index finger connected him to a machine that monitored his heartbeat and blood pressure; plus there were other tubes and wires for which Alex had no explanation. The whole picture was sobering, and for a few moments the two housemates stood transfixed.

Steve's eyes opened then, and he smiled tiredly. "Hey, don't just stand there," his voice sounded weary. "Come and say hello. I promise not to bite."

Matthew was the first to move. He went straight to the bed and took hold of Steve's right hand. "How are you? Are you in pain?"

"I'm fine, don't worry. Pull up a chair."

Matthew did so and sat as close as he could to the bed.

"Alex." Steve saw her standing where Matthew had left her. "You're allowed to touch me, you know," he reassured her.

Alex went forward and kissed his cheek. "I'm so glad you're back with us," she said gently. "I don't want you to worry about anything. I'm looking after the garden. I'll bring you some roses tomorrow when I come to visit, okay?"

He smiled tiredly. "No problem, my dear." Then, he frowned. "But you both look so worried. I want you to be happy for me. I'm not in pain."

Neither Matthew nor Alex trusted themselves to speak in case they broke down and wept. Finally, Alex managed to talk, but her voice was shaky. "I'm going to leave you with Matthew now so you two can be alone. I'll be back tomorrow." She leaned over Steve again and kissed him on the forehead. "Rest well."

Steve reached out with his left hand and caressed the side of her face, and Alex felt the peg of the heart and blood pressure monitor brush against her skin. It sent shivers down her spine. "I will rest well," he told her. "I know you're looking after Matthew, and I thank you for it."

She smiled at him tremulously and softly touched his face with her fingers. "This is probably not going to come as a surprise," she remarked, trying to lighten the mood, "but he's still so messy that I spend most of my time picking up after him."

"Yes," he responded with a soft laugh, "that's my Matthew

through and through."

Alex kissed his face again. "I'll see you tomorrow."

"Okay, my dear." His eyes closed for a moment's rest.

Alex turned to Matthew and before she could stop herself, she ran her fingers through his hair and smiled at him in encouragement. Then, she left him alone with his partner.

Steve's eyes opened at the sound of the door closing. "She loves you very much," he remarked.

This was the last thing Matthew had expected to hear. His eyes registered surprise. "What do you mean?"

"She's always been afraid to love because of her past, but with you it's different. She may not even realise it, but she loves you."

Matthew was silent. He had no idea what to say to this.

"Don't worry," Steve went on, "I'm not jealous." He smiled, and Matthew smiled back, seeing the humour in the remark.

"Love her back," Steve continued, now serious. "You're her only chance at finding happiness."

Matthew was puzzled. "I'm not sure what you mean."

"You will when the time comes. Just be sure you won't hold back. She's terribly fragile inside and she's going to need you before she finds the courage to get on with her life."

Matthew nodded. "Whatever it is you mean, I promise I'll be there for her if she needs me. It's just like you, Steve, to be thinking of others when you're the one we should all be thinking about right now," he protested.

Steve gave Matthew's hand a squeeze. "I don't think about myself, but I do think about you all the time. You know how much I love you, don't you?" Again, Matthew nodded. "Well, I want you to promise me something."

"What is it?"

"We talked about this before—about selling the house. The mortgage will be paid off when—"

"Why are we talking about this now? I want you to get well and come home!" Matthew's voice sounded like a little boy's, insisting that Santa Claus was real.

"There's nothing I would like better than to come back home, but you have to face reality," Steve's voice was firm. "We both know this is my time, and I need to know you'll do the right thing for yourself."

Tears rolled down Matthew's face, but he didn't bother to wipe them away. "And what's that?"

"That you'll use the money for LA. I want to see your name in lights; and I'll be watching, you know."

Steve's eyes took in his beloved, and he wished he could reach out and cradle him in his arms, but he felt so weak he had to make do with holding his hand instead.

Matthew could not answer. He did not trust himself to speak. He simply wept silently.

CHAPTER 20

For the next three days Matthew practically lived at the hospital and Alex dropped in from time to time, bringing in roses from the garden to decorate Steve's room. Although he was no better, Steve was no worse, either.

Alex noticed the veiled hope in Matthew's eyes that a miracle would occur and Steve would recover. She felt pain deep within her heart for Matthew, for she knew Steve's life was hanging in the balance and his time was drawing nearer the end.

At night, when she lay in bed in the empty house, she thought of Matthew and an inexplicable emptiness filled her soul. She could not explain why she felt this way. Her only certainty was that she did not want to see him suffer while he watched Steve's life ebb. She felt his pain as if it were her own and wished there was something she could do to erase it.

Sometimes, her feelings were so intense she could not sleep. She would pace the house, wondering whether Matthew was getting any sleep in his visitor's chair at the hospital. Then, she felt guilty about being so concerned over him when Steve was the one who was dying. But whenever she thought of Steve, she felt at peace. She knew it was right for him to leave—the time had come.

Steve had had enough suffering in this life and he deserved better. He admitted he was ready to go and wasn't afraid of death. His main concern was about leaving Matthew behind—his beautiful Matthew—the angel with the bright blue eyes and the heart of gold. The angel who haunted Alex's days and nights.

* * *

Spring was in the air when Alex made her way to the hospital on the fourth day of Steve's stay. It was a crisp and clear morning with a soft breeze carrying the fragrance of flowers.

Alex loved this time of year when things were beginning to grow again. In her mind, it was a time for clearing the cobwebs of winter and making way for the renewal of life. She had always felt this way about spring. For her it was a time of new expectations, and on this morning she felt hopeful, even in the face of Steve's illness, that everything would work out as it should.

As she pulled into the hospital car park in Matthew's car, she thought anything was possible on a day like this, but her mood of optimism soon vanished when, alighting from the car, she saw Mark waving to her from a short distance away.

"So we meet again!" he called out cheerfully.

Alex locked the car door and walked up to him, pasting a smile on her face to hide the fact that she wasn't yet ready for this meeting. "Nice to see you, Mark."

His eyes regarded her for a moment. "You're looking good."

Alex was wearing a pair of jeans and a white cotton shirt that accentuated her figure. For some reason, she hadn't felt like wearing her usual baggy clothes, and now she regretted not having done so. "Thank you," she said quietly.

She began to walk toward the entrance to the hospital building with Mark walking beside her. "I just saw Steve, and I was on my way home when I saw you pull up."

Well, don't let me keep you, Alex felt like saying to him. Instead, she remarked, "How did you find him?"

"Not as well as I'd hoped." He looked sombre. "Life can be cruel sometimes."

Alex regarded him with interest. This was the first time she had seen him in a wistful mood. "Yes, it can."

"Matthew's looking pretty much under the weather, too," Mark added.

"He's been sleeping in a chair for three nights now," she told him, feeling a little defensive. "I'm going to try and get him to come home tonight."

Why bite Mark's head off, thought Alex, regretting the tone of voice she had used with him. It wasn't his fault Matthew looked stressed.

Sensing her prickly mood, Mark said, "Look, I won't keep you, but perhaps we can have coffee sometime?"

"Yes, perhaps we will."

He gave her one of his boyish smiles. "I'll call you."

Alex nodded and watched him walk away. She still found him attractive but felt the black wall of fear standing in her way.

* * *

"Matthew, please listen to me," Alex begged. "You have to get some proper rest."

They were standing outside Steve's room, talking quietly so as not to disturb anyone.

"I'm not leaving him alone," Matthew declared. "What if something happens while I'm not here?"

Alex sighed in resignation. She knew she had no argument for this. "Okay. But did you at least have breakfast this morning?"

He smiled at her and for a second his eyes lit up. "God, you fuss, Alex."

"Yes, I do," her voice was firm. "So go and have something to eat while I'm with Steve."

Matthew had not had anything to eat for hours, and his stomach felt hollow from hunger. Of course, he would never admit this to her. "All right then. I'll be back in half an hour."

Alex watched him walk down the hallway, pleased he would at least get something to eat. He looked exhausted and she was worried about his health. She waited until he was no longer in sight before entering Steve's room.

Steve looked frailer than ever, if that was possible, and she did not blame Matthew for wanting to stay with him at all times. He seemed ready to slip away at any moment. His eyes were closed and his breathing had become quite shallow.

Alex felt a sudden prick of fear and just as she was going to go back out in search of Matthew, Steve's eyes opened. "Alex." His voice was a whisper. "Come sit by me, my dear."

She breathed a sigh of relief and went to him, kissing his cheek as she sat down on the visitor's chair next to his bed. "How are you, my friend?"

"I was dreaming about one of our gardening sessions," he said weakly.

She took hold of his hand. "The roses are doing especially well,

Steve," she reassured him.

"I know." He managed a smile. "I selected my gardener with care, didn't I?"

"Yes, you did."

He closed his eyes for a moment and seemed to concentrate on his breathing. The grip of his hand on hers was weak, and Alex's fears returned. She wished now she hadn't told Matthew to go and eat, and pondered whether she should call him on the mobile. He would never forgive her if anything happened while he was absent. Then, Steve's eyes opened again and Alex smiled at him, not wanting him to see the worry on her face.

"Alex. His voice was so soft now, she could barely hear him.

"Yes, I'm here."

"There's something I must say to you." He paused and closed his eyes again for a few moments. Alex waited tensely. His eyes opened once more and looked directly into hers. "Alex," he murmured softly, "it pains me that all this time you've been afraid to love."

His words affected her deeply, going straight to her heart. Alex felt a lump rise to her throat as tears welled in her eyes and for a moment, Steve looked fuzzy. Then, she blinked and he was back in focus.

"Don't be afraid to let yourself love someone," he continued, his breath laboured. "Love's the only thing worth living for. Nothing else in this universe is more important." The effort of speaking seemed to tire him and once again he closed his eyes.

Alex's voice was croaky when she spoke. "Steve, I'll never forget your kindness to me."

Steve smiled weakly and drifted off to sleep. Alex regarded him for a moment to make sure he was still breathing before standing up and walking over to the window. She looked at the bright blue of the sky outside and the shining rays of the sun, and she allowed her tears to fall unchecked at the beauty of it all. Somehow, the simplicity and truth of Steve's words found their way into her soul and she was filled with hope. Hope for a future without fear.

Matthew walked into the room at that moment and saw her crying by the window. His face registered alarm at first and he glanced at Steve; but when he saw he was merely sleeping, he relaxed and walked over to her. Alex didn't move away when he reached out and dried her tears with his finger. He did not ask her what had happened; he simply let her be.

In the silence of the moment she gazed up at him, and as she looked into his eyes she suddenly realised she loved him. She felt a love so deep and complete that the shock of it brought fresh tears to her eyes.

Matthew, unaware of the reason for her tears, gently pulled her into his arms and held her. She closed her eyes, afraid to think any further about her realisation. There would be time for thinking later. Instead, she enjoyed the luxury of his touch and the nearness of his body. She savoured the moment for a few seconds and then gently pulled away.

"I'm okay now," she assured him. "I'll go home and come back this afternoon."

Matthew nodded. He searched her face, making sure she was all right.

She felt herself blush under his scrutiny and looked away. "I'll see you later." She moved away from him and went to Steve. "Bye for now, Steve," she whispered so as not to wake him; she leaned over and gently kissed his face.

* * *

Matthew drifted into an exhausted sleep after Alex's departure, and he slept through until noon when a nurse came in to check on Steve.

Sister Trent was a petite middle-aged woman with bright orange hair and soft brown eyes. "So you're still here, love," she addressed Matthew.

Over the last few days, Matthew and Sister Trent had settled into a mother-son type of relationship. She was forever clucking around and looking out for him. Now, Matthew regarded her with sleepy eyes. "These chairs are a killer on the back."

"Exactly the reason why you should be at home getting proper rest," was the cheerful rejoinder.

"Can't leave him, Sister. Not now."

The nurse took in his tired demeanour, the weariness in his eyes, and the hopelessness in his voice. She spoke gently, "Why don't you step out for a cuppa while I give our patient a sponge bath?"

"A sponge bath?" a soft voice echoed from the bed. "All my fantasies *are* coming true."

Sister Trent turned to Steve with a bright laugh. "And someone around here hasn't stopped flirting with all the nurses since he arrived!" she teased. "I've been warned about you. What a dirty mind you have, *Mr Wicks!*"

"Don't be so coy, Sister," was the comeback. "Call me Steve."

Matthew looked at Steve and noticed the effort it took for him to speak. "Is it okay if I step out for ten minutes?"

"Sure, just leave me to enjoy my sponge bath with this sex-crazed woman."

Sister Trent gave a whooping laugh at this. "See what I mean?" She winked at Matthew. "He's dangerous, he is."

Matthew smiled at Steve and winked back at the nurse. "I'll be back soon."

The moment he left, Steve's laboured breath became more noticeable. "Never mind the bath, Sister," he said. "I won't be needing it."

An understanding look passed between nurse and patient, and Sister Trent took hold of Steve's hand. "Do you want me to go and get him, love?"

"Not yet," Steve whispered. "Let him have a cup of coffee first." With this said, he closed his eyes.

Sister Trent made sure he was comfortable and left the room quietly.

* * *

Alex sat in the quiet of the courtyard, soaking up the midday sun while she reviewed her emotions. How ironic that after all these years of being afraid to allow herself to love somebody she should fall in love with a gay man.

From the first time she'd laid eyes on Matthew, she had been affected by him. At first, it was the predictable reaction to his extreme good looks, but as time went by she came to know the kind and sensitive person he really was—the one who gave of his love just as unselfishly as Steve.

She remembered his many kindnesses to her; his actions of chivalry when trying to shield her from the catty models; the time he offered to drive her to the meeting with her mother, and the way he had comforted her afterwards. Then, there was the dress he gave her as a gift for Steve's party and his non-judgemental and protective attitude when she flew into his arms after the episode with Mark.

All those things and more made Matthew what he was—a kind and beautiful soul. Steve had been so right when he'd said Matthew had a heart of gold. The more analytical side of her, however, told her she had come to love Matthew because she'd never perceived him as a threat. He had never expected anything from her and because of this, she had felt safe in opening her heart to him.

Alex had never had the opportunity of getting so close to a man before; her fear had always stood in the way. With Matthew it had been different, but what was she to do now? If he ever found out how she felt, he would be embarrassed. He would despise her. She shivered at the thought. He must never know how she felt. So far, he knew she found him attractive—Steve had told her this much. As for the rest, he need only know she loved him as a friend. The burden would be on her to conceal her true feelings.

Then, her thoughts momentarily turned to Mark. He still had the power to disturb and frighten her. She found him attractive, but she didn't love him. She only loved Matthew, and she was convinced he was her soul mate in this life—one she would have to let go. Painful as the knowledge seemed to her right now, Matthew was not meant to be with her in this life, except for a brief time. Their paths had crossed for a purpose and further down the line they would take them in different directions.

Alex hugged herself, feeling cold despite the sun's warmth, and her thoughts turned once again to Mark. How could she still have a feeling of attraction for the disturbing Mark if she loved Matthew? Had her mother been right when she had called her a slut?

Cecilia had accused her of leading her stepfather on. Was this what had happened with Mark? Had she led him on? Feeling agitated, Alex forced the frightening thoughts away before they had the power to bring on another panic attack. Instead, she focused on the flowers in the garden. The roses were doing fine and the shoots of jasmine she had recently planted seemed to have taken well.

Why couldn't life be like a garden, where one pulled out the weeds of dark thoughts and only planted and nurtured the positive thoughts that grew into lovely flowers? It would be too easy this way, she thought—and life was not easy.

Alex sighed, feeling forlorn. All she wanted right now was for Matthew to hold her, and go on holding her, until the pain of the past and present was wiped away. But Matthew had his own pain to bear. If anything, it would be she who would need to wipe away his pain.

The ringing of the telephone from inside the house interrupted her thoughts and she was up in a second, rushing to answer the call.

"Alex," Matthew's voice was barely recognisable and Alex felt her stomach plummet. "Come and pick me up. Steve's gone."

CHAPTER 21

Alex regarded Matthew thoughtfully as he sat on the sofa in the loungeroom. He hadn't uttered a single word since they had left the hospital.

When she had gone to pick him up, she'd found him waiting in Steve's room. Steve's body had already been taken away. Dr Benning had come in to express his condolences and to give her some sedatives for Matthew.

"He'll need them," he'd said, leaning over to whisper quietly in her ear.

After this, Alex drove home with a silent Matthew sitting next to her. When they arrived, she led him to the loungeroom and left him sitting on the sofa while she went off to make a cup of tea.

Now, as she sat next to him, she noticed he had not shed any tears. Meanwhile, the tea sat untouched and had grown stone cold. Not sure what to do, Alex tentatively laid a hand over his and felt surprised at the response. He intertwined his fingers with hers, holding her hand in a tight grip.

"He waited for me to get back," Matthew finally spoke in a low voice that held a tone of desolation. "I went for a cup of coffee," he continued, "and the nurse was going to give him a sponge bath." He paused, reliving the events in his mind. "When I came back, he was waiting for me."

Alex noticed the glazed look in his eyes, staring at some imaginary point in front of him. She waited silently.

"He took hold of my hand and smiled at me, really peacefully. Then, he said: 'I love you. Never forget that.' And his eyes closed; and before I knew it, he was gone, his hand still holding mine."

Alex felt tears roll down her face while she mentally said goodbye to Steve. "He's at peace now," she consoled him. "His pain is over."

He turned to glance at her, a sad smile on his face; then, he went back to looking at nothing.

She stayed with him, her hand in his, and they sat for a long time, neither saying a word. Sometime later, the thought registered in her mind that evening was upon them and they had been sitting in the dark for hours. She gently disengaged her fingers from Matthew's and switched on one of the table lamps, noticing the time. It was 7:30.

"Matthew," she called softly. Matthew looked up at her. "I'm going to make us something to eat."

"I'm not hungry." His voice was quiet, without emotion.

Alex felt a stirring of worry. She had been expecting tears or a strong emotion of some kind, but not this total lack of feeling. Matthew seemed shell-shocked. She debated as to whether to call Dr Benning to ask him what to do, but her thoughts were cut short when the telephone rang. She winced as the ringing noise pierced the silence in the room. Matthew did not even blink.

She rushed to answer the call. It was Mark.

"Alex, I heard a few hours ago. I'm so sorry."

Alex was still worried about Matthew and did not want to stay on the line. "Mark, can I call you back? I can't talk right now."

"Of course," he said. "I'll be at home all evening. Ring any time you want."

"Thank you." She replaced the receiver and walked back to where Matthew was sitting. "I'm going to make you some soup, and then I'm taking you to bed," she announced firmly.

This must have had an effect on him because he regarded her with a brief smile. "Taking me to bed," he commented softly, but there was no emotion whatsoever in his voice. "Are you going to take advantage of me in some way, I wonder?"

Alex was astounded at his remark and her face grew hot. Seeing her reaction, Matthew assured her, "No need to blush, Alex, I knew what you meant. Put it down to my dark sense of humour." Then, he went back to looking at nothing.

* * *

Alex made a very tasty vegetable soup mixed with Mexican spices and was relieved when Matthew ate his share without complaint. Afterwards, true to her word, she went upstairs with him

189

and waited till he got ready for bed. She tried not to stare at him when he came back from the bathroom wearing only pyjama bottoms, as was his habit, and climbed into bed.

"Okay," he uttered, still in a detached way. "I'm in bed. Now what?"

She was ready for him this time and produced one of the sedatives Dr Benning had given her earlier. "Now, you take one of these and go to sleep."

To her surprise, he did not argue. He asked for a glass of water and obediently took the tablet she handed him.

"I'll look in on you before I go to bed," she told him.

He nodded, and it suddenly struck her that he was behaving like a little boy with his mother. She repressed the urge to lean down and kiss him good night before leaving the room and made her way to the kitchen where she did the dishes. Later, she telephoned Mark.

"Sorry about earlier," she explained. "I didn't want to speak in front of Matthew. He was close by when you telephoned."

"No problem," Mark replied. "How is he?"

"I just put him to bed."

"You seem to have your hands full at the moment. So I want you to let me take care of the funeral arrangements."

"Well," she uttered with some relief, "I never even thought about that. It's been a difficult and strange afternoon."

"I can imagine," Mark sympathised. "I'm sure Matthew won't mind if I take it upon myself to do this. What do you think?"

"You're right," she agreed. "I don't think he's up to this sort of thing right now. Do you know what you have to do?"

"Yes. I spoke with Gazza tonight," he informed her. "You may not have been aware that he and his partner have been away on holidays in the UK."

"No, I didn't know."

"They only got back this morning, and as soon as I found out what had happened, I rang him."

"How did he take it?"

"He was deeply shocked and upset, of course. You know, he was Steve's best friend."

"Yes."

"He couldn't get over the fact that he didn't get a chance to say goodbye."

"These things happen," Alex replied, too emotionally exhausted to say any more.

"He told me Steve discussed funeral arrangements with him some months ago. Apparently, he didn't want to upset Matthew so he asked Gazza to arrange things."

"And?"

"And Gazza's going to do as Steve asked; but I insisted I wanted to help."

"Why?" Alex asked before she could stop herself.

"Because Steve was my friend, too." He paused for a moment. "Besides, I told Gazza that I knew you and it would be best if I liaised with you."

"You make it sound like a business project." Her voice was tart.

Mark sounded exasperated all of a sudden. "Come on, Alex, be fair!"

"Okay, I'm sorry."

"Why do you have to be suspicious of everything I do?" he exclaimed, the frustration evident in his voice.

"I'm not suspicious," she assured him, regretting her earlier reaction. She knew he sincerely wanted to help. "Look, I'm just really tired."

His voice softened. "Okay. Get some rest and don't worry about a thing. Gazza and I will look after all the details. Ring me if you need anything, day or night."

"Thank you. I appreciate it."

"I'll let you go now. And remember—ring me any time."

"I will. Good night." She put down the phone and realised how very exhausted she really was, but before she went to bed she wanted to look in on Matthew.

She switched off the lights downstairs and when she got to the top of the stairs, she switched off the stairwell light. Alex realised with sadness that it would no longer be needed. Steve had never told her why this particular light was left on every night, but she now knew it was for the times when he was sick and Matthew had to rush up and down the stairs in the middle of the night. Steve probably feared Matthew wouldn't bother to switch on the light and that he might trip and fall.

Expelling a long sigh, she went to take a much-needed shower and then changed into her pyjamas. It couldn't have been later than nine o'clock, but her eyes felt heavy and her mind craved sleep. She came out of the bathroom and made her way to Matthew's room in the dark. The door had been left ajar earlier on, so she stuck her head in to see whether he was sleeping. The curtains were undrawn and the room was bathed in a soft semidarkness as light filtered in from the streetlamp outside.

Matthew lay face up in bed, his naked torso outlined in the shadows, and his breathing even. Alex made to leave the room when suddenly he spoke softly. "Alex."

Her heart skipped a beat. "Yes?"

"Will you stay with me tonight?"

Her mouth went dry. To lie next to him all night would be sweet torture, but the need to be of comfort to him took over and she didn't hesitate when she replied. "Sure, I'll stay with you."

She walked into the room feeling like an intruder, thinking Steve should be here and not her. But then she remembered Steve was gone and he could no longer comfort Matthew. She had inherited the role now.

Matthew lifted the bed covers for her to climb in and she did so in silence. Her skin tingled all over and he hadn't even touched her. She felt like a traitor but realised this was totally innocent, at least on his part. He simply needed to be with someone and she was happy he'd asked her.

When she settled next to him, he pulled her into his arms, and they lay on their sides, spoon fashion. Alex must have been holding her body stiffly because he whispered in her ear, "Relax. I'm not going to do anything." He sounded sleepy.

Alex forced her body to loosen up as much as possible, though her whole being burned with desire and she hated herself for it. Matthew was asleep within moments, but tired as she was, it took her hours to drift into oblivion. During the whole of that time, she kept telling her traitorous body to stop feeling so alive.

* * *

Alex awoke with a feeling that something was not as it should be. She looked around the room and realised she was alone in Matthew's bed. The morning light shone bright in her eyes, and she blinked a few times.

One glance at the clock on the bedside table told her it was almost ten and before she could get out of bed, Matthew entered the room. Fresh out from the shower, he was wearing a pair of track pants. His hair was damp and his upper body looked glorious. Alex flushed.

"Morning," he said, unaware of her reaction. "I left you some coffee downstairs." He started to rummage through the wardrobe. "Did you sleep well?"

Alex felt like laughing hysterically; the whole thing was so surreal. She had slept with the man she loved, who happened to be gay, and who had just lost his partner—and she had spent half the night burning with desire at his nearness. So how could she possibly have slept well? But in response to his question, she replied casually, "Reasonably. What about you?"

He turned to look at her and his eyes did not hold their usual brightness; but other than this, he seemed fine. "Under the circumstances, I slept well." He paused for a moment. "I suppose all those nights at the hospital really took their toll."

Alex was truly amazed at his sense of detachment. He sounded like he was making an observation about an event that affected someone other than himself. Alex felt mounting concern for him.

Matthew went on, "By the way, thanks for staying with me last night. I hope I didn't inconvenience you."

She felt like she was listening to a stranger, thanking her politely for having joined him for afternoon tea. It was time to telephone Dr Benning and tell him Matthew was in total and complete denial. She tried to answer him as neutrally as possible. "Well, anything for a friend." She must have grinned at him because he gave her what could pass for a smile and turned to the wardrobe to resume his search. She felt foolish behaving like this.

"What exactly are you looking for, Matthew?" She was suddenly curious.

"My weightlifting belt."

"Your what?"

"Weightlifting belt. I'm off to the gym to do weights."

For the time being, she decided to treat everything he did as normal since she did not know what else to do. "You're off to the gym?"

"Yes. Time to tone my body."

Tone his body? As far as she was concerned, he had never looked anything but toned. "Did you have breakfast?" she asked, trying to keep things in perspective. It felt like all sense of reality was slipping away from her, and she didn't like it.

"Yes, but I didn't do the dishes," he answered. "I'll do them when I get back," he added, surprising her.

He finally found his belt and stuffed it into his gym bag. Then, he put on a T-shirt, threw on a tracksuit top, and sat on the edge of the bed to tie up his sneakers while Alex watched in fascination at this young man who was Matthew and yet, not the Matthew she knew.

Of all the ways he could've reacted to Steve's death, she had never prepared herself for this one. Why, he hadn't even asked about funeral arrangements or anything connected to Steve's death.

"Matthew." She waited until he turned to her. "Do you feel all right?"

"I'm fine. I just want to pump some iron."

"When will you be back?"

"In a couple of hours. Are you making lunch today?"

"Yes, if you want me to."

"Good. I'll see you then," he replied, and having finished with his sneakers, he picked up his gym bag and left the room.

The minute Alex heard the front door slam shut, she was on the phone to Dr Benning. It took about ten minutes to be connected with him as the hospital had to have him paged.

"Alex," he said when he finally came on the line, "how may I help you?"

"Dr Benning, I'm sorry to disturb you, but it's urgent I talk with you."

"No problem," replied the doctor. "You sound troubled. Is everything all right?"

"I don't think so. It's Matthew, you see. He's acting strange, like he's in complete denial. And since Steve passed on, he hasn't even shed one tear."

"People have different ways of coping with the death of a loved one," Dr Benning explained. "I would say Matthew's repressing his grief at present, but it'll come to the surface eventually. The only thing I advise you to do is act as normal as you can around him and watch out for any destructive behaviour."

"You mean like throwing things around?"

"Yes, violence of any kind; even upon himself. Keep him on the sedatives at night, at least for another week or so. If nothing changes by then, I'll be happy to arrange some counselling for him."

"Should I refer to Steve's death in any way?" she asked, wondering what she would do if Matthew became self-destructive.

"Not unless he brings up the subject," the doctor answered.

"But what about the funeral?" She was really worried now. "How do I make him attend?"

"Alex, he's not delusional. He knows Steve passed away, and he'll go to the funeral. Just break it to him gently and make sure you have support around you if you need it."

Alex sighed, feeling helpless. "Okay, Doctor. Thank you."

"Call me if you have further problems. Goodbye for now." Dr Benning rang off.

Thoughtful, Alex put down the phone. Her instincts told her to call Mark. He might know what to do, and before she could change her mind, she dialled his number.

* * *

They sat out in the garden drinking morning coffee while Alex related to Mark everything that had happened since Matthew returned from the hospital. The only thing she omitted to tell him was the part about sleeping in his bed. This was her secret.

Mark listened in silence and only spoke when Alex finished her tale. "I had an uncle who reacted in exactly the same way when his wife died," he told her. "It's called delayed shock, or in this case, delayed grief."

"So what do I do?" Alex sounded desperate.

"Dr Benning's advice is correct. Just give him a few days to get used to the idea."

"What happened with your uncle in the end?" She wanted to know because she wasn't yet fully convinced all Matthew needed was time to come to terms with Steve's death.

"Nothing happened. He simply broke down and cried at the funeral service," he answered. "Going there brought the whole thing home to him." Mark took in her worried looks and smiled reassuringly. "Don't worry, Alex. Give him time and he'll be okay. Be yourself around him and act normal. You're the only person who can make him feel safe now."

"How do you mean?"

"Well, it's like when someone has a bad experience, say a car accident or getting mugged. When they come home, they're surrounded by familiar people and things; and it's this semblance of normalcy that they hold onto until in time they start to heal from the shock."

Alex felt more reassured now. "So as long as he's home and I'm around, he'll feel safe?"

"Correct. Simply be there for him." He drained what remained of his coffee and regarded her thoughtfully. "Steve was right about you. He told me he'd been sent a guardian angel just in time."

Alex was touched. "Did he really say that?"

"Yes. He was very concerned about leaving Matthew behind, but once you came along he knew he could leave in peace."

She felt tears sting the back of her eyes. "How do you know this?"

"He told me the last time I went to visit." He reached across the table and took hold of her hand. "You're doing a wonderful job taking care of Matthew, just as Steve would've wanted."

Alex drew back her hand gently and finished her coffee to cover up her uneasiness at his touch. "Thank you for your help," she said at last. "I really appreciate what you're doing."

"I'm glad you called," his voice was soft. "No one should have to go through this alone."

She nodded; feeling like the weight on her shoulders had been lifted. "What's happening with the funeral arrangements?"

"Gazza's been to see Steve's lawyer so he can release some money from the estate to cover costs."

"What about the reading of the will?"

"The lawyer thought it best to wait until after the funeral to give Matthew a chance to come to grips with his grief."

"Good idea."

Mark glanced at his watch. "Didn't you say Matthew would be home by noon?"

"Oh! Is it that time already?"

"I'm afraid so," he said regretfully. "I guess I better go before he arrives."

"Yes. He mustn't know we've been discussing him."

They stood and Mark hugged her gently, tilting her chin up with one finger to look into her eyes. "You know where to reach me, okay?"

She nodded.

"I'll call you when I have a date for the funeral."

"Thank you."

He leaned down and kissed her mouth softly. "Take care."

CHAPTER 22

Mark called the following day to inform Alex of the funeral arrangements. "How's Matthew?"

"Still the same." Alex sighed, frustrated. "He carries on like nothing's happened."

"Want me to be present when you tell him about the funeral?"

"No, it's okay." She told him she'd call him if there were any problems and rang off.

Matthew was at the gym again. It seemed all of a sudden he was obsessed with working out. Alex continued with the vacuuming, which was what she had been doing when Mark had called, and mused about the events of the last twenty-four hours.

When Matthew had arrived home from the gym the previous day, he had been glowing with energy and in a good mood. During lunch he was in a chatty frame of mind, and Alex had managed to keep up a façade of normalcy for him. Afterwards, he'd helped her with the dishes.

In the afternoon, he spent time in his room packing away all of Steve's clothes. When Alex went up to check on him, she had to resist the overwhelming desire to scream at him to stop. Instead, she left him alone and forced herself to do some weeding in the garden. Any kind of physical work was welcome rather than watch Matthew carry on like a man with a mission—his mission being to obliterate Steve's presence from the house.

Much later, when he was in the shower, Alex sneaked into Matthew's bedroom to see the end result of his labours. She was amazed to see that not only had he packed away all of Steve's clothing and personal effects, but all the furniture had been rearranged with pieces placed in different parts of the room. The French impressionist paintings were also gone, replaced by a variety of colourful contemporary ones. Alex wondered where they had come from.

Matthew's behaviour was worrisome, but at least he did not exhibit any aggressive or destructive tendencies, and for this she was grateful. At dinner that evening, Matthew kept up his lively chatter and afterwards had gone to bed early, taking the sedative prescribed by Dr Benning. When Alex checked on him later, he was fast asleep.

Now, while she finished the vacuuming, she wondered what else Matthew might do upon his return from the gym. Just as she thought of this, he walked in.

"Hi, I'm back," he announced, gym bag slung over his shoulder. "What's for lunch? I'm starving." Without waiting for a response, he ran up the stairs to his room.

Minutes later, Alex heard him in the shower. She was unnerved by the extent of his denial and, making her way to the kitchen to prepare lunch, the goose bumps she noticed covering her body provided a clear testament to this.

It was a lovely warm day again and Alex decided they would eat outdoors. She planned to tell Matthew about the funeral arrangements during lunch. When he came back downstairs, he joined her in the courtyard. Alex had laid out cold cuts, salad and crusty bread rolls.

"This looks good," he commented. "You know, if I was straight, I think I'd probably marry you." Although his chatter was lighthearted, Alex sensed the flatness in the tone of his voice. It was the same tone she had been hearing since Steve's death, so she feigned a calm outward appearance.

"That's nice, Matthew," she humoured him. "Now, dig in."

They ate in silence, and she watched him; not really knowing what it was she was trying to find. He looked healthy enough; the only hint of emotional turmoil was the opaque look in his eyes.

Matthew wore casual khaki pants and a white cotton shirt and once again, Alex felt the devastating effect of his good looks. Sometime in the last couple of weeks, he had acquired a deeper tan. Alex noted he was one of those lucky individuals whose skin tanned naturally at the slightest bit of sun and stayed this way all year round. In contrast with his skin, his hair seemed lighter and his eyes, though not possessing their usual brightness, were still as blue as the sky above them. Even his teeth looked whiter these days, she observed and was inexplicably annoyed with him for looking so attractive for someone who was in mourning.

"Are you thinking about my proposition?" Matthew spoke suddenly, jolting her out of her thoughts.

She flushed, knowing she had been caught staring. "Not at all," she answered flippantly. "You're too young for me."

"Only by seven years," he replied as if he was taking the whole thing seriously.

She ignored his comment and thought about what she was about to do. She didn't know how to tell him, so she decided to get straight to the point without preamble. "Matthew, we have a date for Steve's funeral," she blurted out; then looked at him for a reaction.

He kept eating his sandwich as he casually asked, "When is it?"

"This coming Friday at ten o'clock."

"Okay."

She didn't know how to respond to his emotional emptiness so she carried on by telling him some of the details. "Gazza and Mark arranged everything. They said Steve didn't want a wake or even a conventional service," she informed him, relieved the whole funeral discussion was over and done with.

There was the slightest hint of surprise from Matthew as he remarked, "I would've thought he'd want a final farewell from his friends, but I do remember he always liked the thought of a graveside service. He wasn't a religious person, you know." His voice sounded distant.

Alex sat there, no longer knowing what to say. Remembering Dr Benning's advice to let him talk of Steve's death when he was ready, she realised the best thing was for her to say nothing at all. She waited for him to navigate his own way—but he changed the subject entirely.

"Do you feel like going for a walk on the beach this afternoon?"

She nodded. "That'll be nice." Perhaps, he wasn't quite ready, she decided.

* * *

For the four days leading up to the funeral, Matthew's routine did not change. He went to the gym every morning, came home to have lunch with Alex, and found some sort of activity to keep him occupied in the afternoons. Then, after an early dinner, he watched television or read; at about nine in the evening, he took one of the sedatives Alex gave him and went straight to bed.

Alex, in the meantime, made sure she was around him much of the time. She carried on with her façade of normalcy when he was around, and when not, she was able to mourn her dear friend. With the stress of coping with Matthew's new behaviour, she hadn't had time to grieve because she could not do it in front of Matthew.

The only time she could be herself was when Matthew was at the gym or at night, when she was in her own room. By this time, however, she was too tired to even think. So it was while she worked in his garden that she could freely think of Steve. This was where she felt closest to him and where she communicated with him in thought.

Alex had no doubt he was resting in peace now, but she worried that if he was able to see Matthew's behavior, he might not be enjoying the hereafter. She berated herself for being fanciful. Who was to say where Steve really was at this time? Still, being out in the garden made her feel she was communing with his spirit, and this was her way of mourning the loss of a very special person.

* * *

Mark dropped by to see Alex the day before the funeral. He knew Matthew would be at the gym, so he arrived without warning. Alex was surprised to see him.

"Come on in." Wearing her gardening gloves, she motioned him into the house. "I'm out back working in the garden."

He followed her in. "Sorry to drop in unannounced. I was at the market and suddenly had a desire to see you."

Alex hoped he had not come around to talk about the night of their date. "Coffee?" she offered.

"That would be nice, thanks."

She took off the gloves and put on the kettle to boil. "Why don't you go outside? I'll join you in a moment."

Mark went out to the courtyard, and Alex watched him through the kitchen window as he inspected the flowers in the garden. He seemed deep in thought, and she wondered whether he was also communing with Steve's spirit. When the coffee was ready, she joined him, and they sat at the table.

"Is everything ready for tomorrow?" she asked. If they were talking about the funeral, Mark could hardly turn the conversation into something more personal.

"Yes. We're driving from the funeral parlour directly to the cemetery at South Head. The service will be conducted by one of the local ministers, and Gazza will be saying a few words afterwards."

"Did anyone ask Matthew whether he wants to say anything in Steve's memory?" Alex was surprised no one had consulted with Matthew about this.

Mark read her thoughts. "Steve was a very special person, Alex. He had the gift of being able to see into people's innermost thoughts." He looked over the garden as if his message to her was coming directly from Steve's spirit.

Alex waited for him to go on.

"The thing is Steve always seemed to know a person's feelings about something. It was like he was able to sense a person's fears and joys. Do you know what I mean?"

"I think so." She knew Steve had that gift. He had certainly sensed how damaged she was, and she had a feeling he had known this from the very start.

"Anyway," Mark continued, "he knew Matthew better than Matthew knows himself. He told Gazza he didn't want a big fuss at the funeral, and knowing how very sensitive Matthew is, he also said he didn't think he'd want to make a speech. He thought it would make things more difficult for him."

Alex wondered whether Steve had truly been able to foresee how Matthew was going to react after his death. Perhaps, he had not been so very accurate about the feelings of the one closest to him after all.

"I think Matthew *would* feel uncomfortable making a speech at the funeral, and I believe Steve was right on this point," Mark went on. "Don't be fooled by Matthew's present behaviour. His grief is so tightly coiled inside him that it's bound to come out with a tremendous force sooner or later."

Alex took exception to this comment. "I think I know Matthew fairly well by now. I've been living in the same house with him for months, you know."

"I'm sorry. I don't mean to imply you're not aware of how he's feeling," Mark returned apologetically. "What I'm trying to say is I simply agree with Steve's observation. No matter how Matthew looks to us now, I don't believe he would be up to making any speeches."

"Well," she answered, more in control of her emotions, "I suppose it's best to trust in Steve's judgement. He always knew best about all of us."

"Did Matthew say anything about the funeral?" Mark asked. He wondered if perhaps it was Matthew who had taken exception to the fact that no one had consulted him about the arrangements.

Alex responded with a bleak look in her eyes. "He hasn't mentioned it at all."

Mark saw the strain of the last few days showing on her face. "Try not to worry too much about him. Remember what I told you about my uncle."

She smiled weakly. "Delayed grief."

He nodded briefly and decided it was time to go. "Thanks for the coffee and sorry about the intrusion. If you like, I can ask Gazza to talk to Matthew about making a speech."

She smiled, grateful for his consideration, and shook her head. "Let's leave it as it is and follow Steve's advice." She then saw him to the front door.

"You know," Mark said as he turned to her on the doorstep, "Matthew's really lucky to have a friend like you." He gave her a searching look and left.

* * *

The following morning dawned too soon for Alex's liking, and by eight o'clock she was already dressed. She had never attended a funeral in her life and had no idea what to wear to one, either. Custom decreed that people wear black, but she didn't think Steve would like a bunch of people gathering around his grave in such a depressing colour.

It was ironic, she thought, how black was considered to be elegant when it came to eveningwear; but at a funeral, it was simply depressing. In the end, she compromised and wore a pair of tailored black pants with a sky blue knitted shirt. She plaited her long hair away from her face and wore no make-up, except for lipstick in a muted red colour. When she was ready, she grabbed a charcoal grey jacket that completed her outfit and went down to the kitchen to prepare breakfast.

The sun was already shining bright and Alex felt its warmth seep into her body, making her more at ease about the ordeal ahead. Minutes later, Matthew strode in with a subdued "good morning". It seemed he felt the same way she did about dress because he was wearing a pastel yellow pullover with black pants and carrying his black leather jacket in hand.

"I made some hot breakfast. It might be hours before we eat again," she said by way of greeting.

Matthew nodded and sat down at the table. They ate in total silence.

* * *

The cemetery at South Head rested on high ground, close to the Pacific Ocean. Alex thought it fitting for Steve to rest among the natural scenery with a constant sea breeze and the gentle sound of the ocean nearby.

There were something like fifty people gathered around the gravesite, and she recognised some of the faces from Steve's party. Michael and Bruce with their wives, all dressed in black; Dennis was alone, also in black; and Gazza and Bazza looked very sombre, each in a simple black suit with a white shirt and dark tie. Mark had dressed in a similar fashion to Matthew: black pants and a pullover in dark green. Everyone waited in silence; perhaps, saying their own personal goodbyes to their dear friend.

The service began with the minister reading a long passage from the Bible, which prompted Alex to wonder why Steve had opted not to have a chapel service instead. The thought occurred to her that it might have something to do with his father having been a minister, and she suddenly realised there was much she did not know about Steve. He had told her about some aspects of his life, but had never shared with her any feelings he may have had at his parents' rejection.

In many ways Steve had been a bit of a mystery when it came to his own life, and all Alex really knew about him was that he had great capacity to love, and his love was unconditional.

The minister droned on, and Alex looked around the gathering and saw tears on many faces while others wore serious or thoughtful looks, probably like her own. She glanced sideways at Matthew, standing a couple of feet away from her, and noted his eyes were dry. He was simply staring at Steve's coffin. Mark stood next to him, a serious look on his face, and Gazza and Bazza were wiping at their eyes with tissues.

The minister stopped speaking and Alex realised she had not heard a single word he had said. In her own way, however, she had been saying her farewells to Steve by being in the present moment and thinking about him in her mind. A cool breeze blew in from the ocean and she shivered. She still could not believe Steve was gone. Yet, here she was, standing in front of his coffin. *Goodbye, my dear friend*, she said to him in thought, *and thank you for loving me.*

Gazza was now speaking, his voice soft and with a hint of sadness. Alex listened. "Steve was a very special friend to each of us," he declared. "He had the gift of being able to make one feel unique in his presence, and I think all here will agree his love knew no bounds." He paused and sniffed as a tear rolled down his face. "On a personal note, I wish to say Steve was always there when I needed a sympathetic ear; and despite his own burdens, he always took mine onboard as if they were his own. He never judged and never made light of my problems. He simply helped me by being my dear friend.

"Lastly, I would like to add that Steve was never one to take praise for what he did; and with this in mind, I will make this a short speech because I know he would want me to say very little on his behalf. Steve was a modest man, and he never boasted about anything. In the end, however, his actions speak for themselves because all of us here have been touched by him one way or another. So please join me in saying farewell to a dear and true friend. May he rest in peace and love everlasting."

Alex felt tears escape her eyes, but the ocean breeze dried them before they had a chance to roll down her face. She watched as the coffin, decked with a large spray of white roses on top, was lowered into the grave by an automatic hoist. This was done in silence, broken only by the sound of the odd seagull flying past. Then, the funeral was over.

Alex stood quietly while one by one, the people who had attended stopped by to pay their respects to Matthew. Mark came to stand next to her.

"You okay?"

She smiled at him. "Yes. It was a beautiful service, Mark. I'm sure Steve would've approved."

"He did want things to be kept as simple as possible, but he wouldn't compromise on the location." The latter was said in mild humour mixed with affection.

"That's Steve all right," Alex responded. "I bet he would've insisted on a rose garden if this was possible."

Mark smiled faintly and regarded her with concern. "Will you be okay driving Matthew home?"

"I'll be fine. I'm only grateful we don't have to entertain a whole bunch of people at the house." The relief was evident in her voice.

Most of the people had dispersed by now and the minister was having a quiet word with Matthew.

"I better take Matthew home," she said. "Thank you for all you've done, and please thank Gazza for me."

He nodded and leaned down to kiss her cheek. "Take care. I'll call you soon."

Mark waited until the minister finished before walking up to Matthew for a few words. Alex, meanwhile, thanked the minister and then went to Matthew, who was left standing alone after Mark's departure. "Let's go home," she said.

"He's at peace now, isn't he?" These were the first words he had spoken to her since breakfast.

"Yes. He's at peace," she reassured him.

She took hold of his hand and slowly led him away from Steve's grave.

CHAPTER 23

A couple of days after Steve's funeral, Alex accompanied Matthew to see John Barry, Steve's lawyer.

The will was straightforward; Steve had left everything he owned to Matthew—the house, money from investments, the furniture and all personal effects. He also included a clause stipulating Matthew should pay off the mortgage on the house with the investment money left to him; and while Alex lived in the house, he was not to charge her rent any longer.

Alex was both surprised and touched by his gesture. She knew this was Steve's way of thanking her for staying on to look after his partner.

Matthew stayed silent all the while the will was being read.

"It'll take a few weeks to arrange the paperwork and release all monies," John Barry explained when he finished reading the will. He was in his mid-thirties, and his slim features reminded Alex of Steve; and by his mannerisms, she could tell he was gay.

"I've also confirmed with the bank the outstanding amount on the mortgage," he went on, mainly looking toward Alex since Matthew seemed to be paying no attention, "and after the discharge of it, this will leave about twenty thousand dollars in the kitty. How would you like me to disburse the funds?" He addressed this question to Matthew.

Matthew did not answer, and John Barry waited patiently. When the lawyer began to fidget with his paperwork, obviously uncomfortable while Matthew continued to gaze into empty space, Alex turned to her companion. "Matthew, what do you want to do with the leftover money?"

The sound of her voice seemed to snap him out of his trance, and he glanced at the lawyer. "Just put it into the savings account."

"Very well," John sounded relieved. "I'll notify you when the transaction is complete."

With nothing else left to discuss, Matthew and Alex took their leave of John and left the office. The weather had turned after Steve's funeral and as they stepped out to the street, they were greeted by grey skies and a cold, harsh wind. Alex espied a café across the road.

"Come on," she said, taking Matthew's arm. "I'll buy you a cappuccino."

They crossed the road and entered into the welcoming warmth of the café. It was early afternoon and the place was quiet. Alex turned to Matthew after they ordered their coffees.

"Matthew," she said in a serious voice, "I'm very grateful for Steve's gesture, but please don't think anything has to change. After all, I'm still a lodger at your house."

"Don't be silly," he responded, and for a moment he sounded like the old Matthew. "Steve did the right thing, so please don't worry about it. You look after the house in every way; and lately, you're even doing my laundry. So even if Steve hadn't thought of it, I wouldn't have accepted any more money from you." He paused and gazed into her eyes. "Besides," he added gently, "you're the only family I have left."

She felt a lump in her throat and was grateful their coffees arrived at that moment. She took her time stirring in sugar and was in control of her emotions by the time she spoke again. "Thank you," she uttered quietly, taking a sip of her coffee. "And what about LA?" she added suddenly, the thought of him going away tearing at her heart.

She caught the bleak look in his eyes when he replied, "I don't know. I need time to think about things."

Alex experienced a rush of relief at this and at once felt guilty for wanting him with her. She immediately dismissed the thought and turned her attention to what he had said. He needed time to think. Surely, this was a sign that he was beginning to sort through his feelings of grief—at least, she hoped so.

* * *

Since Steve's death, Alex had not had a lot of time to examine her newfound feelings for Matthew. She knew it was absolutely crazy to be in love with him, but she could not help it. There was, however, nothing stopping her from loving him as a close and dear friend; and she would simply have to be content with this.

Therefore, in the days that followed Steve's passing, she became a kind of pseudo-partner to him. She looked after him domestically, she was there for him emotionally, and pretty much took part in most aspects of his life, except the most intimate ones.

They ate together, went for walks or coffee, or spent their leisure time watching films or reading quietly. Neither of them mentioned Steve after the visit to the lawyer, and they seemed to settle into a daily routine that suited them.

Matthew continued going to the gym each day, and Alex worked in the garden. Aside from these individual pursuits, the two of them spent most of their time together.

The days merged one into another, and except when she caught the odd look of sadness in his eyes or when he lapsed into silence with a faraway gaze, Alex saw no sign of real grief in Matthew. It occurred to her that he felt safe in their routine, and therefore he need not face Steve's death—at least, not as long as he could go on pretending everything in his world was fine. He still took a sedative every night, and she realised he welcomed the deep, dreamless sleep that engulfed him as a result of the drug.

As for her, she knew sooner or later things would change, because nothing ever stayed the same for long.

* * *

Spring finally arrived, and with it the inevitable winds of change, just as Alex had expected. It had been a few weeks since Steve's passing, and she and Matthew had become so absorbed in their daily routine that it was a shock to have the outside world intrude in on them. It happened to Alex first.

She was gardening one sunny morning when the doorbell rang, and she was faintly annoyed when she found Mark on her doorstep. She felt he had pierced the cocoon she and Matthew had woven around themselves.

"How are you?" Mark had neither seen nor called her since the funeral.

"Mark," she uttered, trying to keep her voice neutral. "I thought you were going to telephone."

The subtle admonishment was not lost on him. "I'm sorry I didn't. I thought you and Matthew might want some time to yourselves. But this morning, when I went down to the market, I thought of you and knew I had to see you."

Alex smiled, faintly amused. "Is there some correlation between the produce at the market and me?"

His boyish grin still had the power to charm her. "No, nothing of the sort. I only thought it was time we had a talk."

Alex felt her stomach muscles tighten. This was the famous talk he had been after ever since the night of their disastrous date. She knew there was no getting away from it, and now was as good a time as any to get it over with. "Come on in. We can talk in the garden."

They sat out in the courtyard after she made coffee.

"How are things with you?" Mark enquired.

"Fine. Things have settled down around here."

"And Matthew, how is he?"

"He's okay. Just trying to get on with his life, I suppose." She did not want to discuss Matthew's denial problem even though Mark had been very supportive when she had asked for advice in the past. Now, however, it felt like she would be betraying Matthew if she discussed him with anybody.

"I'd like to catch up with him, maybe organise a night out with the boys. Gazza and Bazza keep asking about him."

Alex felt annoyed all of a sudden. "There's no reason why they can't telephone and speak directly with him. Why do they need to go through you?" The moment this was out, she regretted her defensive manner. "I'm sorry," she said immediately. "I didn't mean to sound so horrid. What I meant was the boys are also Matthew's friends, and they can call any time they want."

Mark decided to drop the subject. "Well, I'm sure one of them will."

A small cloud blocked the sun momentarily and the garden was cast in cold shadow. "Mark," Alex decided to come to the point, "about our dinner date; I have to apologise. Perhaps, you thought I was leading you on, and it wasn't like this at all. I'm just not ready to get involved with anyone at the moment."

Mark glanced at her at the same time as the sun reappeared, turning the colour of his eyes into a deep golden green. "It's not you who should apologise," he confessed. "I thought I hurt you in some way, and I was angry with myself for being such an oaf."

The admission surprised her. "That's really sweet of you," she reassured him. "And while you were angry thinking you'd hurt me; I was angry with myself, thinking I'd led you on. So it seems we were at cross-purposes all this time."

He smiled in relief. "Well, for what it's worth, I'm glad you're not angry with me. I would love to get to know you better. But if you're not ready, at least I hope you'll let me be your friend."

Alex shook her head in mild disbelief. "You're an attractive man and can date any woman you like, so why do you bother with me?"

He gazed into her eyes searchingly. "I guess we can't choose who we fall for. It just happens."

Don't I know it, thought Alex.

Mark went on speaking, "Maybe, it's your simplicity of manner. You don't put on airs and graces like a lot of other women do to attract a guy. In any case, I think you're an attractive lady, and ..." He laughed suddenly. "I sound like a sentimental fool, don't I?"

Alex joined in the laughter. "Well, let's just say you're making me feel like we're in one of Matthew's soapies." She sobered up quickly. "Seriously, I would be honoured to be your friend. Thank you for asking."

They exchanged a look that did not need words to convey their relief at having finally reached a compromise, but deep down inside Alex wondered if Mark would be happy with only friendship between them.

* * *

The second sign that the outside world was intruding into their domestic bliss came with Matthew. They were having lunch after his return from the gym when Alex informed him, "Mark popped in this morning."

"How is he?"

"He said he'd call you about organising a boys' night out with Gazza and Bazza."

A hint of brightness lit his eyes. "Great idea," he declared. "I haven't seen them in ages."

It would be good for him to start going out with his friends, Alex thought. It was certainly time for him to get on with his life.

The only thing that worried her was that his grief had not yet come out; unless he was grieving in silence and she was not aware of it. Perhaps, this was the case, she thought with hope. She fervently wished Matthew would truly come to terms with his grief and start to heal. This would make her very happy for his sake. Then, the only shadow over her would be the feeling that things were slipping away, but this was a problem with which she would have to cope.

In any case, the wheel of change was turning, and there was nothing she could do about it. She knew it was necessary for Matthew to get on with his life.

"By the way," Matthew said, interrupting her thoughts, "I went by Brent's on the way home, and guess what?" Alex waited. "He's sending me in for an audition. It's a big American blockbuster, and they have several good parts."

Alex sensed the excitement in him. "That's fantastic!" She managed to sound enthusiastic even though this was yet another intrusion from the world outside. "When's the big day?"

"The day after tomorrow. Brent was about to phone me today with the news, but I called him first. Anyway, I have to learn a whole scene for the audition so I'm counting on you to help me with the lines."

This was the first time since Steve's death that the dullness lifted from his eyes, and as she looked into them, she drew in her breath at their beauty..

CHAPTER 24

The day of the audition arrived and Matthew was nervous. Alex had helped him learn his lines and they'd practised over and over until he could say them in his sleep. Yet, for some inexplicable reason, he still felt uneasy. Alex noticed his anxiety at breakfast.

"Why so nervous?" she asked. "You know you're ready."

Matthew played with the food on his plate. "I don't know." He sounded uncertain. "Maybe it's because this is a good, solid part that I'm trying out for. It could mean so much for my career."

The film was an action-thriller blockbuster with a big star in the lead. Rumours had it Tom Cruise was starring; others said it was Bruce Willis. Brent related this to Matthew when he'd gone to the agent's office to pick up a copy of the script that he was to learn in preparation for the audition.

"It could be the rumours you've been hearing about the lead actor," Alex pointed out. "Hell, I'd be nervous, too, if I knew I might be working alongside a big name."

"Yes, you're right. That could be it."

"Try not to think about it. Just focus on your lines and deliver them as you've been doing here with me," she advised. "After all, it's not like any of these guys will be there watching you."

"I know that, but the film director will be."

"Well, you just go in there, do your stuff, and don't worry about who'll be there."

Matthew nodded at her attempt to reassure him, but he looked unconvinced.

* * *

The audition was to take place at Fox Studios in Moore Park, and since it wasn't so far from where he lived, Matthew decided to walk. He thought the exercise might steady his nerves.

When he arrived at his destination, one of the production assistants gave him a card the size of an A4 page with his name and a number written out in bold black letters.

He was told to wait until his name was called, so Matthew took a seat in the waiting room and looked at the others who were waiting to audition. There were five guys around his age group and with a similar build to his; probably all trying out for the same role. With nerves mounting, he decided against checking out the competition and instead, he studied his audition script.

The role was that of a young agent entangled in a major conspiracy involving Australian and American intelligence organisations. Though secondary, the role was of importance because it supported the lead. In the film, the young agent was in possession of certain information that was vital to the main character. This meant there would be several scenes played opposite the lead actor.

A production assistant appeared in the waiting room, interrupting his thoughts, and called out the name of one of the other actors waiting to audition. Matthew sighed with relief; he still had time to compose himself. He closed his eyes and mentally went through his lines and was satisfied he had them down pat. Even so, he kept repeating them in his mind over and over again.

"Matthew Davis," the production assistant called out suddenly.

Matthew started; sure there were still other guys before him. But when he looked around the room, he realised the guys had all gone. In their place, were female actors waiting to audition for some other part. Matthew wondered how long he'd been sitting there with his eyes closed.

The production assistant led him down a long corridor, then turned and opened a door to her left. "Good luck." She smiled at him and was gone.

Matthew found himself inside a small studio. At one end, there was a well-lit white wall, which would serve as the backdrop for the screen test. A piece of bright blue electrical tape was stuck to the floor, marking the spot where the actor was to stand; and a few feet away fiddling with the camera, was a young guy wearing baggy jeans and a black T-shirt.

A skinny red-haired woman held a clapperboard, and at her side, sitting in a black canvas chair, was the film director—a man somewhere in his fifties, wearing a crumpled pair of khaki pants and a white T-shirt. His hair was longish and mostly grey, and he sported a bushy grey beard. His manner was relaxed and friendly. "Matthew, is it?" The man addressed Matthew with an American accent.

"Yes." Matthew felt his throat go dry, and his voice sounded hoarse.

The director nodded a greeting but did not introduce himself.

"Please hold up your card," instructed the red-haired girl before Matthew could nod back.

He did this and noticed the young guy at the camera was already filming him.

"Okay, Matthew, here's how it goes," the director said. "The bad guys are onto you. They know you have vital information and you're going to try to contact the hero in our film. The question is: will you get to him before they get to you? In this scene, you're with your girlfriend, a last visit to her in case you never see her again. You're telling her what happened." The director paused and looked at Matthew for feedback.

Matthew nodded in acknowledgment. He understood everything that had been said to him, but the only thing he was aware of was the tension building up inside him.

The director eyed him curiously. "Do you want some water before we start?"

"No," Matthew managed to reply, "I'll be okay."

"Good. In that case, Katrina," the director gestured toward the red-head, "is going to read the lines of the girlfriend."

Matthew nodded, struggling to swallow through his dry throat. He knew he should've taken the offer of water.

Katrina stood close to him, holding the clapperboard in front of his chest. When the cameraman nodded, she said, "Matthew Davis— number two zero eight." She snapped the clapperboard bar and moved out of the way.

"Okay, we're rolling," the director called out. "You're on."

Matthew was about to deliver his first line when suddenly the whole room disappeared from his view, and standing in front of him, only a few feet away, he saw Steve.

* * *

215

Alex had a meeting with the editor of an airline magazine who was interested in some of her outback articles. She had decided only a few days previously that it was time to get back to work and was pleasantly surprised when the call had come through from the editor's office.

She arrived ten minutes early to the meeting and while she waited, she telephoned the house, hoping Matthew would be back from his audition. The answering machine picked up the call and she hung up.

The meeting with the editor dragged on for close to three hours and by the time she arrived back home, it was late afternoon. The house was quiet and she found a note from Matthew on the kitchen counter. *Gone for a walk*, it read.

Alex felt a touch of anxiety but was not sure why. She had expected him to be home, waiting to tell her all about the audition. Instead, he'd gone for a walk; and judging from the look of the dark grey clouds covering the sky, it was going to start pouring at any moment.

When Matthew had left in the morning the day had been sunny, but Sydney weather was treacherous at times. Sunny weather in the morning could turn into a violent thunderstorm by the afternoon. It had been unseasonably warm earlier and now southerly winds were blowing in, cooling things down rapidly. Alex knew they were in for a big storm and hoped Matthew wouldn't be caught in it.

A feeling of exhaustion swept over her. She'd spent a long afternoon closeted in a small stuffy office with the editor and now she needed to clear her head. A hot shower would do the trick. She took her time and came out feeling refreshed and hungry. It was almost six o'clock by now and she hadn't eaten anything since the sandwich she gobbled down at noon, before her departure for the meeting.

A flash of lightning lit the room all of a sudden and it was followed by a crack of thunder that vibrated through the whole house. Alex jumped. She looked out her bedroom window just in time to see large hailstones pounding the courtyard and garden below; and she winced at the thought of the damage this would do to Steve's roses. A minute later, the skies opened up, spewing down heavy torrents of rain.

She turned away from the window and dressed in a warm

tracksuit. The temperature had dropped very quickly and it felt like winter once again. Where was Matthew? Alex wondered apprehensively. Just then, she heard the front door open and slam shut, followed by hurried footsteps climbing the stairs.

She popped her head out of the doorway and saw him standing on the top landing. Her mouth dropped open with shock. Not only was he thoroughly drenched, but his eyes looked red and puffy. There was a stricken look on his face, and no words were needed to explain what had happened.

Matthew did not speak. He took one glance at her querying eyes and fled into his room, slamming the door behind him. Alex paled and for a moment felt faint. If anyone had told her grief could look so devastating on someone's face, she wouldn't have believed it.

With mounting anxiety, she realised this was the time Steve had referred to when he'd told her to be there for Matthew, but now she felt helpless. What could she possibly do to make him feel better? Besides, he needed to release his grief, and both Dr Benning and Mark had told her it would come out at some point.

Hesitantly, Alex stepped over to the door of his room and listened, but all she could hear was the force of the storm with its continuing thunder and torrential rain. She tentatively put her hand on the doorknob and in a moment of bravado, turned it and walked in.

Matthew lay stretched out on the bed, face down. His body shook and Alex was not sure whether it was from the cold or his racking sobs. In an instant, her heart took over from her head and she went to him instinctively.

"Matthew," she called softly, but he ignored her. She sat close to him on the bed and, with a hand on his shoulder, shook him gently, motioning for him to turn over. When he glanced up at her, she gasped at the ravaged look on his face. The tears coursing down his cheeks, were a storm of weeping, echoing the storm outside.

"Oh, Matthew," she uttered, her heart breaking for him.

He couldn't speak and seeing the look in her eyes brought on another bout of weeping. He shook like a leaf; and even his teeth were chattering.

"Matthew." Alex was suddenly practical. "You have to change into dry clothes. You're frozen!"

He shook his head like he did not care what happened to him, and she realised that before she could comfort him she'd have to get him dry.

"You're going to have to let me help you get out of those wet clothes."

He didn't respond. His weeping subsided temporarily, however, and he looked both physically and emotionally spent.

Alex summoned up her courage and started to unbutton his shirt. He didn't fight her. In fact, he was like a child, letting his mother undress him for bed. His shirt unbuttoned, Alex pulled out one of his arms, then the other, and it was off. His upper body was covered in goose bumps from the cold. Next were his jeans. Her fingers fumbled a little as she unzipped him, but she managed it without trouble. At times like this, she reminded herself, it was best to remain detached from what she was doing. She then proceeded to unlace his shoes and took them off, followed by his socks. Finally, she pulled off his jeans and was dismayed to find that his underpants were also saturated by the rain. This part was going to be tricky, she knew; her nerves standing on end.

It was obvious Matthew was not in a state to help her, so she went to the wardrobe and pulled out a blanket to cover him. Then, reaching under the covers, she started pulling off his underwear, her fingers brushing against his muscular thighs.

Alex repressed a traitorous wave of desire and turned her thoughts to the damage in Steve's garden so she could complete the task before her without blushing. Once all the wet clothes were in a heap on the floor and he was wrapped in the blanket, Alex rushed downstairs and returned with a bottle of brandy and a small glass. She poured some out for him and made him drink it. As he did so, she took a swig from the bottle to calm down her own nerves.

The storm raged with full force, and gusts of wind and hail kept rattling the windows, threatening to shatter the glass. The room was in darkness, so Alex switched on the bedside lamp and made Matthew move further down the bed to get him away from the wet patch left earlier by his saturated clothes. Then, she grabbed a towel and rubbed at his wet hair vigorously. When she was satisfied she had done all she could, she stopped and smoothed back his ruffled hair with her fingers.

His eyes were red and puffy from the earlier violence of his weeping, and now they gazed directly into hers. "Thank you," he whispered hoarsely. He was no longer shivering and seemed calmer, but the exhaustion was written all over his face.

"Why don't you try to sleep awhile?"

"I don't want to yet. I need to talk to you."

"What is it, sweetie?" Alex was surprised at how naturally the endearment escaped from her lips.

"Alex, I saw him. I saw Steve!" Matthew's voice sounded tremulous, and the tears he was repressing threatened to erupt again.

"What do you mean?" She felt her heart skip in fear for him.

He explained what had happened at the audition: his uncharacteristic anxiety, the waiting, the tension in his stomach once he was in front of the camera, and then the appearance of Steve, just before he was about to deliver his first line.

Alex listened quietly to his account, all the time stroking his hair, comforting him.

"When I saw him there," Matthew declared, "I froze. I didn't know what to do. I must've swayed or something because next thing I knew, I was sitting in one of the chairs with the director leaning over me and asking if I was okay." He paused and sighed at the memory. "It was so embarrassing. The worst part was that I couldn't explain about Steve. I was so shaken up about seeing him that I couldn't even speak." He shuddered as he relived the moment and began to shiver once more.

Alex tucked the blanket more tightly around him while she took in the bleak look in his eyes. "Matthew, I think it's delayed grief," she explained quietly. "Since Steve's passing, you haven't really faced the fact that he's gone. You've been repressing everything. And with the excitement of the audition and the expectations, I believe your emotions finally uncoiled and you conjured up his image in your mind."

Matthew did not seem to hear her; he went on with his story. "I somehow managed to tell them I was ill and left. I came home and couldn't stand being here, so I went for a walk on the beach. All of a sudden, I started to cry and couldn't stop. Then, the storm broke and I ran all the way back." His shivering seemed to get worse and Alex worried for him.

"Do you want me to get you some warm pyjamas? You're still freezing."

"No, no, just come here. Lie with me for a while."

Alex was shocked when he abruptly lifted the blanket and pulled her next to his naked body. She blushed deeply and, despite his exhaustion, he gave her a weak smile. "Poor Alex. I suppose this is a first for you."

She nodded, feeling every cell in her body tingle with electric energy as he tightened his arm around her. "Body heat's the best way to warm up quickly," he explained, faintly amused despite his emotional turmoil.

They lay together in silence, listening to the storm rage. Alex was too tense to truly relax, but Matthew was quite at ease, drawing comfort from their physical contact.

"I'm glad you're here," he whispered suddenly, his face only inches away from hers. "I don't know what I would've done if I had to stay alone in this house."

A solitary tear rolled down his face, and she wiped it dry. "Why don't you sleep now? We can talk later if you want."

His eyes closed and within seconds he was asleep. Alex must have dozed off as well, for when she next opened her eyes she noticed the silence all around them. The storm had subsided.

Matthew was still in a deep, exhausted sleep, and she turned slightly to look at the clock on the bedside table. It was 8:15pm. She'd slept for at least an hour and her stomach rumbled as she remembered how hungry she had been earlier.

Trying not to disturb the sleeping figure next to her, she moved away slowly. In the act of lifting the blanket to get out of bed, she couldn't help but take a peek at his most private of parts. Then, with face burning, she hurried from the room.

CHAPTER 25

Alex stood assessing the garden in the clear morning light. The sun's reflection sparkled off the wet leaves of rosebushes and plants, giving the effect of a thousand glittering lights. It looked magical, but in reality, Steve's garden was destroyed.

The gale force winds, hail and heavy rain of the previous night had stripped most of the rosebushes, ripping some right out of the soil, and rose petals of all colours lay scattered on the soggy earth. The jasmine plant was totally flattened and branches on several of the young trees had snapped while others littered the ground with their roots exposed. Only a few of the hardier rosebushes managed to survive, and Alex was relieved that something had been preserved.

"It's like the storm wiped away his presence," Matthew remarked as he appeared at her side.

He had showered and looked more rested after the night's deep sleep. Only the barest hint of puffiness under his eyes reminded Alex of the maelstrom of emotions, which had swept through him, releasing the pain and grief he had repressed for so long.

"It's a sign of renewal," she replied. "Life begins again."

Matthew regarded the devastation before him, sadness reflected on his face.

Alex felt the inner pain he experienced. "Let's go in," she said. "We'll have some coffee." They turned back without a word and walked into the kitchen. "Did you sleep okay?" she asked and blushed as she pictured his nakedness.

Matthew did not notice her heightened colour. "I was so tired I slept right through."

Alex wished she could say the same thing for herself. Instead, she'd spent most of the night lying awake and worrying about him. The rest of the time, she had done battle with her inner demons, trying to eradicate her feelings of love and desire for him, and telling herself to love him only as a friend.

She was thankful he was not aware of the turmoil of her emotions and relieved he was too busy coping with his own feelings to guess how she felt. She joined him at the table and as they sipped their hot drinks quietly for a few moments, she stole a look at him over the rim of her cup and saw a number of emotions fleeting across his face.

"What you said last night ..." Matthew spoke suddenly. "I've been thinking about it, and perhaps you're right."

He seemed to be struggling with his thoughts and she waited for him to go on.

"What I'm trying to say is that I've been going around pretending like Steve had just gone away temporarily. I've been too afraid to face the reality of what happened. Then, at the audition, I was under so much stress I somehow thought I saw him there. I really felt his presence, you know." He lowered his eyes, not trusting himself to remain in control.

"And now?" Alex asked. "How do you feel now?"

He took a few moments to answer. "I know now he's gone for good. I miss him so much, it hurts," he uttered, the pain in his voice evident, "but I know I wouldn't want him around, suffering like he did toward the end."

Alex felt relieved the old Matthew had finally returned. He was now grieving, as was to be expected, and however painful this might be for him, she knew he had already taken the first step toward healing.

"I think Steve would be proud to hear you say this," she consoled him. "He was always concerned about how you'd cope once he passed on, and now he must be at peace, knowing you'll be okay."

He smiled sadly. "They do say time heals all wounds, so I know I'll carry on living without him, but somehow I can't believe it just yet."

"I know," she agreed, thinking how long her own pain had lasted and how her stepfather still had the power to haunt her. She realised that even though she had never been through a loved one's death, her pain felt like she had experienced the death of her own youth.

* * *

Brent Perry peered thoughtfully at Matthew while he finished drinking a glass of Pellegrino. "I can only say I'm sorry, man," he said finally. "If you'd told me your partner passed away, I would never have sent you to the audition."

Matthew looked contrite. He felt he had lied by omission in not telling Brent about his domestic situation and as a result, his performance at the audition reflected negatively on the agency. "I know I should've told you. The last thing I wanted was to make you look bad."

"Why didn't you tell them what happened? They would've understood, you know. Instead, they think you weren't prepared and panicked." Brent's voice was mildly accusing.

Matthew's eyes hardened. "I don't really give a shit what they think!" He was upset at Brent's attitude. "If you want to call them and explain, go ahead. I don't mind; but don't treat Steve's death so lightly. I was too upset to explain anything at the time. I've already said I'm sorry, so don't push it anymore."

Brent regretted his words as he looked across at his client, an apology on his face. "I'm the one who's sorry, Matt. I shouldn't have said what I did. I *am* sorry for your loss."

This pacified Matthew, and he calmed down. "That's okay," his voice was gruff. "Like I said, I should have told you, but my only excuse is I was in denial about the whole thing."

Brent accepted his explanation. "So what do you want to do now?"

Matthew sighed. "I don't know. The experience at the audition really shook me up. I'm not sure I'm ready to go on acting. Maybe, I should just give up."

"You're not serious!" Brent exclaimed, surprised. "Matt, I realise it'll take time for you to get over this, but don't give up, man. I know you. I know the talent you have."

Matthew did not answer. He was tired of everything at the moment, and all he wanted to do was to go home and sleep. Sleep was the only thing that helped obliterate the whole of reality.

"I tell you what," Brent went on when he noticed Matthew's look of exhaustion. "Forget what happened at the audition. I'll phone them and explain. The casting agency's pretty cool; they'll understand. I want you to take some time off, so I won't put you up for anything for a few weeks unless another opportunity like this comes along. What do you say?"

Matthew took a few moments to think and finally nodded his consent.

* * *

As the days passed, Alex worked hard to restore the garden to some semblance of order, planting new jasmine seedlings along with baby rosebushes. In the afternoons, she worked on the outback articles she had discussed with her editor, and her spare time was spent with Matthew in the evenings.

On a few occasions, Mark visited her at home, and when Matthew was there, he made an extra effort to draw him out and get him chatting. During these times, Alex would disappear on the pretext that she had something to do in the house, leaving the boys to chat on their own. She thought it was good for Matthew to have company other than hers.

Gazza and Bazza also dropped by a few times, and one night they finally managed to drag Matthew out of the house for their boys' night out. Mark went along with them, together with some of his friends from the hotel. This was the only night when Matthew came home very late and, for the first time since Alex had known him, very drunk.

It was about two in the morning when she awoke to the sound of the front door being unlocked. There were a few giggles in the darkness, and Alex tiptoed out of bed to peek through the open crack of her bedroom door. She saw Gazza and Bazza helping Matthew up the stairs and into his room. When they came back out, Alex was waiting for them downstairs.

"Have a good night, boys?"

"It's been a long time since Matthew's been to Stonewall," Gazza confided. "The boy had some serious drinking to do."

Alex smiled faintly. "How serious is serious?"

Bazza laughed. "Well, I don't think he'll chuck up, if that's what you mean, but he'll be nursing a big headache in the morning."

"Charming." She was not amused.

"Oh, come on, darling." Gazza patted her shoulder. "Be happy for the boy. He needed to have some fun."

"Yeah!" Bazza agreed, adding, "And just think how interesting it was for Mark to be at Stonewall surrounded by a whole bunch of boys who found him irresistible. Is that sacrifice for friendship or what?"

Alex had to laugh at this. She could just imagine Mark trying to look unperturbed while surrounded by gay males checking him out. "Okay. I get the picture."

After the boys said their good nights, she checked on Matthew and found him stretched across the bed, out like a light. She covered him with a blanket and left him. This time, she was not going to undress him.

The following morning, while she was in the garden, Matthew joined her, still wearing the clothes from the previous night. She took one look at him and knew he was suffering from a huge hangover.

"Morning!" she said in a bright and chirpy voice. "Want some eggs?"

This was enough to send him scurrying back into the house— probably to throw up, Alex thought with a smile.

* * *

A few days later, Alex persuaded Matthew to accompany her to the grand opening of a new musical followed by a private supper with the cast, courtesy of one of her editors who wanted her to write an article for Gourmet Traveller magazine.

Knowing how important it was for Alex to get him out of the house, Matthew reluctantly agreed to accompany her. On this occasion, it was a very late night for them, arriving home sometime after three in the morning.

"Aren't you glad you came?" Alex asked while they sipped jasmine tea in the kitchen.

"Of course I'm glad," Matthew replied, having enjoyed the outing despite his state of mind. "It was a great show. Thank you for asking me along."

Alex flushed at the warmth in his voice. "It was nice to share it with you."

He smiled in response, but his eyes told her he was thinking of Steve and how he would have loved it even more if he could've shared the special moment with him.

"I better go to bed now," Alex said almost abruptly, a wounded look in her eyes. "Good night."

She left the kitchen so quickly that Matthew wondered if he'd said or done something to offend her. He had only thanked her for asking him along to the show—a show he had thoroughly enjoyed. Of course, if Steve had been with him, he knew he would have enjoyed it all the better.

Then, it struck him. Alex was in love with him. How blind he had been! She could probably tell he'd been thinking of Steve just now. How could he have been so thoughtless?

Now he recalled with sudden clarity Steve telling him, *"She loves you very much"* and *"Love her back; you're her only chance at finding happiness."* Matthew thought of Alex, who shivered every time he touched her and who'd looked uneasy when she had undressed him on the night of the storm.

His mind suddenly opened up and he realised Alex was like a partner to him: always supportive, consoling, and loving. Why had he failed to see this? Steve had certainly recognised it.

Matthew's heart cried out with pity for her—poor Alex, falling in love with a gay man. What could he possibly offer her in return? And what had Steve meant by loving her back? Matthew examined his feelings for her. He knew he loved her as a special friend, and he even found comfort when he had physical contact with her. She made him feel safe, but he didn't have sexual feelings for her. *Love her back; you're her only chance at finding happiness.* Steve's voice echoed inside his head. Surely, he had not meant for Matthew to become Alex's partner in every sense of the word. So what had he meant? *Love her back; you're her only chance at finding happiness.* Steve's words kept repeating themselves in his mind.

How could he be Alex's only chance at happiness? Alex could not possibly want to be with a man who was gay. She needed someone like Mark, someone who could love her as a woman—except she was afraid of intimacy. She broke out in a panic when Mark so much as touched her. Steve had told him she needed to express her sexuality in a "safe" environment. He had also said Matthew would know what to do when the time came.

Finally, it dawned on him. It was suddenly clear why he was Alex's only chance at finding happiness. Matthew smiled to himself.

He was rusty when it came to women, but he would try his best to help Alex face her worst fear.

This would be his gift of friendship to her—a gift to someone who had done so much for him.

CHAPTER 26

John Barry telephoned Matthew. "I'm calling to let you know the mortgage's been discharged and the rest of the money's now in your bank account." Matthew said nothing, and John went on. "The deed of the house is now in your name and everything's in order."

"Thanks, John," was all Matthew could manage to say through the lump that rose to his throat; memories of Steve crowding in on him. They quickly discussed the lawyer's fees for services rendered and John would email his invoice to Matthew; then, they rang off.

Alex saw the bleak look on Matthew's face when he walked into the kitchen to join her. "What is it?" she asked, her voice tinged with concern.

"That was the lawyer," he replied, accepting a cup of coffee from her. "Everything's settled." He couldn't keep the pain of loss from his voice.

"It's best that everything's out of the way. At least, now you can start afresh."

"I can't see it this way yet, Alex. The pain's too raw."

She patted his arm gently. "I know."

He sipped his coffee in silence, and his eyes filled with tears. He hated feeling so vulnerable and spoke while staring into his cup. "It's just that little by little, I'm losing pieces of him. And when the day comes that I sell this house, there'll be nothing left."

"You'll always have the memories inside you," Alex pointed out. "It's just the material things that are disappearing. The essence of Steve will be there for as long as you keep him in your heart."

The silent tears rolled down Matthew's face, and she reached out and wiped them dry. "Look at me," she uttered in a soft voice. He gazed into her eyes, and she went on, "I know no one will ever replace Steve in your heart, but you have to carry on with your life. You can't stop living because he moved on. His spirit's with you.

Your time together was wonderful, so hold on to that. No one can take it away from you—ever."

There was a lost look in her eyes when she said this. Matthew noticed it and remembered his thoughts of a few nights before. This time, it was he who reached out to her, caressing the side of her face. "Poor Alex," he said. "Here I am, unburdening myself to you, and I keep forgetting how much you've lost."

Alex couldn't find an appropriate reply but knew Matthew referred to her past and the absence of love from her life. The two looked into each other's eyes, sharing their sorrow in silence. Matthew's nearness disturbed her peace of mind, but the moment was so tender she dare not move. They stayed suspended like this for what seemed a long time when in actual fact, it was only a few seconds. Then, Matthew's face moved closer to hers, with his mouth only a couple of inches away from her own, and his breath softly fanned her face. Alex couldn't look away. She was mesmerised by the deep blue colour of his eyes. Her body tingled with an expectancy that threatened to undo her self-control and her lips parted slightly as she held her breath.

The jarring ring of the telephone startled them both. Alex jumped, blushing. Matthew snapped out of his trance-like state and went to answer the call. Meanwhile, Alex, her whole body shaken by the experience, started to do the breakfast dishes. She wondered what would have happened if the phone had not rung.

She felt confused and tears threatened to escape her eyes. Surely, Matthew was not attracted to her in that way. He was mourning Steve. He was gay. And even if he were straight, she thought, he was too good looking to be attracted to someone like her.

By the time Matthew returned to the kitchen, she'd managed to compose herself and was glad of it because he looked totally in control as if nothing had happened.

"Things will never cease to amaze me," he declared in wonder.

"What happened?" She was pleased her voice sounded normal.

"That was Brent. Remember the audition I stuffed up?"

How could she forget?

"Well, it turns out there were some delays with the shooting schedule. The director wasn't happy with the actors he saw, so they're doing another casting round." His eyes were bright all of a sudden.

"And?"

"Brent explained to the casting agent about my circumstances, and they want to see me again."

Alex smiled, happy for him. "That's wonderful! You didn't miss out after all."

A shadow of doubt crossed his eyes. "I only hope I can do it right this time."

"You will," she answered confidently. "Now that you've acknowledged your grief, you can do anything you like."

"I hope so, but it's only been a few weeks. I don't know if I'm ready."

In the face of his doubt, Alex forgot all about her own emotions and knew she had to encourage him to go on. "Matthew, this is a wonderful opportunity for you; and it's come around again. I think it was meant to be," she reasoned. "So don't let it go now, not after all the hard work you've put in. Don't let go of your dream!"

Matthew continued to look pensive.

"When's the audition?" she asked.

"In two days' time."

"Good," she said, taking charge. "We have time to brush up on your lines."

"What would I do without you?" he remarked, giving her a warm smile.

"You'd manage," she stated in a matter-of-fact tone while her heart broke at the thought.

* * *

That evening, they worked on Matthew's lines and this time Alex was the one to go to bed early. She was exhausted by the roller coaster of emotions brought on by her feelings for him.

While she lay in the dark trying to fall asleep, she told herself to detach from the situation. It was insane to be in love with a gay man, and more insane to expect him to return her feelings. She didn't understand what had happened in the kitchen earlier that day, but whatever it was, it couldn't have been anything serious on his part. In any case, he would be moving on soon; his need for her was at an end. Even in his grief, she sensed his increasing strength, and it was obvious he was gradually getting on with his life as she must get on with hers.

She had no doubt that sometime soon Matthew would put up the house for sale and set his sights on LA. What would she do then? A feeling of loneliness descended upon her. Would she go back to her rolling stone life or settle in Sydney? Now that she had spent so much time in one spot, she didn't feel like uprooting herself all over again. Once Matthew was gone, though, what would she have left? Steve was gone; Matthew would be gone; the house sold—and she would have to find another place to live and start all over, alone as always.

What about Mark? a small voice popped into her head. Mark was just a friend, nothing else. He was charming and attractive, but it was Matthew she loved, not Mark. Are you sure you love Matthew for himself or because it's safe to love him? the voice persisted. Who knows, Alex thought in frustration. All she knew for sure was that her body tingled with desire every time Matthew touched her. She didn't seem to be afraid of his touch; in fact, she yearned for it. But you tingled with desire when Mark touched you, too—only you ran away in a panic, the voice challenged her.

Stop it! Alex told her wayward thoughts. She knew for a fact that she didn't yearn for Mark like she did for Matthew. In any case, there was no point in thinking about Mark, or any other male, as long as she was afraid of intimacy. An image of her stepfather rose to her mind, but instead of breaking into a panic, this time Alex was filled with a hatred so strong she bunched her hands into fists and punched the mattress several times, pretending it was his face that she was hitting.

I hate you! I hate you so much, you bastard! The words filled her head, pushing out everything else as tears of helplessness rolled down her face. Suddenly, she remembered a conversation she'd had with Steve a long time ago. It was something about forgiveness. She'd told Steve she could not imagine ever being able to forgive her stepfather for what he had done.

The thought now occurred to her that forgiveness did not mean she had to condone his actions; she only needed to release him from her mind so she could go on living without the deep hate she held in her heart. As long as she hung onto her hate and anger, she knew she would never be able to find happiness with anyone.

Desperate for resolution, Alex burst into tears of frustration, turning her face into the pillow in case Matthew heard her. How could she forgive what had been done to her? Searching for answers that would not come, she cried for a long time, only stopping when she was totally spent. In that silence, she became aware of a peaceful feeling taking over her body and soul. *Let it go, Alex*, a voice spoke inside her mind; and from the depths of her being, she knew the voice belonged to Steve.

A fresh wave of tears overcame her, but instead of crying from desperation, she cried with gratitude. She felt Steve's presence all around her, his pure love enveloping her, dissolving her hate and anger. All that was left was a kind of acceptance, and with acceptance came the realisation her stepfather was a very sick man. He was a man who did not know any better, a man tormented by secret demons of his own; for nothing short of evil could have made him do what he did.

Alex actually felt pity for this sick man—pity he was living with the burden of his sick acts—because she knew he would have to confront his actions within his own conscience some day. She felt pity for him because he was not capable of loving anyone or anything, including himself. He was a prisoner of his own twisted desires; and seeing all of this clearly for the first time in her life, Alex's newfound pity for her stepfather was transformed into forgiveness.

Steve's presence was still all around her, and she wished she could reach out and hug him.

"Thank you, my friend," she spoke into the darkness; and before she fell asleep, her mind was filled with the beauty of the compassion she had always seen in Steve's eyes.

* * *

If Matthew noticed her puffy eyes the next morning, he kept any comments to himself. Alex seemed distracted with her thoughts, and though they chatted over breakfast, he could tell she was only half listening. They finished eating in silence, and he rushed off to the gym.

In the evening, he offered to help with making dinner. They were standing side by side, Alex peeling potatoes and washing vegetables and Matthew getting the chicken ready for their favourite curry, when the telephone rang.

"I'll get it," Alex said, drying her hands with a tea towel.

Matthew carried on with his task but could not help overhearing her conversation on the phone.

'Hi, Mark, how are you?" Alex sounded tired. A pause while Mark was speaking, and then, "No, I don't really think it's a good idea." Another pause. "I know I said we could be friends; and we are, aren't we?"

Matthew could not hear any more. Alex must have lowered her voice. When she returned to the kitchen, she carried on with her work and did not speak again until they sat down to dinner.

"How are you feeling about the audition tomorrow morning?" she asked.

"Nervous," Matthew answered, "but I think I'll be all right."

"Sure you will. You'll see."

They ate in silence for a while before Matthew spoke. "Alex, is there something wrong between you and Mark?"

She looked at him guardedly, but replied casually, "No. What could possibly be wrong?"

"Come on, this is me you're talking to," he reminded her.

"All right," she sighed with exasperation. "If you must know, he's asked me out, and I said no."

"How come?"

She felt suddenly irritated. "What's the point, Matthew? He keeps hanging around, hoping I'll become more than a friend; and you know I can't do that. It's not fair to keep the guy hanging on forever."

"But how do you feel about him?"

"I don't know." She sounded confused. "Surely, it's better to forget all about him, don't you think?"

"Are you asking for my advice?" He searched her eyes and only read more confusion in them.

"Maybe."

He smiled faintly. "You either are or you're not."

"Okay, I am!"

"Well, calm down first."

She took a deep breath and smiled at him. "I'm fine now."

He looked at her warily. "I think if you like him—and it seems to me that you do—you should give it another chance." He waited for her response.

A look of disappointment crossed her face, followed by one of resignation and then apprehension. "I don't know," she said finally. "Maybe I'm just not ready."

Matthew did not pursue the subject further. He knew exactly what she had been thinking. She was disappointed her love for him was something impossible and was resigned to the fact that he was gay and nothing would change this. At the same time, she was apprehensive at the idea of giving Mark another chance because of her fear. Once again, Matthew thought about his role in helping her overcome this.

"You're disappointed with me, right?" Alex cut into his thoughts.

"Of course not. What you do is up to you. I simply hate to see you like this."

"Like what?" She frowned.

"Don't get upset," he placated her. "I meant this whole thing of your past. I just wish I could help you erase it somehow."

"Thank you for saying that," she responded gently, "but I don't think any of us can erase past hurts so easily. But we can learn to forgive ... I guess."

Matthew was surprised at this statement. He had expected to hear words of bitterness. "You sounded like Steve just now."

A secret smile played on her lips. "Maybe I've been getting good advice from him."

He gazed at her quizzically, but she did not expand on her comment.

* * *

The following morning, Matthew set off early for his audition while Alex slept. He left her a note to tell her he would be going to the gym afterwards.

Alex was sorry to have missed him as she had wanted to wish him good luck. After breakfast, she worked in the garden for a couple of hours and found the exercise stimulating. The day was warm, and by the time she finished she had worked up a sweat and decided to take a shower.

In the bathroom, she undressed and was suddenly overcome by the urge to look at her body. She stood naked in front of the mirror and was amazed to feel nothing, except for a general curiosity about her looks. In the past, she had never been able to look at herself. She'd hated the body that had attracted her stepfather.

Now, all these feelings seemed to have disappeared and what she saw was a slim woman with full breasts and a firm body. Though not a great fan of exercise, she had kept fit by years of hard work in the outback, all the walking she had done during her travels, and most recently, the work she put into Steve's garden. She had no opinion to offer on her looks, though. Living in a society where pressure was put on women to look almost anorexic, she thought she would never make model of the year, but she felt her body was okay. At least, Mark certainly thought so. She blushed at this thought and quickly jumped into the shower.

* * *

Brent called a couple of days after the audition and gave Matthew the good news. Alex was in the garden when he rushed over to her, picked her up from the waist, and swung her round.

"I got it, Alex! It's mine!" His eyes were lit with excitement.

Alex was thrilled for him. "Congratulations! I knew you'd get it," she exclaimed when he put her down.

His arms remained around her body and he grinned at her. "Well," he told her, a wicked sparkle in his eyes, "what are you waiting for, woman, aren't you going to kiss me?"

She smiled and went to kiss his cheek, but his hand snaked out at that moment and came to rest at the back of her neck, guiding her lips to his. She tried to pull away immediately, but he kept her there through his superior strength.

He kissed her full on the mouth. It was a firm kiss, but the kind of kiss that could have been shared by close friends and not necessarily lovers. When he released her, he saw the hot flush across her face and could not help saying, "Don't tell me you found the kiss distasteful." Alex was speechless, and he laughed. "Are you going to be a prude now?"

"No," she finally stated with dignity. "I simply didn't expect it."

"Well, I thought the occasion called for something more than a peck on the cheek." He gave her a dazzling smile. "I'm off to have a shower now."

She watched him disappear into the house while she still felt the imprint of his mouth on hers.

$* * *$

"Gazza called," Matthew announced during dinner that evening. "When I told him about the audition, he invited me to Stonewall to celebrate with the boys." He searched Alex's face for a reaction. "Sorry I can't ask you to come along, but it's a boys' thing."

"It's okay. I'm not into getting pissed drunk, anyway." Her tone was dry.

He glanced at her, a smile on his lips. "You disapprove, don't you?"

"Why should I care if you decide to drink?"

"Oh, listen to you, Alex," he protested. "You sound like I do this all the time." He sounded affronted but was only teasing her.

She knew this and looked at him with mock severity. "Well, don't come crying to me later when you're suffering from a huge hangover."

"Don't worry. I won't let it happen."

"We'll see," she told him, totally unimpressed.

They looked at each other and laughed.

"Okay," she uttered. "Go, and have fun."

"We'll celebrate tomorrow night," he said. "I'll take you out to dinner."

"You don't have to," she remarked casually but could not help feeling excited at the prospect.

CHAPTER 27

Matthew left for Stonewall straight after dinner, and Alex decided to work on the last of her outback articles. It was around eight when she finished. The weather had changed in the afternoon, bringing gusty winds and grey clouds laden with rain, and she hoped there wouldn't be a repeat of the storm that had destroyed the garden last time. Even as she thought this, she heard the first drops of rain beginning to fall outside.

She felt chilled and played with the idea of having an early night, but instead decided to watch television for a while. She got comfortable on the sofa with a throw around her shoulders and switched on the TV set. A documentary on ancient Egypt was playing and she became so engrossed in the program that she was surprised, a short while later, when she heard a key turn in the lock and the front door opened to reveal Matthew, looking wet from the rain.

"What happened?" she exclaimed, thinking about what ensued the last time Matthew came in during a storm. "I didn't expect to see you till sometime tomorrow morning."

Matthew wore a look of sadness when he replied, "I decided to come home early."

Alex felt she could almost reach out and touch his emotions; they were so plain to see. "Not much fun, huh?"

He paused for a moment, not knowing what to say. "It wasn't that so much as the fact I was in the middle of a cheerful crowd, the boys happy for me, you know—and then, I thought of Steve."

She nodded with understanding. There were going to be many moments like this for Matthew, and her heart went out to him. "Do you want something hot to drink?"

"No, thanks. I think I'll go to bed." He wished her good night and went upstairs.

Alex returned to the program she'd been watching but did not take anything in. She felt depressed for Matthew. Finally, his dream was becoming a reality and Steve was not here to share it with him. She sighed and her eyes closed for a moment from the warmth in the room. She dozed off for a while and when she woke up, the program had already finished. She glanced at her watch, it was past midnight, and she switched off the TV and lights, and headed upstairs to the bathroom. She decided to have a hot shower before bed to take away the chill she felt.

Later, while she was making her way to her room, she noticed a light peeping from underneath Matthew's door. She hesitated for a moment, then went to the door and knocked softly. A faint "come in" told her he was still awake. Alex entered the room and found him sitting up in bed. As she moved closer, she noticed his eyes looked a little red. He had been crying.

"Are you having trouble sleeping?" she asked. "Do you want a sedative?"

"No. I don't want any drugs. They only take the edge off the pain, but when the effect wears off, it feels worse than before." His voice was subdued.

"I'm sorry you feel sad on your night of celebration," she said softly.

"That's okay. These things happen. One minute I'm up, the next I'm down. It'll get better one day." He then noticed her standing barefoot. "It's cold out. Why don't you climb in here for a while?"

Alex's senses came alive in that instant and she hated her body for betraying her calm demeanour. "I think I should let you sleep."

"I'm not sleepy yet. Stay and talk with me."

His offer was too hard to resist and she climbed into bed without a second prompting. The rain still fell outside, though not as strong as on the night of the storm, and she was grateful for the warmth of the bed. She ignored the fact that Matthew wore his habitual pyjama bottoms with nothing on top, and she told her body to shut up and stop tingling.

"Alex, there's something I want to talk to you about," Matthew remarked, his voice serious.

Alex braced herself, somehow knowing this would be about her. "What is it?" Her mouth went dry all of a sudden.

He hesitated for a moment. "I don't know how to say this

without sounding presumptuous or even condescending."

She waited for him to continue; her stomach tight with nerves.

He turned to her so he could look into her eyes. "The thing is ... I think I know ..."

A feeling of mortification crept over her instantly and she suddenly knew what he was trying to say. "I'm sorry if I've embarrassed you," she cried before he could go on. "I'll move out as soon as possible." She made to get out of bed. All she wanted was to escape to the safety of her room, but Matthew reached out and caught her by the arm, pulling her back against the pillows. He was laughing softly.

"You're a real nut sometimes, you know that?"

She was confused. "What is it then? I'm trying to understand what you want to say."

"You're not embarrassing me. My only concern is you're wasting your feelings on someone who's always going to be gay."

Alex closed her eyes in shame. He had seen right through her. He knew she loved him. Why didn't the mattress just swallow her up? Instead, she jumped with shock when she felt his lips kiss her closed eyelids. Her eyes flew open; he was smiling.

"You're a real goose, aren't you?" he said affectionately. "You shouldn't be ashamed of how you feel. I'm honoured you feel this way. All I'm trying to say to you is that I can never be what you want me to be because of whom I really am." He caressed the side of her face. "I love you in my own way, too. You must know this; but my kind of love isn't the kind that would fulfill you."

Alex closed her eyes again. Matthew's directness hurt her, but she knew he was being honest and realistic. All this time, it was she who had been fantasising about something that could never become a reality. To her horror, she felt tears well up in her eyes and escape through her closed eyelids.

"Aw, don't cry." Matthew's voice was so gentle it made her tears worse, and then he was kissing them away.

Alex let him do this for a while, enjoying his touch, but then she opened her eyes and gazed into his. Her emotions in control now, she spoke, "Please forgive me. I never meant for this to happen."

"There's nothing to forgive." He reached out and brought her closer to him. "Come here."

They snuggled close together, and she found the warmth from

his body comforting. For a while they said nothing; they simply enjoyed the physical contact. Then, Matthew spoke again, his voice almost a whisper. "About this fear of yours—I want to help you." He felt her body tense up.

"What are you saying?" She was wary.

"I want to share with you the experience of making love. I want to show you there's nothing to fear."

Alex was stunned. "But ... I mean ... You just said that ..." She didn't know how to put it into words. She was afraid and excited at the same time, and her thoughts were a jumble of confusion.

"Making love's about expressing yourself and your feelings for your partner," he explained patiently. "It's about giving and getting pleasure from a beautiful act that's intimate and very special."

"But ..." She finally found what she wanted to say. "Why would you want to do this? You just said you'll always be gay."

"Yes, I'm gay. But I wasn't always with men. Steve was my first." Matthew was amused now. "I have made love to plenty of women before, I'll have you know."

Alex's body relaxed in his arms, and he knew she was trying to understand even though she still looked puzzled.

"You're my best friend, Alex," he went on, "and you've been hurt by something that's still affecting you to a huge extent. I care about this very much, and I want to help you get past it. So will you trust me?"

As if in a trance, Alex nodded slightly. She could not look at him because she felt painfully shy. Her body, however, ached for his touch even if she still felt some fear at what was to come. And yet, she wanted this more than anything else.

"I promise I won't hurt you," he spoke softly.

Like a child afraid of the dark, she asked, "But what if I panic?"

He smiled reassuringly. "Then, I'll stop. If there's anything you don't like, simply say so. I'm your friend, remember this. I'm not here to hurt or take advantage of you in any way."

Again, she nodded shyly, barely able to maintain eye contact with him. Matthew sensed her feelings and reached out to switch off the bedside lamp. The room was cast into darkness, and the only visible light came from the street lamp outside. Alex tensed again, waiting for him to make a move. He couldn't help but laugh softly, and then he kissed her lightly on the lips.

"Relax," he whispered and kissed her again gently.

Alex closed her eyes and surrendered to the pleasurable sensation of being touched by him; a wonderful warmth spread right through her body.

When Matthew felt her relax, his mouth became more insistent and his kiss turned deep and searching. Alex moaned with desire and her mouth opened under his as their tongues met in erotic play. The familiar black wall of fear did not rise up to meet her, and Alex instinctively knew what they were doing was right. This was meant to be and no matter what happened in the future, she would always look upon this as an act of unconditional love—given to her by her dearest and closest friend.

Matthew's hands began to undress her and she followed suit, abandoning herself to the feelings coursing through her. Her hands touched him with eager fingers as she helped him off with his pyjama bottoms, seeking his nakedness underneath. She ran her hands all over his body, enjoying the feel of skin and firm muscle. She ventured further into what she considered to be forbidden territory and her fingers wrapped themselves around his hardness.

Matthew's body arched toward hers in pleasure, but he gently moved her hand away. "Not yet," he whispered in her ear.

Alex was thrown into a myriad of intense and pleasurable sensations as his hands travelled to her breasts and his mouth kissed her nipples. His tongue tasted them and teased them. His mouth then moved lower over her stomach while his hands slid off her panties. They came off in one smooth move; his mouth now played across her belly.

Alex moaned again; the heat of desire rushed down to her pelvis as his mouth found her secret place and his tongue started to explore the moist darkness within. She gasped in shock at the mounting feeling of heat and thought she would faint from the pleasure of it. All of a sudden, her body became engulfed in a series of overwhelming spasms, which lead to a wonderful sense of release that was beyond words. Matthew had played her body like a master violinist, exacting the exquisite music of love—the kind of love that had the power to melt away everything ugly and gross in the world.

Alex was left in wonder at this beautiful act of intimacy and felt no fear whatsoever when his body moved on top of hers. She tasted herself on his tongue when he kissed her. This was a sensation so erotic, there was an instant rush of wetness between her legs, and the now familiar heat of desire gathered in her pelvis once more. Matthew slid into her, moving deeply; each thrust bringing her closer to release. She wrapped her legs around him and rose up to meet his every thrust, and this time the spasms were deeper. When she felt the wonderful sense of release, she became aware of a hot rush permeating her inner depths—Matthew had climaxed into her.

She opened her eyes and gazed straight into his, and even in the darkness of the room she could still make out the tenderness in them. He smiled and kissed her softly while he moved to lie next to her.

"No panic?" He grinned, knowing very well that he had left her entirely satisfied and without any fear whatsoever.

Alex shook her head. "I never knew it could be like this," she uttered in wonder, her voice soft, still shy. Her body felt light and alive in the aftermath of their intimacy.

"And now you do."

She kissed his face. "Thank you," she said. It was a childlike gesture, like kissing an uncle after being taken to the circus.

Matthew was touched. She seemed so innocent, and yet her innocence had been brutally taken long ago. He felt for her but lightened the moment by remarking, "That's okay. You'll get my invoice in the mail."

They laughed, and Alex rested her head against his chest and smelled the musky aroma of their lovemaking. She sighed with contentment and closed her eyes, thankful that no images of fear had risen to haunt her. She was finally free of the darkness.

"Oh, no!" Matthew exclaimed suddenly.

"What is it?"

"God, I'm sorry, Alex. In the midst of it all, I forgot to use protection." His voice reflected his concern.

A lump rose to her throat and her voice was tinged with sadness when she replied, "That's all right. I can never have children—there was too much damage."

Matthew felt hot anger course through his body. "That bastard," he muttered.

"No matter," she replied. "It wasn't meant to be."

"Maybe not, but I hate the fact that he took so much away from you."

Alex exalted in the luxury of being able to run her hand across his chest in a soft caress. "But you gave so much more back to me," she uttered, her voice soft.

"You're a beautiful person, and there are plenty of straight men out there who'd want to make love to you."

"Perhaps so. But in all these years, I could never stand having a man touch me—except for you."

Her total honesty and trust affected him more than he cared to admit. "Well, we can be thankful to Steve," he said to cover up his feelings. "He was the one who opened my eyes."

Alex raised her head to look at him. "About what?" she asked, suspicion creeping into her tone.

Matthew wondered if he'd said the wrong thing, but it was too late to take it back now. "What I meant was Steve made me aware of your love, and during his last days he told me to love you back. He said he wouldn't be jealous."

"You mean to say he told you to make love to me?" Alex suddenly sat up in bed, astounded.

"Not in so many words. He only hinted that I should be here for you."

"Yes," Alex remarked, lying back down but sounding almost disappointed, "but you knew what he meant." Why couldn't this gesture have been Matthew's idea? Why did it have to come from Steve?

"Honestly, Alex. I didn't know what he meant." Matthew knew he had upset her.

"So why make love to me, then?" She was not quite ready to believe him.

"It was because of that night when we came back from the musical. I said or did something to hurt you, when all you were trying to do was thank me for sharing the time with you."

Alex remembered. She knew Matthew had been thinking of Steve, and she had behaved like a self-centred idiot. "Matthew, you didn't do anything wrong. You were only thinking of Steve. I was being selfish."

"Well, it doesn't matter. The point is I did a lot of thinking since then and realised how you felt. That's when I knew I wanted to share this experience with you. You've done so much for me and gave so much of yourself. But it wasn't until that night that I realised I hadn't given anything in return."

Alex was moved by what he said. "True friends love unconditionally," she pointed out. "I didn't expect anything back. I was happy to be with you, and that was enough." Then, she added with an impish smile on her lips, "However, I would like to say I'm glad we did this."

Matthew laughed, relieved the moment of tension between them had passed. "If you keep going on about it, my ego will never fit through the door."

"Okay. I'll shut up now."

They lay in silence, listening to the steady fall of rain, and in a matter of minutes, they fell fast asleep.

* * *

Alex awoke with a start, feeling disoriented before realising she was naked and lying next to Matthew. Only a few hours earlier they'd made love. Her face grew hot at the thought. It was still raining steadily outside. The luminous clock on the bedside table showed it was 4:15. She needed to go to the bathroom.

Matthew was fast asleep so she picked up her discarded pyjama top and noiselessly climbed out of bed. In the bathroom, she stood in front of the mirror and examined her naked body. Nothing had changed. It still looked the same. She shook her head at her fanciful thoughts and smiled. Lovemaking was not going to turn her into a toad after all.

Matthew was still asleep when she returned to the bedroom. Looking at him, Alex felt a renewal of her deep love for this man. She accepted the fact that he was not meant for her, but she loved him all the same and always would—no matter where they went to from here.

CHAPTER 28

Alex escaped to her room to dress in the morning. She wasn't sure how she was going to face Matthew after their lovemaking, so she continuously reminded herself nothing had changed between them, except that Matthew had simply "helped her out", as he put it, with her fear.

Down the hall, she heard the shower running. Matthew was up, and it was time to get breakfast ready. As she turned to leave the room, her eyes came to rest upon the picture above her bed. With a smile, she pulled off the cloth covering the print of the two naked male bodies. She stood back and took a long look at it. The picture no longer had the power to disturb her.

Alex silently said goodbye to her fear of the past and left the room.

* * *

The aroma of freshly brewed coffee wafted through the air when Matthew entered the kitchen. Alex was busy cooking breakfast.

"Hi," he said by way of greeting.

Her cheeks flushed red. "Hello." Her voice was barely audible.

They smiled shyly at each other, not knowing how to behave. Matthew took the initiative and with a wicked glint in his eyes, asked, "Did you sleep well?"

"Like a log." She smiled at him, feeling more at ease. "Why don't you help set the table?" They worked in silence until breakfast was ready.

Despite the awkwardness of the situation they were in, Matthew did not mind. He acknowledged he had derived pleasure from making love to Alex. It brought to mind the days when he had been with Erica, his ex-fiancée, and other girls before her. Making love with Alex did not change the way he felt about her even though he'd enjoyed what they'd shared. He still only loved her as a friend and knew their relationship could never be as it had been with Steve.

Matthew was surprised, however, as he admitted to himself that he would be happy to go on having a physical relationship with Alex for the time being, as long as she wanted it. Of course, he would never intentionally hurt her feelings or raise her hopes. She would have to understand the arrangement could end at any moment. If she found this to be difficult or she felt the need to move on, he knew he would be equally happy for her, no matter what she decided.

He would never have imagined himself becoming sexually entangled with a woman again. Perhaps, in his loss of Steve, Matthew depended on Alex for too many of his needs. This was hardly fair to her, and yet he knew he filled needs within her at the same time. It was as though fate had brought them together so they could survive through this time in their lives—a time filled with fear, loss, and the need to face an uncertain future.

"Brekkie's ready," Alex announced, breaking into his thoughts.

They ate in silence, both of them quite hungry; and once they finished, they relaxed over coffee.

"When did you find out you couldn't have kids?" Matthew asked, still harbouring a deep anger for the monster that had damaged her so profoundly.

A shadow crossed over her eyes. "When I ran away from home, I went to see a doctor. I was having terrible pains in my pelvic area. The doctor checked me out and couldn't believe the damage to my womb. By that time, it had all healed, but there was still a lot of scar tissue left. The short of it is that I can never bear a child." Pensive, she sipped her coffee. "The thing is, I was only fifteen at the time, you know; so not being able to bear children didn't really bother me. And since I couldn't stand the touch of a man, anyway, I'd already resigned myself to a life of being single and without kids."

Matthew regarded her with concern; however, she seemed quite in control of her emotions. "And now?"

"And now what?"

"Well, now that you *can* stand being touched by a man, you may want to get married one day."

She laughed suddenly. "I don't think I'll ever get married."

"Why not?"

"I'm too used to being on my own for one thing. Besides, I don't know if I could share my life with another person." Wistfully, she added, "I don't think I'll ever find my soul mate, as people call it, and I really don't want to be with second best."

"What about Mark?"

"Mark's not my soul mate. He's just a friend."

"You find him attractive, don't you?"

I find you attractive, she wanted to say, but the look in her eyes said it for her.

Matthew wasn't sure how to handle the situation. The last thing he wanted was to hurt her feelings, and yet, he felt he had to be honest with her. "Alex, what happened between us—"

"I know, I know," she interrupted. "You're gay and will never be anything else." She said it for him without any feeling of resentment, only a little sadness.

He smiled faintly. "That's not exactly what I was going to say, but yes, you're right." He noted the disappointment mixed with fear in her face. Could it be fear of what lay ahead for her? "Alex, I want you to hear me out," he said carefully. "And please let me finish what I need to say before you respond. It's difficult enough as it is, but I need to say it."

She nodded, waiting for him to explain.

"Through my whole life, I never really loved anyone," Matthew paused, thoughtful for a moment. "Well, as a young child, I did love my parents, at least until they started putting me on show. Then, I loved Conchita, our housekeeper, because she was the only one who used to hug me. But as I grew up, I never knew what real love was like until I met Steve and my whole life changed.

"All this time, I'd been walking around with a chip on my shoulder because people always reacted to my looks and never took the time to really see me. I used to hate the way I looked, until Steve taught me to accept myself the way I am. He taught me about loving unconditionally, which is the only way he knew how to love. I was so very lucky to have found him. Finally, here was someone who loved me, not for the way I looked but for who I was. Before Steve, there was Erica; and before her, there were other girls. But they were all shallow. All they wanted was to get me into bed. None of them saw me as I was; they never saw past the looks and the body. Besides, it just never felt quite right for me to be with a woman."

Seeing the pain in his eyes, Alex realised that being attractive could be a curse rather than a blessing. In a way, it was like being rich—you never knew who your real friends were.

"I was happy with Steve," Matthew went on. "With him, I could be myself, and I knew no matter what happened in my life, I always had his love. Nothing could hurt me, you know. I felt invincible." Tears gathered in his eyes and he paused for a moment before continuing, "When he died, I felt so frightened. All of a sudden, I was back on my own, like I was before I met him; and I was certain I wouldn't be able to carry on.

"But all through this time, without my realising it, there was someone in the background watching over me, supporting me, caring for me, and finally, consoling me when Steve passed on." His eyes held her gaze, imparting the emotion he felt. "That someone was you. Steve died, but I wasn't left alone. You became a true friend—one who not only helped Steve during his illness, but also helped me get through the tough times. You're still helping me; so in my own way, I love you, too."

Alex looked into her cup, feeling the pinprick of tears. "I know you love me in your own way," she spoke softly. "I also know there may never be another Steve for you. You loved him totally and completely—he was your soul mate, and you were blessed to have him." She sighed, feeling so alone even though she had Matthew, at least, for the moment. "What I'm trying to say is you don't have to tell me why you can't love me like you loved Steve. I don't expect that. I also know I'm not your soul mate, not in the way Steve was. I'd like to think, though, that I'm your *soul mate in friendship*." She smiled at the idea, and continued, "I must admit I was guilty, just like all those girls in your past, of being initially attracted to you for your looks. I built a stupid fantasy about you in my head because of it, but this helped me move a step closer to healing; and the more I got to know you the more I knew I loved you for who you really are. So even though it can never be for us, and I accept this, I want you to know that no matter what happens in the future, I'll always feel the way I do about you. I'll never ask for something you can't give, though." She confessed her innermost thoughts and now waited for his reaction.

"I admit I did resent you for a time when I felt you were reacting to my looks," he responded, moved by what she had just said. "But thanks to Steve, I began to realise you weren't after my body for sex. Well," he added, giving her a cheeky smile that eased the tension between them, "at least not then. I realised you found me safe to be with and that you trusted me. You also craved physical comfort and for some reason, I was the only one who could provide it. So in the end, I'm glad I did. And in the process, I came to care very much for you, just as you do for me." Cocking one eyebrow in an impish manner, he asked, "You do care for me, don't you?"

Alex laughed. "You know I do, so don't make this difficult."

"Okay, I was only teasing. Opening our hearts to each other is heavy going."

"I know. But it's got to be done, right?"

He nodded. "Yes. And this why I need to ask you one more question."

She tensed. "What's that?"

"Well, until I decide about LA, what is it that you expect to happen between us?"

LA was like a slap across the face for her. It stood for reality and for the fact that in a short time Matthew would be going off to America—away from her. She tried to ignore the pain of this and knew when the time came she would have to let him go for good.

"I ..." Her breath caught, and she could not answer his question. The thought of LA was too much to bear at present.

He came around to her side of the table, drawing her to her feet. Alex stood facing him, hating the tears that rolled down her face. He took her in his arms and held her, stroking her hair. "I'm not going away just yet, but you know eventually I will. It's what I've always wanted to do."

She nodded, burying her face in his chest.

"But no matter where I go, you'll always be my friend. We'll keep in touch. Maybe, when I'm famous, you can even visit me and write your stories from there," Matthew remarked, trying to comfort her.

She laughed, but it only came out as a muffled sob.

"Hey," Matthew uttered, "look at me." Slowly, she raised her face to his. "Let's not think about LA for now. I'm not ready yet to make that kind of decision. In the meantime, I want to remain your friend if you want me to."

Alex looked puzzled. "You already are my friend."

He kissed her lips gently. "You know what I mean."

Suddenly suspicious, she drew away from him slightly. "Why would you want this? I don't want you having sex with me because you pity me!"

He sighed. This was such a difficult thing for him to explain. "It's not about pity. It's about wanting to be with you. I'm human, too, you know. You're not the only one who's found our lovemaking enjoyable." He saw her flush. "I know I sound selfish when I say this," he added, "but for me, being with you has been comforting and wonderful. I want you to know, however, that no matter what you decide, I'll be your friend under any circumstances. I don't want to put you under any pressure."

Alex gazed into his beautiful eyes for a long time, weighing what he had said. Matthew was obviously in need of physical comfort to help him cope with his loss, and she was in need of physical comfort to help her erase her past. They were two peas in a pod.

Right now, he was asking whether she would be strong enough to let go once he decided it was time. She knew he didn't want to hurt her feelings, so the choice was hers—she could live with him as a friend or as a lover; and if the latter was her choice, then she would have to release him in due course.

She didn't have to think about it twice nor did she have to communicate her answer in words, either. Slowly, she brought her lips to his and kissed him, gently at first. Then, as desire swept through her body, she thrust her tongue into his mouth in search of his.

Matthew responded eagerly, and it was his unrestrained physical response that caused him to wonder if he had done the right thing by becoming involved with his best friend.

* * *

They spent all day together talking, eating, and making love. It was as if they had just discovered sex and couldn't stop.

For Alex, this was somewhat true. For Matthew, after so many months of repressing his own sexuality due to Steve's illness, it was as though his whole being had suddenly come alive and his newfound energy needed to be spent.

"I think I've unleashed a sex fiend," he teased her after one of their lovemaking sessions.

"You asked for it," was the rejoinder.

They were both looking up at the ceiling while they lay in bed, watching spots of light reflected from the street outside.

"Matthew," Alex said, her voice no longer teasing.

"Mm?"

"Why haven't you been to visit Steve's grave yet?"

The question took him by surprise and he raised himself on one elbow to look at her. "What makes you ask that all of a sudden?"

"I don't know. I just thought of it. It's been over six weeks since ..." She hesitated, not wanting to upset him. "Well, maybe I shouldn't have asked."

"It's okay." He lay back on the pillow. "I guess I don't believe Steve's inside that coffin anymore—at least not his soul, anyway."

She thought about his reply. "It's true what you say, but more like something I would expect Steve to say."

Matthew smiled. "Maybe a lot of Steve's rubbed off on me."

"I guess so." She was quiet for a moment before suddenly asking, "Do you think Steve would disapprove of what we're doing?"

Matthew could not help smiling at the concern in her voice. "There's a lot about Steve you don't know. He was a very open-minded person. Besides, he never once doubted my love for him. While he was alive, I never looked at anyone else. But even if I had, it wouldn't have worried him. He told me so once. I remember his saying that what we had was so strong it transcended the physical aspect of our relationship."

"So then you think it's okay?" She did not sound very convinced.

He raised himself on his elbow again. "Alex, if for one minute I thought what we're sharing would upset Steve, I'd never do it. There are many ways of expressing love, and there are many different kinds of love. What we have is unique to us, and if Steve knew—well, maybe he does know—he would be happy for us."

Alex sighed in relief. "Steve was such an unselfish person."

"He was, and still is." Matthew's heart ached for Steve all of a sudden, and a fresh wave of emotional pain hit him like a floodtide. He was thankful it was dark enough in the room so Alex could not see the tears filling his eyes. There wasn't one single day in which he did not think about his partner. Even now, with the physical

251

relationship between him and Alex, he missed Steve even more. He missed the old days when they had shared their own physical love.

Outside, it began to rain, and the temperature inside the room dropped. Matthew pulled the bedcover over them. Sensing his pain, Alex cuddled up to him, wanting to provide some comfort. Her own heart was overwhelmed by the love she bore for this man who had changed everything.

Life was so mysterious sometimes, she mused. If she had not decided to share with a gay couple, she would not be here now. If Steve had not encouraged her to open up about her past, she would never have turned to him, and later to Matthew, for comfort.

The cumulative result of the circumstances surrounding their interaction since the day she had moved in had led to this—her love for Matthew, and through her love, the release of her nightmarish past.

As for Matthew, like he had said earlier, if she had not been there for him, he did not think he could have coped with Steve's death. But what about Steve? What had he achieved as a result of their interaction? Peace of mind, knowing Matthew would be okay after he died.

Alex remembered once asking herself why she had been led to this household—now she knew.

CHAPTER 29

Alex opened her eyes and stretched slowly and luxuriously like a cat. She smiled when she looked at Matthew, who was still asleep. His profile in sleep was beautiful, like the rest of him. She watched him with loving eyes, admiring his face and muscular upper body. She felt awed. Her life had changed overnight, and all her fears had dissolved, leaving her with a sense of freedom.

She had released all hate of her stepfather, and with Steve's help, had managed to find it in her heart to forgive him. As for her mother, she no longer held any ill will toward her, either. How could a woman living with a lie ever be happy? She was sure deep down inside, her mother suspected, perhaps even knew, what her husband was. Her denial and her accusing Alex of leading him on were just ruses designed to keep her from facing her own fears.

Alex felt pity for her and, at the same time, sadness—sadness that a mother and daughter could never enjoy each other because of the man who had come between them. In her fear and denial, her mother had chosen the man, letting go of the daughter, her own flesh and blood. This was something Alex would never forget but could now forgive.

Matthew turned toward her in his sleep and the sun shining in through the window turned his hair into molten gold. She was not surprised his parents had put him on show from an early age. He must have been exquisitely beautiful, but her heart ached for the small child he had been. In their pride and ambition, his parents had neglected to give him the love and care he deserved, so instead he'd turned to the housekeeper for the human contact he needed. It was amazing how simply hugging a child could provide so much love and safety.

At least, Matthew had been fortunate to have the housekeeper. Alex could not remember ever being hugged until she met Steve and

Matthew. Her natural father had died too early in her life for her to remember him, and her mother had never been very demonstrative with her feelings, though Alex knew she had loved her once. With the difficulties of raising a child on her own, however, Cecilia had not had much time for her. Then, when her mother married John, all love for Alex had stopped, traded in by her mother for the security of having a husband. The pain of this rejection would never really go away, but at least Alex felt she had now started to heal.

A sudden thought clouded her happiness as she refocused on the sleeping figure next to her. The time with him would inevitably come to an end. Matthew had made it clear this was their stolen interlude, so to speak, and she had not objected. She could have chosen to call it quits after they had first made love without losing Matthew as her friend. Yet, she had not been able to help herself. Even if her time with him was limited, she was prepared to risk a broken heart. She would miss him terribly when he went to America, but she would always have this time to remember.

When Matthew had asked how she felt about Mark, he was probably hoping she would fall in love with him. This would certainly be the saner choice. Alex knew, however, that Mark was not her soul mate; he was just a good friend. Perhaps, something would develop between them after Matthew left; but only time would tell.

Alex remembered Matthew's words: *There are many ways of expressing love, and there are many different kinds of love.* In her own way, she may come to love Mark one day. But right now, she didn't want to think about a future without Matthew. She only wanted to live in the present.

"You look thoughtful," Matthew remarked, startling her out of her reverie.

Alex noticed his eyes searching hers, so close to her face. She smiled. "Good morning. Just thinking about the meaning of life. Nothing important."

He grinned. "You know, between you and Steve, I could never make up my mind which of you was the most philosophical."

"Steve. Definitely Steve," she replied.

His face went serious all of a sudden. "When did your stepfather start molesting you?"

Alex was startled by the non sequitur. "Why do you ask?"

"Ever since you told me about the damage he did to you, I

haven't been able to get it out of my mind." He looked troubled. "I need to understand what happened."

Alex was touched. "Steve always said you had a heart of gold, except you didn't know it. He was right."

"I don't think I need a heart of gold, as you put it, to be outraged at what was done to you."

"You'd be surprised how many people wouldn't really care, Matthew," she pointed out. "Look at all the so-called friends who dropped Steve when they found out he had AIDS."

"What's that got to do with it? AIDS is a disease people are afraid of, at least those who don't understand it. Child abuse is something entirely different," he reasoned.

She agreed with him, but she went on, "What I'm trying to say is a lot of people in this world can be so cold or they simply go into denial when they see or hear something that disturbs them. I suppose we can't blame them, though, can we? We're all guilty of it to some degree. Look at the kids starving in Africa, we see them on TV and tell ourselves it doesn't affect us because they're so far away or it somehow doesn't seem real seeing it on television. So we easily justify our decision to look the other way."

Matthew glanced at her questioningly.

"The thing is I'm touched that you care enough to be angry at my stepfather," she stated. "I've never known caring from anyone, except old Harry, and he didn't know anything about my past. So you and Steve have been the only ones who've really cared about me."

"You still haven't answered my question," Matthew reminded her.

"Is it that important for you to know?"

He nodded.

"Okay," she said resignedly, taking a moment to compose herself. "When my stepfather came to live with us, he was nice to me for a short while. He tried to convince me that he could be the father I never had. He used to buy me toys and played games with me." The look in her eyes was far away now. "But once he gained my trust, the games we played began to change. I was seven years old by this time. We'd play catch, and somehow he would always manage to hold my body too tight against his own or he'd run a hand up my leg. He always made it look accidental, but even at that age I began feeling uneasy with him." She paused, gathering her thoughts.

Although the pain in her eyes was clearly visible to Matthew, he knew this was all part of the healing process, and he needed to understand what this damage had done to her.

"One day," Alex continued, "when he caught me in hide and seek, his hand slipped under my skirt and all of a sudden I felt his fingers between my legs. I tried to pull away, but he was too strong for me. I struggled to get free of him, but he held me firmly and whispered in my ear that this was a new game, and if I didn't play with him, he'd hit me.

"I was so frightened I stopped struggling. He then told me if I said anything to my mother, she would not believe me and she'd kick me out of the house. By this time, I was weeping in silence, afraid my mother might hear me. So I forced myself to relax against him and that's when he stuck his finger inside me." Alex felt tears well in her eyes, and Matthew put an arm around her and brought her close to him. His naked body against hers was a source of comfort.

"I almost screamed when he did that. It hurt so much. He saw the pain in my face but didn't stop. He kept moving his finger in and out of my body until I felt something wet between my legs. It was blood. When he saw it, he stopped and took me inside the house to the bathroom. My mother was preparing lunch in the kitchen and didn't see anything. He cleaned me up and told me to put on fresh panties. He took the ones stained with the blood, and I suppose he disposed of them somewhere so my mother wouldn't find them.

"He left me alone for a few days after this, and I thought he realised how much he'd hurt me and was sorry. I was wrong. One night, he came to my room. It was late, and I remember it was a moonless night, so it was really dark. He locked the door behind him and came over to my bed. I was shaking with terror and began to whimper. He slapped me hard across the face and told me to shut up. Then, he pulled off my pyjama pants and spread some sort of cool lotion between my legs—it was some sort of lubricant, I guess. Of course, I didn't know this at the time. In my innocence, I thought he was applying some sort of medicated cream to heal the hurt from a few days before." Her voice cracked at this, and her tears fell unchecked. She cried for the little girl she had been—the one whose innocence was destroyed. "Do you really want to hear the rest?"

He held her closer to him. "I want you to tell me all if you're okay with it. I'm here for you," he reminded her tenderly.

"Very well," she continued in a soft voice. "After he applied the lubricant, he stuck a towel under me so we wouldn't stain the sheets and then got into my bed. In the dark, I couldn't see his penis, but when he opened my legs and pushed it into me, I screamed with the pain of it. He clamped a hand down over my mouth to stifle my screams and just kept pushing himself into me. I almost passed out from the pain.

"When he finished, he threatened me again with violence if I told my mother. Then, he cleaned me up and left. This went on every single night for a whole week, and I became like a frightened dog that had been beaten too many times. I watched his every move during the day. I jumped if I heard a loud noise near me, and finally, I withdrew into myself, hoping the horror of it would go away. After a few weeks of this, things got worse." Alex stopped, she could not go on. She held onto Matthew and cried for a long time.

Matthew felt terrible for putting her through this, but he truly believed she needed to talk about it. He had been so lucky to have Steve help him through the time of his parents' rejection. He felt he owed the same thing to Alex; so he went on holding her close and waited until she calmed down. At the same time, he wondered how things could have gotten worse for her. What could be worse than a grown man forcing himself onto an innocent child?

Alex sniffed and wiped at her tears. "I'm a mess, aren't I? I guess forgiving him wasn't enough. I have to release all the hurt, too."

Matthew was glad she understood this and continued to hold her close, reassuring her through their physical contact.

She spoke again, "Anyway, things got worse. He started putting his thing in my mouth, forcing me to suck on it. I used to run to the bathroom and vomit after it was over, but I didn't dare vomit while he was still with me. Then, came the final humiliation; he ... um ... he ... " She could not say it.

"He sodomised you," Matthew filled in for her, feeling such deep hate and disgust for that bastard that he could have killed him with his bare hands.

Alex nodded. "Yes; and this completed his little routine." She hid her face against his chest, too embarrassed to look at him.

He caressed her hair. "Oh God, Alex, it's so much worse than I thought." He felt tears in his eyes. "What kind of a sick and twisted monster would do something like that to a child?"

"I'm okay, Matthew. I survived, didn't I?" Her muffled voice had a childlike tone to it.

"You did, sweetheart, you did." He kissed her hair. "Alex, no matter what happens in our lives I want you to know I'll always be there for you." He felt an overwhelming need to protect her.

Alex nodded. No further words were needed.

That evening, he took her out to dinner for their belated celebration of his audition success. They went to an expensive Italian restaurant in Double Bay and shared a lovely meal, drank smooth red wine, and relaxed in each other's company. There was no need for much conversation. They had both said everything that needed to be said.

Matthew felt they had put the past firmly behind them, and there was no longer any need for either of them to look back. From this point forward, they could enjoy the present and look to a better future.

CHAPTER 30

Time passed and spring started to give way to summer. The days grew warmer and Alex saw life through a haze of sweet contentment. Matthew began filming and was out of the house at the crack of dawn, often returning after dinner time. She missed his company and their lovemaking, but she kept busy working out of doors.

Steve's garden sprouted back to life under her capable hands and even the small jasmine plants produced fragrant blossoms, which filled the air with an exotic scent. If only Steve could be here working alongside of her, Alex mused, then stopped short—but if Steve were here, Matthew would not have become her lover. The thought made her feel guilty.

It had taken Steve's death to bring her and Matthew together. Life was like that sometimes, she reasoned in her mind. Out of sadness came happiness; out of bad came good. The whole cycle of life was a series of ups and downs.

Alex had more time to think about her future now that Matthew wasn't around during the day, and she made the decision to stay on in Sydney. When the time came for Matthew to leave, she would rent a place for herself and have a go at writing a novel. The days of writing travel articles were over as far as she was concerned. She had finally sprouted the roots for which she had searched all this time, and there was no longer any need to keep running away from life.

Early one morning, Mark dropped by the house. He brought with him coffee and croissants. "I've missed you, Alex. I thought we could have breakfast together," he said when he greeted her.

Alex led him into the sunny kitchen.

"I'm not keeping you from anything, I hope?" he inquired.

"No, it's okay," she answered. "Matthew left around five thirty this morning and won't be back until tonight. I was just about to do some gardening." She took out butter and strawberry preserve from the refrigerator. "This is a nice surprise."

Mark gazed at her pensively. "You look different somehow," he commented.

Alex was sure she flushed. "How so?"

"I don't know exactly," he replied, still searching her face. "Your eyes look alive, and you seem to be vibrating with energy."

"Maybe, it's because I've been doing so much exercise working in the garden," she lied.

"Maybe." He sounded unconvinced. "How have you been, anyway?"

"Good." Alex busied herself buttering a croissant.

"And Matthew, how is he?"

"He's happier." At least, she didn't have to lie about this. "He's over the moon about the film and he's already talking about going to LA."

"So the worst of his grief is over."

"I'm not so sure about that; some nights he cries in his sleep." As soon as she said this, she flushed a deep red.

Mark noticed her discomfort but had the sense not to remark upon it. His feeling that there was more to the relationship between Alex and Matthew was not wrong. He wished he could ask Alex what was going on, but knowing how defensive she was about Matthew, he didn't want to risk her anger. Instead, he decided to skirt around the issue. "So how do you feel about his going off to LA?"

Alex was relieved he let her slip go by. "I think it's a wonderful opportunity for him," she forced herself to say brightly. "It's always been his dream."

"Is he going to sell the house?"

"That's what Steve wanted. If Matthew's serious about LA, he'll have to give it at least a year minimum to see if things pan out for him; so he's going to need the money. Things are expensive over there."

Mark thought about this before asking, "But to sell the house when it's totally paid off; isn't this a big risk? What if things don't work out over there? He'll have nothing to come back to."

"I don't think he'll blow all the money. Besides, he can always buy something smaller if he comes back." She reflected for a moment. "In any case, I have a feeling he'll want to sell the house. Too many memories for him here."

"Yeah, you're right. What about you, will you keep on travelling?"

"No," she said to his surprise. "I decided to stay on and look for a place of my own."

"Well, that's great! You'll make Sydney your home, then."

"I think I've had enough of travelling and living out of a suitcase," she confessed. "I want to have somewhere to belong. Plus I decided to write a novel, too."

"A complete change," he remarked, looking impressed.

"Yes." She gave him a smile, but he noticed she still looked troubled.

"At least, you'll have one friend left in Sydney," he declared, meaning himself.

"Yes, I will. So you're stuck with me, Mark."

"I'll be glad to be stuck with you any time," he returned. "If you want that, of course," he added quickly.

She glanced at him, looking serious. "I know I haven't been the easiest of friends, and I can't think why you still want my company. But, yes, if you still want to be my friend, I'd be honoured."

Mark was not ecstatic at her response. He'd hoped she would see him in a more romantic light, but her admission about wanting to continue their friendship was a start.

Alex went on, as if knowing what he was thinking. "There are a lot of things you don't know about me. Perhaps, one day I'll be able to share them with you." Her voice held a tone of sadness, and Mark guessed she was referring to a painful past.

"I hope you will," he uttered.

* * *

Alex woke up and heard Matthew crying out in his sleep. It instantly made her think of her slip with Mark earlier that day. The bedside clock read 3:32. He would have to be up in about an hour to get ready for another day at the studio. Alex wondered whether she should wake him, but before she could decide, he started awake with a jerk.

"Are you okay?" she asked.

He seemed disoriented for a moment and then flipped on the bedside lamp. "I'm sorry, did I wake you?" he uttered as he wiped

261

away tears from his eyes.

"No worries. I'm a light sleeper."

"I had a dream about Steve," he told her, looking troubled. "He was in the garden working on his roses when a big storm broke out. The wind was destroying everything while he reached out to me, but just as I tried to take hold of his hand, the wind blew him further away. I tried again but couldn't reach him. I kept crying out his name, and all I could see were the dark clouds engulfing him. Then, it started to rain really hard and he disappeared."

"It isn't the first time you've had this dream, is it?" Alex stated knowingly.

"You're right," his voice was barely audible.

Alex thought of the night when a storm really had destroyed Steve's garden. That was also the night when Matthew's grief had come to the surface. Lately, he'd been so busy with the film she wondered if his grieving was taking place at a subconscious level. He certainly had little or no time to think about it during the day.

"I'm sorry about the dream," she said consolingly. "It's like reliving the whole thing again, and I can relate to that." She referred to her own nightmares regarding her stepfather.

Matthew glanced at her, a beseeching look in his eyes. "The pain gets less as time goes by, doesn't it?"

He sounded so lost that Alex felt old and used up with the bitter wisdom that lifelong suffering often brings. She reassured him, "It will get better, Matthew."

* * *

It was another week until Matthew finished filming, and he was elated but relieved that it was over. He still needed time to work through his grief and could now look forward to a few weeks' break.

In the end, the rumours about the star of the film had been unfounded. Neither Tom Cruise nor Bruce Willis had played the main part. Matthew had found himself playing opposite Denzel Washington, and the experience had not disappointed him. The actor had been both professional and a really nice guy. He'd made Matthew feel at ease from the moment of their meeting and the two struck up a friendship. So much so, that Denzel told him to "look him up" should he ever come to LA and he would see what he could do about introducing him to the right people.

When Brent heard about this, he got on the phone to his contact in the States and shortly thereafter called Matthew in for a meeting. "I've been talking to a colleague of mine in LA," Brent explained. "He was very interested to hear about your work with Denzel. He says if you go to LA, he's prepared to co-represent you."

"He's an agent?" Matthew exclaimed, trying to keep the excitement out of his voice.

"Yes. I know him from my university days. Ian went to live in the States when he married an American girl and he set up shop over there."

"So why does he want to help me?"

Brent shook his head in frustration. "Because I told him you've got potential, Matt! And now that you worked with Denzel Washington, you have something solid to add to your resume." Brent paused and looked directly at Matthew. "I think it's time to make that decision. Nothing's holding you back now, and you're going to turn twenty-nine soon. You have to establish yourself or it'll be too late."

Matthew regarded his agent thoughtfully and with a sinking feeling in his stomach, he realised Brent was right. He wasn't getting any younger. If he passed up this opportunity, he knew he would never go to the States.

"Okay, give me a day to think about it," he told Brent. "I have to talk it over with someone, and I have to plan things. I'd have to put up the house for sale, too."

Brent nodded. "Fine. Ring me tomorrow and let me know what you want to do. If you decide to go, I'll need an estimate of how long it'll take you to wind things up over here."

Matthew promised he would call the following morning and left Brent's office. On his way home, he thought about Alex and how the news would affect her. But, he reminded himself, they'd both known it would come to this eventually. Even so, this did nothing to make him feel better about deserting her. Yet he could not stay with her and be what she fantasised him to be. It was time to make the break. He had to be fair to Alex and true to himself. The only way he could do this was by moving on to follow his dream and leaving Alex to establish a new life.

That evening over dinner, Matthew told her about his meeting with Brent. The fact that she forced a smile to her face broke his heart. "Of course you should go," she feigned enthusiasm. "It's what you've been waiting for."

He sighed, feeling guilty. "What about you?"

"What about me?"

"What will you do?"

"I'll carry on," she assured him. "I've decided to stay in Sydney and rent a place for myself."

Matthew felt exasperated with himself. "I'm so sorry, Alex. I've been a real shit to you. I should've insisted on our remaining friends," he confessed. "But I enjoyed what we had, and I needed you. So I've been a total bastard."

Alex could not help smiling. "You forget it takes two to tango."

"I know. But I feel I played with your feelings for me."

"Hey, I'm a big girl, you know. I think I can make my own decisions." She regarded him tenderly and added in a softer voice, "Besides, I wouldn't have had it any other way."

"Are you sure about this?" He needed her reassurance.

"I've looked upon our time together as a stolen interlude," she answered. "And now time is passing by and things must change."

Matthew searched her face, wondering if she felt as confident as she sounded.

That night in bed, it was not Matthew who cried but Alex. She hoped he would not wake up and hear her.

CHAPTER 31

The house was put up for sale, and Matthew informed Brent if it sold before Christmas, he'd be ready to fly out to LA early in the New Year. "I want to spend Christmas in Sydney plus wrap up a few things," he explained.

"I'll let Ian know you'll be arriving sometime in January," Brent said. "Do you have a place to stay over there?"

"I haven't even thought about it yet," Matthew replied. "Maybe Ian can recommend an inexpensive apartment for me to rent."

"I'll get onto it." Brent smiled encouragingly. "You're making the right decision, Matt."

Matthew's heart still ached for Alex. "I hope so."

The house was open for inspection on Saturday afternoons, so Matthew and Alex went for drives or out for coffee while the real estate agent showed prospective buyers through the property.

"I'm glad you decided to stay on for Christmas," Alex told him as they walked along the beach one Saturday. The weather was balmy and there were several swimmers in the water.

"It wouldn't feel like Christmas unless you were with me," he replied. "You're my family, remember?"

"What about your real family, Matthew; did you tell them you're going?"

"Why should I tell them anything?" he uttered, sounding upset. "My mother would just gloat, happy Steve's finally dead. And my father, well, he doesn't give a shit."

"Do you seriously believe that?"

"You don't know them, Alex. My mother's changed a lot since I left home. All she does now is play the victim and drink herself into a stupor. For a while, I thought she cared about me, but she was trying to get me to leave Steve in your care so I could go off with her to LA and try my luck."

265

Alex was astonished to hear this. Steve had never mentioned anything to her, and she was positive he must've known. "I would've done it, you know."

He smiled at her. "I know you would, but that isn't the point. If Steve had lived, I wouldn't be going off to LA now." His voice sounded hoarse.

"He really wanted you to realise your dream," she reminded him.

"Yes, I know. He was like that—always thinking about others instead of himself—but I would never have left him. My career's important, but not so important I would've deserted him."

Alex felt a knot of anguish in her stomach. What would it be like to be loved so deeply by Matthew that he would give up his career in the name of love? She forced a smile to her lips when she glanced at him. "Why don't we go to the cemetery? I know Steve's soul isn't there, but I still want to go."

He gazed at her with understanding. "You need to draw on his strength, don't you?"

So Matthew had read her anguished thoughts after all. She didn't mind. "Yes."

They drove in silence to the cemetery at South Head and when they found Steve's grave they sat down next to it. The headstone read: *In Loving Memory of Steve Wicks. A Loving Partner. A Loving Friend.*

"We should've brought some roses from his garden," Alex said.

Matthew did not speak. He gazed at the headstone, lost in his own thoughts.

* * *

On the third weekend that the house was open for inspection, Matthew received an offer.

"It's a great offer," the real estate agent told him and Alex. "In fact, it exceeded our expectations." He was correct. The offer made by a newly married couple was ten thousand dollars above the market value. "They were charmed by the whole place," the agent informed them, "and they absolutely adored the garden."

Alex felt a twinge of pride. She had worked so hard to recapture the beauty of Steve's garden after the terrible storm, and now it was full of life.

"I promised I'd call them back if you agree, Matthew," the agent went on. "They're ready to put down a deposit on it straight away."

Matthew looked at Alex for a moment, indecision in his eyes. Then, he nodded. "Do it."

The real estate agent left immediately to secure the deal.

"So it's done," Matthew stated. "I didn't think it was going to be this easy."

"Why not? You and Steve kept the house in immaculate condition. It's a great buy."

He looked around the kitchen where they were standing. "I'm going to miss this place."

So am I, she reflected silently.

Matthew caught the sadness in her eyes and put an arm around her shoulders. "Why don't we get a pizza for dinner?" he suggested. "Then, we can watch a mushy movie. What do you say?"

Alex could not help smiling. "All right, but only if you promise not to cry," she teased.

A look of indignation crossed his face. "I don't cry at movies!"

"Yes, you do," she laughed. "Remember the night we watched *The Shawshank Redemption?*"

"Well," he admitted reluctantly, "that was a one-off."

"Yeah, right!"

They watched a golden oldie, *Casablanca*, and when the movie ended, Alex caught Matthew with suspiciously damp-looking eyes. He glanced away, pretending he had something in one of his eyes.

"Can I help?" She asked on purpose. "You won't be able to see for yourself if there's something in there."

"Thanks." He went along with the act.

She leaned toward him and looked into his eye. "Nothing there," she pronounced, "except a bad case of nostalgia."

He made a face at her. "You're horrible sometimes, Alex. You never give a guy a break."

"You had that coming to you, Matthew Davis, superstar extraordinaire!" she said in jest, and then was serious. "I decided I'm going to write a novel," she announced.

"When did you decide this?"

"I've been thinking about it for a while, but I suppose it was since I decided to stay on in Sydney."

"I think that's great," he replied, and added with mock importance, "and will I feature greatly in this story?"

"Aha!" she exclaimed. "I knew there was an ego in there somewhere." They laughed. "I'm going to call it *The Soul Bearers*." She explained, "It'll be a story about great human courage and unconditional love in the face of adversity." They both went silent, thinking of Steve. Then, Alex added, "It'll be dedicated in his memory."

Matthew kissed her hair. "I wish you all the best success with it, my dear."

For a moment he sounded just like Steve and Alex remembered fondly the way he used to call her *my dear.*

* * *

The sale of the house was confirmed, and Matthew and Alex planned to hand over the premises after Christmas.

Alex began to hunt around for an apartment and decided to move away from Surry Hills. The suburb held bittersweet memories for her. So when Mark telephoned one evening and she told him about the sale of the house, he offered to help her look for a place to live, and she accepted gladly.

It would be better for her to go looking with Mark. Going with Matthew would only make it harder to disassociate from even more memories being shared. She needed to choose her new home without him. So while Matthew kept busy packing his belongings, Alex went around with Mark to look for apartments.

Two weeks before Christmas, she found a charming one bedroom in Centennial Park, only a couple of suburbs away from Surry Hills. The apartment was on the second floor with a balcony looking out onto the big park and with plenty of natural light coming in through the windows. There was no garden except for the lawn around the building, but the balcony was large enough for potted plants. Alex planned to take some of Steve's roses with her and replant them in a large pot. She signed up for a twelve-month lease and made arrangements to move in a couple of days prior to Christmas.

When the last night at the house in Surry Hills arrived, she looked around the room where she had lived since she'd moved in. She had asked Matthew if she could keep the picture that hung above her bed, the print of the two naked male bodies. "Of course you can have it," he'd said, "but I thought you didn't like the print."

"I do now," Alex answered mysteriously. She was no longer afraid of anything sexual, thanks to Matthew, and the print would serve as a reminder of the gift he'd given her.

The rest of the house was pretty much packed up by now and most of the furniture, aside from a few pieces, had been put away in storage. All that remained were a few cooking utensils, clothes, and a spare mattress on the bedroom floor.

Matthew and Alex dined on Chinese food and went to bed early. The removalists would be coming for Alex's belongings in the morning. Although she had not wanted anything from the house, Matthew insisted she take all the electrical appliances and whatever furniture she wished. She reluctantly agreed.

"There's no point for me to put absolutely everything in storage," he'd argued. "You need to furnish a whole apartment, and I can't take anything with me except my clothes and personal things, in any case."

So Alex had accepted the offer and set aside a few items. She absolutely refused, however, to take Matthew's bed.

"Why not?"

"I have my reasons, Matthew. Besides, I already bought a bed I like. I have to have something new."

Matthew did not argue.

Now, as they lay on the mattress in the dark room, covered only by a bed sheet in the warm night, Matthew spoke. "I've a favour to ask of you."

"What is it?"

"I don't fly out till the eighth of January, but I have to be out of here by Christmas. I gave permission for the new owners to paint indoors before they take possession."

Alex tensed, and he felt it. "I can always stay at Gazza's place," he said quickly.

"No," she exclaimed. "There's no point in my fighting it. I may as well be with you until you go. There'll be plenty of time to get used to your absence afterwards." Though sad, her voice sounded normal. She had accepted the inevitable.

"Are you sure about this? Maybe I shouldn't have asked."

"But you didn't," she answered.

"I kind of did."

She propped herself up on one elbow and gazed into his eyes. "There's no point pretending I won't miss you." Her voice choked up with emotion. "You know I will. But I don't hold a grudge against you for going away. I love you for who you are, and I don't expect anything in return." She paused and smiled faintly. "It's like loving unconditionally, isn't it? I think I learned a lot from Steve."

Matthew watched her tenderly. He had been so lucky to have found this *soul mate in friendship*, as she called it. He knew no matter what happened during their lives, the bond between them would never be broken. They would always be together in spirit. He reached out for her and pulled her to him. "I think we both learned a lot from Steve." He kissed her gently. "Alex, if I stay on in LA for longer than a year, will you come and visit?"

"Is that an invitation?" She gave him a mock leer and licked her lips.

"You know you'll always be welcome," he declared in a sincere voice, ignoring the jest.

"Even when you're rich and famous, and surrounded by thousands of fans and little chickie-babes running around, trying to get you into bed?" She persisted with the leer, and Matthew laughed.

"Of one thing I can definitely assure you," he stated. "No other woman, aside from you, will ever get me into bed."

Alex felt an inner glow. "I'm flattered, Matthew. I always knew I would make a great lover."

He grinned. "You're still so wicked, you know that?"

She nodded.

* * *

Christmas Eve arrived, and Alex settled into her quaint apartment. She had spent the last two days unpacking. Then, Matthew came by to pick her up and they drove to Gazza and Bazza's place for Christmas Eve dinner and a going away party for him.

"Is it still okay if I come and stay with you tomorrow?" Matthew asked her in the car.

"Sure."

"Then, we can have Christmas day together," he said. "There's no point staying in an empty house. I can go back after the owners finish painting and give it a last minute clean before I leave."

"God, to think you're finally going to do some real housework for a change," she teased him.

He smiled sheepishly. "Who would've thought? By the way, do you want to keep this junk of a car while I'm gone? It's so old there's no point in selling it, and you might find it handy."

"I'll tell you what," she told him, "I'll keep it for one year and if you stay on in LA, I'll trade it in and buy myself a nice new one."

"Deal."

The dinner party went well. Apart from Gazza and Bazza, Mark was the only other person present. After dinner, Matthew was given a going away gift from the boys. They had all chipped in and bought him a couple of elegant Louis Vuitton suitcases.

"So you can travel in style, darling," said Gazza.

Matthew was pleased. Then, the others exchanged Christmas gifts. Alex and Matthew had bought the boys a Venetian glass vase to add to their collection of Venetian glassware. For Mark, Matthew bought a music CD and Alex bought him a new golfing umbrella.

"This way, you don't have to use hotel giveaways," she teased, and only the two of them enjoyed the private joke.

Alex received a coffee set of Mexican earthenware from Gazza and Bazza as a housewarming present. Mark gave her a delicate gold bracelet with little charms in the shape of dolphins. Alex loved it and thought this marked the promise of a closer friendship between them in future.

CHAPTER 32

Matthew arrived at Alex's apartment early on Christmas morning. When she opened the door, he thrust a flowerpot at her, which held a couple of baby rosebushes. "From Steve's garden," he announced.

While she put the pot out on the balcony, he brought in his two new suitcases and a couple of overnight bags. "I have a few boxes out in the car that I'll be shipping over to LA before I go," he informed her when she joined him in the room.

Matthew looked around the place quickly, ending in her bedroom, which was a large airy room with wall-to-wall wardrobes and an ensuite bathroom. The furniture consisted of the chest of drawers and Queen Anne desk that had come from Matthew's house, plus a queen-size bed with a scrolled iron bedhead mimicking the Edwardian era.

"Nice," he commented, "but can I ask why you insisted on a new bed? We had two back at the house."

Alex decided to tell him. "The bed in my room was where I had the nightmares and the memories of my past. Your bed was where my whole life changed." This last statement came out in a whisper. Matthew noticed the colour in her cheeks as she went on, "And though it was wonderful to be there with you, I felt I was the interloper. After all, the bed belonged to you and Steve. So now, I have a bed of my own to start my new life and make my own memories."

Matthew remained silent but put his arm around her shoulders and kissed her cheek. As they were about to leave the room, his eyes came to rest on the picture hanging above the bed. It was the print of the two naked male bodies, but it had been reframed in antique wood.

"So give me the official tour," he requested, deciding not to comment about this one memory Alex had insisted on bringing along with her.

Alex took the loungeroom furniture from the house at Surry Hills so the only changes Matthew noticed in the room were a new rug under the coffee table and some bright modern prints decorating the walls. The kitchen was small with pine cupboards and pale yellow walls, lending it a country feeling. Alex had purchased a pine table to fit in the room and four matching chairs.

"Small, but cosy, don't you think?" She waited for his reaction.

"I like it. You've made it your own; and yes, it's very cosy." He grinned sheepishly at her. "So where do I sleep? Not in the bathtub, I hope."

"You'll sleep in my new bed," she said confidently.

"Won't that make more memories for you?" He was serious now.

She turned to him and put her arms around his neck, kissing his lips softly. "I'm not running away from my new memories, Matthew. It's only the old ones that I've left behind. I'm glad we have this short time together before you go. When you're no longer here, you'll still be with me in my thoughts. Nothing can change this, not even a new bed."

He held her against him, resting his chin on her shoulder so she could not see the pain in his eyes. He felt guilty about having to leave her behind.

"Hey, it's Christmas today. Let's be happy," she remarked and pulled away from him. "I have something for you. Come."

She led him back to the loungeroom and told him to wait before disappearing into her room. When she came back, she was holding a small package wrapped in gold leaf paper with a small envelope. "Merry Christmas." She held out the package to him.

Matthew asked, "Do I open it now?"

She nodded and he unwrapped the package to reveal a small black velvet pouch. A fine gold chain slipped out onto the palm of his hand. It was a neck chain of delicate gold links and a yellow gold pendant in the shape of the sun with a half moon in white gold superimposed over it.

"It's beautiful," he stated as he admired her gift. Then, he opened the envelope to find a small white card inside. It read: *You are the sun, I am the moon—we may be divided, as day is from night, but we cannot exist without each other. All my love, Alex.*

Matthew was moved to tears. "God, this is really beautiful. Thank you." He kissed her tenderly and then put on the pendant. "I'll never take it off." He then motioned for her to sit on the sofa. "Now, it's my turn," he announced, went to his luggage and drew his gift to her from one of the overnight bags. "This is for you." He gave her a small jewellery box and waited.

Alex opened it slowly and gasped with delight at the beautiful Russian friendship ring inside. It had three intertwined bands of gold. Each band was in a different coloured gold: white, yellow, and rose. She slipped the ring on the third finger of her right hand. It fitted perfectly.

"The white is you, silver like the moon. The gold is me, the sun," Matthew explained, linking the colours to the symbolism of the pendant Alex had given him. Then, he added, "And the rose is Steve, bringing us together in friendship."

How ironic that Steve was the rose, just like the rose garden he had always loved. Alex could not speak. She was too choked up with emotion so she turned into Matthew's arms and let her tears fall.

* * *

Matthew had two weeks before he was due to leave for LA, and neither he nor Alex mentioned the trip. They simply enjoyed their time together and saw no one.

On New Year's Eve, they had a picnic in the park under the Harbour Bridge and enjoyed the fireworks at midnight. The rest of the time they spent walking on the beach, picnicking at Centennial Park, going out for coffee, discovering new restaurants, and making love.

For Alex, this last interlude would leave her with the memories to last a lifetime. She knew she would ever love anyone like she loved Matthew. Therefore, she lived for the moment as if trying to store up each thing they did so she could savour the memories after he left.

Matthew also enjoyed their time together, Alex sensed, but there were a few times when she caught a look of distraction in his eyes, and she wondered whether this was part of his grief for Steve or if it was anxiety about what lay before him.

On the day before they were due to go back for a last clean of the house Matthew seemed more distracted than ever. That night, Alex awoke to find him sitting up in bed, taking big gulps of air into his lungs.

"Are you okay?" she asked sleepily.

He had tears coursing down his face. "God, Alex." His voice was croaky. "I couldn't breathe. I was suffocating!"

"It's all right now," she reassured him gently. "You had a bad dream."

"It was the same dream, the one about Steve disappearing into the storm; but this time, when the dark clouds engulfed him, they got me, too. That's when I couldn't breathe anymore, and then you appeared. You were holding out your hand to me, but I couldn't reach you. I just kept choking."

"I'll get you some water," she said and went to the kitchen.

She was right, she thought, Matthew was in deep anxiety about the trip, his future, and leaving all that was familiar behind him. She was not surprised his dream had been so disturbing.

"Here, drink this." She handed him the glass when she returned and climbed back into bed.

He took a few sips but still looked troubled. "I don't know if I can go through with it," he confessed to Alex's astonishment.

"What are you saying?"

"I don't even know myself. Everything's moving so fast!"

For a moment, Alex realised she could be selfish and manipulate him into staying, but this wouldn't be right. She had to be strong for him.

"Matthew, listen to me," she said firmly. "You're just having an anxiety attack. It's only natural," she reasoned. "You're leaving behind everything that's familiar: your home, friends, the place where Steve died. You're simply in fear of the unknown." She had his attention now. "But you were meant to follow this dream of yours. You'll hate yourself if you don't at least try."

His breathing had returned to normal by now and the anxiety in his eyes started to subside.

"You'll be fine once you get there," Alex assured him. "Don't give up now—not when you've come this far." She felt like someone was cutting out her heart with a sharp knife. She was telling Matthew to go when all she wanted was for him to stay. But she knew this was the right thing to do. "You're okay now," she consoled him. "You'll be fine." She made him lie back on the bed. "Let's get some sleep."

* * *

The following morning, they drove over to Surry Hills and cleaned up the newly painted house. When they finished, they packed away the cleaning equipment in the car and went back inside for a last look. They stood in the empty kitchen, the doors to the courtyard wide open.

"The garden still looks so beautiful," Alex remarked.

"You did a great job with it," Matthew replied and then sighed. "I suppose we better say goodbye to the house and return the keys to the agent."

"Yes," she agreed, a little sadly.

They continued to stand in silence for a moment longer, each saying goodbye in their own way.

The sun shone bright in the azure blue sky. It was a perfect summer's day. Alex said goodbye to her memories and thanked Steve for everything he had done for her—including bringing Matthew into her life. She wished him peace and happiness.

She could not read Matthew's thoughts while he said his own goodbyes, but she imagined how he must be feeling. The house was his last link to Steve, and all Matthew could take to LA with him were the memories.

"Let's go," Matthew said all of a sudden, his voice just above a whisper.

They turned to go, but Alex stopped. "Hold on. We forgot to shut the doors."

They turned back toward the kitchen doors, and as they did they saw something moving out in the garden. They stood, frozen, hardly breathing.

Outside, hovering above one of the rosebushes that had survived the storm was a beautiful blue and black butterfly.

The butterfly circled slowly around the rosebush and landed on a red rose. Matthew and Alex watched, transfixed, as the butterfly rested on the rose for a few seconds before it took flight again and circled a couple of times more around the rosebush.

Tears welled up in their eyes, and while they watched the butterfly's movements, they experienced a feeling of deep peace.

Each knew in their own heart that they were watching Steve's *soul bearer*.

The butterfly circled one last time, and then flew gently away.

The End

About the Author

Sylvia Massara is a multi-genre author based in Sydney, Australia. She loves to dabble in wacky love affairs, drama, murder, sci-fi (or anything else that takes her fancy) over good coffee.

Born in Argentina from Italian and Spanish descent (with a bit of Swiss thrown in) and transplanted to Australia at age 10, Sylvia describes herself as a bit of a "moggie" cat by way of mixed pedigree. She is also a citizen of the world as she has travelled widely throughout most of her life and she's the proud owner of three passports.

From a creative perspective, Sylvia has been writing since her early teens and her work consists of novels, screenplays and freelance writing. She has also dabbled in acting on and off, songwriting and even had her own band during her teens/early 20s where she performed at various venues.

As with most authors, Sylvia draws on her varied experience from the often puzzling tapestry of life. A few years ago Sylvia resigned from the human race because she discovered the animal kingdom was a much nicer place to be.

Currently, Sylvia lives with her cat, Mia; and always vicariously through the many characters in her head. Occasionally, Sylvia ventures into the world of humans, and she cherishes genuine friendships as they are a rare find.

Sylvia has recently released her 7th novel, The Stranger, a sci-fi apocalyptic romance with moralistic issues that involve the fight of love vs evil in the cosmos.

Please visit the author's website to keep up with her latest novels or to contact her at: www.sylviamassara.com

About Massara's Novels

The Mia Ferrari Mystery Series

Playing With The Bad Boys

A woman plunges ten floors down an atrium and lands on a baby grand piano in the luxurious Rourke Hotel Sydney. The police rule this as a straight case of suicide; but 48-year-old hotel duty manager and wannabe investigator, Mia Ferrari, thinks otherwise.

As Mia sets out to unravel the mysterious death and prove the cops wrong, especially her archenemy, Detective Sergeant Phil Smythe; she comes up against an unsavoury cast of characters who will do anything to shut her up. But with a little help from her friends, Mia will not stop until she unearths the truth.

Mia Ferrari is a "wiseass", older chick with determination and an attitude, and she never takes "no" for an answer.

The Gay Mardi Gras Murders

Mia Ferrari, smartarse, older chick, super sleuth, is back in her 2nd murder mystery, and this time, she is up to her neck in drag queens, a rare diamond with a curse and murder most foul against the backdrop of Sydney's world famous Gay Mardi Gras.

A female impersonator is found dismembered in her hotel suite bathtub, and a rare diamond worth twenty million dollars is gone. The Gay Mardi Gras is fast approaching and Mia Ferrari, senior duty manager of the exclusive Rourke International Hotel Sydney, has to juggle a bunch of drag queens, a number of fabulously handsome gay men, a transsexual with a dark mystery, a young cop with sex on his mind, a close friend from the UK who is having marital problems and a mounting body count.

As Mia pits her investigative skills against her archenemy, Detective Sergeant Phil Smythe, to solve the case, she not only becomes embroiled in the life of the people around her, but it looks like she is the next target for a serial killer with a grudge against gay men.

The South Pacific Murders

It's a well-known fact that wherever Mia Ferrari goes trouble always follows, and going on a holiday cruise to Hawaii is no different.

A killer is on the loose onboard ship. A number of doctors from a medical convention are being murdered one by one. The captain of the cruise liner asks Mia and her travelling companions to take over the investigation while the ship is in the middle of the Pacific Ocean toward its final destination. A secret sex club and horse racing bets are the only clues that can uncover the identity of the killer, but will Mia be able to solve the mystery before the killer strikes again?

Join Mia and her friends, plus her sexy detective archenemy, on a cruise to murder, mayhem, and sizzling hot sex.

Science fiction romance

The Stranger

The Stranger is a sci-fi apocalyptic romance with moralistic issues involving the fight between love and evil and its repercussions.

Rhys is on a mission on Earth in order to determine Earth's destiny, but his judgement is in danger of becoming clouded when he meets and falls in love with Carla, a human. The balance of life on Earth depends upon Rhys's recommendation to the League of Galaxies. But how will Rhys choose between his mission and his love for an Earthling? Rhys is forced to weigh up the collective evil on Earth and its causal effect on the greater good of other life in the universe against the love he has for one woman.

This is not simply a tale of love between two beings but a story of the unconditional and sublime love, which is the force that drives the cosmos.

The Stranger was dedicated to the Loving Memory of David Bowie.

Romance

Like Casablanca

What does internet dating and Casablanca have in common? Nothing, unless you go to Rick's Cafe and find out what antiques dealer and dating blogger, Cat Ryan, is up to.

Cat's doing research for her internet dating blog gig, and the place she chooses to meet her many dates is at Rick's Cafe in Sydney. But what of its disturbingly handsome owner, Rick Blake?

Cat wonders what he thinks, seeing her with a different male all the time. What's more, why does this bother Cat so much? It's not like she wants any involvement after her recent break up with Josh, her cheating ex. Besides, it looks like Rick is trying to get back together with his ex-wife, Denise. So Cat decides to play it safe, but her heart has different ideas.

The Other Boyfriend

Sarah Jamison is on a mission to find a boyfriend for Moira, who is her lover's partner. And Sarah's best friend, Monica, comes to the rescue with the perfect solution. Enter the enigmatic Mike Connor. Monica is sure that Mike will sweep Moira off her feet, leaving the way open for Sarah to be with her true love, Jeffrey.

Sarah hates Mike on sight despite the fact that her body tells her otherwise. He is a romance novel "hero-type" who is smug and full of himself. But the only way to accomplish her mission is for her to work with Mike so she can be together with the man she loves.

Jeffrey has promised her that the minute he can end his platonic relationship with Moira, he will be with Sarah for good; but he is having trouble letting go of the wretched woman, and Sarah feels her time is running out. She is terrified of the pending big "M" (menopause), and seeing as she's just turned forty, and her hormones are driving her to do insane and desperate things, she is sure that it is not too far off into the future!

So here she is, building a multi-level marketing business in Taiwan, and struggling with it all: a stranger in a foreign country, away from her mother and friends back in London; a reluctant lover; a drop-dead gorgeous man who might have ulterior motives for helping her, and finally, a business that seems to be dwindling.

Sarah is doing it all in the name of love and the last chance to have a family, and if this means scheming and working with the devil himself, then she will do it! What she doesn't take into account is the fact that instead of getting closer to her goal, Sarah's feelings take a turn, and she finds herself increasingly thinking about the very man she despises the most – "the other boyfriend".

Contemporary fiction – drama

The Soul Bearers

Partly inspired by true life events, this is a story of courage, the gift of friendship, and unconditional love. The story involves three people whose lives cross for a short period of time and the profound effect that results from their interaction.

Alex, a freelance travel writer and victim of child abuse, arrives in Sydney in an attempt to exorcise the ghosts of her past. She shares a house with Steve and the disturbing Matthew, a homosexual couple. Alex finds herself inexplicably attracted to Matthew and she must battle with her repressed sexuality and fear of intimacy. Matthew, an aspiring actor, must face the prospect of a potential future without his partner, who has AIDS, and he must deal with the rejection of his socialite parents.

Steve is the rock to which the troubled Matthew and Alex cling while they examine their lives and beliefs in the hope that they will find the strength to face their pain and release the past.

This powerful story explores the true meaning of unconditional love and friendship.

www.ingramcontent.com/pod-product-compliance
Lightning Source LLC
Chambersburg PA
CBHW052018020726
47501CB00004B/1130